11-19

MW00911317

BEAST BLOOD

BEAST BLOOD

Volume Two: Truer Sin

BY M. A. LEVI

Copyright © 2015 M. A. Levi.

All rights reserved. No part of this book may be used or reproduced by
any means, graphic, electronic, or mechanical, including photocopying,
recording, taping or by any information storage retrieval system
without the written permission of the publisher except in the case
of brief quotations embodied in critical articles and reviews.

Archway Publishing books may be ordered through booksellers or by contacting:

Archway Publishing
1663 Liberty Drive
Bloomington, IN 47403
www.archwaypublishing.com
1 (888) 242-5904

Because of the dynamic nature of the Internet, any web addresses or
links contained in this book may have changed since publication and
may no longer be valid. The views expressed in this work are solely those
of the author and do not necessarily reflect the views of the publisher,
and the publisher hereby disclaims any responsibility for them.

Any people depicted in stock imagery provided by Thinkstock are models,
and such images are being used for illustrative purposes only.
Certain stock imagery © Thinkstock.

ISBN: 978-1-4808-1941-2 (sc)
ISBN: 978-1-4808-1942-9 (e)

Library of Congress Control Number: 2015909990

Print information available on the last page.

Archway Publishing rev. date: 6/22/2015

Dedications and Thanks

I dedicate this story to my family. My husband for supporting and
having faith in me throughout this entire process. With the aroma
of coffee swirling in the air and classical music softly filling in the
still morning, he proof read my story aloud every Saturday morning. My mother for being a continuous influence for me regarding anything relating to the supernatural. Without her continuous
loyalty to programs of ghosts, monsters, witches and creatures of
the unknown; I wouldn't have grown up with such knowledge and
probably wouldn't have became inspired to write the story you're
about to read. My father for proof reading the story as well, but
mostly for instilling in me that the world held uninterrupted won
derment, mystery and beauty. That the mystery was there for th
taking and you only had to know where to look to fully appreci
and understand it. Finally, I thank God for blessing me with
wonderful family, friends, great opportunities, insight, an over-
alytical personality, love, laughter and life.

A Special Thanks to:

Boyd & Yvonne; Ray & Annette; Bruce & Linda; Boyd & Co
Tara & Darrel; Lisa, Allen, Rebekah & Emily; Joey & Myran
& Linda; Helen & Darrel; Christine; Joe & Christine; Sarah
Walter. Finally, my Patrick.

CONTENTS

PROLOGUE

Oral Ceremony speech. Originally predated: 1300 A.D, New world

Translated and first written in English: December, 14ᵗʰ 1599 A.D, America

Prophecy: Beast Blood

. . . .

The Great Spirit has blessed our people with his shared vision. With large wings of an eagle, he fell to the ground with purpose in his heart and scars across his white-man face. This warrior of the Great Sky Spirit chose my tribe to be the protectors of their holy talisman. A talisman that we need to keep on our skin and remain hidden from all outsiders. Like a mountain, our honor, respect and warrior's unity have stood proud within time. We have proved our loyalty through our ways, our Shaman's feasts, prayers and sacrifices.

Our people pleased the Great Sky spirits and they rewarded us through their ritual. When the moon rises in the black lake, we hunt with our native wolf. Our people have achieved the gift of shape shifting. We are the guardians. Stronger. Proud. Blessed with immortality. Obtaining a coveted power beyond all men. We are more with nature! The moon, the sun, the earth, water and wind; our power is growing from their power that surrounds us. If we finally wish to seek death, we are to consume the talisman from our bodies and cleanse our blood with fire. Never are we to part from this ritual. Either we die or live forever. Our treasure isn't without trade and danger. The Great Spirit told me another battle will occur and then war. We will not lose the battle. We fight as proud people. Then, when the war comes we will mark our skin, look to the sky and take the shape of a beast to win the war. My people, a lost war is dire to humanity only if we fail to hold the talisman away from the Evil Spirit. A known spirit showing its face of the wild boar with horns sharper than the rams that roasts on our fires. The winged warrior told me a powerful entity will resurrect a demon from the bloody ground. The demon will be a warrior, placed on a different side than nature's balance of Good and Evil. He will cause fear and he will make himself known to some. We wait for the day when we're needed. As we have for hundreds of years, we keep our hearts connected to nature. The warrior gave me these last words to give to you all. I say them now word for word. '*Look toward the sky and behold the red moon. Cast your eyes downward and take notice an army of beasts guarding the newborn who will be one with the guardians in Heaven and Earth.*'

My people, we play a part within this vision. Our angelic talisman's needed. We need to keep it safe until the day comes when the signs reveal themselves and the Hybrid, made by evil and blessed blood, becomes born into the world. Fate is unknown, but the warriors path is paved.

~Chief Fang-Song, Blood of Chief Stone-Arrow

As great, great blood daughter to Chief Fang-Song and Chief Stone-Arrow, I write the first words of many to this noble ceremonious blessing. Documented for when the world falls to ash, people will need to remember.

~Abequea, A sister guardian of the Angelic Talisman

1

THE ORIGIN OF ESCAPE

Scotland, 1515

"Alexandria! Come out, right now, you incorrigible lowlander whore. I know what you have done. All the bloody clans know what you have done. You have made a mockery of me while you lay with him and you are now...Ugh!" Frances let out a loud, raspy scream. "I am going to kill you. Show yourself to me, Alexandria. I know you can hear me from wherever you're hiding." He yelled for his unfaithful wife as he stormed the dark corridors looking for her.

Alexandria's hazel eyes grew larger as she heard her husband's thunderous approaching footsteps accompanied by his roars of vehemence. They echoed murderously through her private parlor, through the connecting wall and sounding clearly into her bed-chamber. She knew her husband would eventually come for her, but she still became paralyzed with immense dread of it suddenly becoming real.

"My Lady, you have to move more quickly. He's moved into the parlor. He'll look in here next. Please hurry and shut the doors. We have to get you to safety."

Alexandria stared perplexedly at her elderly nursemaid with fear radiating through her, but she complied with her nursemaid's hushed, frantic plea and closed the wardrobe doors. Once they were both inside, the nursemaid moved her trembling hands along the inside walls of the wardrobe, trying to find the notch that promised their escape. Alexandria became worried her husband would find them while trying to flee and kill them both with a swipe of his sword across their necks. Through a dry throat Alexandria's voice sounded small and scratchy as she eagerly begged the elderly woman to hasten her search. "Please. Oh God, Nona. Please be swift." Alexandria cried.

Relieved, the nursemaid found the mark and pressed inside the indent to activate the large square panel to open. "I found it, Miss. It's open." They crouched, leaning on the padding of their slipper-covered feet. Momentarily hesitant, they stared into the pitch-black tunnel that promised to lead them to their freedom. "My Lady, you must go first. If he caught me, I would only take a beating from him, but if he caught you he would surely kill you." The nursemaid quickly grabbed Alexandria's head to turn it to face her sensing she was becoming unmoving within her fear. "Now listen to me, Miss. I know you understand and I know you're afraid. You're smart, lass, but you have to buck up! I'll be right behind you. When the panel's closed and locked, I will let you know by grabbing onto you. Go now!"

Alexandria looked at the fragile, but resolute elderly woman in front of her. She had to be strong for Nona and for the growing life within her. She quickly tapered her skirts and went through the opening headfirst with haste. She felt the texture of the floor change from the smooth oak of the wardrobe to the rough floor of the stone tunnel, as it grazed her delicate hands. Alexandria's eyes adjusted to the blinding darkness, but the slight adjustment was useless. It was still too dark. As she started to crawl, she allowed her other instincts to guide her. Moving several feet into the dark passageway, she thought of Laycerath making his way through the same tunnel to see her during the late hours of the night. She quickly shook her head to make the plaguing memories go away. Immediately, she turned her attention to call on divine intervention as she crawled forward deeper into the tunnel. She began thanking God her pregnancy hadn't hindered her to move with ease and quietly begged Him to save all their lives. She finished with a plea. *Lord, if not for me or Nona, let it be for the innocent soul that now grows within me.*

Alexandria became startled out of her prayer as she felt a cold frail hand grab around her ankle. She quickly remembered Nona telling her that was a signal for when the panel closed and locked behind them. Forgetting briefly of her prayer, the nursemaid's icy grasp, and of her scattered nerves, she recalled her husband had no clue about her hidden tunnel. *He won't find us in here,* she thought and almost laughed aloud. However, the guard's would begin patrolling the forest by now and they would search until everything was thoroughly looked over. With that knowledge, she knew the odds were not in her favor, yet she believed that God, despite her recent mortal sin, heard her prayer and gave mercy on her plight. This gave Alexandria a glimmer of hope and comfort of the resulting escape.

After what must have been almost a two-hour stretch of silence and hushed movement Alexandria and Nona became overly tired; they were still fear ridden . Only the sound of their haggard breathing and rustling skirts filled the silence, until they finally reached the ending point of the tunnel. Alexandria saw slivers of moonlight break through the hanging moss and roots, which hid the tunnels' existence from anyone who might have been wandering in the forest. She broke the silence and whispered to the nursemaid, "We've made it, Nona. I'll go out first to see if it's safe." Alexandria could hear the elderly woman's sigh of relief as they continued to crawl out of the tunnel into the clearing. As she poked her head out from the veiled opening, the moonlight blinded her as her eyes adjusted to the well-lit night. Once she could clearly see again, she scanned her surroundings and listened. After a few moments, she neither saw nor heard anything. "It's safe. We can go."

Nona emerged from the damp ground, she smoothed out her cotton skirts and looked over her surroundings. "Thank the good Lord we're out of the tunnel. Where are we headed now my Lady?"

Alexandria turned to answer her longtime nursemaid and friend. "We're in the thick of the forest. We do not have any other means of travel, so we walk from here to the shipyard. The night and the forest will be our cover until we arrive at the shipyard, if we go now, we will arrive just before dawn. There we will disguise ourselves as men and gain passage to England as part of the working crew. With all those trunks laying about, I don't see why there wouldn't be any clothes for men in them."

Nona looked away from Alexandria and sighed again. "But, Miss, your condition, and that's a three-hour walk. What about the babe growing inside you? What if we're caught in our pursuit? Remember, you're pregnant. You can't be working on a ship."

Alexandria, harshly whispered to her ranting friend, "What choice do we have now?" She knew Nona wanted to discourage the plan even further, but fortunately she held her tongue. Nona looked to the ground and nodded her head, agreeing to the impetuous plan. This arrangement was their only alternative, and Alexandria knew it brought a small chance of bringing success. She tried to go to Laycerath, but she found he used her for his greedy pleasure. She thought back on the promises he made; he would love her for all of eternity, taking her away from her neglectful and womanizing husband, and together they would face the world. She could spit on the ground at the thought of his lies. She believed herself a gullible fool for falling so easily into that arrogant bastard's hand. Suddenly, she vowed she wouldn't be so absent-minded again. Her freedom meant everything was going to change. Daybreak would bring her new a start, a new life, and she will grow into her own wherever the Lord led her, Nona, and her child.

Alexandria looked over the vast land of Scotland for the last time. In the distance, she could see her husband's and Laycerath's boarding lands. Feeling a pang of uncertainty, she hurriedly looked away from what she was leaving behind. In the corner of her eye, she noticed the moonlight struck the blood-red eyes of the snarling, silver wolf head, that adorned the small band on her right hand. As she looked into its eyes, Alexandria remembered the brief conversation with her mother the day she married Frances and received the strange heirloom. However, one sentence struck her memory the most and Alexandria impulsively whispered it to herself. "After today, you're forever bound to the wolves; it's your destiny."

She remembered the sad look on her mother's face as she placed the beautiful ring in her hand and closed it with her own long, thin fingers. She gave her adolescent daughter a pitiful smile before she kissed her cheek and walked away. Alexandria did not understand that day, or even now, exactly what the haunting words meant, but she had a feeling she was going to find out soon. The cold wind started to rise. It blew Alexandria's long, blonde hair from her face, bringing her back to the present. She took the brisk wind as a signal to start moving. She looked to Nona, gave her a slight touch on the arm, and started walking. Together they turned their backs and headed to the shipyard.

Meanwhile

Silently, he scouted from inside the treetop to wait for Lord Frances O'Mara to arrive. He knew the man would come to be in the middle of the forest to look for his runaway wife. Amused at the thought of O'Mara running through the woods frantically looking for his unfaithful pregnant wife, made his plan to kill him all the more pleasurable. He smugly thought, *Serves him right, the pious bastard.*

The moon had reached it's highest point and he was at full strength. All the more ready to slaughter those who tried to keep him from completing his goal. Alerted by a faint rustle from the brush line he readied his position to attack. Taken back to see France's wife, Alexandria and her aged nursemaid, scurry from the tunnel in haste, he expected to see the man he was waiting for. *Ah, that's right, the tunnel. Thank you for reminding me, my fair whore.* Relaxing his attack, he watched her with a personal interest as he quietly slunk through the branches of the tree, edging closer to where they stood. She started to speak and he stopped moving at the slightest inclination of detection by the women. However, she did not notice his presence and continued talking to the elderly woman. *Of course, they wouldn't notice me. No one ever does until it's too late.* He followed them with his eyes and smugly smiled, revealing pointed teeth as he jumped from the ground and made his way into the dark tunnel.

2

A MID-OCTOBER'S NIGHT DREAM

Michigan, Modern Day America.

From inside the excessively warm cottage, Esmeralda sat at her favorite window to watch the last traces of the sun's golden color finally fade into twilight and release the night in its place. A routine older than time, the night came to conquer the sky, changing the personality of the land until morning. The wind, which was a subtle whisper in the day's light, had turned vengeful and harsh. The unseen force started to play with the dying leaves of the trees, which lined their vast property. With a rough push from the fall wind, the leaves fell from their rightful place onto the ground. With an underlying anxiousness pulsing under her skin, Esmeralda watched the flighty objects make their way to the threshold of the forest where their journey ended. Switching her line of vision to the trees, she noticed how they swayed against their will. The forming light of the quarter moon began to peek over the trees as it held its steady gaze on the land making the inner forest appear darker and thicker. While watching the completed modification from day to night,

Esmeralda sighed as she nervously bit her the pad of her thumb. As she always did out of habit if she was in flux deep reflection.

A deep voice, which came from behind her, startled her from her uneasy thoughts, "Good evening my darling wife."

Esmeralda turned her head to scan the room for the familiar voice and saw Gabrio leaning carelessly against the door frame. Her feeling of uncertainty quickly fleeted when her body electrified with excitement at the sight of seeing her husband. "Hey, your home early."

Gabrio, sensed his wife's passing concern, but felt her recent rush of excitement and could not help to smile. "Yeah, Marrok and I got off from our posts earlier. So I decided, instead of heading out for a quick drink with him, I would come home to see what my lovely wife was doing. Possibly get her a bit drunk before our run tonight." On cue, Gabrio held up a bottle of champagne.

Esmeralda smiled as she cast her eyes toward the bottle and back to Gabrio, only to smile wider. "Cook's Spumante. Well, it looks like you're going to make great progress in your plan by bringing that home. Do you remember the last time when we had that?"

It was Gabrio's turn to flash a wolfish, lopsided grin. "I remember exceedingly well. That's why I specifically bought it and came rushing home to you.

Esmeralda was silent for a brief moment, then playfully stated. "Well, I don't see you rushing over here now to give me a thorough kiss."

In quick strides he stepped to where she sat. Esmeralda looked up at her husband and gave him a light, throaty laugh as he buried his free hand into the thick, black wave of her long hair. He gave it a light tug wanting her head backward, exposing her throat to his invasion. She looked into his golden-brown eyes through her hooded vision. Esmeralda, felt another swift tug and fully laid her head into the palm of his expanded hand and willingly surrendered to her alpha. She lightly closed her eyes as he leaned down to brush his lips against hers. His quaint peck quickly deepened and slowly parted. Gabrio moved his lips to kiss his wife's forehead to leave a lingering kiss there. He straightened his body upright as he continued to look at Esmeralda's delicate features as she opened her eyes. "Should I go get two glasses for us?"

"That would be great. Thank you." She replied. She watched Gabrio turn from her to walk into the dining room with the bottle of champagne and disappear. She turned her head to look out the window to continue watching the liveliness of the night. After a few minutes, she heard the clank of the glasses, the loud pop from Gabrio removing the cork from the bottle. Then, the soft pattern of his walk as he entered back into the cozy den. Esmeralda turned her head to look at Gabrio handing her a glass of the sweet, bubbly liquid.

"Here you go my love." Gabrio said.

Esmeralda noticed how out of place, his strong, calloused hand, looked holding the fragile stem of the champagne flute. She smiled at him as she grabbed the glass and took a small sip. "Thank you." She said in a muffled voice.

Gabrio noticed the small patch of skin missing from Esmeralda's thumb, which she was nervously nibbled on earlier. *What has you worried, enough to bite the pad of your thumb raw?* Gabrio thought as he placed himself to sit opposite of Esmeralda, sharing the window seat with her. Esmeralda moved to make room for his large, but lean body.

In reply, he stretched his legs and crossed his feet, making himself comfortable. He took a lingering drink out of his glass as he looked at his wife and set the glass on the floor. "Man, that's good. So how's the champagne my dear?"

Her eyes peeked over her raised glass towards her husband and snorted a laugh into the glass as she finished the last morsel of her drink. As if she was a child carelessly, giddily eating ice cream, she licked her lips and smiled. "It's so delicious and cold. I just love the taste and the eventual effect, which I think might be working already."

Gabrio raised an eyebrow and chuckled. "I'm glad it's to your specification and that you're such a lightweight. I can see tonight will work in a way that'll be beneficial to us both, but let's play fair, shall we?" He winked at her as he picked up his glass from the floor, finished his drink in one large gulp and continued. "We're one for one." He looked at their empty glasses, then at his wife. "At the rate we're going I'm thinking I should have brought the bottle in here?"

She nodded her head, but hurriedly stated, "No, you don't have to get up. I'll get it." She swiftly lifted herself from where they sat, quickly climbed over Gabrio's lap.

Gabrio, laughed at his wife's urgency and boldly declared, "There's a good woman. Go '*fetch*' the bottle and bring it back."

Esmeralda paused for only a brief moment to look down at her husband from her straddling position. In a quick strike, she took her fingers and quickly flicked the side of his neck, sounding a loud fleshy pop. Before Gabrio could react, her feet were on the ground and she was rushing towards the kitchen to retrieve the champagne bottle.

"Oh, you bitch. You got my neck, good this time." Gabrio lightheartedly exclaimed while rubbing out the quick abuse. In response to his expletive, he could hear her mischievous chuckle echo in the other room. Smiling, he looked out the window and remembered her expression when had first came home. He finally asked her. "Why were you biting your thumb earlier Essie?" Within the years together, Gabrio noticed the biting of her thumb was her tell when she had been dwelling in flux anxiety. He heard the light pattern of her footsteps grow louder as she entered the room. He turned his gaze from outside the window to the image of Essie prancing into the den.

Esmeralda tried acting dispassionate toward his question. "Oh, nothing; I noticed how the wind kept pushing the leaves towards the woods. Then I couldn't help to think how we're often times like the leaves. Influenced by an unseen force and pushed into the forest."

After hearing her lame explanation, Gabrio shook his head, chuckled and in a light voice of concern, he replied. "Essie, there's a charming quality about you being a horrible liar. Your cheeks flush, your voice falters and you're just plain horrible at it. Honesty, is a great quality I've always admired within you. That said, what are you so worried about that you unsuccessfully lied?"

Head down, she walked to the window seat to reclaim her position on the plush seat. Her soft features turned a bit frayed as her eyebrows furrowed and her mouth slanted on remembering her earlier inner turmoil. She handed him the bottle to refill their glasses and began to make clear of her distress. "I can't remember all of it, but the parts I do remember were vivid. It felt real. I know it was only a dream, but it still didn't feel right and I haven't been able to shake the feeling all-day. Then, as night approached, the feeling became worse, until you came home." She paused for a second as she looked at her husband, waiting for him to interject, but he said not a word as he handed her a glass. He only nodded his head, signaling for her to continue.

"Well, as I was saying. I stood in the middle of our woods. The surroundings were the same, but more beautiful and picturesque. I looked towards the sun as if I could willingly gain power from it. I could feel the warmth of its rays and the birds around me. Then, I remembered closing my eyes to embrace the life of day and when I opened them, the surroundings had changed. The woods became dark as if it were night, but it wasn't like night. It was more of an unnatural darkness. I remember looking at the moon and it was as red as blood. I heard something come from my left. I turned my head toward the faint noise and these eyes, as red as the unnatural moon that hung in the sky in my dream, were mere inches from mine. I could feel the creature's warm breath on my face and smell the foul odor of iron mixed with stomach acid - as if the creature killed something and was digesting it. Suddenly, this creature spoke to me. I could hear its voice in my head as if we're somehow linked." She paused for a split second to recollect her memory.

Gabrio, stared at his wife, intently listening to her speak. "What did it say to you?"

Esmeralda looked from her husband and out the window. She focused on nothing in specific as she continued to recall her dream. "In what I think was a female's voice, the creature told me some-thing like, *'Awake with the blood moon. Turn the father's sun. Death is inevitable'.*" She looked back at Gabrio and seen his expression was just as confounded as she felt. She laughed, "I know, tell me about it. I've no idea what it meant. I'm worried because the crea-ture may be referring to the 'Rite of Transformation' during the Ancient Ritual this Saturday? Is there to be a lunar eclipse? What will awake if there is one? Worse yet, who will death come to?"

Gabrio saw his wife quickly becoming overwhelmed with her over analytical thoughts. "It'll be okay. I admit it is a confusing dream and to my knowledge, there is no prior evidence to a lunar fluctuation this weekend. We would be the first ones to know, right?" He saw her nod lightly and he continued. "For now there isn't a need to concern ourselves over this dream. As strange it maybe, it could be just a dream after all." Gabrio leaned over to grab his wife's hand for further reassurance.

Esmeralda watched his full lips to better comprehend Gabrio's words and found they rang with truth. Agreeing, she nodded while looking down at their folded hands in her lap as the silence grew be-tween them. She could tell he became spooked about the dream, but she took his advice. She would let it go for now. Within the passing moments of silence, she began cultivating a desire inflicted by him and the champagne. She figured she would change the dark mood to a more playful one and knew exactly how to do it. She started by coyly looking up at Gabrio using her crystal blue eyes and long lashes to appeal to his more dominate nature.

"What was that look for?" Gabrio asked with a knowing grin.

Esmeralda wantonly smiled, grabbed the bottle from the floor and took a big swig and set the bottle back to the floor. "You know exactly what *that* look means." Gabrio smiled back at her as he sprung up from the cozy place in front of the bay window. She looked at the clock, which hung above the fireplace. The night was young and the *calling* wouldn't demanded their attention until later.

In a courteous fashion, but with thoughts less honorable running through his head, he extended his hand to her. Esmeralda lightly placed her hand into his to rise from the window seat and started to tiptoe toward the doorway as she looked back, flashing a vixen smile at him. With her back still turned to him, she stopped in the middle of the threshold of the doorway. She placed a hand on the door frame as the other pinched the hair clip to release the silky, bundle. In a throaty voice, she asked Gabrio, "Want to go for our run now?"

He watched her long hair descend in wispy layers from the nape of her neck to brush just under her taut denim covered bottom. He inhaled sharply as she began to tease him with her wanton act of seduction. He started to walk to her and found the words to reply in his own husky tone. "I believe running after you will be more pleasurable in the end."

Esmeralda seen his eyes full of life and wickedly held back a full grin. "That's good, because we start it now." Briskly, she ran through the living room into the kitchen. Rushing through the back door, she was outside before Gabrio had the chance to comprehend what she was doing. However, he caught on quick and closed on her tail. Sensing his presence behind her, Esmeralda shut the door without faulting and Gabrio slammed his lean body into the screen door, breaking through the weak barrier. Not hindered in the slightest, Gabrio was a few inches behind her and Esmeralda squealed when she turned to see he was so close. They ran into the clearing, behind their home and before they reached the threshold of the forest, Gabrio jumped to wrap his burly arms around Esmeralda. Together they fell to the ground with a soft thud masked by the sound of their laughter. In a swift move he flipped, her onto her back to pin her arms above her head as he vigorously tickled Esmeralda's sides and kissed her face.

Through her paralyzing laughter, Esmeralda gathered enough breath, "Stop, you big brute and let me go." As he leaned down to give her another onslaught of playful kisses on her lips, she playfully timed it correctly and nipped at his lush bottom lip.

Gabrio exclaimed. "Oh, you little viper. You bit my lip. Now I'm just going to have to kiss everything, but your lips."After a few more moments of roaring laughter and lingering chuckles, Gabrio let her go and she could finally speak in a full sentence, despite the laughter, still fresh in her voice. "Looks like we both tied."

Gabrio simulated false injury and in his best diplomatic tone, he stated. "My dear Essie, I would have been the true victor if you played fair and didn't slam the damn screen door in my face."

Esmeralda quickly recalled doing what he accused her of and she looked to the house to see the pitiful screen door off its hinges. In a blasé tone she commented. "Well, it looks like the door is destroyed and in need of repair." She looked at Gabrio and continuing with the mischievous mood, she stated, "Looks like you'll be working on that tomorrow since you slammed your body through it."

Gabrio grabbed her towards him, "The hell I am." Esmeralda squealed with delight as he pulled her back down to lay her on the ground as he hovered over her to resume his lighthearted attack, sounding another round of laughter. Nevertheless, their mirth quieted again into a content silence. Still hovering over Esmeralda, the aura of the night turned within the silence between them. With their fleeting laughter, came a hard growing tension, which willed to take action quickly. Gabrio suddenly noticed how unruly

Esmeralda looked under the night's dark veil. Her hair flowed on the ground, her breasts heaving under her red sweater, slowing their tempo with her breathing. He looked at the night sky once more to see the moon was entering its highest point. He both cursed the moon for giving him so little time, but adored how its light played across Esmeralda's flush, soft, creamy skin, illuminating her as if she were glowing from the inside out. Her darkened rosy lips parted, upturned slightly at the corners from their merriment, tempted his thoughts to become sultry, making his growing manhood press against his jeans and her upper thigh.

Sensing all too clearly how the mood shifted to the swirling need growing between them, she looked into his eyes and seen they were alive. The golden-honey color of his eyes began to reflect the light of the moon as a predatory sheen began to make them glow, as most nocturnal creatures do.

He leaned over her, caressing the locks of her hair away from her suddenly excessively warm skin. He wedged his fingers between her head and the damp ground to lift her head. Faces closer, she nipped at his lower lip, then gingerly kissed the slight affliction away. The pain of her lover's bite pushed Gabrio over the edge and as if he were a savage animal overwhelmed by a primitive hunger, over-took her mouth with his. He darted his warm tongue into her submitting mouth as she curled her own with his. Their breath mingled creating steam, when exhaled whirled into the chill night. Grabbing at each other with ferocious untamed yearn, Gabrio splayed his hands from her hair and down over her stomach to find the button of her jeans. Then just as he looped the button from its hold, a stronger, inner demand called to them, forcing them to pause and take notice.

3

THE CALLING

After a few moments of the temporary halt, Gabrio dropped his forehead to rest on Esmeralda's chin. He shakily exhaled from his passion coming to a sudden halt and in a whispered, disappointed voice. "Well, my love, I have to say that this is the first time I've had the moon cock-block me."

Despite her dissatisfaction of having any release, she sniggered to herself. "Serves us right, trying to beat the clock when we both know when the time runs out we have to answer." She lifted herself onto her elbows, while Gabrio unwillingly lifted himself from her and rested on his haunches next to her. She tilted her head back and seen the face of the moon stare back at her, demanding them to stall no longer. Without releasing her gaze from the white orb, she called to him. "Gabrio I think it's time to go for our *real* run with the *Moon of the falling leaves*."

Gabrio smiled wide, kissed her forehead and raised himself off the moist laden ground. Playfully mocking with a dramatic, southern drawl, he put his hand to his heart. "My Lady, much as I love what's to come. I have to say I would rather make-love to you in this field, than to be rudely called away from your lovely blooming 'magnolias'. Unfortunately, I have to agree, it's indeed that time again."

Esmeralda rolled her smiling eyes as he grabbed her hand and lifted her from the soft, dented grass. She forgot the button of her jeans remained undone and paused to loop the button back through the tiny slit.

Gabrio, walking a few feet ahead of her, noticed she was falling behind and understood what for. "Don't even bother Essie. They'll be coming right off here in a few more strides anyway."

She looked down at the undone flaps and figured he was right. She saw he waited for her so she hurried her pace by lightly trotting to him. Reaching out to her, she grabbed Gabrio's hand and together they sauntered to the edge of the clearing, to the forest.

Arriving at their destination, between the thin veil of the moonlit meadow and the cloaked forest. They stood silent, looking, listening for anything out of the ordinary. After a few passing moments of silence, Gabrio gave Esmeralda a curt nod signaling it was safe for them to step over the dividing line and into the darkness. With each passing moment the moon demanded their attention, pressuring them, twisting them from the inside out and signifying the time was passing the point of preparation.

Esmeralda became disgruntled as she felt the weight of the moon's stare. "Gabrio, we have to hurry, before I change while in my clothes!"

Gabrio became almost hostile in his reply. "I know. I can feel it. I am just glad we are already by the marked tree. I'll hurry with getting the trunk and you can start undressing."

She hurriedly started to discard her clothes by shifting out from her already unclasped jeans as Gabrio tore the false bark from the trunk of the tree to reveal its hollowed out center. He fumbled for the handle and once in his grasp, he pulled out an old, wooden trunk and quickly opened its top. Ferociously, he ripped the clothes off his body and carelessly threw them inside the mouth of the trunk. Esmeralda walked to the trunk to place her neatly folded clothes on top of Gabrio's disheveled ones and closed the top. He pushed the trunk back into the oak tree and covered the hidden entrance with the false bark. With their belongings and the trunk hidden from view, they stood gloriously naked, unashamed and free, as if they were Adam and Eve in the Garden of Eden. They looked over each others bodies, smiling admiringly at another. Then, like a Godly command forcing them out from hiding and into the opening, the 'calling' leaded their bodies with an unrelenting force binding their feet to where they stood. The moon was in its between stage of full rise and beginning to set when its silver gaze paralyzed them where they stood. The ancient power demanded their attention. Simultaneously, their heads snapped back, forced to look toward the moon. As if the moon had invisible fingers, it fiercely held their eyes open to stare toward the quarter moon. As obedient as children, they willingly succumbed to the ancient power when the moons' blinding gaze met theirs. The silver beams pierced through their dilated eyes, liquefying to a tangible mass. The cold light ran through their veins, spreading throughout their bodies all the while transforming them from the inside out.

Gabrio yelled an unearthly sound. He clawed down his face and frantically dug into his blistering flesh revealing patches of dark, bloody fur underneath the thin tissues. He pulled at his human form as if to escape a thin, blood-filled cocoon. Dark, red, blood, veins and tendons of Gabrio's human form dripped from his changing, twisting hands. His neck snapped back and broke sideways, as his mortal face distorted and melted to the ground. His spine elongated and broke through the skin, forming his unnaturally long tail.

Esmeralda's bones cracked, pushing through her muscles and ripping her skin. Her eyes popped in their sockets and the creamy, fluid ran down her face. Her legs unnaturally bent backwards and her joints scraped to divulge the form she was taking. Gritting her changing jaw, Esmeralda tried to fight against the unbearable pain. She screamed aloud, having the ear-splitting shriek end as a howl, which echoed through the trees of the forest.

The moon hung high, proud of its creation, watching them before it hid behind the murky clouds. Standing in a puddle of their superfluous human flesh and wet blood, stood the transformed Gabrio and Esmeralda. The life of the forest moved effortlessly through their heightened senses. Illuminated under the moon's beams, the forest began to glow under the midnight sun casting a silver-blue glow on the land. A rodent scampered into its nest nearby, causing Gabrio's ear to twitch to the sound as his nose lifted into the air to inhale. He looked at Esmeralda, whom did the same. Talking not through sound, but through his mind, he spoke in a deeper, calmer voice. "There's a black bear ahead, by the smell of it, it's a male. He's close, just a few miles towards Altman Lake. We are going to go for him tonight and wait to pluck an unsuspecting mortal from their life for Saturday."

Esmeralda's inner voice was as calm and huskier sounding. However, frantic with hunger from transforming, she anxiously replied. "I smell its scent on the wind. Oh god, he smells good. Can you hear the slosh of his pulse? It's strong and healthy. Hearing the blood push through his veins is mouth watering. The bear, if we took the bear... God, he smells so ripe, biting into him would be like eating an overripe peach."

Gabrio paused in calculated thought, and then voiced his conclusion. "Ready for a fight?"

In a raspy, breathless reply Esmeralda answered, "I'm ready."

With one quick, fluid movement, they ran faster than the wind in the direction where the naive bear currently resided. The hostile famine clawed at Gabrio's stomach, causing bile to rise in the back of his throat. He knew the bear smelled mouth watering. He could almost feel the thick, bitter blood of the creature slide down his throat. He snarled and snapped as he pushed harder to get to their prey. As the alpha male, he naturally ran ahead of Esmeralda, leading her through the forest for her protection if anything were to happen. As one, they dodged between the various trunks of growing oaks, pines and birch trees. They moved as if they were part of the fierce, violent wind, which still roared through the dying leaves around them. Except for the sound of their breathing and the howling wind, they moved in quick, quiet stealth. Their paws ran across the soft forest floor in soundless consistency. Gabrio intently listened to the sounds around him as they moved. He lifted his nose to breathe in the brisk air while he ran. In doing so, he knew the bear's location did not change course, nor was he alert to their approach. Gabrio smelled another pack approaching within a ten-mile radius, but they were closer. The bear would be theirs before the other pack would arrive. After a few more advances, they hurdled over the fallen oak and attacked the unsuspecting bear. Gabrio landed on the startled animal's back and clawed into its bulky tissue bracing himself from the force of the creature's retaliation. Afraid, the bear bucked onto his hind legs and tried to move quickly out from the hulking weight of Gabrio's body.

The bear's gurgled roars echoed through the night while the animal turned to grab him with no prevail. Quickly Esmeralda attacked the thick legs of the black bear while Gabrio secured himself by sinking his fangs into its neck, compelling a throaty sound of distress from the dying creature. Suddenly, Gabrio twisted his head to have a long fang puncture the artery in the animal's neck to abruptly, mercifully end the misery of the bear. The animal fell with a loud thud. Gabrio released his hold from the creature and stood over the night victorious kill. They watched the blood pour from the puncture wound and the life slowly faded from the round black eyes of the creature. Once the creature's last warm breath puffed from its gaping mouth and swirl in the cold air is when Gabrio began feeding, leading Esmeralda to follow his suit. Both feasted on the steaming corpse, quenching their hunger to the fullest.

The moon hung low over the western horizon, no longer casting its full glow over the land. The early morning light began to spread its rays into the profuse darkness. Gabrio startled awake from the dream that plagued most of the morning. He recalled waking all hours of the night to make sure Esmeralda was still next to him and as always, she lay in perfect slumber by his side. Lifting his head from his paws, he realized the forests' silver glow was fading back into its rich, luscious color with the approaching day.

Through tired eyes, he looked to the sky and seen dawn was replacing the night. He rose, arched his aching body to stretch, and shook his fur. Esmeralda, who was laying her head on Gabrio's back, was rudely awaken by her head falling to the ground with a thud. When she had risen from the ground, Gabrio looked to his left and seen Esmeralda lifting herself from where she lay. He spoke quickly. "Essie, we need to get back home. It's morning - if we don't hurry, we'll be running half the way home in our human form."

Esmeralda released a lazy yawn revealing her sharp fangs, while she stretched her lean body as well. "Then we better hurry, before we're caught by some passing mortals. We wouldn't want that."

First to arrive, Esmeralda reached the entry point of the forest. She took in the sights and seen the sun's golden rays dominated more than half of the meadow. Gabrio arrived a few moments later, panting hard, slowing his speed to a stuttering halt. Esmeralda moved out of his way before he collided into her. Gabrio's eyes were hard, glazed over as he scanned the space that was between them and their backyard. She saw he was distant in thought and wondered what was bothering him enough to almost run into her like he didn't even see her. After a few more seconds of searching he looked at her and saw the concern for him in her eyes. Not fully intending to tell her until later, he compressed his anxiety and forced to calm himself. "Don't look so worried Essie. I just wanted to make sure there was no one around, especially poachers, but then again we don't look like the average wolf and guns don't affect us."

He was rambling, which made Esmeralda recognize he was hiding something. Though she couldn't figure what could've happened in the short amount of time with her not finding out when she was next to him the entire night. If a drastic event had taken place, she would have noticed it too.

Gabrio spoke, jolting her from her own thoughts. "It's time, get ready."

They readied themselves by standing in the same location where they transformed, standing in their own puddle of discarded flesh. In unison, they watched the sun glide across the brownish-green grass, inching closer until it vigorously engulfed them. They immediately rose from the ground to stand on their hind legs. Encased in a translucent, golden, womb-like entity, their bones snapped back into place. Their faces cringed at the pain they felt as their bodies reformed while their bones were setting into place. The fur that covered their bodies fell in clumps to the ground as the halo of flesh surrounded their feet. New skin took life and crawled up their bodies, mending around each limb, creating flushed flesh. Their sharp fangs fell to the fur covered soil as their human teeth poised to take their place. After convulse twitching and snapping, they were once again whole, returning into their naked human form. Just as quickly, as it came the golden entity faded into the brightness of the day and they firmly landed to the earth.

As soon as his feet touched the ground Gabrio left his position to stride barefoot across the soft grass, heading towards the hollowed tree to recover their belongings from the trunk. Anxiety and hostility radiated from him like a perfume. Esmeralda quickly took offense as he gave her the cold shoulder and keeping her further from telling her what bothered him. She quickly covered herself using her hands and arms, she ran towards Gabrio who had already pulled the items from the tree and assembled their clothes. Gabrio was already pulling on his jeans over his briefs as he watched his naked wife trot towards him at full pace and savagely grabbed her clothes from him.

Gabrio, whom had already frayed nerves, snapped at her. "What's wrong with you?"

Esmeralda scuffed as she furrowed her brow and glared at him. "I should be asking you the same!"

Gabrio turned his attention back towards getting dressed, casting his eyes downward so she could not see the worry behind them. She angrily put on her clothes as she stared unrelentingly at him. She knew the ruse he was trying to convey and she would not allow herself to become misguided. What she felt like doing was throttle him for acting like a complete ass and not confiding her with his concerns.

I'm his wife and an alpha too, damn it. He doesn't need to handle me with kid gloves. She thought. Despite her riled inner emotion, she saw something troubled him and he needed her to be calm. Mustering up a soft voice, she asked him once again, what was bothering him.

He looked at her as if all the sadness in the world lingered within them. "This morning I had a dream."

Esmeralda's eyes became wider at the thought of her own dream and the possible connection between his and hers. Without trying to push him for information or alert him of her rising concern, she would let him do most of the talking, with a few pushes here and there to keep the conversation going. "A dream like the one I had?"

Gabrio nodded his head and continued. "But, it was worse and dark. So much darkness." He sighed.

Esmeralda nonchalantly smoothed out her sweater as she raised a brow and looked at him. "Want to tell me about it?"

Gabrio scratched his head. He knew Esmeralda was the person to take dreams and signs seriously as they proved to become bits of reality within their lives. It was a dream she had that brought them together in the first place. "I think I should since it had you in it."

"Okay, let's hear it." She said.

Gabrio spoke, reflecting the memory of his dream. "We were in our wolf forms. You were ahead of me and I was running after you. But every time I tried to get next to you a tree would appear in my way, blocking me, preventing me to get to you."

Esmeralda hung on every word, looking for something to link between her dream and his. Her thoughts as wild and frantic as her hunger for the bear last night.

He continued, growing more agitated as he recalled the nightmare. "I ended losing sight of you because of some fucking trees. Then I became blocked, surrounded by them. Frantically, I tried finding a way through them, and then I heard a distressed howl turn into a high-pitched, gurgled scream." He looked straight in Esmeralda's eyes. "It was you screaming. I knew you had been injured and worse was happening. The trees disappeared in front of me and with them gone, I knew something horrible had happened and I was too late. I ran and ran, for what seemed like an eternity. Then I ran into this strange alter that sat on a cobblestone floor. I saw you lie naked in your human form upon it, as if someone put you there for me to find. I could smell your blood, still fresh, shiny, pouring from your throat. Then I looked to the sky and seen the red moon. It was full and unnaturally close. I felt it staring down at me. I looked from its gaze and down to your corpse, but it wasn't you any longer. A blond woman lay in your place. Quickly overwhelmed, a mixed feeling of trepidation and confusion overcame me. Then I noticed an object near her open, blood covered hand. As I leaned in closer to see what it was, her piercing green eyes snapped open to look directly at me and she whispered, *"Find him."* I woke, startled and looked all around. All was as it should be.

However, I couldn't shake the feeling of someone watching us. So all through the night I watched you. I made sure you were safe next to me and that no one or nothing separated us." He took a few steps forward and wrapped her into his arms, pressing her head to his bare chest. "It felt so real, Essie. You know if anything… ever happened… I…"

He did not need to say anymore for her to understand. "I know Gabe, I know. I don't know what I would do too." Esmeralda wrapped her arms around him while she suppressed a growing lump in her throat. Quickly she began to process all that he said to find the likenesses that held within the two dreams. However, she couldn't curb the anxiety she felt at the mention of her death in his dream and the statement, 'Death is inevitable', which came through hers. Many, unanswered questions raced through her mind. However, now she needed to reassure him, just as he did for her.

"It'll be okay. It's safe to say though, these dreams aren't just dreams anymore. Call them warnings, or a glimpse of something, but it would do us good to take caution and try to go about our days as normal. If anything is to bear fruit, we'll be together."

Gabrio kissed the top of her forehead. "That seems like a sound plan, but it wouldn't hurt to do a little research about the next occurrence of the blood moon."

Esmeralda smiled. "I agree. I'll do that today while at the candle shop." She placed both hands on his warm chest as she looked up to kiss the bottom of his chin. She lightly pushed herself away and noticed how his jeans hung low on his hips slightly exposing his pelvic bone as well as the black briefs he wore underneath them. Immediately, she became aroused by how his dewy skin and unshaven face made him appear rough and rugged. "Come on, finish getting dressed, we'll go take a hot shower and finish what we started last night."

Gabrio stepped back and looked down at his attire. "I'm dressed enough."

Esmeralda rolled her eyes and smiled. "No, you're not. I don't need you, purposely or not, flaunting your chiseled body in front of Mrs. Screws-a lot, prying eyes."

Gabrio's hardy laugh echoed through the forest. "Essie, are you the jealous sort?"

Esmeralda smiled and smoothly replied. "Enough to kill."

He chuckled again as he bunched his black T-shirt together to pull it over his body. "Okay, you win. We wouldn't want you to kill the insatiable neighbor."

Esmeralda scuffed. "If her husband just doesn't one day become fed up with her and get to her first. I have a feeling he thinks about her *accidental* demise."

Gabrio smiled at her as he walked over to where Esmeralda stood. He lazily wrapped his arm around her tiny waist, pulling her close to his side as he stuffed his hands comfortably in her back pocket. He kissed the top of her forehead. "Come on, my love. We still have a whole day ahead of us at our respectable jobs, like all the other mortals. However, I want to be very thorough in helping you become cleaned up."

Esmeralda blushed as she nodded her head. "Then we shall not waste any more time." She kissed him hard before they walked towards the house.

As they reached the bottom step of the back porch Esmeralda heard the faint crackle of dead leaves grow louder behind them and realized someone was approaching in haste. Esmeralda turned and seen Mrs. Mayer crossing past the border of bright red burning bushes that separated their neighboring yards. Esmeralda's eyes thinned as she looked over the intruder with contempt as she whispered to Gabrio. "As if the thought conjured her out of thin air, here she comes now."

Gabrio did not have to turn around to see whom Esmeralda was talking about, but he did so anyway and seen Mrs. Mayer stiffly walking through their yard. However, he did have to do a double take as he became immediately shocked at the older woman's outlandish appearance. Her auburn curly hair glistened in the early morning sun and hung in loose curls around her face trailing down her back. Gabrio, thought at one time she could have been an attractive woman in her younger years. In addition, for a woman in her late forties, she was still slender enough to become passable in the right light. Despite that small factor, her personality and appearance screamed easy.

She wore heavy black makeup, giving her a raccoon-like quality around her dull hazel eyes. Her full lips, covered in a overdone dark red lip gloss. She tried too hard to draw attention to herself, which was proven since she wore hot pink high heels that sank into the dewy grass causing her walk gawkily towards them. As he continued to look her over in cold, expressionless distaste. He could not help but to notice her leopard print leggings accentuated every womanly curve of her slender figure. While the too tight black, turtleneck sweater looked like she purposely bought the item to be two times smaller than proper. Gabrio was not stupid. She was a selfish, greedy brat who craved attention. She did not care who noticed her; married, single, straight, homosexual, woman or man; she enjoyed the attention and whether it was good or bad, she would take it. Nevertheless, what was worst about her visit today was that he noticed her line of visual direction focused solely on him. She dressed that way to get his attention and he was doing all he could to repress his disgust.

He saw Esmeralda ready her stance. She slightly lifted her chin in a haughty fashion into the air, ready to fight as if she expected the unexpected to arise from the presence of the older woman. The tension thickened like the fog, which floated over the field from which they came. As a side effect of the drastic tension, Esmeralda purposely placed herself between Mrs. Mayer's pursuit and Gabrio. However, it didn't matter. The infamous Mrs. Jasmine Mayer looked beyond Esmeralda. In a high-pitched voice, which held enough contempt for her and just enough sexual drawl for Gabrio, her voice sounded lusty, almost regal in her greeting. "Good morning, Gabrio. Esmeralda."

Gabrio nodded in reply in a brief, curt manner where as Esmeralda's guarded greeting sounded bored in a monotone pitch. "Good Morning Mrs. Mayer. What brings you to the *back* porch this early in the day?"

Without looking at Esmeralda Jasmine answered her question as she continued to stare her unyielding hazel-eyed gaze directly at Gabrio, whom was looking everywhere else, but at her. Jasmine altered her voice to sound helpless. "I came over today because I was wondering if I could borrow your husband for a couple of hours to help me fix the plumbing in my master bathroom. I think a pipe's plugged. Then Bill, won't be arriving home until the start of next month. So, he can't fix it."

Esmeralda clutched her jaw as tight as she could when she saw the glints in Jasmine's eyes held a sexual nature and not one of those in genuine need. To the untrained eye, it would appear as if she was telling the truth. However, Esmeralda saw that the older woman's nostrils slightly flare, her pupils dilate and the tick of her pulse in her neck increase. Giving herself away as she lied to them both. *Yeah, like Gabrio is going into your cougar den so you can try to get your red claws into him.*

Esmeralda was going to outright refuse, but Gabrio interrupted her before she could answer. "I'm sorry to hear about that *Mrs. Mayer.*"

Jasmine straightened herself, offended that Gabrio would use her married name rather than her first name and scolded him for doing so. She hated how old the title made her sound. "Please call me Jasmine, Gabrio." She pressed.

He continued as if he did not hear her request. "I'm going to be very busy tonight as you can see our back door is in need of repair." As if the door had a part in the act, it chose that particular moment to fall to the wooden porch with a thud.

Jasmine took her eyes off him long enough to prove that he was telling the truth. Jasmine replied with a pout. "I see, but..."

Gabrio again interrupted her. "Nevertheless, I know a person, a woman to be exact, who works on that sort of thing for a living. She is a great friend of ours and she will have no trouble helping you right away. Today even. I'll give her a call when I get inside." In a flash Gabrio bent and scooped Esmeralda from her feet and into his arms. Esmeralda released a small cry as he lifted her from the porch and she wrapped her arms around his neck for support. "Now if you would be kind enough to excuse us, Mrs. Mayer. My wife and I have a very busy hour or so in front of us. If you know what I mean." Gabrio turned on his heal and trotting inside with Esmeralda bouncing in his arms. Jasmine speechless and freshly rejected, stood by their back porch steps. Her expression was a mixture of confusion, dismissal and shock. With a huff and a few petulant words, she turned away from the empty space to walk back into her own backyard to slam the door as she stomped inside.

4

PICKING OUT THE PREY
IS IN THE DETAILS

Gabrio turned a sharp left onto M-55, heading towards the small-town of Manistee as he tugged on parts of his uniform. It clung onto his clammy body because of his rushed shower and not allowing himself time to become fully dry. He took his hand to slick back his black mane, which curled around his ears, dripping water onto the collar of his shirt. He regretted at least not taking a minute to towel dry his hair and pulled at the uncomfortable collar rubbing against his neck. At last, feeling comfortable enough he stopped fussing with his clothes, he relaxed and turned on the radio.

The radio station blared the intense, rough voice of Sully Erna as the music behind him increased the strength of the band's hard rock song. Gabrio enjoyed the song wordlessly as he listened to the lyrics. However, when the song ended Gabrio stretched his hand towards the dial to search for a different station. Turning it on the Classic Rock station a familiar song was already playing. He put his hand back on the wheel and let the song play. The smooth, vibrato sound of Warren Zevon singing, poured through the speakers. On hearing the song, Gabrio instantly smirked to himself as he listened to the 1975 classic. Gabrio stared ahead, looking outward to the long stretch of road that lay in front of him. The music faded into the background as his mind once again lingered to the strange dreams, which still plagued his thoughts despite his and Esmeralda's earlier discussion on the subject. He did not want upset Esmeralda any further by lingering on them in her presence. However, now that he was alone, he could without distraction, freely think about them.

As he continued to roll them over in his mind, the more he could not shake the feeling the dreams held a hidden meaning within them. Ironically, they were so similar as well different. Nevertheless, the odds of them happening in succession were cause enough to pay close attention to their inner meaning. Other than the blood moon and the sense of death occurring in both dreams, he could not find a definite connection between them. Nevertheless, he was certain Esmeralda was the center of whatever might be going on and he contended that he would make sure she was safe at any cost. A distant thought of his parents faded into his mind, but quickly had become invaded by the radio station cutting out and letting in the shrill sound of his cell phone.

Ringing over the speakers of his 2012 Chevy Malibu, Gabrio clicked a button on his steering wheel immediately accepting the call. "Hello, Gabrio here."

The deep, regal voice of a man sounded throughout the car as he replied "Officer Mackley. I assume it's safe to speak, for you should be on your way to work."

Gabrio smirked in great admiration and respect on hearing the voice of his longtime friend-like-father and replied. "Judge Crownwelm. Yes, it is safe to speak. I got the message and I figured I would be hearing from you today."

The judge lightly chuckled in a deep, slow drawl. "Yeah, it's that time again. Can you believe it's been almost five years since the last one we had."

Gabrio reflected, "I know. We had a great showing last time. Twenty different packs and about thirty new *Beast-bloods*. How many are we expecting this year?"

Crownwelm was briefly silent, except for the sound of him fumbling through a few papers on his desk. "We have at least a hundred and twenty *Beast-bloods* showing the signs of turning this year."

"Holy shit! Why are there so many this year? Don't get me wrong, it's great that we have increased in our number, but they couldn't be at the normal age of first transformation. Come on George, it's only been five years. They're born Beast-bloods or made?" Gabrio asked taken back by the large number. He couldn't believe the increase of his kind almost tripling.

"They're all born in the blood and they're young. Most are in the age range of three to eight years old. I think only a couple of children are above the age of ten." He stated.

Gabrio absorbed the information calculating the number of people who would be at the Ancient Ritual. "How many for the pickup?"

The judge was silent on the other end of the receiver while Gabrio waited patiently for his friend's orders. The deep voice once again boomed over Gabrio's sound-system. "Only one this year. He is a fat fuck. So he'll go far and he won't run long enough without becoming quickly winded." The judge cackled at his own crude scrutiny then lightly sobered to continue. "His prisoner number was 25489. Name Carlos, Miguel 'Sin' Garcia. He has a shaved head, brown eyes and the word *El Diablo* tattooed on his neck. He's 5'11 and weighs 280 pounds. This son-of-a bitch was charged for the assault, rape, and murder of a woman and her seventeen year old daughter."

Gabrio cringed on hearing the man's crime. After all these years hearing the felonies the prisoners have committed against their own kind still made him sick to his stomach. Sick enough to leave a revolting taste in his mouth. That's why he felt no remorse when he would get the chance to take one and release them to the wolves, literally. Gabrio continued to listen patiently to the judge speak.

"He committed the crime a few years ago in Detroit. However, he scurried up here and one of our boys brought his sorry ass in for starting a fight at a place in Detroit called Scotty's Tavern. When they ran his name through the system, he had a notice detailing he was a suspect, armed, dangerous so on and so forth. I don't know the many details of the trial, because it was Judge McMatty's case. However, after a long process, he still pleaded not-guilty on all accounts. Long story short, his lawyer got all the charges dropped, claiming there wasn't enough evidence to rightfully charge the man. Someone tampered with the existing evidence and the jury couldn't convict properly because of unreliable testimonies. So he became acquitted. With that said, the system failed. A fucking wet-behind-the-ears lawyer got lucky with his first case and released an insane criminal back on the street, despite the evidence against this guy. So, this is where you come in. The other night, after Sheryl and I completed our transformations and hunted, I scouted his place to see if he still lived at the address we have on record and he still does. However, he wasn't alone. I saw he had some tawdry woman with him before they walked into his shanty of a house. I don't know if the woman lives with him or not; but I'm sure you could handle any complications if they should arise. I trust your judgment. Nevertheless, tonight you will make him the pickup. After you're done, meet me at our usual place to contain him until Saturday night, where I'll place him as bait for the newcomers."

"Where does the man live?" Gabrio asked in a monotone voice. The same voice he uses in deep concentration and consideration for the given state of affairs.

"He lives on River road, just past the Coho Bend campground in a decrepit modular. You'll know when it's his house. Especially with his subtle salute to the confederates by hanging an oversized rebel flag like an ornament over the front door of the establishment." The judge took a moment's pause. "Gabrio please be careful. Wouldn't want anything to happen to you and leave Esmeralda in a vulnerable state."

Gabrio thought what George said to be strange. As if it was a hidden threat or a concerned warning. Either way it didn't raise Gabrio's suspicions, he trusted the man with his life and so did his parents. "George, I remember the procedure. It's the same as it was last time with that other fellow who was guilty of murdering his grandparents for their money." Gabrio paused to ease his churning stomach. "God, that guy was a stroke of pure evil. Now this guy-what's the world coming to?"

The judged tiredly laughed. "I don't know, kid. I just don't know."

After a moment of silence between them, George sighed. "Well have a good day officer and tell Esmeralda that Sheryl says 'Hello'."

"Will do judge. You have a good day too, and I'll see you tonight."

"Tonight."

After the subtle click of the phone call ending, the radio station turned on once again and revealed the silky voices and music of The Eagles while singing the dark story of 'Witchy Woman'. Gabrio pondered about what he had to do as the music played in the background.

Driving down North Mitchell Street in downtown Cadillac Esmeralda pulled her red Chevy Equinox in front of the candle shop that she's owned for the past four years. Gathering her belongings in her purse, she exited out of the car, shut the door and paused for a moment to look at her building. She swelled with a sense of accomplishment and pride every time she would arrive in front of the brick structure. She remembered the sorry condition it was in when she first bought the little store from the previous owner, who used it as a pet shop. The chubby older man, whom she bought it from, was slowly losing his business, letting the condition of the shop go with it. After selling the various animals and product to another pet shop, he was more than happy when Esmeralda came to him and made him an offer. She saw the potential of the building. Nonetheless, she didn't think everything needed repair, but it did. The floors had paint splattered across them, the walls were gaping holes from an incompetent electrician, there was water damage, and mold and it smelled of cat urine. It took almost two years to get it into immaculate shape. However, it was well worth the money because it shined among the other buildings, making the surrounding shops drab in comparison. It was warm, inviting and always smelled of fresh flowers and sugar cookies because the mixture of the different scents and waxes she used to create the candles. The large, white scroll lettering on the doors and bay windows read, '*The White Wick*'. Courtesy of Patterson Flowers, a floral shop down the street, the colorful mums in front of her shop reigned in a flood of luscious golden yellows and reds. Each color complimented the various sized planters she bought from the antique shop, which connected next to her building.

She walked to the doors fumbling with the ring of keys and found the one that'll unlock the shop's doors. She flipped the closed sign to open and turned on the track lighting. She looked around the store and saw everything was just as she left it. She looked at the large wrought iron clock that hung on the honey-colored walls. *Eight-fifty. I still have time.*

She ran behind the counter to press the button of the sleek, black desktop. The gentle humming sound of the spinning fans and the passing traffic filled the silence of the shop. She trotted to the break room toward the coffee machine. Claiming a large container full of ground coffee from the cupboard she began making coffee for her and the two other women that she hired. She knew at any moment they would arrive to work. She pressed a slender finger against the 'brew' button and began to wait. After a few moments of waiting for the coffee to fill the glass container to the twelve cup line, she looked at the less impressive clock in the break room. *Two minutes till it's nine o'clock.* She thought.

Even though the coffee hadn't filled the container fully, she hurriedly poured herself a cup and accidentally burned herself on the slow stream. She hissed from her pain as she estimated the desired amount of cream and sugar. She stirred the ingredients together and walked back into the main part of the shop. She rushed sliding behind the sales counter and made herself comfortable in front of the computer. After a few clicks of the keys and mouse Esmeralda opened the browser and began her search for anything that was about the blood moon. After typing the words *Blood Moon* into Google's search bar, multiple links instantly listed. *Ugh. 83,800,000 results, seriously?* Esmeralda sighed in hopeless annoyance. *Well, might as well start with the first link.* After she searched through the fifth site in growing frustration she still found little that pertained to her. Nevertheless, she noticed the employees walked in together and was grateful for the interruption. Esmeralda looked up from the computer to smile at the young women while she saved the page for later reference and closed the browser's page. With a light singsong voice, Esmeralda greeted them. "Hello Sandra. Hello Eva. How are you both doing on this lovely Friday morning?

Sandra flashed a wide sterling smile, half waving her long manicured hands at Esmeralda as she walked toward the break room. "Hey, lady! I'm beyond walking on clouds this morning. Give me a second and I'll tell you about it. Coffee brewing?"

Esmeralda smiled at the lively attitude of the self-certified diva. Sandra was the first person Esmeralda hired. She loved having the woman around because she constantly remained positive in any given situation, her great work ethic and how she handled the customers. Esmeralda raised her voice so Sandra could hear her. "Yeah, coffee is fresh, hot and probably done. So, what's so special about today that you're walking on the clouds?" Esmeralda asked.

Eva rolled her eyes smiling. Esmeralda became thrilled that her employees were in such great spirits this morning. "She's been like this all morning would not shut up about it. Constantly talking, talking, talking…" Eva made a hand gesture as if it was blabbing away.

Esmeralda smiled. Eva was the second employee that she had hired. The woman was smart, witty and kind. Despite her being a shy beauty, Eva carried herself in a reluctant way and it added to her overall charm. Esmeralda and the customers loved the hidden peaceful aura, which illuminated around her. On top of this, she too had a great work ethic and customer service qualities. Esmeralda was impatiently curious about what the girls were talking about. "Okay. What's going on? What's the good news?"

Sandra came jogging out of the break room, her tight, brown spiral curls bouncing with each step. Excitement bloomed through her brown eyes as she spoke. "I'm getting married!"

"Oh, my God! Congratulations Sandra! When, how did he do it?" Esmeralda spoke with enthusiasm ridding in her voice.

Sandra and Eva spoke in unison. "Last night under the moon; after we made love in the tall grassy meadow is when he proposed. It was so cold, but worth it!"

Sandra looked at Eva and glared at the other woman's mocking impersonation. Unaltered Eva smiled and laughed, her green eyes twinkling with amusement and love for her happy friend and co-worker. "I've heard it so much I can predict what you're going to say."

It was Esmeralda's turn to laugh. "I understand how you both feel. When I became engaged to Gabrio, I became ecstatic! It was hard for me not to talk about anything else until after the wedding. I'm sure there were some days people wanted me to shut up, but you're becoming a bride for a short while, then you're a loving wife. I say enjoy the hell out of it."

"See!" Sandra said and stuck her tongue out at Eva, playfully.

At that moment, Sheryl Crownwelm walked into the shop, making the door sound off a twinkling signal, which usually occurs when a customer pulls the door open. Sandra was the first to speak, switching gears to a relaxed, professional stance.

"Good morning Mrs. Crownwelm. Is there anything you would like to see today of our candle stock. Earlier this week we began selling gourmet chocolate. Perhaps you would like to see what we have in that department instead?"

Esmeralda could tell that Sheryl had something urgent to say to her. "Eva, I think Mrs. Crownwelm is here for a different reason." Esmeralda said.

Sheryl looked thankful to Esmeralda. "Yes. Essie I just need a few moments of your time to speak with you about something. Is there a place we can speak in private?"

Esmeralda replied. "Of course; we can go to the break room." She grabbed her coffee. "Sheryl would you like some coffee?"

A few moments later Esmeralda and Sheryl were sitting at the wooden table in the break room with their cups of coffee resting on the table between them.

Esmeralda spoke first. "I'm glad you're here, I have a question for you, but you go first."

Sheryl started to speak with a kind smile touching her thin lips. "I don't have much time to talk. I have a long shift at the hospital today. However, I just wanted to give you the details for tomorrow night." Sheryl took a thick, manila envelope out from her purse and gave it to Esmeralda.

Just as soon as it touched her fingertips, Esmeralda opened the package and started to read vigorously through the first page of notes. After a few seconds she looked at the older woman in front of her. She could hear her heart beat differently than her own, but she knew Sheryl's made by the blood the night George and she became man and wife. However, she stopped aging when she was in her early sixties, where as George stopped when he hit early seventies.

She had crystal blue eyes and pure white hair. Her skin was clear, firm, yet a little weathered. However, born in the late 1600's, she always wore her hair in a fashion from that period of time. "You want Gabrio and me to lead over a hundred '*Beast Bloods*' into their 'Rite of Transformation' and into the *First Hunt* tomorrow with you and George?"

Sheryl nodded. "Yes. George and I thought about it and out of all the alpha couples you two seemed the most right for it. You both are the strongest, fastest and savviest during your methods of hunting and hiding your transformation from the mortals."

The compliment touched Esmeralda deeply as she flipped the first page to see the start of a long list of names, ages and sex. "Good God, this page is nothing but male and female three and four year olds. Three and four; Are you sure they're that young?" Esmeralda asked disbelieving.

She nodded again. "Yes. I couldn't believe it myself when I got the phone calls to make the list."

Esmeralda shook her head. "I was about nine, almost ten when I transformed for the first time and I stopped aging when I turned twenty-two. The pain these children are going to experience. It'll be heart wrenching to watch. Will they even understand why?"

She smiled at Esmeralda. "Essie, you know when it's a pure instinct that you're born with. You already understand without any further explanation. As for the pain, their bodies must be ready for it for the signs to even appear."

Esmeralda knew she was right, but couldn't understand why such an increase of *Beast Bloods* and why they're going to be transformed at a younger age. "Do other elders have a record about this occurring before?"

Sheryl sighed and shrugged her shoulders. "I have no idea, but it wouldn't hurt to find out if there's a few scrolls laying about the monastery." She laughed as she started to rise from her seat, pushing her chair behind her as she rose. "Thank you for the coffee and for agreeing to lead with us. I'll now leave so you can get back to work."

Esmeralda smiled and gave her longtime friend a hug. "To be an elder is an honor we're more than happy to accept, Sheryl. I'll see you out." She walked out of the break room and seen Sandra showing a customer the unique sculpture candles as Eva was ringing another customer's total at the cash register. "Have a good day Sheryl." Esmeralda called to her friend as she headed out the door. Sheryl waved back as Esmeralda once again slid behind the counter. Suddenly remembering, she thought. *Oh shit! I forgot to ask her my question.*

Sheryl walked to her car, opened the door and slid herself into the driver's seat. She looked toward The *White Wick* to see if Esmeralda was watching her leave, but there was no one there. She fumbled with her cell phone as she pulled it from her purse and started to make a call. "Pick up, you old bastard." Sheryl said impatiently. The line clicked over. "Hey, it's me. They did. Yes. Yes. I love you too. No, I have to work late tonight. Okay. I love you too." The line went dead and Sheryl ended the call. She put her phone into her purse, grabbed her keys to start the ignition and drove away. She began to hum and old song, pleased that after so many years of waiting and planning the signs were showing. It's finally beginning. Enacting her plan, she picked up her phone again. Now, was the time to gather the coven.

5

THE GUEST

"It was one hell of a day today, Officer Armstrong." Gabrio stated, talking to Marrok as they walked through the doors of Correctional Oaks Facility and into its surrounding parking lot.

"Tell me about it. I was taking a prisoner back to his cell and the son-of-a-bitch decided to spit in my face. Of course, he did it once he was behind the safety of his bars. Thank God I moved my head in time or else it would've hit me and not my shoulder."

Gabrio shook his head as he looked at his Superman keychain. "Was it the new prisoner that came here last week? Brown, crew-cut hair, handle- bar mustache, goes by the nickname '*Quiet-Man*' because of the John Wayne tattoo across his back?"

The blonde hair and crystal blue-eyed man looked at Gabrio and grinned. "He got you too?"

Gabrio shook his head again, smiling. "No. He got Jimmy though when he first came here. The guy seemed calm walking through the doors, and then he saw Jim and quickly kicked him right between the legs and dropped him right to the ground."

Marrok started to laugh. "Oh man. Doesn't it seem like Jimmy always gets the worst of the prisoner's antics. First, he received a hard fist to the face last month, which started the uproar in the cafeteria. Then a kick in the pants last week; He better keep a close eye out for number three it might be the one that keeps him away for a few days."

Gabrio and Marrok were at their own separate automobiles when Gabrio received a phone call from Esmeralda on his cell phone.

Marrok caught on to Gabrio's ring tone. "Bump-N-Grind. R. Kelly. Seriously Gabe?" He flicked a golden brow.

Gabrio smiled and raised a finger in the air, telling him to hold on. "Hold that thought Marrok, it's my wife calling."

Marrok nodded his reply while smiling at the absurd ring tone and patiently waited until Gabrio was no longer occupied.

"Hello my dear. Everything okay? Good, good. I don't know. It's Friday, so how about pizza and beer?. No, don't worry, I'll pick it up. You go home to get everything ready." He looked at Marrok, who was swiping at something on his phone. He spoke a little lower to Esmeralda. "I'll be bringing a guest home for dinner. Yeah, he did call me. Yeah, but that's not for a while. Okay. I love you too. Please be careful and drive safe." Gabrio hung up the call and tucked the phone back into his pocket as he asked Marrok. "Have any plans tonight?"

Marrok was silent for a brief moment. "No, not really. I was thinking about getting a few drinks at the bar in town."

Gabrio interrupted. "Do you want free beer and pizza at my place?"

Marrok chuckled. He and Gabrio had been friends for years and never was he invited to his home. He knew he was always a private man, but the invitation made gave him a slight pleasure that made the offer seem special. "Yeah, company sounds like a better change of routine than hanging out at some rickety bar. Since it's getting colder the women are going to the bars less and it has been slim pickings since last week and Jenna hadn't call me back since we last hooked up."

Gabrio laughed. "Looking for love in all the wrong places?"

Marrok chuckled."Shut the fuck up, man." He laughed again. "Let me go home and get a few things situated. I need to get out of these damn clothes."

He knew what he meant. When the work day ended, nothing was better than to rid yourself of your work gear. "I don't blame you. Do what you need to do. Remember where I live?" Gabrio asked.

"Yeah, I think I do. I have your number if I need directions. What time should I be there by?" Marrok asked.

Gabrio looked at his phone. "It's six now. So, I say in about an hour and a half."

"Sounds great, I'll see you there." Marrok happily said.

Gabrio nodded. "Okay. See you later, man."

Each climbed into their own cars simultaneously. However, Marrok was the first to back out, then leave. Gabrio followed his lead and drove behind him, eventually taking different directions leading to their own destinations. As Gabrio drove he thought it through and figured it was time to further his friendship with Marrok by inviting him over. He did have an ulterior motive to invite the man over. He wanted Marrok to meet Esmeralda. Within Gabrio's a hundred and thirty four years, he had befriended countless mortals in his different lines of work. He had seen them eventually wither down and die as Gabrio stayed forever young, forever moving from place to place with Esmeralda. However, he's always kept his distance with them and he never brought one of them home for obvious reasons. Despite that fact, he had known Marrok for years and from the first time he met the man he knew there was something different about Marrok. Something recognizable was underneath his skin. However, he had a feeling it lay hidden, waiting to break free and take a breath. Gabrio wanted to see if

Esmeralda's would sense it too, confirming what he felt was not all in his head.

Esmeralda saw Gabrio pull into the curving driveway to park his car in the already open garage. "Don't rush. Let him walk in the house." Esmeralda kept looking out the window to see if another car was trailing in behind Gabrio, but she noticed no one else was driving into the driveway, yet. She heard the garage door closing while the connecting door to the garage in the kitchen began opening. Esmeralda left her post from the couch to rush towards Gabrio.

"Hey, you." Essie gave him a quick kiss as she took the hot pizza boxes from his hands and rushed towards the kitchen table to put them down.

"And a sexy *hey* to you too." Gabrio responded in a playful tone.

Esmeralda turned toward Gabrio as he was wrapping his arms around her waist to land a kiss on her neck. However, he missed his mark when he turned into him and backed herself into binding arms. "No. Wait a second. I don't know how much time we have left until your guest gets here, but I need to ask and tell you a few things before he does."

Gabrio determined to give her a kiss and did so a bit forcefully and briefly on the lips. "Okay, shoot."

Esmeralda shot him a look at his brisk kiss while she took a deep breath for all that she had to say and in a large exhale she began. "Sheryl came by the store today and gave me a manila envelope detailing all the new 'Beast Bloods' this year. There are over a hundred of them and they start at the age of three! Can you believe that three year olds are already showing signs of changing form? Sheryl asked me if we'll lead the 'Rite of Transformation' and the 'First Hunt'. I told them it would be an honor to do so and that we accept to become elders with them. Second, I couldn't find anything regarding the blood moon that pertained to us, yet. There are some links that feel the blood moon is the sign of the end of times or a great change will come to mankind. Then someone said the blood moon is a symbol used commonly in witchcraft when issuing a blood circle or a time when a coven can cast their most powerful, influential spell. Also, the next blood moon is not until the middle next year. So it would be for a little while longer until a lunar eclipse will occur. Third, when are you supposed to meet with George tonight? Finally, what on earth are you doing bringing a mortal around here?" Esmeralda was wide-eyed and winded when she finished talking. She took steady, deep breaths to pace her breathing.

Gabrio looked at her in amazement. "Wow."

Esmeralda laughed as she poked his chest. "Don't *wow* me, Gabe. Like I said, I don't know how much longer we have until your guest is here."

Gabrio focused his vision on the face of the grandfather clock in the den while placing the case of Budweiser on the table behind Esmeralda. "Yeah, you're right, he's to be here any time now. Okay, so I'll try to be as quick as you and just as thorough in my answers. I'll start with answering the questions."

Taking a deep breath as well, Gabrio began. "I'm supposed to meet George after two in the morning after we've transformed. We'll hunt together, but you have to stay here while George and I capture the prey." Esmeralda gave no protest and nodded in compliance. Gabrio continued. "I have my reasons for asking Marrok over tonight, but I'm not going to tell you until after he leaves."

She rolled her eyes and was going to defiantly assert her thoughts, but Gabrio interrupted her before she could. In a soft voice he said. "Essie. Trust me."

Esmeralda searched his handsome features for any inkling of doubt that maybe there. However, only his obnoxious confidence radiated from him. Her skepticism dissipated and she sighed. "Okay Gabe. I trust you know what you're doing."

She leaned in to kiss him lightly on his full bottom lip. She looked up at him and smiled as her eyes became distant, as if she was concentrating on something. "We'll talk more later on the subject. He'll be here in five... four... three... two...." As she hit the one mark, Marrok pulled his truck into the driveway.

Gabrio promptly kissed her nose as he let go of her to meet Marrok at the door. "You couldn't have timed that any better."

Then she gloated. "I heard him approaching from ten miles away."

Gabrio chuckled as he walked toward the front door. "Sonic hearing is part of the life."

Esmeralda smiled as she trailed behind him. "You make us sound like superheroes"

As his hand touched the doorknob as he flashed a grin and quickly stated, "You can call me Superman."

Esmeralda shook her head, grinning at how ridiculously charming he could be.

Gabrio waited for Marrok to knock a few times before opening the door. "Hey. Come on in."

Marrok walked into the house and quickly took in the open layout of their home. He became impressed by the insides of the home, which wasn't what he expected based from the outer appearance of the establishment. Styled as a modest brick manor house in the countryside of England, the outside came complete with lush gardens on either side of the pathway leading to the front door. *This, on our salary?* He thought to himself. Accompanied the gardens were overlapping ivy clutched to the walls and lighted coach lanterns. However, once stepping inside, the scenery whisked to a more elegant Mediterranean design. He looked at Gabrio and smiled in slight embarrassment since he found himself gaping at their house as if he was a mindless dolt. However, he shook it off rather quickly and greeted them. "Hey, Gabe. Mrs. Mackley. What a beautiful home you have."

Gabrio smiled wider and swelled a bit with pride. He noticed Marrok's surprise turned to embarrassment, but to ease his friend, he feigned not to notice. "Thank you. I owe the credit of this cozy abode to my wife. It was her designs and decorations that made it as you see it."

Esmeralda took that as a cue to step forward, reaching out to shake his hand, despite him being a human. "Hello. You must be Marrok. I'm Esmeralda. It's so great to finally put a face to the person Gabrio mentions so often."

He leaned forward to grab her extended hand. As soon as their hands touched electricity rushed to her heart. It caused her heart to skip a beat to match his steady pulse and their hearts began to beat as one. Esmeralda became immediately startled. She quickly looked in his eyes and seen there was no fluctuation in his demeanor. He didn't seem to notice the strange connection. Unless, he did and became skillful at hiding his emotions. Flabbergasted at what just happened, she instantaneously wanted to pull her hand back and wipe her palm on her jeans to rid herself of the sensation, as if it would help. However, she ignored the rude impulse with her teeth clenched. Though her smile was less genuine, she held it firm. She lightly, but rapidly released her grip from his hand to put it behind her back as if she was keeping it from his reach. In a light voice of warmth she spoke to him again. "Pizzas are on the table next to the beers. You are more than welcome to help yourself to whatever we have available. You don't have to worry about being overly coy or shy, because we're not."

Gabrio looked into his wife's eyes as she looked at him. He noticed the small ticking pulse in the base of her throat was rapidly pounding against the skin and thought. *She felt something.* Gabrio smiled inwardly *I knew she would.*

Marrok already out of his shoes started to take his coat off. "Where would you like me to put these?"

Gabrio pointed to a dark oak door. "In that closest to your left. You can leave your shoes next to ours where you stand."

Esmeralda left the gathering by the door to prepare the pizzas and beer for the inevitable invasion. "Come on and eat before they start to switch their temperatures."

After a couple of hours of lively jokes, laughter and trivial conversation through their meal, Esmeralda thought it was time to get to know Marrok on a slightly deeper level. She started with a simple question. "So Marrok, Gabrio told me you went to U of M for a few years and played football?"

Marrok momentarily looked at the bottle in his hand, then back at her as he replied in a casual tone. "Yeah, I went there for about three years. I was lucky enough to gain acceptance and play football because of my scholarship."

Gabrio's eyes lit up over the turn of conversation. Gabrio was hardly in his twelfth year of life when football was first formed around 1892. When it began growing in popularity, his love for the game grew with the franchise. Resulting into a deep, oftentimes raging passion for the game. "I bet that was an experience beyond belief." Gabrio stated with a knowing leer as they had conversations before about the sport..

Marrok smiled wider. Reminiscing about his experience brought past feelings into full view as he spoke. "Oh, man! It's an incredible high playing on the field with the crowd roaring. A pulsing beat of the chants, screams and stomps. It was staggering to take in all at once!"

Esmeralda courteously interrupted, her voice filled with cheery curiosity. "What did you study while you were there?"

Marrok slightly sobered from his ecstatic memories. "I took courses in Medieval and Early Modern studies. I figured it was sensible to choose something that I had a passion for, just in case something happened where I couldn't play professional football."

Gabrio spoke with calm enthusiasm. "Really? A great friend of mine teaches those courses for the university. Did you have Professor Hartman?"

Marrok smiled. "Yes, I did. He was a great teacher. One of the coolest, nicest men I've ever met. Too bad my freshman year was his last year of teaching before retirement."

"Oh, I didn't know he retired. It's been almost ten years since we've last spoken." Gabrio said.

Esmeralda's interest became piqued even further. She assessed him closely while trying to understand what Gabrio saw in the tall, blonde, blue eyed-man that he invited into their home. In addition, she needed to know why there was an immediate connection between them when they touched hands. It wasn't a bond of abrupt soul attraction, like how she felt towards Gabrio when they first met. No, this was a strange connection of familiarity. Their hearts beat as one giving the illusion Marrok was a werewolf and part of the clans. Yet, he reeked of mortality and contradicted the syncing of the hearts. Frustrated, Esmeralda grew confused because she was not being able to quickly understand the connections between them. Without missing a beat in the conversation she asked. "What inspired you to choose that field of interest?"

Marrok looked a bit taken aback with the series of questions, but he was happy to continue. "The courses thoroughly covered the events that occurred in the time frames that most interested me. I was taking other history classes as well, but this course was my favorite. What inspired me? I would have to say it was a combination of things, but mostly my grandfather. He told me stories from his youth, days of the war and I loved listening to them all. I've come to realize the events of the past collides with future events. If you know the origin of past events you'll have a better understanding of the future. Then hopefully a knowledge to know how to deal with what may come." He noticed the room remained silent. Feeling it was because of what he had said, he made a joke. "Plus, I thought it would impress the women." He chuckled.

Esmeralda chuckled, remaining impressed with Marrok's insight and nodded her head in silent agreement. Then, she said just as much. "I agree with that wholeheartedly. The understandings of the past and future and how they truly affect one another."

Gabrio said as he stealthy tapped Esmeralda on her arm enough for her to notice and look up at him. Their gaze met and she could read within Gabrio's eyes. *See. I told you there's something about him.*

Esmeralda smiled as she shook her head to look down at their folded hands and back at Marrok. Gabrio noticed Marrok finished the last swallow of his beer with a gulping swig. He quickly finished his as he rose from the couch. "You're ready for another beer, Marrok?"

"Yeah, that would be great, thanks." He replied.

Gabrio walked into the kitchen, leaving Marrok and Esmeralda in the living room together. After a few moments of silence between them, Marrok spoke, unable to deal with the silence, he decided to show is gratitude. "Thank you Esmeralda for welcoming me into your lovely home tonight. It was cool to let me come and hang out with you guys."

Esmeralda looked at him and flash a smile as she looked at her half-full beer. "I know you guys been great friends for a while. It's really no problem Marrok." She quickly thought. *Because if you were a problem I would just kill you now and eat you later.* Despite her inner stirrings Esmeralda continued to speak politely. "Maybe next time you could bring your significant other and we could go out and eat." She almost smiled as their usual meaning of going out to eat was after transformation and getting the first kill of the night.

Marrok chuckled. "No, I don't have anyone that claims either of those titles right now, but I wouldn't mind doing this again. You two have been wonderful."

Esmeralda raised an eyebrow, nodded her head as she gave thanks and analyzed the man in front of her. Through the awkward passing silence they looked everywhere, but at each other. Both unsure what to say next.

Gabrio walked in the living room holding a beer for each of

them. As Marrok reached with his right hand to grab the beer from Gabrio's offering hand, Gabrio noticed a flash of silver wrapped around Marrok's index finger. As he was about remark to see the item, Esmeralda spoke before he could. "I'm curious Marrok, how did you begin working at the prison with Gabrio?"

He looked a bit worried at which route the conversation was about to take. "What you do you mean?

Esmeralda imperturbably explained. "You went to college for history, played football on a scholarship. What made you change your mind about your passion for history and a chance at professional football to get into the line of work you're into now?"

Marrok's face slumped as his brow furrowed in his now sporadic thought. Esmeralda thought she had crossed a line and felt bad for making his thoughts turn time to a distressing occurrence. Gabrio shot her a look which Esmeralda could clearly read. She shied a bit from her husband's scolding glare. However, there's much at stake of not knowing him further. Also, she needed to know why she would have any feeling toward this stranger, this mortal, anyway. Esmeralda quickly interjected."I'm sorry I don't mean to pry. Sometimes my impulsive curiosity makes me speak -."

"Don't worry about it." Marrok forcefully said. Then calming his voice he repeated his sentence in a softer tone. "Don't worry about it. It happened a long time ago. But you know, some things are impossible to forget and can't get over. They shape who you are."

Esmeralda and Gabrio silently gave each other a look as they waited for Marrok to compose himself.

After a few seconds of silence, he took a deep breath and exhaled as the darkness of his eyes widened in recollection. "I'll try to keep it short as possible. When I was younger, I lived with my mother with my grandparents on our family's horse farm in the most secluded part of Wisconsin. On my tenth birthday, my mother took me for a horse ride in the middle of the night. For God knows what, I don't know."

Gabrio noticed Marrok's nose flare and quickly thought. *Oh, there's more to that incident. I wonder if Essie picked up on it.* Gabrio turned from his thoughts and tuned back in Marrok's voice without missing a beat of the conversation.

"The horse became spooked and we fell off his back. My mother instantly broke her neck and died. My grandparents raised me since that day. However, after her death, I became lost and troublesome." Marrok's emotion began to edge past his control. "God bless their souls, my grandparents raised my troubled ass as best as they could. Even after they pushed me into football, my studies, dances, and other endless happenings; I was still restless and bitter. After I graduated, they thought it best I should apply for colleges outside Wisconsin and see what I could have the world. 'Live it up' as best as I could. I thought it was a great idea to escape. I was so sick of seeing the same things every day, the same people, the routine of it all. Out of all the applications for scholarships and entry into countless schools, the University of Michigan accepted me first and I took it." Marrok's eyes darkened as his lips thinned. "When the time came I told my grandparents, I love them, I'll see them soon and I packed up and left. I still went home for breaks and so on. However, when I was in the middle of my junior year, I received a phone call. It from the sheriff's department. The sheriff at the time, a fat, lazy fucker, told me that my grandparents' farm burned to the ground and that they died trying to escape. They were too late to help."

Marrok's lips began to curl as his teeth clenched. "It took two days to get the flames down." His voice became shaky as his throat was choking him. "The house, hay barns and fields were all aflame. Nothing of the house or of our lives there survived. All turned to ash, except a few things. The only set of parents I've known, who took the role as my parents were gone. My mother was their only child and I was an only child. After all those years of feeling alone, I now truly was. I learned from the sheriff that a fucking mental patient, who was an extreme pyromaniac, became blamed for the arson of my family home. The man had already been in prison for a similar set of crimes, but somehow escaped and found his way to Wisconsin. While *vacationing* he fucking burnt down twenty homes in three days. Twenty homes, twenty different families, who all survived, but mine and my family's home was the worst fire of them all.

What put the cherry on top of the shit pie of that day was the warped son-of-a-bitch was proud of what he did. I heard they found the man rocking back and forth on the ground, several hundred yards away screaming about how beautiful it was. Screaming, his creation of the massive fire was perfect. On hearing that, all the old bitterness, anger and hate came rushing back in full force, but it had a reason to thrive. No one was going to be a victim like me if I could control it. If I had a hand at controlling the lives of innocent people like my grandparents, to keep them safe from sick assholes like that guy, then so be it. I did whatever it took. So, after selling the horses, which all incredibly survived and my grandparent's other salvageable assets, I devoted I would avenge them, but I was going to do it the right away. That's when I changed my course of life. I busted my ass off and with my endless supply of raging motivation I became who I am today."

With those last words, the room stood still and silent. Esmeralda found her voice as she wrapped her head around the horrific visions that danced around in her head. Marrok's story held one big similarity as to how Gabrio's parents died. Fire, had been a wicked tool used to kill their kind for thousands of years. She understood that pain. Whereas Gabrio could relate, but for Marrok's people, there hadn't been justice for them. In a tiny voice she asked, "What happened to the man who did that to you and your family?"

Marrok looked at her with the residue of the past still lingering through his eyes as he comprehended what she asked. "After his trial, which he pleaded guilty for, he was sentenced to a lifetime of solitary confinement. After a few days he died by slitting his wrists with a piece of metal from his bed. A life for their lives; It all works out the same, I guess."

The grandfather clock in the next room loudly rang the chimes, resting on the eleventh mark, which sounded through the music that still played on the radio. Feeling it was time for him to go, Marrok ascended from his seat and stretched. "Well, I guess it's about time for me to get going."

Gabrio and Esmeralda were already out of their seats following him to the door as Marrok fetched his coat and shoes.

"Thanks for coming over Marrok. I hope you enjoyed yourself." Gabrio said.

Marrok smiled at his friend. "I did - I had a great time. Once again thank you for your hospitality. You and your wife are great people."Once his shoes and coat were firmly in place he gave a short, but genuine wave goodbye to Esmeralda. "Thank you Esmeralda. It was great finally meeting you. Hope you have a lovely night."

Esmeralda smiled. "Come back anytime. It was fun."

Marrok gave a curt nod of his head and walked out the door. Gabrio followed him leaving the door open behind him as he quickly descended toward Marrok.

"Hey, wait a second!" Marrok turned around. Gabrio spoke quickly. "I hope what happened in there didn't...."

Marrok chuckled. "It didn't. I just thought I should head home before the clock struck twelve. You know that fairy godmother can be a real bitch sometimes."

Gabrio snorted at his friend's dud of a joke, but he didn't become fouled by Marrok's nonchalant attitude. However, he let it go. "Okay, if you say so. You have a good night Marrok and thanks for coming over."

"Yeah. You too, Gabe." Marrok said as he jumped in his truck and shut the door tightly.

Gabrio gave a short nod and a wave to Marrok as he started his truck and pulled out of the drive way and drive down the road until he couldn't be heard anymore.

6

PREPARATIONS

Gabrio walked backed into the house. Instantly, he noticed the house was void of music they had playing low and Esmeralda standing, waiting for him with a look of excited nerves fluttering across her beautiful features. After Gabrio shut the door, without delay, she blurted. "I felt something. There's more to him than he knows or is giving away. Overall, he's genuine, but there's something more. I just don't know what yet."

Gabrio smiled. "I knew you would notice it too. It's almost like he's one of us, but then he isn't."

Esmeralda exclaimed at his understanding. "Exactly; do you remember ever feeling the strange sensation of familiarity, like electricity when you first shook his hand or anything like that?"

Gabrio scanned his memory. "No, I didn't. Did you?"

Esmeralda bit her lip hesitant to tell him, and then figuring it was better for him to know, she replied. "Yes. I did, but I don't know why. I've never seen him before tonight." She scanned her thoughts of the different possible theories about what might be the answer, and then remembered. "I should add that when I touched his hand our hearts started to beat as one."

Gabrio arched an eyebrow. "You know that doesn't happen unless we're in the company of those born werewolves and those made, which have a undeniable, different heartbeat that won't ever match ours, like Sheryl."

Esmeralda walked into the living room and plopped on the overstuffed leather couch. Becoming increasingly irritated she replied. "I know, I know. God, no wonder you invited him over tonight to see what I thought." Esmeralda dove into a quagmire of contemplation. "Let's say he's like us. He would have a distinct smell to him, but it doesn't exist when it comes to Marrok. He smells too sweet. Therefore, he's human. Right? He reminds me of a child that has the blood, but hasn't gone through the sickness yet." Esmeralda abruptly, stopped her thoughts to focus her contrasting almond shaped eyes straight at Gabrio's. "What tipped you off about him? If you didn't feel what I felt, how did you know?"

Gabrio looked straight ahead at nothing in particular and took a pregnant pause. Then he looked at her. "I would've said, it's my gut telling me there was something about him. Pure instinct, so I acted on it."

Esmeralda laid her head back down on the arm of the couch as she stared at the patterned tiles on the ceiling. "It seems like something building and it's going to happening at once. Doesn't it? It's like a swirling vortex, hiding in a storm, ready to land its point, but you don't know when."

Gabrio plopped down next to Esmeralda and pulled her into his arms to hold her tight. "Yeah, it does seem that way. Overall, it's just the gathering tomorrow that has us all excited. Then, it will pass."

Comfortably squished in his hold, she took refuge in his arms and snuggled her face into his chest. "Possibly, but you and I know the aura had changed. There's a different power swirling through the air, like when a storm is coming and we can feel it. Somehow it's different with the dreams, the Ancient Ritual and now Marrok. However, I guess with Marrok we can keep him close, keep an eye out for anything suspicious and try to prepare for the worst. He is only mortal after all. One day he will die of old age. Sickness. A bus. However, if he proves a risk to us and our kind…"

She didn't have to finish for Gabrio to understand. He nodded. "We'll deal with him sooner than expected."

Gabrio felt Esmeralda's head nod against his expanding chest. "We would have to change him. So, he's in danger as well."

He agreed with Esmeralda. The aura has changed as if someone added a strange, foreboding energy into the air. *Something's coming, but only God knows what.* Gabrio thought.

Esmeralda released her silence. "It's almost time again. The *calling* is a subtle whisper right now, but maybe we should start heading to the meadow. You have to prime and ready yourself to get the prey after we hunt together."

Gabrio lifted her head as he placed a lingering kiss on the corner of her mouth. "The lark is gone, let the nightingale call."

Esmeralda laughed as Gabrio lifted himself from the couch and scooped her up in the motion. "You're such a poetic oaf!"

He smiled at her as he nuzzled her neck. "Yeah, but you love it."

Esmeralda rolled her eyes as they headed outside to answer to the call.

Meanwhile

Sheryl was in a hysterical state of excitement as she set her large, crystal blue eyes on the wondrous moon. She admired its beauty as it hung suspended like a white globe in the blackened night sky. Her person became with its silvery illuminating caresses that shined across her pale, aged skin. She looked to her left toward the group of women and seen all dressed in the same black hooded robes as she. However, the only difference between the sisters of the coven were the various symbolic seals they wore on a long silver chain around their necks over their plain attire. Seals special to their specific powers.

"The moon's entering its highest point. We have to prepare our circle before the moon starts to descend. Move, now!" Sheryl shouted to them. She was soon to transform into a Beast Blood, but she fought against until the time came when she no longer could.

The chattering women quieted as they sauntered in the dark forest, creating a shadowed swaying mass that broke into seven sectors. Peeping pale, bare feet poked beneath their robes as each woman gathered the black material the bottom from their robes to step on the large primeval stone circle. Sheryl was the last woman to step on the stone as she readied herself to talk in a voice of command. "My sisters, I gather you tonight for it's time for the summoning of the guardian's of Heaven and man. Using my visionary power, bestowed on me from the power of the angels. I've had visions of greater importance than our coven have already succeeded. They tell me the signs have set into motion and I know this to be true since I have seen the blood moon with the destruction and the glory that shall come."

Collectively the women gasped and words of disbelief released through their whispers, except for a few that broke free into loud voices.

"How can this be?" A woman asked as she held her protective medallion.

"No! What you say is a lie!" Another woman yelled, looking at Sheryl in fear.

Sheryl's sudden rage became apparent as she looked at the younger woman, who called her a liar. "You better control your sister, Victoria! Or I'll give her a disgraced death."

Victoria gasped and complied fearfully. "Julianne, hush your tongue!" She pleaded for her sister by smoothing the verbal injury with liberal logic. "What she meant to say mistress is that how do we know that your visions were not only dreams because of stress or other mental influences?"

Sheryl's eyes became wider from the defiance of her coven. "Do you doubt me? The strength of my mind. Overall, my power." She snarled as her eyes sunk into black holes as they looked to each woman.

The older woman, who spoke for Julianne, lifted her hands up and cowered in fear of Sheryl's greater power. "No, no Mistress. It's not that she doesn't fully believe what you say is true, but what other proof, than your words, do we rely on? Our visions show nothing of that degree. The blood moon affects all of mankind and all the creatures that inhabit this world. You know our coven has always aided the side of the heavens. We have to be sure because what we do tonight can aid the world or if it's too soon we will face punishment or worse, by our own power or the ultimate power."

Sheryl's rage slowly subsided at the cautious speech of the second oldest sister. Her eyes returned to their icy blue normality as she responded in a cold voice. "The werewolves have increased their number by triple fold. There 're over hundred born Beast Bloods that are to transform for the first time tomorrow night. All of you know what the prophecy details as well as I. This is why it's necessary to prepare ourselves for the worst! The battle will break soon, and then war will come."

Julianne, usually a timid woman, couldn't contain her impulse to voice her opinion once again. "Something about it doesn't feel right, Mistress. How do we know that you have no alternate motive behind your summons for us tonight? Or you're not influenced by a darker evil, which our kind is even more prone to demonic possession."

The women felt an apprehension fill the atmosphere as their faces held expressions of astonishment toward the outlandish woman. They fearfully and eagerly paid attention to the conflict between their mistress and the newest, youngest sister, hoping that their beloved sister would keep her mouth shut so she could live.

Sheryl's face was unreadable for the briefest of moments. When her face became shadowed by the passing clouds covering the light of the moon, the sisters could see the glowing whites of Sheryl's eyes and her wide malicious smile under her hood. She could hear their hearts beating quicker, but Julianne's heart began to beat frantically in her chest. Sheryl's contriving lure. As the clouds released the moonlight once again, Sheryl's smile was gone and a plain expression took its place and her voice was a deathly calm as she spoke. "So you think your mistress has been a liar and a deceiver for the past four hundred years?"

Julianne swallowed hard to find her throat was scratchy and dry. "N... no, but..."

"Good, then we shall proceed?" Sheryl interrupted coolly, even though she was trembling from fighting the urge to transform. Her coven never knew she contained the blood of the werewolves and she wasn't going to let them know until they were running and screaming from her hunting them. Sheryl firmly commanded. "We'll no longer waste any more time of this frivolous talk. As your entrusted mistress I have given you enough proof for all of us to call on the angels. So, ready your positions!"

The sisters became even more stupefied at Sheryl's casual reaction, but it didn't ease their heightened vigilant state of the situation. Hesitantly they began by taking off their silver seals and placed them on the ground in front of where they stood. Once the seals were in place on the stone-ground an unearthly beam of white projected skyward from them. A low pulsing hum sounded from the beacons of light. The night fog began to gather motion and swirl around them. Sheryl looked to the sky. *It's time.* She thought. "Undress. It's time to be part of the nature that surrounds us. Become as vulnerable as the earth and as naked as the wind." She yelled through the rising wind.

The women began to disrobe revealing their scantly covered bodies. They knelt on their knees and swayed to the pulse of the beams raising their arms into the air. Sheryl disrobed as well, however, she stood above them as the spell and her status as a leader dictated. The wind whipped the sisters' hair all about them as they began to chant their mantra in high tones.

"Take our life's nectar. Use us to gain your strength. We summon thee." Sheryl screamed through the wind with her hands raised above her head. Her face was a vicious snarl as she spoke the words of old. "Come and see thee. The time has come of your need. The wicked are near. We call on our protector and together speak the name that we seek. Come forth to greet us with your presence. Hear our hearts. They are yours for the taking. Hear our voices. Let them lure you here. Follow them. Follow them. Follow them Laycerath." She yelled deceitfully. As soon as the spell was complete the white beams that burst from the seals busted into seven columns of flames. A lower hum came from the shaking ground. The sisters began to rise, confused and even more afraid.

Julianne looked at Sheryl. "She's a traitor of the coven! She has raised a demon in place of an angel. We are all doomed to death."

The women began to scatter in horrid screams. Julianne tried to run, but Sheryl extended her hand and pulled back. Julianne lifted from her feet as she flew back into Sheryl's grasp from the invisible force which propelled her backward. Sheryl looked to the moon once again as her fingernail elongated to cut the struggling woman's throat. She let her drop to the ground with a heavy thud. The blood poured from Julianne's stretched neck in the middle of the stone circle. With a life of its own, the puddle of blood shaped into a perfect circle and began bubbling. Sheryl watched with exhilaration at what was happening before her eyes. The blood gathered upon its self, rising from the ground and forming a tall, writhing shape. The flames faltered and extinguished. The forest seemed darker than before and nature stilled to silence. The low hum and shaking ground subsided and out of the blood stood a magnificent naked man. Sheryl looked at him. He was as perfect as the day he died.

Laycerath stood before her as the residue of blood glistened over his muscular body. His dark hair was long down his back and his square jaw, set in a stern expression. He looked around him and noticed he stood within a darkened forest. He remembered dying elsewhere.

Sheryl squinted and looked into his blood red eyes. She smiled wide as she gave him a heartwarming, loving look. "My son."

Laycerath stepped forward from the darkness and into a ray of moonlight. In a heavy Scottish slur he spoke coldly. "Mother."

7

CATCHING THE PREY

When the night came the world was Gabrio's playground. He could freely roam at night because of his jet-black fur, which made him nearly invisible, even in plain sight. He could thank his father for the trait as his coloring worked like a charm when it came to stalking prey. He could get as close as he wanted to his prey without them ever noticing. Until it was too late for them. However, never was he foolish with his advantage of stealth, not like when he was younger. Careful, not to alert the motion light attached to the rusting metal barn, Gabrio moved from the edge of the woods, lightly creeping toward the side of the house. He stopped under the first window he came to peeping through its sullied glass.

As Gabrio's eyes scanned the room they reflected the light of a solitary lamp, which sat atop a cardboard box next. It sank into the box and looked like it was going to fall onto to the only piece of furniture in the living room of the home. An old, plaid couch. Gabrio sniffed the air to see what he could pick up. Within the fresh night air, he inhaled the failing condition of the home as black mold, rotting garbage, human and the scent of various rodents living under the home filled his nose. He looked away from the window as he snorted into the air, making a face of disgust from the stronger, fouler stenches that raided his nostrils. Recovering from the burning sensation that affected him, his ears perked up from the sound of heavy steps echoing from inside the nearly empty room.

"Carlos, bring your fucking sorry ass out here now!"

Gabrio looked inside the house again. His warm breath started to swirl in the increasing cold night's air, creating a small foggy patch on the window as he watched a young woman start passing through the living room.

"Carlos. Now!" She screamed again in a raspy voice.

Gabrio assessed the sloppy woman as he saw her face. Her greasy brown hair sat in a messy bun atop of her head. She vigorously puffed on the cigarette she held in her left hand, indicating her stress. She blew white smoke from her pressing lips and took a swig of the cheap beer that occupied her other hand. As she walked away, her tight white shirt showed her girth through the flimsy material. While the overly large gym shorts kept falling off her hips to reveal a turquoise colored thong, pressing tightly on her hips. Gabrio heard even heavier steps slowly walk into the living room area as he seen the larger and taller person dominate the area. He was the exact image George described him to be.

"What the hell do you want, woman?" Carlos responded equally severe to the woman's call.

"Who the fuck is she, Carlos? Who is she?" She screamed at him. Carlos rubbed the back of his neck, stretching the skin where his tattoo rested.

"Who? What are you talking about you crazy bitch?" He said in a hostile tone.

"Don't play stupid, you fat motherfucker!" She threw a cell phone trying to aim for his head.

Coming close, the phone smacked his shoulder, as he moved in time before it made the initial contact point. Carlos's eyes became dark as his anger began to increase. He was starting to see in tunnel vision. In an eerie, deep calm voice he spoke. "If you throw anything else at me, I will fucking kill you with my bare hands and you know I will! Now, what the fuck are you talking about?" She ignored his threat as she screamed again.

"Amanda, the fucking whore at your work, you've been screwing her behind my back! I have seen the pictures of your tiny ass dick you've sent to her over your shitty phone. I've seen the text messages! What you think I'm stupid? You think I wouldn't notice the fucking pictures, the texts, the afternoon and nights you've been away at work. You don't work, there's never any money. You're a fat loser! A fucking dead beat!" With those words she threw the beer bottle that she had been holding, trying to aim for his head once again. However, this time it blasted against the wall behind him, shattering glass and liquid over the wall and floor.

Carlos looked at her as his whole body trembled with rage. "You fucking stupid bitch!" Swiftly moving for his abundant girth, he overpowered her as he quickly punched her in the face, knocking her out with his single blow. The young woman fell to the ground. Carlos didn't stop there. Kneeling to the ground, he grabbed her throat as her body lay limp and unconscious in his gripping hands. Carlos started strangling her.

In a flash, Gabrio jumped through the window to attack him, knocking the lamp off the box in the process, shattering the light bulb inside its shade. The room became engulfed in darkness. Gabrio was so close he could hear the racing pattern of the man's overworked heart. He knew that Carlos was trying to process what was going on, but fear, passing anger and increasing adrenaline made the man's mind scattered. Gabrio began to salivate, dripping his saliva on the floor as he hid in the corner of the dark living room. Gabrio could almost taste his blood sliding down his gullet like a thick malt drink. He was happy he had already hunted earlier, satisfying his hunger in the process, or else reasoning would be nonexistent and become a distraction.

Carlos breathing was heavy in the silence. He looked all around him, straining his neck as best as he could as he began to rise off the ground. Gabrio could clearly see the man in the dark with apparent trepidation altering his face. He slowly tried to move from off the ground, but Gabrio released a low, gurgling growl, making the man look in the corner where Gabrio was and stop his advancement. Carlos signed himself in the shape of the cross for protection. Gabrio could've smirked as he counted down in his head. *Three... two... one...*

Carlos impressively jumped to his feet and started to run into the kitchen, heading toward the back door. Gabrio was faster as he leaped from the corner, snarling. He grabbed Carlos's shoulder, sinking his claws deep into his soft skin, preventing him from going any further without his arm becoming torn from his body. Carlos screamed.

"Here it comes." Gabrio bellowed in his head. Sounds and images flashed through Gabrio's head as he saw the sins of Carlos Garcia replayed for him as if it was flashes from a horror movie. Gabrio sneered and snapped into the air as the fast movement of the descriptions took him from one crime to the next, ending in the murder of the beautiful middle-aged woman and her daughter. Gabrio snapped out of his trance. He became more outraged. Hearing the sins of men were one thing, but seeing them committed made Gabrio uncontrollable in his beastly form. He looked at Carlos.

"No. Please have mercy on me." Carlos pleaded through gasping sobs of fear still unable to see who had a hold of him.

Gabrio released his hold from the man's shoulder only to grab him by the shirt instead. He began to drag him through the house heading outside.

"No, please don't. Please let me go." Carlos tried to wriggle from Gabrio's hold as he slid across the ground and onto the grass still screaming his echoing pleas through the silence of the night.

Gabrio dropped Carlos on the wet, grassy ground, leaving him lying on his back, motionless, bleeding and starring at the night sky. Gabrio circled him and crawled above the man, breathing his hot, steamy breath on his face. Carlos knew the creature was above him, but his tear filled eyes remained tightly closed, refusing to see what attacked and dragged him from his house with such ease. Gabrio became irritated that Carlos wouldn't even look. "You're not a cold killer now are you?" Gabrio spoke to the man, even with the knowledge that Carlos couldn't hear him.

Gabrio loudly roared in his face and grabbed him by the neck, causing Carlos to open his eyes. When Gabrio brought him close enough to his face, he stepped out of the shadow and under the moonlight so Carlos could see the face of the intruder. Carlos stared in soundless horror at the sight of Gabrio. His heart began to pound even harder as his body shook at the fear that overrode him. It became beyond his comprehension and the world started to fade as he passed out from the lack of air and abundant fear. Gabrio got the result he wanted.

"Now, I won't have to listen to your screams until tomorrow night." Gabrio dropped to all fours and flung the man onto his back as he walked through the threshold of the forest to meet George.

Meanwhile

George waited anxiously for Gabrio's arrival as he slunked through the slivers of light that shined in pools on the forest floor, which illuminated his pure white fur as he passed through them. Treading his usual trail he paced the invisible perimeter of the small patch of land that became the designated area to deliver the prey. Despite George's agile footing, he had to make sure he was far enough from the empty, gaping seven foot hole that he patrolled. Ages ago, Gabrio suggested the idea of holding the prey in a hole in the middle of the forest until morning and since then the tradition held strong.

Snapped from his memory, George's ears perked as he picked up on a faint sound of twigs snapping from a few miles away. He suddenly stood alert as his body hardened and coiled to make quick work of whatever was approaching him do so with alacrity. He smelled the wind that swept by and only could detect the nature that surrounded him. Nothing appeared out of the ordinary, but he stood still, waiting for the creature to reveal itself from the thick of the forest. After a few moments a woman, covered in mud, blood and scant clothing ran hysterically from the thorn filled bushes outside the perimeter. She was panting hard from her exertion. She looked behind her as if she ran from something or someone. He watched the woman run by him without a single glance toward his way. *She didn't see me.* He thought.

Half expecting to see Gabrio behind the woman, chasing her, no one appeared as she disappeared into the darkness of the night. George thought it to be a vision, then figured she could've been running from another werewolf that was hunting nearby. Turning around, he came face-to-face with Gabrio.

Immediately he roared, ready to fight, until he realized who it was. "Holy hell, you startled me!" George snapped at Gabrio.

Gabrio gave George a look of amusement as he dropped Carlos into the deep abyss. "Sorry old timer."

"I'm an old dog now. You can't be doing that shit." George stated as he peeked into the hole and seen the man leaning against the dirt wall in an unconscious state. "Was he much trouble?"

Gabrio rested on the ground looking at George. "No. He was easy to deal with. He became distracted enough when he started to strangle his old lady on the floor. So I rushed him then. She laid subconscious on the floor, but didn't see me. I took him out of the house quick enough."

George looked at Gabrio and replied in finality. "Good. We'll leave him here till morning. No one will find him. Let alone hear him, but I'll stay with him tonight, just to make sure. You can go home if you like. You did a great job, Gabrio. You remind me so much of your father when we would hunt down the occasional demon-filled mortal."

"We learned from the best." His mood changed a bit at the reminder of his father.

A sound of thunder rang in the distance, causing Gabrio and George to look up into the night sky.

"A storm that came out of nowhere. I didn't even feel the storm. Did you?" Gabrio asked George.

"No. What a strange night. First the woman and now the storm, wonder what will come next?"

"A woman came through here?"Gabrio said with a furrowed brow.

"Yeah, I thought it was you chasing her, but I think another Beast Blood might've picked her out. She didn't look like a Half-Breed, though."

At that moment, Gabrio and George heard the woman's dying cries echo through the trees, between the roars of thunder. Then all remained quiet.

8

MOTHER KNOWS BEST

"Wake up honey, wake up. Marrok you have one more birthday surprise, but you have to get up to get it my darling boy."

Marrok felt his mother's dainty hands lightly shake his shoulder. "Mom, stop. It's Saturday. I don't' have school today."

The woman chuckled. "No darling, you have a surprise waiting for you, for your birthday. It's waiting for you."

Marrok opened his eyes. Through sleepy vision he had seen his mother's hazel eyes and broad smile. She leaned to kiss his forehead. "Come on, my love." She grabbed his hand to lift him from his bed.

"Where are we going?"

"To the stables, but your surprise isn't there."

Marrok rubbed his eyes. The scene flashed. Marrok watched her ready his favorite horse Sugar. He named her Sugar, because that's what she reminded him of.

"Marrok let me help you up first."

"Okay."

A dark flashed occurred again. He was no longer in his room, but sitting behind his mother, riding into the moonlit darkness of the night.

"The woods are scary tonight. Huh, Mom?"

"They can be honey, but your surprise will make them better at night."

Marrok became confused. "Like a flashlight? I already have a flashlight."

The mother laughed at her son's innocence. "No. Not like a flashlight, It'll make things clearer about a part of you I've never told you about."

The faint snap of a twig broke somewhere close in the woods and Sugar became spooked. She began to trot harder down the dirt path.

"Mom, I think something is in the woods with us." Marrok tucked his head into his mother's shirt.

"Easy, Sugar." The woman spoke to the horse, trying to calm her, and then spoke to Marrok doing the same. "It's probably a deer honey. They're in rut this time of year. Don't be afraid." The woman clicked her tongue and lightly lunged forward to keep the horse moving ahead. In an instant, a black, heavy mass with such brute force knocked them to the ground. The woman released a short, high-pitched scream.

"Mom!" Marrok screamed as he fell to the ground.

He smacked his head on a rock. He's bleeding. He sees his blood on the rock. His vision is getting foggy again. He sees his mother lying next to him. He sees Sugar running from them. She's too far away now. Marrok tires to crawl to his mom. He's too sleepy. He reaches for her arm, but it falls to the ground. He hears her whisper to him.

"Look, Marrok. Take... My necklace. Your surprise. Your father..."

Darkness engulfed his vision. Then a burst of light comes from the darkness. Fire. His grandparent's farm is on fire. His home, there's fire. It's on fire. Marrok sees them inside screaming. They're pounding on the windows.

"Why can't they get out?" Panicking, Marrok's voice became riddled with distraught. He placed his hands on his head as he looked around for help.

He sees a flash of white run past him. It's a man. He follows the man into the woods. He can't find him. Looking closer he spots him on the ground far away. He quickly runs to the man to find him rocking on the ground with his face covered with his folded arms. He speaks to the man with his lips curled over his teeth. "You mother fucker." Marrok tried to pick the man up, but his hand goes through him. He becomes confused and angry. "Why can't I touch you?"

The man slowly peeked an eye over his arm and lunged at Marrok's neck and screamed. "Mother said, "Wake up. Wake up. Wake up.""

Marrok awoke, launching himself off the pillow as he gasped in mouthfuls of chill air. His hand dug into his sheets as the other clutched to his tense throat. Removing his hands from his throat and sheets, he rubbed his face to wake himself up even further. He felt his heart threatening to burst into his chest as sweat soaked his naked body. He dropped his hands from his face to rest on his lap as he began to calm himself. "Just a dream, It's just a dream." He whispered aloud in the moonlit room. He saw dawn was approaching and took comfort knowing the sunlight would fill the dark. Taking deep breaths, he blinked rapidly to wake and rid himself of the nightmare. Looking downward, he opened his eyes and glimpsed at his shaking hands. He did a double take upon the sight. Long claws protruded from his fingertips and were descending back into normal fingernails. In disbelieve of what he saw as he sat in shock. "I... I must be dreaming."

Later

Curled in her soft, ivory and gold patterned comforter, Esmeralda awakened to the warm sun shining through the wall of windows.

The cream walls, even the dark contrast of the oak furniture, beamed brightly under the cascading sunlight. Little by little she blinked with increasing ease as her tired body lagged behind in waking up with her already racing mind. Reaching behind her, she tapped the fluffy mound of blankets realizing that Gabrio wasn't in bed with her. She rolled over and seen his side of the massive bed was empty. Esmeralda sat up in bed, glanced around the room and seen no sign of Gabrio ever entering their room. She expected to see his clothes thrown to the floor and most of the blankets taken from her during the early morning hours. However, all was how she left it.

Did he come home last night? She lightly tapped her fingertips against her lips as she began to think. Thinking was a mistake as anxiety coursed through her reasoning. She envisioned something going wrong and he lay rotting, chard in the middle of the woods, dead. *God, I hope he's okay.* She swung her legs over the side of the bed and scooted herself forward until her bare feet touched the ground. She peeked into their connecting bathroom and saw everything was in its place, unmoved. Gabrio hadn't been there either. She quickly walked to the loft and briskly stepped down the stairs. She glanced throughout the living room and saw Gabrio's leg, limply hanging over the back of the couch. Esmeralda felt a rush of relief, assured fully when she saw parts of him had remained un-touched by flame. She descended the steps and tiptoed to the back of the couch, looking over him.

Immediately, she put her hand to her mouth to control a spout of giggling laughter on seeing the rest of him. Spread eagle and stark naked, Gabrio laid crookedly on his back. His arms were thrown over his head as one leg rested on the floor and the other still hung elevated. The only part that had become partially covered was his eyes because of the shaggy cut of his hair. She watched his parted lips puff outward with every deep, snore he released. She looked over him with great admiration. His muscles, even in their relaxed state were firm. His skin was a beautiful dark tan color, even in winter. He was beautiful and striking. She knew a long time ago that her love for the man that lay in front of her would never grow lax. She smiled as her character was becoming mischievous. She yearned to take advantage of his exposed vulnerability. After a few moments of battling with her greedy desire, she thought better of it as she looked him over and sighed. *I should just let him sleep. He looks tired.*

Esmeralda walked to the den and carried back with her a soft, wool blanket. As she thoroughly took advantage of looking at him once again, she noticed he was, in a sense, alert for being asleep. She stifled a chuckle again. "Well, it is morning." She whispered aloud. In a comedic way, she lightly tossed the blanket over his exposed and very ready to act manhood. She walked around the couch to fuss with the other end of the blanket, pulling it upward to rest under Gabrio's chest. After lightly kissing his lips, she walked away, heading into the kitchen.

Gabrio, awoke once he heard her laugh quietly at him, now looked at her from under his shielding hair. He did not move or say a word. He just watched to see what she would do. However, he found himself disappointed, expecting more would come from her finding him so exposed. Yet, she covered him with a blanket and only kissed him on the mouth. He spoke to her as she was walking away from him, heading for the kitchen. "I noticed you checking me out." His smile was increasing with his throbbing desire. He grabbed her arm and pulled her to him. She fell on top of him as his mouth savagely found hers and with equal passion she kissed him back. Through a ragged whisper, he exclaimed. "It's been too long."

Esmeralda gave a sultry laugh as he suckled on her throat. "Gabrio, it's only been a day."

With his teeth nibbling on her collarbone, which became exposed as her nightshirt fell over her shoulder, his reply became muffled. "That's an eternity in our world."

She found amusement out of what he said, but it stoked as more fiery desires burned to become satisfied. His touch began to scorch her as her skin became sensitive to the passions he stirred within her.. When his hands left her shoulders and his mouth left her neck, her skin chilled. Until he placed them elsewhere.

Before succumbing to their passions, little traces of logic delayed as Gabrio suggested a thought. "The couch isn't comfortable for being as thorough as I want to be. You want to take this to our room?"

Esmeralda nodded her head. He didn't need much more of a reply. He wrapped his arms around her waist as he tossed her over one shoulder to lift them together from the couch. He swiftly moved up the stairs. Laughing as she lay, belly first, on his shoulder and had an ample opportunity to free her hand and slap him on his tight bouncing bottom. "Go, go. go!" She playfully teased.

When Gabrio passed through the threshold of the master bedroom, he stopped. He hooked his foot around the open door to kick back forcibly, slamming the door shut. In a fluid movement he tossed her from his shoulder onto the plush covers and mattress of their bed. He quickly climbed over her, pressing her petite body into the cushion of the mattress. He covered her with his body as his mouth greedily, skillfully tasted her lips. Their tongues swirled in a slow, tantalizing dance while his hand worked at the trailing buttons of her white, silky nightshirt. Unbuttoning far enough down, he then pushed the silken material to the side, revealing her creamy, rosy tipped breasts. He placed a rough, calloused hand over a perky mound taking his forefinger and thumb to pinch and roll her nipple between them. She arched her back into his greedy hand and released a small mewling sound as a shot of pleasure headed to her already moistened womanhood.

Gabrio pressed her hardened nipple between his lips and gently suckled in taking her nipple farther in his mouth. She groaned as she began to nod her head, liking every sensation she could feel with that swift movement. With his hot mouth and luscious lips around her succulent globe, Gabrio began gently nibbling and suckling to create an intoxicating mixture of pain and pleasure within her. She moved her hands up his chest as she wrapped her slender legs around him, crossing her ankles to keep them in close contact. She began to tighten, she was more than ready as she bucked and could feel his elongated erection against her inner thigh. Through heavy breathing, she bit his earlobe and whispered to him two simple words. "Dominate me."

He looked at her as his eyes dilated wide and a deep aggressive sound came from his throat. He reached up her legs and pulled her panties around her ankles and tossed them to the side. Gabrio pushed her legs open to see every inch of her revealed to him. Her eyes slanted in pleasure, her lips parted in want, need and her breast heaving in growing expectation. From his intrusive hands, her hair became fanned behind her in an unruly array. She was wanton and he was wild with her. He couldn't wait any longer as he plunged himself deep into her, gritting his teeth. He knew it was going to be quick, but hard and thoroughly. She gasped as he invaded her, pushing his throbbing erection deep into her slick folds.

"God! You're so damn tight." He rasped.

She rocked against him in an age-old rhythm, wanting him to go deeper, harder. She dug her nails into his back. With a slapping sound he grabbed her hips to elevate them higher, plunging deeper into her. She matched every vigorous thrust that he gave. Gabrio thrust harder, but rocked back and forth skillfully against her clitoris until she couldn't take it anymore and found her release in gasping breaths. Gabrio felt her tighten in spasms as he drove harder into her, releasing his seed as he swirled in his own pulsating ecstasy.

Several moments of blissful silence passed, Gabrio rested his head on her chest and listened to her rapid heartbeat slow down to a normal beat. She ran her fingers through his thick, black hair as they enjoyed the afterglow of their lovemaking in embracing silence. In a husky, well-satisfied voice, Esmeralda stated. "You know Gabrio, you didn't need to surprise me the way you did to make love to me." She looked down at him and saw he lifted his head to rest his chin in the valley between her breasts as he looked up at her and smiled. Esmeralda loved how his white smile complimented his dark features. It always made his eyes brighter, especially after becoming physically satisfied.

"The result of my nakedness was a bonus. One we both completely enjoyed. Multiple times." He said cockily.

She gave him her own flashy grin as she chuckled. "True, but why were you naked. Just so you know, I'm not complaining about your nakedness. Ever."

Gabrio kissed the smooth skin on her chest and looked up. "It rained early this morning and my clothes became soaking wet as I ran to the house. When I got inside I stripped naked, threw the clothes in the laundry room and crashed on the couch. I was so damn exhausted."

Esmeralda nodded her head in understanding. A silenced passed between them. Yawning wide, she began to play with his hair again. "Are you exhausted now?"

Gabrio smiled even wider. "Round two?"

Esmeralda blushed and chuckled. "No. Not yet at least. However, since we have a long night ahead of us because of the *Ancient Ritual…*"

Gabrio interrupted her. "We have nowhere else to be or nothing better to do. I don't see why we can't laze around a bit longer."

She put her head to the side and gave him a look of disagreement.

Gabrio chuckled. "Well, what do you have in mind?"

Esmeralda overplayed a look of consideration and then lifted her closed hand, palm up, extended her pointer finger and made a bending motion, signaling Gabrio to come closer to her. He scooted upward, his ear next her mouth. She smiled as her voice slicked over in a husky whisper.

"I think it would be really sexy… if you were shirtless…"

Gabrio interrupted unsure of what she was going to suggest, since he was already shirtless. Hell, he's still naked. "Yeah?"

She continued, "… downstairs… fixing the back door…

"Is that a dirty joke or a request." He said through a lopsided smile.

She laughed as she took an open hand and smacked his back, continuing to speak to him. "While I made coffee and breakfast." She added with a sexy, needy groan. She mocked a look of pleasure to add to the act.

Gabrio dropped his head on the bed. "Ugh, that's right. The door." He exclaimed, but then he quickly switched his tone, thinking of a way to get something out of this bargain too. "Okay, but you have to make French toast with the works. I mean orange juice, three types of meat- the works. Agree?"

Esmeralda shook her head. "Agreed."

"Good." Gabrio flipped the covers off their naked bodies as he got out of bed and sauntered to the closet.

Happily, she gazed at his Greek statue physic as she lazed in the warm comforters a while longer. When Gabrio began to slide on his clothes is when Esmeralda presumed she should get up and ready as well.

Meanwhile

Cleaned and clothed, Laycerath sat stiffly at the kitchen table like a stone statue as he watched his mother flutter around the spacious kitchen gathering various cooking utensils. He's never seen so many tools for making damn food to supply the morning's meal. Bothered by the lack of understanding of this surface life, he looked to out the window. Quickly, he shut his eyes and put his hand over them to cut out the light. His eyes still burned as they adjusted to the striking white light of the sun. Used to the darkness of the underground and the orange glow of flames, he knew he could only linger within the darkness of twilight. At least until he adjusted to the light. Sheryl, remained in an ignorant bliss of his sinister mood, as she hummed a song from her childhood. A lovely song her father would sing to her was the same tune she would sing to him when she nursed him in back to life. In a flat tone he finally spoke to her. "Why slave yourself when you can transform and hunt. There's woods all around and I'm sure there's a fat little human nearby that would be a plump meal. Satisfying more so than chicken eggs and wheat."

Sheryl looked up with warmth in her eyes and for a brief moment she stopped humming. "The world is a smaller place than when you were last alive, Laycerath. We can't be free as we once were when there are mortals everywhere."

Laycerath became outraged at her reply, startling her as he raised his voice. " Free! We can't be free when we're stronger than the fucking mortals. We kill the weak and tame the strongest. I watched them from hell and seen them fall past me. They've become overweight, greed-filled blood-sacks. They're begging for death. They want someone to rid them of their miserable lives. I can do so quickly." He grumbled

Sheryl raised her voice, but admired her son's passion. "No, you're weak! You couldn't catch the women in the forest last night and I had to kill her for you!"

He glared at her with his eyes turning a glowing red as he interrupted her. "Five out of seven isn't bad."

She retorted quickly. "It was sloppy. You're weak, Laycerath, but you are going to be strong soon enough. Then, we can utilize that passion of yours, but my way. A few mortal hearts and you should have all your strengths. Yet, you have to be careful. I've remarried since your last death and I've brought you back in a world that documents everything. Strategy, stealth and remaining part of society is important to get what we want. Not drawing attention to yourself in the meantime. You should know how to use those skills to your advantage. You used them to take the O'Mara whore."

He smirked as he looked out the window. "Alexandria. What a fine beauty she was. Young, innocent, desperate and stupid." Then he gloated. "I killed that rat-bastard Frances going through the same tunnel I used to get into the chamber and fuck his wife." He laughed darkly at a conjoined memory. "He didn't suspect me emerging from the wardrobe when he opened its doors." Laycerath coldly laughed at the memory, his laughter filled the room. Sheryl didn't even smirk as she continued to cook. Laycerath sobered after a few moments and a steady silenced passed between them. Laycerath looked from the window back to his mother. "Where do you plan to hide me when your husband wakes up?"

"He stayed overnight with the captured Half-Breed. He won't be home today, but I'll be meeting him tonight. There is a guesthouse on the back lot of our property. You'll stay there. It has everything you need, but food. You can hunt, but nothing human. I mean that, Laycerath. We work very hard to keep ourselves hidden." She said as she began to flip the fried eggs.

"Yet, you feast on the corpse of demon filled mortals and I'm left to the wildlife for game. I thought the host was to provide the best for the guest." He stated.

"The Half-Breed isn't for me. It's for the newborn Beast Bloods." She looked at him and saw he caught on to the tone of her voice, hiding something from him. His thick eyebrow raised, in calculating thought.

He said coolly, darkly. "Why did you summon me here, now? I'm sure there's more of a reason than you missed your adopted son."

She stopped whisking the wheat mixture and looked at him. In a stern voice she spoke to him. "Don't you dare say that. Since the day I found you on that accursed battlefield, slaughtered by your enemy, a thin line, pouring crimson across your throat and you lay dying; I was the one who saved your life. I have treated you like my own and loved you in the same manner. I made you who you are today, Laycerath, remember that and don't ever forget it."

He glared his eyes, looking out the window as his mind swelled over the memories of that day when he died and became resurrected by her forbidden spell. His soul forever damned to return to hell for his actions in his prior life. The actions that destined him to become Lucifer's demon werewolf. The tool that's meant to destroy man, beast and everything between. Broken from thought he then realized she didn't answer him. She evaded the question, but he asked again. "No need to use that overplayed instrument. There's more to me being here? What do you need me for, *Mother*?"

Sheryl sighed, "Yes, there is."

He chuckled as he relaxed in his chair and crossed his feet atop of the table. "Of course there is. Go on. Proceed to tell me."

She shot him a sharp look as she started to explain. "I've had visions of the blood moon, Laycerath. The werewolves are increasing in number, which leads me to believe the prophecy is beginning. Soon the '*Blood Tasters*' will run rampant, suckling like the leeches they are and after that we won't have much of a chance."

Laycerath looked at her with a strange mixture of uncertainty and blankness. '*Look toward the sky, behold the red moon. Cast your eyes downward and take notice an army of beasts guarding the newborn who will be one with the guardians in Heaven.*' He quoted from the prophecy in his head. He looked to her as he began to snarl. "The time is coming. That's why you have summoned me back. Do you know who the carrier is yet?"

Sheryl shook her head slowly as she routinely continued to make breakfast, pouring the mixture into the hot skillet. "No, but as you well know the carrier has to be a werewolf for the prophecy to become fulfilled. Tonight is an Ancient Ritual. A tradition, I created to find the carrier of the Hybrid soon. It's been over hundreds of years strong and I'm going to make damn sure that I find out what I need to know."

Laycerath spoke darkly. "Then we will kill the Hybrid."

Sheryl shook her head once again. "No. I know of a better way that will benefit us both. If accomplished successfully, it'll right all the wrongs that have accumulated in our long lives."

"I take it you have a plan then, once you find out who the carrier is." He stated knowingly.

Sheryl nodded her head as she smiled maliciously, walking to him with a plate of eggs, pancakes and a slab raw meat that still dripped blood, mixing within the other food.

"It's human, the meat. It's from that fucking Julianne. She was a lean little thing, but she was tender in her ways." Sheryl said tongue in cheek.

"From the sludge of hell bound souls to a morning meal in the realm between. How an appetite varies by location." He dryly commented as he bit into the bloody meat, ripping a chunk with his dagger like teeth, he chewed, blood dripping from the corners of his mouth. "While you're investigating for pregnant werewolves, I'll go into town and see what this place has to offer."

She nodded quietly as she walked over to him to dab a napkin over his salivating mouth. He growled. "Leave me be, you overbearing woman from hell. I'm not a cripple."

She stepped back to rest against the countertop, smiled and watched her son devour his blood soaked meal, thinking, *Mothers always know what's best for their children before their children do.*

9

ALEXANDRIA

Alexandria screamed in horrible agony as she lay in her bed soaked in sweat, blood and cooling water. She clutched the sheets and clenched her teeth harder from the pain. "God. God, make the pain go away. Please, please God."

"Breath. You're doing well. Just keep on pushing, Miss. Push harder, now." Covered in bloodstained clothes, Nona tried to ease Alexandria through the birthing practices she learned over the years. She firmly yelled over Alexandria's expanded belly while she sat on a milking stool, watching for a baby's writhing head to push through Alexandria's expanded womanhood. She dropped the blanket for a quick moment. "Breath, like how I taught you. Breath and push at the same time." Nona shook with fright for the girl, whom Nona took care of since she was a little bonny girl. Now that Alexandria was having a babe of her own in a longhouse, fashioned into a cabin like structure, in the middle of the woods, Nona was beyond afraid for the young woman's life. There was no doctor around to aid if she was dying from blood loss or a turned fetus. No one else was around for fifty miles. except for herself, Alexandria and a native local woman named Abequea, who recently joined several months ago from the tribe they befriended. Nona lifted the blanket to see the crowning babe between Alexandria's thin stretched legs. "I see the head! Oh, what a fine head of hair it has. You're almost done; you've passed the shoulders, just one more push!"

Alexandria, had only begun and felt drained of all energy. She had spent almost nine months in horrible, anemic pain and was thankful to have the time finally come where she could birth, then return to normal. She grunted, then with a scream and a final push, a little body fell into the aged, wavering hands of Nona. She looked at the breathless babe, covered in birthing fluid and streaks of blood. She gave a few firm pats on his bottom, shocking the babe into taking its first breath. The baby wailed at the new sensation.

"Oh Lord, Alexandria, It's a beautiful baby boy." Nona exclaimed.

Alexandria nodded her head as she saw crimson rush from her. She still had contractions and could still feel an inner movement. Alarmed, she jolted herself forward, eyes wide in fear and uncertainty. "Nona. I still feel like there's movement. I'm still in pain. My muscles are squeezing in my stomach. What's wrong with me?"

Nona looked to Abequea. "Here, take him, wash him well and keep him warm in a clean blanket."

The dark haired, native woman complied with the order and whisked the whimpering child away as Nona raised from the stool to rush towards Esmeralda, pressing on her belly. "It might be the afterbirth, Miss." As she pressed on the left side of Alexandria's stomach, she felt a hard spot. Her eyes became wide as she whispered. "I don't believe it."

Alexandria shot a look to Nona and pleaded nervously to her for an answer. "What? What is it Nona?"

She replied calmly, taking control of the situation. "Miss, you're going to have another baby today. You're birthing twins and…"

Alexandria felt as if she was about to faint. "T… twins. I'm having twins. No, no I'm not having…" A sudden pain shot through her body. "Oh, my God in Heaven! Make it stop, Nona, please!"

Sympathetic to her pain, she replied. "I can't Miss, it's -."

Struck with another sharp pain, Alexandria heard Nona address her formally again. Beyond annoyed, she yelled. "Stop calling me fucking, *Miss*, Nona! We're not in Scotland, anymore!"

Nona let the last comment go as she readied herself sitting on the stool once again. She understood the pain-fueled anger and irritation. Experienced in such dealing, the words women used during childbirth no longer surprised her. "Alexandria, you have to give a few more great pushes when I let you know."

Nona leaned forward to spread her hand across Alexandria's belly and could feel the baby moving, shifting into place. "Ready yourself."

Alexandria sat up, resting on her hands, leaning forward to give her leverage as she pushed.

"Push again, now!" Nona shouted through gritted teeth.

Alexandria complied Nona's commands until a baby girl, who was a bit bigger than the boy, came into the world. New warmth took over Nona as she smiled lovingly at Alexandria in a motherly way. "You did well, Alexandria. You brought two lovely children into the world tonight. A handsome boy and a lovely girl."

Alexandria smiled, seeing her baby girl was healthy and crying loudly in Nona's arms, she finally gave into fainting and the world went dark.

After a several hours passed, Alexandria awoke. She dazedly looked around the room. Immediately, she noticed her body felt comfortable, yet horribly ached. Looking down, she noticed they stripped of her soiled gown, skin cleaned her with perfumed water and changed her into a fresh, thinner nightgown. Even the blood soaked bedding exchanged to the cleaner, newer set that rested on her, keeping her warm. She scanned around the room and seen the fire blazed even hotter; to keep her newborns from the late spring chill. Alexandria looked to her right and noticed Nona had a bundle in her arms, cooing and gushing words of love to it as she leaned over the coveted treasure. Alexandria smiled. *It's my treasure.* She looked to Abequea, who was doing the same to the other tiny bundle, but in her native language. Alexandria weakly snorted as she watched the two women in their glory cuddling to each sleeping child. Nona must have sensed her watchful eyes, because she looked at Alexandria.

"Oh, you're awake." She said cheerfully. She began carefully lifting herself off the wooden rocking chair, clutching to the bundle as she steadied herself to walk. "Do you want to hold your daughter?"

Alexandria was as ready as she would ever be. She nodded her head and raised her hands to accept the bundle that weighed as light as air in her arms. She looked down at the little baby girl that engulfed her arms, then overtook her heart. She moved the white blanket a little farther from the baby's tiny nose and seen she had the most beautiful features. Rosy cheeks, creamy ivory skin, pink soft lips and a tuft of bright blonde hair, made up the beautiful little baby girl. "Just like your mama." Alexandria said softly to the sleeping baby.

Abequea walked over to Alexandria with her son in her arms. She knew little *white* language, as she loved to call it, but she could put together simple sentences that were easy to understand. "Do you want the boy?"

She nodded her head eagerly. "Yes, yes please hand me my son." She opened her arm to make a mock cradle for her son to be placed in and against her warm body. She looked at the boy who was just as light, just as pink and soft and who was just as beautiful with olive skin. She openly wept at the wondrous sight of her sleeping innocent children in her arms. "Oh, my children, my babies, here in my arms. No longer tucked away in my belly." She began to laugh through her sobs. "You guys were a mischievous bunch in there. Causing your mama so much pain. Draining me of my life!" She joked, chuckling. "But it's okay. You're here with me now. Out here, with me. I can protect you further." She chuckled.

Abequea spoke in a whisper, careful not to wake the babies. "What are the names for them?"

"Are you going with the tradition of using family names, miss?" Nona asked.

Alexandria shook her head. "No. No family names. They are different, completely special and unique. They will have names that'll match them."

She paused in thought and announced, "My daughter will carry the name Rosella Jane Huffman."

"Miss, Huffman is your maiden name." Nona asked.

Alexandria forcefully interjected. "I'm no longer with my husband and my husband is not their father, so I'm hardly in any position to use either surname."

Nona nodded. She knew she was right given the circumstance. It would be more fitting for them to revert to a more stable and well known name. Alexandria spoke with undeniable certainty.

"For my son, he will have the name Xavier James Huffman."

"Those are right sounding names." Nona sighed in contentment.

Alexandria nodded as she looked up at the women who stood next to her and smiled as she looked back at her children.

Ten Years Later

Alexandria sat in the rocking chair in front of the fire surrounded by garments of clothes and different patterns of material. She slowly rocked back and forth as she leaned forward, squinting her eyes to finish sewing a beautiful little surprise dress for Rosella to wear in celebration of turning ten. Holding up the powered pink creation, she admired the embroidered lace detail and placed it on the new navy blue outfit she made for Xavier. She dreamily and deeply sighed. "Can you believe it Abequea? Tomorrow my babies are going to be ten years old. No longer babies anymore; they're now a young man and a little lady. If only Nona was here to marvel in this experience with us."

Abequea watched the children play in the evening light, through the window as she prepared supper. Within all the years she learned the English language with proper clarity and spoke fluidly. She loved and cared for the family, she quickly became accepted in so many years ago. "I can't believe it myself, Alexandria. Ten years of cuts, scrapes, crying, laughter, and toads in the house."

Alexandria laughed. "Remember how the children put one of those nasty creatures in Nona's pillow. That blasted toad stayed there, patiently waiting until Nona laid her head down as if he was in on the joke." She chuckled. "Nona, until the day she died, swore that toad put its slimy hand on her lips on purpose, causing her to go mad and fall out of bed."

They laughed hysterically at the memory, then after a few moments they sobered in a lighthearted aura.

"The children, boy, did they get a sound tongue-lashing from her. Well-deserved it was, but the children- they felt so horrid about making her hurt her hip when she fell." Alexandria said through her twinkling laughter.

She nodded her head. "They were even more sorry when they had to do her chores for two weeks."

Alexandria chuckled. "Nona was perfectly able to do her work the very next day, but it taught the children a few good lessons." She paused switching her thoughts around. "Where are the children? Still outside playing?"

Abequea looked up and seen Rosella lying, unmoving on the ground while Xavier was running toward the house. In an alarmed voice Abequea alerted Alexandria. "Alex! Something's wrong!"

"What?" Alexandria responded in a distressed tone.

Xavier forcefully opened the door, screaming. "Mama! Mama! Hurry Rosie is sick. She's sweating everywhere and she said she doesn't feel right."

Alexandria wide eyed and full of fear followed Xavier outside as they ran to where Rosella laid. "Xavier did she eat, touch something poisonous? A berry, a flower, anything?" She began to panic as she looked over her daughter's pale little face. Her long curly blonde hair fanned beneath her, her body trembling with sickness, her chest expanded rapidly with each deep shaky breath she took.

Xavier became just as afraid for his sister's health In tears, he began to reply. "No, Mama. We were playing and running around. Then, suddenly she said she didn't feel too good and passed out. I was with her the whole time. She didn't eat anything bad, Mama."

Alexandria fell to the ground, confused as to what might be wrong, as she took her little girl in her arms and ran back into the house. Alexandria yelled for the young woman. "Abequea! Abequea! Ready her nightclothes, some hot water and her bed. Rosie is sick."

Abequea, who stood outside by the cabin, hurriedly ran inside to gather all that asked of her with haste. Alexandria nuzzled her little girl as tears fell down her face. "It'll be okay, my love. It'll be okay, my darling girl." Rosie lay limp and unresponsive in her arms as she ran inside the house, into the young girl's bedroom and laid her on her bed. Xavier followed them trying not to whimper as the fear overrode him. His big blue eyes were glassy and strikingly clear because of the tears that filled them. Alexandria began to strip Rosie of her dirty play clothes.

She turned to Xavier and in a shaky, but calm voice she spoke to him. "My son, be strong and give us a moment to get Rosie clean and in her night clothes. Sit by the fire and get warm and ready for supper." She rubbed her hand through his long black hair to comfort him further. "It'll be okay, my strong little man. It'll be okay." She gave him a quick hug and sent him on his way. He obeyed his mother's orders.

Alexandria turned to see Abequea had already braided the Rosie's hair back to keep her cooler from her feverish sweat, which worsened with each passing minute. Alexandria began unbuttoning the white, cotton slip dress to change her into a thinner nightgown. "Abequea, the children haven't been sick ever. Not once in their lives have they ever come down with the common cold!" She scorned the situation as she passionately spoke louder. "Do you recognize any illness that could result this quickly?"

Abequea's dark brown eyes were glistening deep with confusion, fear and understanding. "I've seen this just once from a traveling tribe, who was coming down from the land of the north. Their chief asked my father to share our food and shelter in trade of furs and other valuable items that they carried."

Alexandria asked impatiently, "Did it pass? Did they survive?"

Abequea's eyes stayed wide as she looked at the sickly child and looked Rosie over once again. She noticed Rosie's ashen colored skin, her profuse sweat beading over her flawless features, her shallow, but deep intakes of breath and her hot skin. All the signs were there. "Yes, it'll pass and they will survive. However, she might be a bit different after it passes."

Alexandria didn't understand and was about to say as much, but stopped by a loud crash in the parlor room. Alexandria moved with haste. She gasped as she saw her little boy face down on the floor, lying next to the rocking chair, not moving like his sister Rosie. Alexandria let the tears flow. "My son. My little boy. What happening is all of this?" She raced to pick him from the ground. "Abequea, Xavier caught it too. What is this damn accursed illness? I'm being punished by God for my infidelity. He's using my children as punishment against me." She yelled, frustrated at the grief she felt for her poor children. Like she did with Rosie, she held him close to her chest as she raced into his bedroom and aided him as well. Watching over both children throughout the long hours of the night until she conformed to the overwhelming exhaustion she felt and had to finally take rest.

After a few hours of deep, dreamless sleep, Alexandria jolted awake when she heard her children's echoing screams coming from outside. The cabin was dark as the roaring fire had fell into dying embers. She stubbed her toes as she raced to her son's bedroom first to see he wasn't in bed. The disheveled sheets and pillows lay on the floor in a heap. She ran to the other room and noticed Abequea and Rosie were both missing. She gripped her head as the thought she was going mad. "Where are all of you?" She screamed in the darkened house, with only the full moon pouring into the windows. She flung open the door as she ran barefoot outside. Her feet thudded with each hard stomp as she flew across the damp, cold grass heading at full speed to where she thought the children could be. Their screams of horrid pain fueled her adrenaline. The wind whipped her hair back and blades of tall grass didn't stand a chance against her advancing run. As she held up her skirts to run with more ease, but it was to no prevail. She tripped, slamming her body hard on the ground with forceful momentum. Alexandria, scraped her face across the ground, groaning and coughing as she gained breath from her fall. She heard something quickly scurry toward her, then saw its large shadow leaning over her.

"I'm sorry for making you stumble, but you have to remain quiet, Alexandria. We have to be still and not alarm the children!" Abequea whispered.

Alexandria rolled on her back, making it easier to gather air into her lungs. "Abequea, the children, where are they?"

"Please be still. The children are just beyond this patch of grass." She replied. She took her thin arm to silently move away the tall grass that blocked their ground base view. Alexandria rolled back onto her stomach and slithered to the opening Abequea created. She saw the children, standing perfectly still looking at the full moon. Then unnaturally saw them start shifting. Cracking bones, popping joints and strange liquefied squishing sounds came from the children's distorted movements.

Alexandria's face became even paler in the moonlight. Her mouth gaped in true horror. She was speechless. Little gurgled, choking sounds left her mouth as her mind went blank at the supernatural wonder. Finding her courage she began to rise.

"No, Alexandria!" Abequea pulled her back onto the ground with unnatural strength.

"Let me go! Those are my children!" Alexandria said angrily through clenched teeth.

Abequea calmly shook her head. "No, this has to be. It's their destiny."

Alexandria became dumbfounded at her choice of the word 'destiny'. She looked to the children once again. They were turning into something. Creatures, that looked like dogs or more like wolves, but stood on their hind legs. Both creatures had beautiful silver fur that glowed brighter under the light of the moon. Still silent, Alexandria watched with confused wonder. However Abequea spoke in a voice almost lower than a whisper.

"They are what the tribes call, *shape shifters*, Alexandria. They're both of man and beast. Know they're not the first to do this, but it's not a common practice. Many tribe elders pray to the sky spirits that their destiny is with the wolves."

Alexandria snapped her head to look at Abequea. "What did you just say?"

Abequea innocently answered her. "They're fated to live the way of both man and wolf. They're born with this, Alexandria. It can't become undone when it's a blessing from the Gods or passed in blood. By their father, obviously."

Alexandria blankly looked to her children. Her mother's long ago words echoing through her head. *Your destiny is with the wolves.* She blindly took Abequea's still gripping hand from her collar, rised out of the tall grass and approached her malformed children who still unwaveringly looked toward the moon. Alexandria slowly shuffled toward them. She was about to reach out to touch the furry pelt of the beast who stood before her. Then suddenly both of the creatures, her children, turned to face her. Their eyes glowing white in the dark. Alexandria's overworked nerves caused her to collapse to the ground, as the night swirled into darkness and her vision clouded to black.

10

BEAST BLOODS

The night brought another unexpected, rushing thunderstorm over a greater portion of Michigan. The thunder rumbled through the charcoal tinted sky as shimmering white-blue streaks of lightning cracked against the air. The bolts came streaking through the sky, creating a strobe light pulse, which quickly lit the darker parts of the land and inside Gabrio and Esmeralda's car. Despite the pushing wind and hard slanting rain, Gabrio drove through the wild elements smoothly. Relaxed with one hand on the steering wheel and the other in his lap, he almost looked sleepy. He calmly sang to the song playing on the radio.

Esmeralda relaxed as she listened to his soothing, deep voice going with the flow of the lyrics and music on the radio. She loved to listen to him sing and sat in silence as she grabbed his hand to hold. Without missing a note or a word of the song, he smiled at her as he finished the last lines of the chorus. With the last note of the melody, it ended. Esmeralda deeply exhaled. "You have a great voice."

"You know it." He cockily replied and winked at her.

Esmeralda laughed, rolled her eyes and looked outside the

passenger window. Another lightning bolt lit up the world around them. "Oh, there's the old farmhouse. We're almost there. Are you excited to be leading the new Beast Bloods tonight?" She excitedly asked him.

He pondered her question with a humming sound coming from him as he thought. "Yeah, I'm excited. It'll be cool watching their eagerness and inexperience become skillful. Can you just imagine our children out there? Oh man, that'll be cool."

Esmeralda slightly frowned and the mood changed. The excitement in her eyes dulled a bit as she replied. "One day we'll have them, my love. One day."

Gabrio could've kicked himself. He knew this was a tricky subject to talk about. Many years they've tried to have a family of their own. Playing the game of stop-and-go, they would lose hope, yet try again to conceive. However, not once were they successful. Several months ago Esmeralda suggested having tests done to see if all appeared right. Despite them being werewolves and their lack of anything ever being physically wrong with them, didn't stop her from wanting them. Nevertheless, the tests came back and showed results of them being in perfect health. Gabrio remembered the words of Dr. Heartsteader, whom remained a lesser werewolf within their clan. He understood their plight. *Esmeralda's in perfect health and will always remain so. Nothing is wrong with any of your organs. Everything came back immaculate. Damn, with your results you can have thousands of children if you wanted.*

However, the good doctor's words didn't ease Esmeralda. It only made her more uncertain to why they couldn't start a family. Gabrio knew at times she felt as if a stronger divine kept them barren, but he knew she was of such strong faith, she would never blame it on heavenly divinity. Gabrio softly squeezed her hand and calmly stated, "Maybe we should start trying again."

Esmeralda looked at him in vacuity. For a brief moment he thought she wasn't going to answer him, but then she spoke. "I thought we established that this morning when I found your butt naked on the couch." She gave him a wide, dazzling smile.

Gabrio looked ahead while he charmingly issued a lopsided grin. "Yes, we did, didn't we." New warmth filled his heart as well as a new hope. He was happy to be trying again.

They turned a left onto a hidden dirt road. The car's headlights illuminated a crooked, nearly sunken barn in the distance. Esmeralda gave a short unnoticeable snort.

"What?" Gabrio asked.

"With the roaring storm above us and the creepy looking chainsaw massacre barn. It almost feels like we're heading into a scene of a 1980's horror movie." She observed.

He looked toward the barn and as soon as he did a bolt of lightning struck the sky behind the deep-rooted structure as a clash of thunder sounded. "It does, but ironically the monsters are us." He vibrantly smiled at her.

She laughed. "Shut up. We're no more the monster than a mortal. The difference is, is that we look the part at night."

Gabrio pressed his lips together and nodded. Finally, they arrived at the gaping entryway of the rickety barn and pulled their car slowly forward inside. The car quickly became engulfed in a pitch-black shroud. They gradually drove through the barn's length to pass through to the other side. They emerged on a field filled with glittering cars.

"It must have rained heavily here." He stated.

Mouth agape, Esmeralda commented at the sight. "That's the first thing you notice. There has to be at least two hundred cars here. It looks like... I don't even know right now, there are just so many."

It was Gabrio's turn to snort. "And tonight we lead all of them for the first time." After finding a makeshift parking spot, he turned off the engine. "Let's go."

Holding hands, they walked through a small, well hidden opening between the thicket of the woodland, which surrounded the field of cars. Stepping through the other side, they entered a whirlwind of swirling life that seemed otherworldly. Despite the passing rain, large bonfires roared and shined their dancing light throughout the span of the barren patch of land, which was now littered with large tents. The perimeter of thick trees, and thorny bushes that surrounded them, shielded them from becoming noticed by the outside world. Men, women and children of all various characteristics huddled with their clans, around the large handful of raging fires.

Esmeralda smiled widely as she noticed the Romanian Gypsies had shown. The women dressed in their traditional grab of rich, lush material and long strands of gold and silver wrapped around their arms, neck and feet as they danced. The men, dressed more modernly, provided the music that brought on sounds of laughter, singing and dancing. It clashed in joyous life, filling the night as the storm roared above them. The way everything meshed together in a collaboration at this traditional event, made the scene almost pagan. Gabrio and Esmeralda walked tall through the crowd of people, who began to step aside out of their pathway automatically. Fear of their presence wasn't the reason people repelled away from them. It was because Esmeralda and Gabrio held an authority that made them on a higher level than most. They were *Alpha-mates* and holders of the title demanded honor and respect from all equal or lesser werewolves. However, tonight Esmeralda and Gabrio would lead the hunt, which signified they were to become Elders, the highest of all honors.

Esmeralda noticed Sheryl sitting alone by a fire, with a furrowed look of deep thought residing within her expression. She noticed her eyes were scanning the horde of people that walked freely in front of her. *I wonder if she's searching for me.* Esmeralda thought. As soon as she completed the thought, Sheryl stared right at her. Not comprehending who she was for a brief second, but then realizing it was Esmeralda, Sheryl smiled and nodded a greeting to her, then went back to continue her search. *Guess she's not.* Esmeralda pondered.

Gabrio grabbed her attention and pointed to a man, who was charming a pack of beautiful young women with a joke or two. "There's your father, honey. He's over there enchanting the giggling debutantes and making rather quick work of it."

Esmeralda snapped her head immediately in the direction he pointed. She honed in closely. "What is he doing over there with them?" She asked, letting go of his hand and walked briskly away. She heard Gabrio heartily laughed at her stomping departure toward her innocent, yet horribly flirtatious father.

Raul Sumer, a carefree man, loved his everlasting life and all the pleasures within its glorious hours. Most of those pleasures he endeavored, involved the company of the fairer sex and oftentimes caused trouble for him. Comparable to his youth, he still was a handsome man of tall stature, pure black hair, glittering green eyes, and still looked like he was in the mortal age of thirty. If that alone wasn't enough to make him alluring to werewolf and mortal women, he had the blessed ability to wield a silver tongue. He could charm anyone when it struck his favor. Over the years, Esmeralda heard stories of her father's rowdier days and learned he often swayed the shrewdest of women into bed and in the same breath get himself out of trouble with them.

Also, within those days he claimed he would never settle down. His life's motto always encouraged a singular lifestyle as life was too rich and too full to become contained by any limitations. Especially when he had all the time in the world to experience every new happening. Yet, when he saw the most beautiful woman named Isabel, Esmeralda's mother, Raul became bewitched by her. He instantly fell in love with the enchanting beauty and stayed within its sweetest passions. The wild days of his youth were forever behind him as his mind became compelled with Isabel. She didn't go to him as easily as the others did either, which drove him even more crazy within his pursuit. She made an honest man of him. However, his charm always came forth and it always got him into trouble now and then. Esmeralda walked up to the nervous laughter of the admirers her father acquired and stood silent, listening, waiting for the right moment to make her presence known.

In a slow southern drawl, her father spoke to the babbling women. "Now, my fair lovelies, you need not to look far for a vibrant, strapping man."

The group became still, hoping he talked about himself. However, he continued. "There is a group of young, reliable men, waiting for your company right over there and I'm sure they would love your gorgeous faces surrounding them."

Disappointments from the girls were obvious. Yet, a woman with large doe eyes, white creamy skin and long silky red hair voiced hers. "Are you not a young, reliable man waiting for some company?"

Esmeralda decided that it was time for her to rule her authority over these lesser werewolves, whom she felt sorry for and increasingly began to loathe their boldness. "My father already has the continuous company of my mother. It's been that way for over two hundred years." Esmeralda spoke regal, firm.

The red headed girl blushed in embarrassment with the others. "Alpha, I did not know..."

Esmeralda cut off the young woman off in mid sentence, using her sharp tongue. "No, of course you wouldn't know. You're fresh out of the schoolroom and looking for another, let's call it, educational distraction. All of you are only several years into your overly horny stages of the blood. Pups with no self control." She clicked her tongue and shamed the newly quiet group of young women as her father beamed proudly at his daughter.

"Ladies, meet my daughter, Esmeralda." He said happily.

Esmeralda scanned the group of women in silence and then spoke assertively to them. "I think it would be best to converse with those men that my father mentioned to you *lovelies* earlier. They can take care of your eagerness for intimate company."

One by one the women left the bonfire with their heads cast down to move elsewhere. Esmeralda shot a look to her father. In reply, he gave her an innocent, cheeky, white smile. "You're mother had to cast them off earlier too. She just left only five minutes ago. They flocked over here, she came back, and left again and again they regrouped."

Esmeralda relaxed and rolled her eyes. "Dad, I know that you were living it up during the time of Scarlett O'Hara, but you don't have to act like Rhett Butler around every flashy skirt."

Raul deeply, laughed at his daughter's sarcastic sense of humor. "Esmeralda, you know your mother is the only woman for me. Also, you know how it is with our kind. We love for life when we find our match. In my defense, they approached me, twice! Instead of an Ancient Ritual, I think it's time our clan adopted the ways of a fertility ceremony."

Esmeralda chuckled, humbled and nodded her head. "We can't arrange our youth's marriages anymore. It's impossible to break that bond once you found it. Not even death can separate it." She looked at him straight in the eye and poked Raul's arm. "However, it's not you that I don't trust, it's the other women."

Her father's eyes softened. He found her protectiveness endearing since it was an old childhood habit of hers. "Esmeralda, you know for something to occur the other party has to be just as compliant."

Esmeralda agreed. "That's true."

"The woman next door. What's her name again... Jasmine? Is she still bothering you and Gabrio?" Raul asked, knowing Esmeralda had claimed a hatred toward her and remained irritated for a few days time when she encountered the woman.

Esmeralda gave him a confirming glare and added spitefully. "Yes. I wish she would just turn into a Half-Born soon, so I can take care of her."

"Oh my God, Essie! You're supposed to protect the mortals, not wish anything harmful would happen to them." Raul said with a chuckled as he watched her face smooth over with laughter. A stillness crawled into the conversation and created a lulling silence, but Raul cleverly and quickly kept the conversation alive."So, now that line of sinister wishing has ended. How's my little wolf? I overheard a certain couple is leading the hunt with the Elders tonight. That's a big deal, especially for Gabrio."

Tucking back her loose hair behind her ears, she nodded her head. "Yeah, Sheryl asked me and I agreed for myself and behalf of Gabrio."

Her father looked down at her and raised an eyebrow. "But." He said, knowing there was more she wanted to say.

Esmeralda paused for a moment and then gave in to confide in her father. "I'm happy to be leading the hunt. I am. It's just lately Gabrio and I have been beset by these dreams and they have many similarities between them. It's almost like we share them, but they're so different. I began having them a couple weeks ago, but they were flashes of strange images. It wasn't until recently they've been a full dream. They were intense, like death was there and something about the blood moon with some other stuff. It's just made me nervous about tonight." Esmeralda wasn't going to tell her dad about the riddled message at the risk of him thinking she might be going crazy. However, she wanted to confide in her father. "I told Gabrio about the most recent one a couple nights ago. Then yesterday morning he had one that startled him. I just don't understand what they mean. It feels like something bigger is coming, but I just don't know. What do you think?"

Her father was about to speak, when the flames of the raging bonfire dimmed and snuffed themselves out into dying embers. The cold moonlight quickly replaced the golden orange glow from the fires. A calm silence filled the once noisy crowd. Only the sounds of the passing storm sounded, releasing soft grumbles of thunder in the distance. Esmeralda lifted herself from the large tree trunk to turn around, but stopped immediately preventing herself from bumping into her mother.

Isabel's long wavy brown hair blew in the soft cool breeze as her face was as unmoving as a marble statue for a split second. Quickly she realized, her daughter stood before her, Isabel's expression turned warm as she spoke softly, but rapidly and hugged her daughter. "Esmeralda, there you are! My God, I hardly recognized you for a moment. You seem different, but I don't know what it is or maybe I've grown tired from trying to fight the women without life mates from your father. You would think they would see the ring and leave him alone, but no. hey have to act like the horny little bitches they are!" Isabel gave them a quick glare before she looked back at her daughter, chuckling.

"Mom!" Esmeralda exclaimed as she burst out laughing. That's what Esmeralda loved about her mother, she was gentle, charming, every ounce of a high-bred lady. However, mess with what was hers and she became a scrapper.

Isabel's large almond shaped eyes looked over Esmeralda's face, she smiled. "Well, it's true, isn't it? If you two weren't an alpha couple, you would be going through the same as me. They know to leave you both alone! I wish I knew you were here sooner, we could talk more, but the *calling* has already begun."

Isabel then turned to face the moon and began to walk. Raul placed himself at Isabel's side and held her close. "Come, my darling."

Esmeralda turned to look for Gabrio and saw him pushing through the crowd to get to her. Esmeralda stretched her hand outward to him as he grabbed it. Together they moved as a group, huddling closely, but spaced far enough apart from each other as if choreographed. As everyone collectively faced the large moon, George and Sheryl separated themselves from the group to stand in front of them as their position dictated them to do so.

George looked to his wife Sheryl and smiled largely. Then he began to speak in a loud, clear, commanding tone to the others. "My brothers and sisters, tonight is the night of the Ancient Ritual. A time we celebrate our *Rite of Transformation* along with the *Rite of the First Hunt'* with the newest *Beast Bloods'* in unity with the hunter's Moon. We celebrate a time where the calls of the moon are stronger. It raises the blood of the beast to the surface, creating the sickness in our offspring. A time when the mortal blood we have is changing and no longer existent in our veins. Men, women of the moon, stand tall, let forth the newcomers and present them to the silver light of the ancient power."

Preteens, children and toddlers, dressed in pure white robes began to expand from the porous crowd in sporadic order, to regroup in front of George and Sheryl. Esmeralda looked at their pale, innocent faces as they brushed past her and seen the mortal sickness was evident within them. With their slow, shuffled movements, sweat gleamed and dripped from them. Their large, dazed eyes sunken and their little bodies hunched in the increasing agony they felt. It pulled Esmeralda's heartstrings to see them in such distress. However, it was the way of it, one intense moment of pure agonizing sickness for a life full of immortality, strength and vibrancy.

George commenced. "Alpha-mates, Gabrio and Esmeralda, join us in the acts of tonight's rituals.

Hearing their names called, Esmeralda and Gabrio looked at each other as every ounce of love they had for another, lingered heavily in their eyes. Gabrio gave her a slight smirk and once again stared ahead. Following his lead, they walked together from the horde of men and women, through the mass of children, all whom parted a path for them with each forward step they took. Esmeralda could feel their eyes casting on them as they walked. She knew they were noticing their strength, their status among them. As they passed the children, Esmeralda could feel they already had them under their command. She swelled with the knowledge of such power and promised herself she would lead them well, all of them. She glanced at Gabrio and noticed he felt the same as she. Arriving, they stood next to George and Sheryl, facing the two massive crowds.

This time it was Sheryl who spoke with firm command. "Tonight, we will follow these two new Elders into the forest with our hearts beating as one."

The mob of people, including the children, began to shift in expectation as the intensity of the energy of the night increased. Sheryl spoke again. "We remember, with tradition, those who came before us. Honor those whom gave themselves in willing sacrifice during the great war between our kind and the Half-Born. A vile creature of man and demon, which rose into command and betrayed the Holy Order of St. Micheal. Betrayed our people! We remember those poor innocent, but possessed mortals whom tried to create a genocide of our kind with the great fire that once plagued these lands. We remember them every time we transform, every time we hunt down a Half Born and rid him of this earth. The tradition of these rituals is to never forget where we come from, who we are and that we will always be."

Sheryl spoke to the children. "Beast Bloods the Half-Born mortal is somewhere in these woods and will be for your consumption only. Their ancestors have feasted on our kind and tonight you shall feast on a tainted descendent. For the rest of you, help lead the children, help them use their powers, their strengths and hunt with them. Consume whatever the forest gives you. Now, is the time to change from the moon's ever rampant command. It is time to undress now." She shouted the last words to the eager group. Sheryl could feel the need overcome her as she began pulling at her own clothes, tearing them off her body in the process. Her ragged breath, releasing in short puffs into the air as her body crumpled into herself.

Items of clothing dropped to the ground as everyone began to shed their garments. In a moment's time, women, men and children stood naked before the moon waiting for the piercing, paralyzing sensation to change them from the inside, out. As quick as lightning it came over them. The moon released engulfing shards of light into their watchful eyes and initiated the *Rite of Transformation*. Screams filled the night as every individual changed into large, brooding, creatures.

Esmeralda stood still, waiting for the effect to take a hold of her as she looked helplessly at the moon. She turned her head and noticed Sheryl, distorted and twisted, she was half beast and half human. She stared at her in awe. Esmeralda's confusion flooded her features, and then suddenly the transformation came over her too, pushing her body forward from the impact of the ancient power.

Gabrio rolled his shoulders as they cracked into place and took off running initiating the *Rite of the First Hunt* as well. Transforming right in time, Esmeralda took off running with Gabrio and all the rest of the werewolves, including George and Sheryl, followed them as if attached to an invisible string. They moved in fluid motion through the woods. Thundering paws ran across the field. Their claws dug into the damp, black soil, added speed and traction to their already unstoppable movement. The children were shaky, but they kept up with the more experienced werewolves. They were strong, eager and quick to learn.

Gabrio looked back. He could hear their frantic, incomplete, racing thoughts echo through his head. Releasing a telepathic message, Gabrio spoke to them. "Calm your thoughts *Beast Bloods* and use your senses. Adjust your eyes to the night. Notice everything around you. What can you see? Sniff the air. What can you detect?" He sniffed the air and caught the scent of a large group of deer ahead, but Carlos's smell was faint, signifying his longer distance from them.

Esmeralda picked up on the scents as well. "Smell the deer. Locate them. Listen hard. You can hear them. Their breath, their pulse, their movement, but learn to control your hunger. Find a target to concentrate on. Now concentrate on the sweet smell. That smell is human." Esmeralda looked behind her and most of the newborn *Beast Bloods* obeyed their commands. However, a tiny child's voice emerged inside her head and stuck out from the rest.

"I'm hungry. My belly hurts. The deer. They smell yummy. The deer, I want deer." The child said.

The voice faded and Esmeralda looked behind her again and seen a copper figure leave the group and head toward the deer. Esmeralda looked from George to Sheryl, who ran behind them. They didn't give any sign as to hearing or seeing anything amiss. She looked to Gabrio. "Gabrio, I heard one of the children pine after the deer. I saw him leave the group. No one else noticed his departure, but I have to go after him so he doesn't become lost."

Gabrio ducked under a low branch, evading impact with it and looked at her. "Are you sure? I didn't hear anything."

"Yes, I'm sure." She answered quickly.

"Do you want me to go after him?" Gabrio asked her.

"No. You continue onward and we'll meet with you." Esmeralda tried assuring him.

Gabrio looked back at the group. If one did break, away he wouldn't be able to tell right now and then it might be too late. "Okay. Go, but be quick, Essie."

Esmeralda pushed herself harder to get ahead of the group and turned sharply to break away easier, before the swift moving swarm trampled over her. Esmeralda ran at full speed in the opposite direction. She could feel the forceful wind of the others swipe against her. She breathed in the air and noticed the deer moved farther away, but she couldn't pick up the scent of the missing werewolf. She abruptly stopped, letting the remainder of the werewolves pass by her.

Once they were far enough away, Esmeralda closed her eyes to pay attention to the sounds of the forest. She could hear the faint shifting sounds of a barn owl wings swooping onto a branch several yards from her. Other than that, the night was encountering the calm after the storm. The calm, allowed her to listen well and she was thankful that it chose that moment to become dormant and re-cover from the common abuse of the elements. Esmeralda became part of the silence, unwavering from her stand still.

Then, a quick snapping branch on her left made her snap open her eyes. Her pupils dilated as she swiveled her head to the sound and seen the figure once again. He quickly ran through a group of small growing trees. With ease, he knocked them over from his weight when scurrying into the deeper, thicker part of the forest.

"Stop!" She yelled to the ambitious figure. However, he contin-ued to run toward the deer. Esmeralda began gnashing her teeth at the disobedient werewolf as she ran through the forest after him. After a few moments, she caught up with him. The more they pushed deeper into the forest, the less the moonlight lit the surroundings. Eventually darkness surrounded them, but it was still easy to see for them. Luckily, she was trailing right behind him. A few times she lunged forward to tackle him down, but he would evade her just in time. She could see him right in front of her. Esmeralda noticed she was approaching a large oak tree. With quick thinking she lunged toward the tree, using the base to push off from and lunged for the final time onto the moving figure. She fell with the thud to the ground as she went through the apparition, which dispersed around her in a cloud. Esmeralda scurried to her feet.

What? What's going on? A rise of nerves came rushing to her already rapidly beating heart. She heard the blood curdling screams of Carlos echo in the distance, which increased her alarmed state. *I have to go back!* Esmeralda turned quickly, but before she could move any farther, a paralyzing sensation stilled her body as then pure black darkness over came her vision.

Meanwhile

Gabrio watched the *Beast Bloods* with great satisfaction as the first line of the newly turned werewolves tore into the overlarge belly of

Carlos Garcia, spilling his insides onto the forest floor. He knew they wouldn't eat much of their first kill, which made enough go for around for the remaining a hundred and thirty.

Sheryl approached Gabrio. "You both did well tonight. Your parents would be proud of you. Elder Santos."

Gabrio smiled inwardly. "Thanks Sheryl. That means a lot to me."

She nodded and looked around and eagerly changed the subject. "Where's Esmeralda. I would like to talk to her, but I can't find her. Where did she go?"

He looked around as alarm set in. "She's not back yet?" He jumped to his back legs as his snarling figure stood close to ten feet. Sheryl became startled as well. Her eyes began to glance around to help locate her.

"What do you mean? Where did she go to?" Sheryl asked alarmed.

Gabrio searched around and couldn't see her. He answered her question in haste. "She went to go get a rogue 'Beast Blood'. She heard him wanting to go for the deer and saw him leave the group to go get them."

Sheryl became confused. "I don't understand. No one left the group."

He ignored her and took off running to go look for his wife. Backtracking from which they ran from, he sniffed the air, trying to find her scent. He became even more savage as he became ever more distraught as he tried, but couldn't pick up the scent of her or the 'Beast Blood' she chased earlier. He ran past the area where they were at when she made her departure from the pack. He looked a little further ahead, he saw the broken trees. They created a path into the forest and without a second thought, he entered the dark abyss. He was frantic with worry as he ran into low hanging branches and jumped over the trunks of fallen trees. He couldn't find any sign of her. Not paw prints, not a scent, nothing. He stopped and seen the trees were growing closer and closer together, which forced him to slow his pace. With the last few steps he was at a dead end. He was in a cage made of trees and they enclosed him in all directions. Déjà Vu hit him like a bus. *This is my dream. I'm living my dream. I'm in my fucking dream!* He knew in the pit of his stomach that someone or something had her and she was in grave danger. Purposely lured from the group, they signaled her out using the ritual. He could feel it in his stomach. *Why? Why would they take her and not me? They could've had me.* He thought. "They could have had me!" Out of pure anger, his frustration gathered like a hot ball of flame within his chest. Gabrio yelled as loudly and as hard as he could toward the clear night sky. To the untrained ear, his yell was nothing, but a lonely howl to the moon.

11

BLOOD RITUAL

The sporadic pattern of icy water droplets fell from the leaky ceiling to hit the skin on Esmeralda's dirty, blood covered face causing her to stir awake. In a mid-state of awareness, she felt stiff and uncomfortable. She lolled her head to one side and started to move her body, which she immediately regretted as she greeted with a sharp pounding pain against her skull that shot through her entire body. Her hand, rushed to the source of the throbbing discomfort on her head, but the chain tether around her wrist prevented her from doing so. Confused, she pulled her arms down towards her and heard the clank of the heavy chain rattle as she felt the pulling resistance of not being able to go any farther. She felt a heavy shackle hang loose around her neck as well.

Oh my God, I'm chained. Where am I? She thought as panic commenced to rise like bile in her stomach. She could only reach far enough to press her fingertips onto the sore spot, which the paralyzing pain came again and revealed a partially scabbed over wound. Now fully alert from the pain she felt, she tried to open her eyes to see if the wound was still bleeding from looking at her fingertips. The task proved to be difficult within her current position, she couldn't open her eyes and figured she was still too groggy to open her eyes. In quick, tired defeat, she gave up opening her eyes for now. Her body couldn't catch up with her mind fast enough. Nevertheless, she knew the wound had to be bleeding a little because the smell of fresh blood surrounded her. She could feel a trail of the sticky substance trickle slowly down the left side of her face.

Freezing, she shivered as her skin prickled against the constant cold draft that engulfed her. As she gained more awareness of her physical status, she realized she's naked, chained and wounded. With that revelation, her heart started to pound hard against her chest as her adrenaline bolted through her veins. Unable to open her eyes fully still she quickly started to scan her memories to find what she could recall about last night. *Ancient Ritual. I was running through the woods. Yelling. Someone was yelling. The prey... the new Beast Bloods must have had him. Gabrio was behind me. No, he wasn't behind me, but someone was. Who was behind me? The apparition faded around me, I became attacked and then it went black.* Increasingly frustrated from lack of sight while remaining prevented from fully remembering, she started to pull her chains harder trying to break free despite the pain that plagued her body and her lack of sight.

"Don't bother with the chains, my little she-wolf. You are not strong enough yet to break the chains that now bind your wrists and neck."

Esmeralda stood silent at the mysterious, booming voice that echoed through the room giving the space more expansion than she thought it had. She tried lifting herself off the stone floor beneath her to rise if she had to defend herself. However the chains that bound her wrists and her neck prevented her to stand on her feet, but they had enough give to allow her to rest on her knees. Once again, she stilled as she sat with her head lowered waiting for the man to speak again. She could feel his eyes raking over her naked superficially submissive bow as she was raging like a caged animal internally. She heard his shoes heavily thud against the ground as he circled her like a predator stalking his prey. As he began to speak, Esmeralda could hear the man's smooth, deep voice glazed in a heavy Irish slur, but he spoke slow and clear, making his voice husky and exotic.

"Good girl. Now that I see you have awakened and calmed yourself. Why don't we start getting to know each other even better." He heard her draw a sharp breath inwardly at his statement of *'getting to know each other'* as she braced herself expecting to fight him. He boisterously laughed, loud disturbing laughs. "I love how your mind turned to a more relating desire. Do not worry my little she-wolf; I will not take advantage of your human form just yet. Even though the idea of taking you every which way has occupied my thoughts since you have arrived three days ago." He said silkily. His words dripped with desire.

Frantically, Esmeralda's thoughts began scattering, searching for lost time she couldn't remember. *Three days. I have been here, like this, for three fucking days.*

The man walked in front of her, stopped his slow pace and continued to talk. "Since we're on the subject do you know how hard it is-." He paused to chuckle at the perverted inner joke at the statement he just voiced. "I'm sure you know to some extent how hard *IT* is, but I mean to look at a glorious naked woman and can't do anything about it at first sign of savage impulse. Then again, being a slight masochist, I enjoy the torture of not touching you for now. Not that I lack women, it's just I like to fuck. So when we do, it will be with you, covered in your blood and dirt. I think it'll make it that much more thrilling, raw and savage. What do you think? Think you would enjoy me?"

Esmeralda could no longer take the sickening chatter of this man and spoke for the first time in three days in a raspy, soft voice, cutting the man off from his ranting. "What do you want with me, you sick fuck?" She heard the man's pulse increase with excitement as he exclaimed in a mocking tone.

"She speaks. You have a voice of an angel with the tongue of a demon. I love hearing your throaty voice using such naughty language gives me even more immense pleasure to think of how much of a spitfire you must be in bed." He walked closer to her until he was only a few feet away. "But I'll just have to keep those entertaining thoughts as the reoccurring fantasies they are, for now, because you asked me a question that I have rudely not answered." As he continued to speak, the tone of his voice switched to one of playful consideration. "What do I want with you? Well, my bonny lass, there are two reasons to be exactly what I want to do with you, regardless of the obvious one, which sadly has to come second." The man paused to gather his thoughts. "The main reason you're here is because of the blood that runs through your succulent skin. As you can see my dear -." The man stopped in mid-sentence as his brain shifted his train of thought. "Oh, I almost forgot where my manners are."

He closed the space that lay between them to crouch on his knees in front of her. He lightly put his hand under her chin to lift her head so they were face-to-face, inches apart. He placed his hand over her eyes to press and swiped his hand upward from her face, mumbling words that were inaudible under his breath. He was close enough that she could smell his breath, which smelled of a mixture of sweet wine and honey. Esmeralda thought that to be an odd mix-ture coming from the sick, erotic bastard that now held her captive.

As soon as he lifted his hand from her eyes, Esmeralda could freely open them to see once again. They fluttered open and squinted against the intruding light from the thousands of candles that surrounded her in a primitive glow. As her vision cleared, she saw the man that knelt in front of her and she became shocked to see his appearance. She expected the man to look twisted, balding and frail. However, he was the exact opposite. He was beautiful in an exotic way. In the light of the candles, she could see he had fashionably slicked dark brown hair and his eyes were so blue; they could pass off as white. His striking features, including his olive skin, contradicted the Irish accent he spoke. Nevertheless, despite his siren features, he was sinister, perverted and he was still crouching next to her staring at her as if he was searching for something within her eyes.

"What a lovely creature you are when you're surprised. I can see by your reaction you were expecting me to look different." He smiled as if it amused him, revealing straight pearly white teeth. Then he continued. "I get that reaction a lot when I give people back their sight."

Esmeralda's eyes gave away her confusion. Even with her trying her best to conceal any emotion from him, he still caught on.

"Don't worry, I'll explain." He rose from his spot in front of her, turned his back to her and started to walk towards the table that held a brass chest that glittered with encrusted jewels of all kinds.

She watched him closely and suspiciously as he stepped away from her. She noticed he wore all black from the tight fitting, black T-shirt with belted black jeans. Even the tribal tattoos that covered his arms and neck were black. Esmeralda saw that he was not frail as she once thought, but lean and well-built. Assessing him further, he sensed he was a fighter and he won most of them. He carried himself with arrogance and strength, which made her observation about him factual. Tearing her eyes away from him, she looked around the room that was to be her prison for the duration. Surprised to see the room looked to be a luxurious dungeon, which only held one prisoner at a time. Since the only chains and restraints that were in the room were already used on her. On that sad fact, she looked down to see what other torturous devices could be around her.

Apart from the large stone platform she knelt on, the floors were a beautiful dark, oak. They shined in dull reflection of the lit candles that rested all around the room in various styles of candle holders. Scanning the room, she noticed the lengthy red and gold silk curtains hung from the top of the stalls, ending in cascading pools of red and gold on the floor. They hung alongside the various old tapestries, which depicted scenes of bloody knights fighting in battles or of young, madly in love men wooing half-naked women. In her search, she noticed a tapestry that held her inquisitiveness longer than the others did. Surprised, she didn't notice the tapestry sooner because it's abnormally large size, which expanded across the entire wall right above the mysterious man and the table he was heading towards. Esmeralda became astounded by the beautiful artwork and its immaculate detail. Like the rest, it too had a red and gold curtain on each side of the tapestry. Although unlike the others, this tapestry was of a glorious angel fighting a demon. The picture beautifully caught the scene, frozen in time during an epic battle of good versus evil. The theme of this tapestry was so different from the others. She did not know why, but a distant, forgotten memory came forth as she fixedly stared at the picture.

Esmeralda looked at the tapestry even closer and recognized the warrior angel was the Archangel Michael. He was fighting the devil with the aid of a wolf. His sword of fire rose in the air as if to strike the demon as the angel's magnificent ivory wings fanned behind him. His ebony and silver armor, held a sheen of a yellow aura that surrounded them. It protected them from the advances of the demon's weapons. She noticed the demon also had a wolf next to him aiding him against the angel. She focused on the wolves and immediately saw the wolves were not just average creatures, but they were werewolves. On continuous close examination, there was seldom difference between the werewolves except for the color of their eyes and a slight difference in the size of the already overly large creatures. The demon's werewolf had blood red eyes as the one belonging to the angel had golden yellow eyes. "Gabrio's eyes." She whispered is breathless awe.

Esmeralda heard the man's footsteps halt, breaking her from the trance just as quick as it occurred. She quickly scanned the room, knowing the man was going to focus his undivided attention to her once again. She followed the chains around her wrists, which kept her arms above her head to see they protruded from the top of a stone wall and securely bolted. She noticed the cold chain, which hung around her neck to rest down her back and between her naked breasts, had been just as powerfully bolted to the stone floor on each side of her. Each chain only gave her so much room to move. He was right; she could not break free just yet, but why. Hurriedly, she looked back at the man to see if he was watching her looking around, but he was unlocking something from the brass chest. Esmeralda watched him pick up the item up, take off its red silk covering and turned to face her. Instead of walking back to her, he folded his arms and leaned against the table.

"See my beautiful wolf, there are signs forthcoming of a bigger purpose. An unfilled prophecy, which my kind can sense rather quickly when it starts to become fulfilled. My instincts led me to your little town. Knowing exactly what I was looking for, I watched your ritual. I watched all members of your pack turn rather quickly, but yet you stalled for a second and that pricked my curiosity. I led you away from the group using an ability I have and here you are today, with me."

Esmeralda became increasingly irate as she asked. "My clan will look for me. I will break free from you and when I escape, I am going to fucking kill you."

He snorted at her threats. "I love your feisty little personality. First, my love, your clan won't find you here. I've heard that line many times and the person saying it, is never found. Second, you can't kill me. You're in my lavish castle, located in the most remote part of this lovely country. Most importantly of all, I am what some used to call a Blood Taster. It's my duty to seek out the wicked in mortals and since the prophecy has begun, your kind as well."

Esmeralda coldly stared into his blue eyes in silence at the man as he continued talking. Confusion took over her when he mentioned her kind in connection to the prophecy. She sensed he was going to have the answers she needed to understand what was going on to her and Gabrio. Perhaps there were more like them having these visions.

"See, before the Order of Draco, in different regions of the world, many diverse names have used to name my kind. Lilitus, Vetalas, Baobhan sith, the list really goes on. Yet, it has became narrowed to one word since the early nineteen hundreds. My people became known as vampires, because of the constant courtesy of the obtuse and imaginative work of Bram Stoker. However, he did get a few of our traits right. We are immortal, which means you can't kill me, ever. Horribly sad for you, because by the look in your eyes you undeniably want to kill me. Second, we do drink blood and we crave it, but we do not shun the world. Also, we do not have venom to change people, as one would believe. They have to drink our blood willingly. We blend so very well into the world just as we always have. We can go out in the middle of the day and we can eat mortal food and drink. Unlike, what the mortals have depicted us to be, we have no weakness to stakes, sun, fire or crosses. We're a mixture of both good and evil. Created to even out the score, just like your kind."

Esmeralda was stunned, but skeptical. She only heard the stories of her people. Never did she hear of another group being made with the creation of her kind. Outraged and yet, too curious, not to ask him a few questions she had racing in her mind. In addition, she figured if she kept him talking that she could at least find out where she was. Settling for one question, in a sarcastic tone she asked him, "Are you telling me you're Dracula?"

The man heartily laughed once again and chuckled as he spoke. "If I were the infamous Dracula you wouldn't be talking right now. His usual methods of dealing with interrogations would to be just ripping your throat out, drink you dry and leave you to rot. Unlike me, my dear, I love to play with my food." He gave her a wink accompanied by a sly sickening smile that now revealed his pointed teeth.

Esmeralda stared at him with disgust. "Tell me your damn name and what a *Blood Taster* is."

He pouted for a second, then thought better of it to let the predator and prey game drag on any further. "You really shouldn't be so demanding, given the position you're in, but I'll comply with humoring you. My name is Conlaoch. My kind, created by the guardian angels of heaven, occurred during the great battle resulting in Lucifer going to his fiery confinement. During the battle, demons found a way to camouflage themselves as humans to live among them. The angels knew demons were disguised as humans. However, they couldn't fully detect them within the crowd because of the little sliver of evil within all mortals. Nevertheless, to avoid the horrible slaughter of innocent mortals, they came up with a plan. They searched for mortals with the strongest wills, physical abilities, hearts, minds and souls to ensure they survived the archangel's experiment without dying or eventually becoming monsters the angels would have to kill. The chosen mortals willingly accepted for their own various reasons and therefore the angels enacted the *Blood Ritual*. They mixed their own blood with the blood of the demons they killed and fed the mixture to the mortals turning them into what I am today. I was the first they created." He took a slight pause and continued. "The angels needed to know who was clean of demon blood and the only way to know was by drinking the mortals blood. Clean blood is bitter, but sweet and it would not affect the angels, but tainted blood is rancid, sludge. Thick and incredibly hot. It is worse than rotting flesh in the hot sun."

"Why couldn't the angels drink the tainted blood? They're protected by the Creator." Esmeralda asked incredulously.

Conlaoch continued, shaking his head and still taping the blade he held in his hand against his folded arms. "If the angels drank the blood of the fallen they would have tainted souls and could turn into demons themselves. Lower-rank angels took the risk for the greater cause and drank the mixture, but they eventually reached a point where God couldn't save them. Eventually, they became infected as well. Twisting into a demon and eventually murdering other angels. Best case scenario, they would become too dark to turn back and fall from heaven. So when it comes to me and my kind, we are a concoction of true good, true evil and mortal, God can save us if we ever died. Our mortal side is already corrupted by the evil of original sin. However, if the more sinister side of the blood-lust were to overrule someone like me, they wouldn't be saved. Being a group of forty, we are only a measly thirteen because corruption overcame them and they had to become destroyed. Before then, we were successful in our aid and Heaven reigned victorious with your breeds' helping abilities as well. Over time, my kind became dormant, but we existed in an endless life still craving the blood of corrupted mortals. It is a driving force, if we don't answer to this overwhelming desire the pain is unbearable and the consequences are dire for us. We lose our minds and slaughter thousands. Ironically, saving the mortals from demons to only become as a source of food for us through the years. However, it's not all gruesome. We did find a few other perquisites than distinguishing a demon from a mortal. Within our dormancy some of my kind, including myself, developed different abilities that prove useful. Some can alter their victim's thoughts and actions and others can shape shift into whatever creature walks this world. Some found they could take someone's senses away, making them blind, deaf, mute and paralyzed for as long as they want. Like I did with you."

Esmeralda grew even more confused and angry and she snarled her reply. "I've heard enough! I'm not a Half-Born. I'm a Beast Blood. A leading elder to my people. What does all of what you've said have to do with me?"

He mysteriously smirked at her. "Well, my darling, I'll have to taste your blood to figure that out."

12

BLOOD TASTER

In a flash of movement, he moved from the table to grab her by the head. With his large, forcible hands on each side of her face, he quickly bent her head back to bite into her salty flesh. Esmeralda's high-pitched scream echoed through the dungeon as he viciously sucked on her pierced artery. The floor began to shake as several drops of Esmeralda's blood hit the stone alter. The flames of the candles shot several feet into the air to dance in a vicious pulse around them. Esmeralda saw flashes of images of her and Gabrio running through the woods. Then the image changed to a smiling blond woman. The blonde was a mother running through the woods with her two children. The two children dived into the air and landed as the werewolves they were. The image then changed to the blood red eyes of a snarling wolf as another flash landed on the image of a great big blood moon in a black sky.

Conlaoch released her neck from his biting hold and immediately flew backwards with enough force, breaking the stone table in half. He stared at her in distressed horror. With a ring of bright red blood dripping from his mouth, he choked on his words. "Your...

blood… burns…!" He grabbed at his throat as he inhaled on the words releasing the shiny object from his grasp.

Esmeralda began to shake uncontrollably as her skin began to fall to the ground. Her body bent awkwardly as her bones began to shift making popping noises as a result. From the puncture wounds he inflicted, scarlet streaks of her blood cascaded down her ivory skin. She was quickly transforming into her wolf form while writhing in pain. The chain around her neck and wrists broke free and fell to the ground as her body expanded twice her normal werewolf size. Esmeralda screamed in a gurgled, panic strain at Conlaoch before her face finished transforming with her body. "What did you do to me?" She screamed.

He continued to watch her as he scurried backwards to lift himself from the floor. Through the rumbling shake and Esmeralda's screams of torture, he yelled his reply. "You have the blood of Laycerath. Born of his blood. You are worse than any demon. You are directly from the resurrected devil!"

Esmeralda could no longer use human tongue to speak, but she understood and howled in a feeling of overwhelming dread. She became frantic as she turned around looking for an escape.

Worried, she would pull her chains from their holds, Conlaoch needed her here with him and he was not going to let her go. Acting fast he shouted his angelic words, "*Fasck- Plauole.*" Releasing a wave of plasmid energy from his entire body to engulf Esmeralda's she became paralyzed.

She fell to the ground as she released another howl. Her head bent backwards with the rest of her body as her arms hung limply behind her sides. She lost all control of her body, but she could feel a strange fuzzy tingling sensation spread throughout her. She recognized the sensation as if an arm or a leg fell asleep from lack of circulation.

Conlaoch picked the shiny object from the ground as he lightly approached her. Suspended from any movement, she listened to him drawing nearer and speak to her in a firm, cold voice as he stood over her. "Your blood is like fire down my throat and the taste is indescribable. You are not like any werewolf, nor of any ordinary mortal blood. You are kin to Laycerath, the demon werewolf of Lucifer." He moved away from her to circle her once again. "My, she-wolf, you have put me in a confounding position. My instincts tell me to slice your pretty fucking throat." As he circled her, Esmeralda could see the glint of the long silver blade he held in his hand. "However, the child that grows within you is pure and can't become tainted with your blood. Certainly, I would go to a place worse than hell for killing you, hence preventing the child's existence. Nevertheless, I do not know your fate if you were to remain alive." He said scathingly.

Esmeralda could not believe what she just heard him say. Her mind started to swirl from the burden of the information she obtained in a short amount of time.

"I'm of demon blood, not just any demon, but Laycerath, Lucifer's demon werewolf and I'm pregnant. No, I don't understand what this means. He lies." She felt she could faint to suddenly become violently ill.

He continued to speak. "When your son's born, he'll be the first of a new breed of werewolf. He will be Michael's werewolf guardian, marking the beginning of it all. He will become a warrior and surpass all boundaries between the fight of good and evil. Your brother has abilities that will secure the grown child during the war that will eventually come."

Esmeralda's pupils dilated from the hysteria and confusion that raided her senses. *I'm an only child. I do not have a brother. How does he know all of this? He's a pathological liar for his sick sadistic pleasure. It cannot be true.*

As if he read her thoughts, he answered. "The blood gives away more than you think. It does not lie. It holds ingrained memories from the past that reveals the future if one has the ability to decode it. If I drink from one, I see into the lives of those around them. I can see how your blood links and spreads across your family. Those that you know of, those that you don't."

He flicked his eyes towards her as he stopped. "You are to remain my prisoner until I have summoned the rest of the Order's members to deal with your fate." Simultaneously, in a flash, the candles lost their flames and the room went dark. While Conloach's paralyzing hold on Esmeralda released and he was gone with the light. Esmeralda's eyes quickly adjusted to the shadowed parts of the dungeon as the rays of sunlight poured in from the cross-shaped window's that lined the top of the stone walls. *I transformed in the day? What the hell is going on?* She was once again alone, a prisoner left to think about all that now plagued her mind.

13

A DARKENED TIME OF MOURNING

Three Weeks Later

Gabrio awoke, lying in a litter of whiskey bottles, broken furniture and shards of glass, as the shrill rang of the telephone sounded through his pounding head. He grunted as he rolled over onto his back, cursing at the telephone. "Fuck no. No, not getting that. Just need to lie here... And not move... Too weak from... The whiskey" Gabrio spoke.

The answering machine clicked on and Esmeralda's soothing voice echoed through the darkened house on the prerecorded greeting. *Insult to injury.* Gabrio thought, then he heard the piercing beep that followed and then Sheryl's voice.

"Hey, Gabrio, It's Sheryl, I just wanted to call to make sure you're okay and if anything else came up in the search. Well, call us back. We love you, Gabe. We're here for you."

After a robotic, '*Thank you for your call*', the darkened house became silent once again. Gabrio laid there, listening to the ringing in his ears, as the memory of the night Esmeralda disappeared came flooding back into his sobering mind. He searched with George,

Sheryl, Raul and Isabel. Combined, they couldn't find a trace of her. Gabrio remembered that lonely drive home, looking at the empty passenger seat, holding back tears from the loss he felt. However, when he entered their empty the house, he was truly without her. Within his heartache he fell to his knees and unhindered anger rose within him. Seeing red, he went unhinged.

Since that lonesome night, he called work, claiming another week of sickness and holed himself inside the house. Only leaving its walls to answer to the *calling*, search for Esmeralda and when he couldn't find her he would get more alcohol. Raul and Isabel had visited him a few times already while Sheryl had called several times a day, but after the first few times, they became redundant enough to ignore them. He never cared too much for Sheryl as he grew older. It's true he once loved her since he looked up to her has a mother figure. She was the only one he knew, but she was always distant. She always kept herself secretive. When she thought she was alone, he would see her talking to herself, speaking somebody's name as she looked at the locket she kept hidden in a drawer. Slowly, he began to distrust her throughout the years as her nature remained shaded. However, for George's sake he said nothing.

Gabrio lifted himself off the ground and looked around the disarranged interior. Staggering forward, he stepped on a picture frame that crunched under his weight. He looked down and saw the silver engraved frame contained a black and white photo of Esmeralda. Gabrio reached down to pick up the broken item. Smirking, he recollected that day clearly. As the memory played on, he saw her rolling around in the tall grassy meadow and remembered capturing that moment with the result being the only photo he now held within his hand.

His eyes glistened with springing tears and he rubbed them away with the palm of his hand. He talked to the photo as she could hear him. "I'm sorry, my Essie. I'll find you. I will. I promise. Stay strong. Please, stay strong for me."

Gabrio wiped his tearing eyes and took the broken frame and placed it on the nearby bookshelf as tears fell down his cheeks. Taking another look around the house, he knew it was time to stop burrowing into his sorrow and pull himself together. Walking to the utility closest he figured he would begin by cleaning the glass and opening the blinds to let the afternoon bring light into this darkened time.

Meanwhile

"Fuck!" Sheryl banged her open palm onto the counter as a reaction to the pure fury she felt rising within her. She threw the cordless phone across the room, which shattered into pieces on the hardwood floor. Back and forth, she walked as her irate mind calculated and rolled over the hindrance thrown into her illicit plan. "I fucking know a *Blood Taster* got to her. I know it. I can feel it. I said they would be swarming around, all over the fucking place. Didn't I say that? Damn it! If she's the one the prophecy is talking about then we won't see her until the child's born and it'll be protected. Oh, it will become under the protection of the *Blood Tasters* and *Beast Bloods*. Then our plan will become shot to hell, unless we can find her and take her from wherever she's at."

Laycerath was nonchalantly flipping through a book. His expression was of grim boredom, as nothing in the words of the book held interest and as he listened to his mother's ranting. In a tone that matched his expression, with a tinge of added sarcasm, he spoke. "Oh, no. What are we going to do? Just calm down mother. We'll find her. Don't get your petticoats in a whore's bunch."

Sheryl snapped her head to the offending comment he made towards her and walked over to him to slap him across his chiseled face. "Don't you ever talk to me that way again, Laycerath. Know your place!"

Laycerath kicked back his chair and in speedily movement

grabbed his mother's throat and with full force slammed her into the light brown, modern chic couch, splintering the wood inside the upholstery. Hovering over her, his face became demonic and his voice quickly deepened into an unearthly, distorted voice. His face was so close she could smell the rotting human flesh from his escapades the night before and the heat of his breath only made it worse. "You fucking ever touch me like that again, you graceless cunt, I will rip out your still beating heart through your hollow chest! Shove it in your throat, causing you to choke and die, before I burn you to ash! Then, finally, you'll deal with what you've been trying to conquer all of these years Do you understand me, *Mother?*"

Sheryl nodded her head. She tried speaking her agreement, but his gripping hand was cutting her windpipe and his long nails bit into her skin. She mouthed it instead, hurriedly getting her point across, before he followed through on what he said.

"Good." His face returned to normal and released her from his pinning grasp.

Sheryl fell to the floor, while making a wheezing noise as she quickly sucked in air and choked on the intrusion. Through her coughs, she spoke with venom. "I should have let you die when Frances cut your throat. You deserved it; feeding you're dead clansmen to your breathing soldiers for their meals. No, I used a blood of a werewolf to give a Half-Born life."

Laycerath snickered impersonally. "Did the pot call the kettle black? Wasn't it you that fed a certain something to a certain someone that got you into the position you're in now."

He struck a sore spot. Laycerath had a verbal knife, twisted it and he knew exactly what and where her weakness was. Sheryl began to sob, her body in a bowing position on the floor and her head in her hands. She screamed at him. "I fucking hate you right now!"

Laycerath stood over her looking at her shivering, crumpled body on the floor. He lifted her up by her hair. "You love me. You need me, like I needed you then when you saved my life when I was a mere man. In return, I let you seduce and marry my lonesome father before he died. However, I didn't know at what price it cost for me to return. My soul's forever damned to the pits of hell for the sins that I have committed, but I crave a power of my own and you crave revenge. Together, our abilities and knowledge, we can have both. That's why you brought me here, mother and I am grateful again that I'm no longer in the seventh pit, surrounded by fucking flames. Yet you treat me a child when we both know that I'm the brawn and I'm not a babbling fool. With one more mortal consumption to go I will be unstoppable. However, I think it would be best if you remember, mother, who's stronger. Remember who can destroy you without a second thought. I know my fate and all these years you've escaped yours!" With that last snarl he walked to the front door, tugged on the knob and ripped the entire door from its frame and hinges, sending scattering wood and screws across the floor. He dropped the door to the ground and walked across its threshold.

Sheryl laid where he left her and cried even harder. After a few moments passed, she heard someone step on the front porch steps in quick haste.

"Jesus, Mary and Joseph; what happened to the door? Sheryl? Are you okay? Are you hurt?" George said in a concerned voice, kneeling next to her.

Sheryl sniffled and rose from the ground. She wiped her dripping nose with the back of her hand. George took a handkerchief from his pocket to dry her tear filled eyes as he helped her get to her feet. She didn't respond right away as she quickly came up with a lie to tell her oblivious, but ever loving George.

Through her sniffles she replied. "I just miss Esmeralda so much and I'm just so worried for her. I'm worried for Gabrio too, he hasn't responded to my calls and I'm afraid for them both. I was going to drive over to Gabrio and Esmeralda's home to see if he was okay, but I became overwhelmed with grief that I took it out on the door and the phone. I'm so sorry, honey." Sheryl sold the lie to her husband as she made herself tremble and sob with more force.

George picked her up and held her close to him as he comforted her, rubbing her back and stroking her hair. "Hush, now. It's okay. I'm worried too, but it'll be okay. We'll find her. Don't worry." He spoke softly and soothingly to her.

"I know we will." Sheryl said aloud, thinking of her and Laycerath.

He looked around the room and seen the broken phone, front door and seen no fault in her explanation. Until he moved her long wavy hair and seen the bruising marks of large hands and dug in fingernail marks around her neck. Then he noticed the back of the couch was convex. He suddenly pushed back from her and Sheryl became confused of the abrupt disconnection from him. George was deadly calm as he spoke to her. "I understand about the door and the phone, but tell me what the hell happened to your neck and the couch?"

Sheryl touched her throat, looked at the couch and back towards George's waiting gaze. Her mind began to scurry, looking for a successful to lie to him. Then it stopped, shredding the last ounce of moral standing she had as it came down to the ultimate choice of solution. She had to remove him from the picture sooner than she thought and after all these years of a loving marriage.

Meanwhile

Fixing the slashing gouges in the back of the couch with a few strips of brown leather, patterned duct tape, he was grateful that it matched perfectly to the material's color. Finished with restoring the salvageable items back into working order, Gabrio looked at the clock and seen that another day was practically over. The night was entering the horizon and the air became cooler with the descended sun. He, felt alone in the large empty space and needed to remove himself before his urge to reach for the tequila bottle set in. He placed the duct tape on the counter, grabbed his coat and decided he would go for a walk in the woods.

Walking out the back door, which he fixed, he remembered how Esmeralda seduced him with her charm and promises of the lavish breakfast in order to motivate him to fix it. He tested the door out again by waving it back and forth. The door groaned and squeaked, but it closed all the way and locked properly. He shrugged and walked off the porch onto the grass and scattered leaves. He looked up trying to find the moon, but remembered the moon wasn't going to show tonight for it was a new moon.

Gabrio felt even emptier, knowing he wasn't going to change tonight. The werewolves never changed during a new moon. How could they, the moon couldn't call to them or initiate the ancient power. Their strength would lessen, but never fully. It was their one night of being almost human. Gabrio walked the trail that he and Esmeralda religiously walked, through the meadow and into the clearing, where he became surrounded by the trees. He slowed his steps and stood in the middle of the dark woods, but he could see just fine.

He looked at the hollowed out oak, took out the wooden trunk and used it as a seat. He listened to the life around him. He lingered in the woods more often now, than ever before. Being in the places where they last were, made him feel as if she was right next to him. He longed for it to be true, but he didn't know where to start looking. He had no clue where she was, who took her and there wasn't even a speck of evidence left behind. Knowing the odds were against him pissed him off even more, but his longing for her was even stronger. He slumped forward and put together his hands and in a hushed, strained whisper he spoke. "I know I haven't talked to you in a long time. I.. I'm sorry for that. You've blessed me well all these years with a wonderful life and a wife I don't deserve. Yet, I feel there were times you weren't there. Maybe you were and I was too deep in whatever to notice your presence. Despite it all, I feel I need you more now than ever. I would give my soul to have my wife next to me again. I love her... I miss her so much." He placed his head in in hand. "Please, God, I beg you. Give me a sign how I can find her. Know where she's at and if she's okay. Or if you're even here."

Gabrio waited and listened to the silence around him and his glimmer of hope began to fade with the increasing stillness. Sardonically, he snorted. "Guess that says it all." He heard a few faint cracking noises, as if the wood was splintering and unexpectedly, he fell through the wooden trunk. Crushing it underneath his weight, he landed on the hard ground. After the initial shock and lifting himself off the ground, he exclaimed loudly. "You know, it fucking figures." He stopped in mid-sentence, while he brushed off the dirt on his jeans and coat. Suddenly, a dull shine of an object peeked through the interweave planks of the wooden trunk and caught his eye as well as his curiosity. Gabrio bent down to move the wood from around the object. Surprised, the dull object that rested under the small pile of rubble was a tarnished silver latch that held firmly attached to a very aged leather book. Incredulous at what he found, picked it off from the ground and looked it over. It was in great condition, except for the tarnished silver. He saw the latch had an engraving on it, but the dullness of the silver kept it from being readable. He figured it must have been somewhere, hidden inside Esmeralda's old trunk.

Did she hide it in there? It doesn't look like Esmeralda's. It looks older. He studied, pondering as he looked to the ground again. He kicked around a few pieces of the splintered wood and couldn't find anything else. He looked to the book one more time and rubbed the top of the cover, when he heard a phone ringing in the distance. He listened carefully and recognized the shrill tone was resonating from his house. Eager to read what he found, he headed back to his house at a speedily pace. As he approached the property line of his backyard, he heard the answering machine take the call for him.

After the piercing beeps, Isabel's soft voice came through the speakers. "Gabrio, It's Isabel. Something happened at George and Sheryl's house today. There was a fire. The whole house is gone and George was inside and - Oh God, Gabe. I'm so sorry. Sheryl barely made it out, but George. George; he didn't make it. The roof collapsed before he could escape and his body wasn't recoverable. I'm so sorry, Gabe. We love you so much. Please call us back."

Gabrio stood inside the doorway as shock waved through his unmoving body. The only father, he'd ever known, died. So many memories flashed through his mind as he ran to the bowl that sat on the counter. He grabbed his car keys and left the book on the counter to read until he returned.

14

AN OPEN BOOK

Gabrio's silver car was a dim streak going through the thick darkness of the night as he raced to the charred house of the only father he knew. He couldn't believe that George, whom lived his entire existence within that house, became lost within the fiery rubble of the family home. His heart ached harder. He didn't think it was possible, but it did. Hardened from another loss, Gabrio was numb. He couldn't think anymore as pure rage boiled past containment within his chest. He continuously slammed his hand on the steering wheel and screamed as he became overloaded by the extreme occurrences happening in rapid sequence. He needed to shut himself off to it all, but he couldn't. Still lost to him, Esmeralda remained missing and he remained George's only heir. Now, with the man gone, everything had an even more surreal essence. Hope seemed unattainable.

Gabrio wiped the tears from his eyes as he turned a hard left and swerved down a dirt road. Arriving at the property that once held the beautiful white colonial home in record time and sharply turned into the driveway scattering dirt and pebbles from his tires. Gabrio drove up the elongated driveway, turning into the circle

drive that encircled a large flowering garden, complete with a lavish fountain. Gabrio shut off the engine, stepped out of the car and
looked at the house, which was a hollow shell of a home. The stark
white exterior was a contrast to the black singeing that surrounded
the windows and the doors. Gabrio noticed the roof had collapsed
inward, just like his mother-in-law said it did.

Glass glittered across the ground from the busted windows
and muddy trudge marks remained on the grass of the fire truck's
wheels digging into the water soaked earth. He envisioned the
disaster of it all and imagined he saw it from the start as if he was
there. The small spark of flame, the black-gray swirling smoke suffo-
cating the land and everyone inside and the hotter than hell flames
licking up the walls destroying everything it touched. Including
George. Then, he imagined he could see George's struggle through
the smoke and flame, trying to escape before the angel of death
finally took him home

*The only way to kill a werewolf and it happens on a day where our
kind is weak. It almost seems as if the fire was on purpose."* Gabrio
thought sadistically with based reason. He sighed as he sniffled
looking over the rubble. Seeing enough of the haunting image of
the burned place he once called home, he went to his car, started it
up and left. As he was leaving he looked in the review mirror and
seen the guesthouse, which sat far from the main house on the back
of the property had a few lit windows. He stopped the car, figuring
Sheryl was using the lavishly quaint structure as a new home. He
battled with himself wondering if he should give his condolences to
Sheryl. He could only imagine how she would be taking the tragic
event. However, the decision happened to become made for him.
He saw the lights go out and with that final note, he left.

As he left, Sheryl looked through the blinds and seen Gabrio's
car parked at the end of the driveway. When she noticed he had
stopped suddenly she moved with haste and turned the lights off

and held her breath. Once she saw him leave relief flooded through her and she released the spent air in a rush. She couldn't meet him now. Would meet him now and absolutely refused to do so since she couldn't get the smell of George's blood off her. He was an alpha and if he questioned her just right, she would have to tell him the truth despite her inner turmoil not to do so. Sheryl glared into the darkness talking to the empty space where Gabrio's car once stood. "You're not going to catch me. Not when I'm so close to having it all." She left the window to finally get some sleep. She could do so easier since the ties were broken and she knew Laycerath was searching for his last victim.

Later

After a few steps of walking into his home, Gabrio noticed the entire house was extraordinarily dark as he naturally was going to flick on the light switch. However, for the briefest of moments he became startled. Walking further into the sheer darkness, he remembered clearly leaving the lights on as he rushed out the door. He scanned the room as his heart began to race and his defenses began to respond to the possibility of an intruder. He began to coil ready for an attack. Gabrio observed all the cupboards and drawers in the kitchen were open and seen the dining room chairs turned over as if someone flipped them onto their backs, crashing them to the floor. He slowly crept through the open floor plan of his home and every room was the same; open cabinets and overturned furniture. Yet nothing seemed out of place, just overturned. As he rounded the corner of the wall to enter the den he listened, while his ears rang from the intense silence.

Suddenly, he heard a loud bang with thuds going up the stairs onto the second floor. Whipping his head toward the noises, he glimpsed a woman's bare legs and feet running up the steps. "I see you! Don't think I can't catch you trespassing bitch!" He growled to the scattering woman, chasing after her. Gabrio was quick to catch up to the woman. He reached out to grab her trailing, long blond hair, hoping to pull it back to stop her in her tracks. As soon as he went to grab the silky strands his hand passed through the cold, smoky apparition and she faded into the darkness.

Stopping in his tracks, he disbelieved what he saw. In a ringing blast, an ear piercing scream surrounded him in the darkness as all the doors in the house began to slam in unison. Gabrio's heart thump hard against his chest. The room began spinning. The scream became louder and louder. Gabrio couldn't take it and shouted back to the phenomenon. "I've seen you! What the fuck do you want from me?" The screaming of the mysterious woman and slamming of the doors ceased. Gabrio felt a cold breeze cool his skin and linger on his neck. The hairs on his arms and neck rose on end. Something was behind him, but he seemed paralyzed, unable to move, even though he tried. Then a faint puff of air trickled on his left ear as it was a subtle breath. Gabrio felt the pressing lips of a woman brushing against his ear.

"Read it. Go to him to find her." The woman quietly spoke to him. As soon as those words registered their cryptic meaning within his calculating thoughts, Gabrio's body tingled with goose bumps. In a flash of light all the lamps in the house flicked back on, beaming through the receding darkness once more. Being able to move again, he turned around and ran downstairs to grab the book he found earlier. When he looked for the book on the counter where he left it, it wasn't there. Looking around, he spotted the book, unlatched and already open on the dining room table, waiting for him to read it's dusty, dirty, but readable pages.

15

THE INTERTWINING TIES

Gabrio pulled out a chair and sat at the dark oak table. The book sat on the glossy tabletop as if it belonged there. As if it was as natural as breathing. He looked at the worn leather of the book and the perfect preservation of the parchment and writing on them. He could smell a mixture of treated wood and the earth wafting from the musty item. After smoothing his hands across the pages he grabbed the cover with both hands, almost afraid it would crumble into dust, but he pressed on. Then, he began reading the first page.

January 2

"~~Dear me? Dear Journal. Hello… Me?~~

"I don't know what to really write in this rather lovely journal, my bothersome nursemaid is forcing me to write in. I find it such a miserable pastime to endure. I rather go outside in the fresh air fishing, gathering snips of herbs and flowers. Maybe taking my beautiful Jade, who's an Arabian thoroughbred bred, for a neck breaking run through the land.

However, it's snowing here in London. There's nothing to do in the Winter, but freeze and stay in bed for weeks on end because of a nasty cold. And I'm not going through that again! Nevertheless, even now as I write my nursemaid, Nona, peeks over at me from her stitching to see if I'm making use of her birthday present. When she gave it to me, I thanked her, as a lady always should, but I asked her what it was for and she gave me such a vague and wretched answer. She told me for whatever I wanted, but suggested I keep track of my days, memories, hopes and dreams; so I can look back and reflect for when I'm older. When I can understand and appreciate it; whatever that bloody means. I hate that saying, 'When you're older you'll understand.' As if I'm just a dolt now and when I become a spinster hag, I'll miraculously understand everything.

I understand I'm a child in society, but I'm so much more than a silly twit, but they chose to see me in an inferior way. Bloody hell! It's almost hypocritical. One day I'm a child, then I hear talk of my betrothal to a Highlander, which means I'm to become a wife. I'm too young for the brandy at parties, but old enough to become a wife and mother. Push out those heirs, Alexandria. Keep up with our bloodline, Alexandria. I shouldn't put words in their mouths. No one had ever said that to me, yet. However, that's what I feel like they're saying to me.

Apparently, the standing treaty between King James and our beloved King Henry, with the relation of marriage between the two kingdoms, has finally made an impact down to their lords as well. However, if they have to look beyond their own eligible women and come to England to find a woman to marry, it might be because of the obvious union. Or else no one there wanted them, which forced them to wander about looking for a spouse.

I believe I should make this clear, of course, for future reflection. As if I wouldn't remember. I damn well should remember, I lived it. Yet, to continue, today I am seventeen years old. *'Practically a woman'*, so I'm continually reminded by those around me. I turned this ripened age yesterday and had a pleasurable gathering with my family. My mother even asked Mrs. Anderson if she could make my favorite meal and dessert for the celebration. It went splendidly! Despite the merriment, my father who's a kind and gentle man, compassionately told me that I'm not to have a first season. No longer will I present myself among the eligible nobles of English society. By Spring, I'll become married to a man who's only a few years older than me. That's all I know about him. Not a name, a description of what he looks like, but I'm sure my hand's promised to that Frances fellow that I've been hearing about. Mother becomes sad when I mention it and father tells me it's because I'm the only child. Also, it'll be just her and him when I'm starting my life in the rocky lands of Scotland. Mother loves Father, of course, but he told me she gets rather sad in an empty house. That's why we have many guests all the time.

Honestly, I'm excited about getting married. Yet, I did want a season. At least one where I could dance, drink bubbly wine and possibly take a try at the art of flirting and maybe even get a kiss or two. However, I must be rather well with flirting for the stable boy tried stealing a few kisses from me when I would go visit Jade. I don't mean to tease him into thinking he has my interests, but it's hard not to when it's horribly fun. I just hope my betrothed isn't old, where he wouldn't be much fun or morbidly father-like. Possibly even maddeningly old, like Mr. Hopps, the family carriage driver. The poor old man, coughs and wheezes every time he moves. His entire body is lanky and slumped from the years of dedicated hard labor.

I've impressed myself. I've written a lot down already and it was just pure thought. We'll I guess I'm going to have to eat crow when I tell Nona, she was right about me getting used to the idea of it. However, I don't think it'll be an everyday occurrence. Then it'll become tedious.

February 13

Tonight, I've met the man who will be my husband and I couldn't be happier with the arrangement! He's not horribly old at all, only by five years at most. He is a handsome man. Finely built and strong. I like that about him. He has the most beautiful of features. I could become a bard writing about his face. Adorned his head is thick dark hair, which I compare to a raven's black wing. He has beautiful golden skin as if the sun permanently bronzed his flesh. It sends shivers through my body as the idea of him being shirtless working with the horses or in the fields. Body, covered in sweat. Then his eyes are just as marvelous; an emerald green and they hold such mischievous promise. Then his lush lips are kissable. I'll be dreaming about his lips and how they kiss. When they part, a straight white smile's revealed.

He stirs emotions in me the stable boy never did. Even when I would try to flirt with him, it was never real. Frances must have enjoyed how I looked too. He couldn't stop staring at my hair and bosom, which once I noticed I couldn't help but to giggle a little and flaunt them a little bit more by puckering out my chest. Since it's settled, he is to be my husband, I saw no shame in him admiring his future wife, even if it was a bit too early. However, I have to be truthful and say that since I found him so completely admirable, I was afraid to become rejected by him if he did not find me equally desirable. Mother must have noticed how I was priming like a peacock before he arrived. I felt her warm hands on my shoulder as our reflection shown together in the parlor mirror. She whispered in my ear telling me not to worry because I had the trimmest of waistlines, the most golden hair and the most immaculate, beautiful features. Then added, Aphrodite and all her daughters would be jealous of such beauty. Given the story of Aphrodite, that did make me feel so much better. I'm glad he found me to his liking. He'll soon know, as well as a woman's body, my mind's highly advanced by a rightfully well-rounded education in all subjects. All which were constantly insisted by my father and mother and performed by my tutors.

That being said, I'm never going to bore Frances by lack of understanding. Just writing his name, as well as about him, makes me smile uncontrollably.

I'm so overjoyed to be marrying this man. I hope our happiness with each other continues throughout the rest of our lives. Mary Elizabeth, my best friend, said her father and mother are not well together anymore. He searches for intimate company with other women because her mother can no longer produce an heir. I don't want a marriage like that. If I worship my husband, I want him to worship me as well. Well, it's late and the candle is starting to burn low. I'm growing very tired and the sooner I go to sleep the sooner I have dreams of my dear Frances.

April 11

This is the happiest day of my life! Here in an hour, I will become Mrs. France's O'Mara. As I write in this wonderful journal, I'm sitting in my wedding dress, listening to the echoing voices of the hundreds of shifting guests sounding through the corridor and into my room. May the Lord bless this union today. During our brief, but productive courtship, I have fallen in love with this man. He's magnificent in everything he does. Even though I haven't met many men, hardly any that wasn't family, I can honestly say that he is my soul mate.

Our fate will become forever bound after the ceremony today and tonight. Well, Mother tried explaining what was to happen in the marriage bed. She began telling me it'll be a bit painful and uncomfortable at first, but once I became used to it, it'll be even more glorious over time. I confided in her about my worries of being unable to satisfy his *appetites*. Confused at first, she caught on a laughed.

She told me not to worry because Frances would know what to do. It's a comfort to know that Frances has experience in what's to happen, but I rather him be just as inexperienced as me. Knowing that he has already experienced that part of life without me makes me furious with jealousy. However, it's the way of this world. The woman's pure in every way possible and has to conform to her husband's liking. I've never minded that much. I found it thrilling to give myself to my husband. My body's pure, which I'm willingly giving Frances, but my mind is my own. That's how I look at it and that's the way it should be. It's one of the values I remember my mother instilling in me since as long as I could remember, no man takes a whore to the marriage alter.

Speaking of mother, she seemed rather sad today. I don't think it's because I'm leaving my home. There's more to it than that. She uttered the most haunting phrase to me, which I don't understand. Now, mother's gifted with certain abilities, which only a close few know about them. Also, she's known to become rather intuitive in the dealings of the unexplained. Rather, they are heavenly visions or negative entities that bother her within the night, she has a gifted perception of seeing the past, as well as glimpses in the future. She told me a vision came to her. She told me with my marriage to Frances, my fate had sealed within an old story about to come true. The entity told her, I'd forever become bound to the wolves. It's my sealed destiny. Then, she placed a beautiful odd looking ring in my hand. I hold it now, twirling it between my fingers.

It's made of silver with a snarling wolf's head with blood red, ruby eyes. The detail is beautiful. It feels like a parting gift. Right now I wear it attached to a long chain around my neck so it can hide under the bodice of my wedding gown. Oh, Nona told me it's time! Oh, it's time. I'm so excited!"

Gabrio reread the woman detailing the ring. "I've seen that ring before. I know I have. Where the hell did I see it?" After a few moments of strenuous thought, it came to him. "Holy hell; that's the ring Marrok was wearing the night I invited him here!" Gabrio heard the grandfather clock sound off two deep chimes. "Two o'clock. It'll be too late to ask Marrok over now, but tomorrow night. Tomorrow night I have to find out more about him and how he got this woman's ring!" Gabrio continued reading the diary of this woman, hoping to piece together the clues it may have within its writing.

April 12

I'm going to keep this passage short because my handsome and naked husband is calling me back to bed with him. So if I ever do grow lax within memory I want to remember the night I lost my virginity. The pain was there, but the sharp intrusion of him taking my maidenhead became supersede. With each movement of his massive manhood the pain eased away. With the pain gone, something else burst into a sensation so incredible. It grew, exploded and sent me to a high I have never imagined possible.

I love my husband for being so gentle and patient with me. I must have pleased him well, for he awakens and calls to me like a siren of the sea. He's begging me to go rest under the folds of our blankets with him to sleep. However, I'm certain that we won't be resting anytime soon, tonight. Despite the fact, we have to get up early to leave this lavish inn he has taken me too. We journey to his castle in Scotland! I'm eager to go, now Frances has agreed I could take my nursemaid. She's been with me since I was a newborn, I would have become stricken with sadness if she had to stay behind. My sister died long ago and I'm the only one left. She would be lonesome without me. A kind man my husband is, asked his two of his men to stay behind and help her to our home. She's making her way to the castle with my belongings to have everything already when I arrive. Apart for one item. I insisted I take my journal tonight. Despite Nona telling me, that I will find no time for it on my wedding night.

I hope they like me there in Scotland. I hope I make friends among their nobles and honor my husband thus in his place. So as well as he honors me too. Frances is calling, I don't know when I'll write again, for I have a feeling I might be busy for a while.

June 15th, 1511

It's been a long while, future me, since I last wrote. My prediction came to bear fruit. The day after our magical wedding night, we headed to his castle. Frances made the carriage ride there beyond pleasurable in his creative ways. After a year, the carriage often became used for our marital delights.

Especially, if the driver was taking too long to get to our destination. However, everything became a bit overwhelming once we arrived at Raven Eye Castle. Another whirlwind of events occurred as I my eyes rested on his large extravagant castle. The gray, gothic castle sat on the dark green hills and expanded over an unfathomable abundance of acreage. As we approached, I remember the drawbridge lowering, as if it was bowing in greeting. Entering the castle walls, the castle's staff stood in a semi-circle around the drive, waiting to greet us. It was as if I were out of my body. My nerves were fluttering through me as I shyly stepped out of the carriage by the help of my loving husband. Since that day, I have had to learn the ways of properly running a large castle with two hundred members within its staff. Yet, I've added my own English touches here and there, but overall everything was beyond perfect. I came to love Raven Eye as if I lived here my entire life. Even when my mother and father came to visit, they couldn't believe the lovely wonder of it all. Surprise, overwhelmed them just as I, when they heard we were only a day's ride from Craigmillar Castle and our old family friends within the ancient castle.

However, I'm a bit nervous of the politics between the country of my youth and the country of which I now call home. There have been rumors turning the gossip mills that Scotland's French allies are going to invade England. There are underlying tensions and I fear that one day it's going to buckle the drawn out civility. However, if Scotland chooses to aid the French, this will infringe with the treaty of England. I hope nothing comes of it, it'll be dire for those involved, but I'm afraid Frances will become called to arms and he won't return to me and our growing child. It has taken us a while to get with child, but the baby grows four months strong as he rests in my womb. Frances is ecstatic as well as me. I have a feeling I'm going to love being a mother was well as I do heartily enjoy being a wife.

June 20th, 1511

I woke up covered in blood during the middle of the night. The gut-wrenching smell of blood still haunts the room. The midwife told me my baby died in my womb and my body cast him out. It was a boy, my son, had died within me. I became informed that it's a common action and it just happens for no reason. She said it wasn't in my control and not to blame myself. It'll be okay, she said, but her words fell on deaf ears. I was too distraught to listen to any positivity. My growing infant was here and then with gushing blood it vanished and I couldn't control it. It seems like an easy escape to cease blaming myself, but... I don't know what to think or feel. I still feel pregnant, but I'm not. I don't want to remember this, but I'm writing it down because I feel that I have to share it and work it through my mind. I just feel so numb. Thank God in heaven Frances has been so thoughtful and considerate of it all. He's saddened, of course, but he told me his mother had several before she had him and his eight other brothers. I just hope I can carry to full term. I would hate for my Frances to see me as barren or worthless and begin finding company with other women.

Women who can provide him sons and daughters.
I pray I could have the comforting knowledge of
what's to occur many years from now. To know if
all will be for naught and I become alone in a once
loving marriage because I can't produce an heir."

Reading page after page, he just started to go through the whirlwind journey of this woman through the words of the summarized
events in her life. Gabrio wasn't sure how to present Marrok with
the incredible and almost disbelieving number of information this
book contained. Also, knowing if Marrok was a missing link to this
intertwining tie of the past and future, he had to reveal it all to him.
Reveal what and who they are, *Beast Bloods*. He needed to save time
because he was running out of it. Gabrio needed to get to Esmeralda
fast and he wasn't about to let Marrok leisurely read the evidence
for himself. Then an idea suddenly struck Gabrio and he rose from
the table, scraping the legs of the chair against the hardwood floors.
He grabbed a piece of paper and a pen from the den, walked back
into his place at the dining room table and began to write the events
within this book on a timeline. Hoping to make it a bit more clear
for himself and to Marrok, he started with what he already read he
mapped it out and went from there, writing what he thought were
the major events. Mumbling out loud as his thoughts raced in his
head, he speedily wrote what he could.

"In 1512, Frances answered his call to arms to battle
the English. August of that same year, the woman
gave birth to a stillborn and told Frances. She sus-
pects her husband is entering a dark depression on
hearing the stillborn was another boy. Also, she
endured the death of her parents, which occurred
several months apart from each other from a mysterious sickness. The woman describes her husband's

letters to be dark, distant and vague. The scenery of war has changed him with a combination of the death of their heir. The woman learns that Frances has made an enemy within his ranks. Doesn't say who. Another comrade has fallen, but this time a commanding officer in his division had died by the hands of enemy spies. The officer's named Laycerath Edwin McKenzie. Frances becomes promoted to commanding officer after Laycerath's found dead in the woods by Frances and a scouting party. After the Battle of Flodden, 1513, The Scottish and French claim defeat and Frances returns to Raven Eye Castle a sinister man. Come to find out the man named Laycerath did not die, but had become saved at the last signs of his life by an unknown woman. This made Frances even more ominous and afraid knowing Laycerath moved his clans on the bordering lands.

Domestic issues occur and the woman claims Frances is loveless, with forcible sex and beatings. She caught Frances having relations with several of the servant women. When she tries to confront him, he beats her into submission and then forces himself on her. The woman orders an escape route to connect to her room. She told the builders it was a precautionary tactic just in case of an enemy raid, but she plans on leaving her husband.

August of 1515, the woman takes comfort in a man she met at an outing and feels an instant connection to him, which quickly becomes sexual. He uses the escape route to enter her room at night. By October the man quickly gets her with child and announces her misfortune through a letter sent directly to her husband. The note held the signature of Laycerath. The woman runs away from her home taking purses full of money, jewels, her mother's ring and flees with her nursemaid Nona. They arrive in the new world, America. She never hears from Frances or Laycerath after that night. In 1516, she gives birth to twins and the boy and a girl survive. Eight years later, Nona dies from natural causes. Two years after that, the children come down with a mysterious illness and then turn into creatures. Monstrous looking wolves. Only the moon and bring the change. Werewolves."

Gabrio couldn't believe what he read and what events took place in this woman's life. Gabrio reflected the events in his head. "So far several ideas were clear. Frances tried killing Laycerath, but Laycerath was a werewolf or had become made by another werewolf and couldn't die by a blade. Laycerath seduced Alexandria to extract his revenge on Frances and leaves this woman to become dishonored. With nowhere to go, she runs away and gives birth to his children. Finally, it's obvious that Marrok's connected to Esmeralda even closer for him to have this woman's ring and for Esmeralda to have the same woman's journal. The question remained was how did they connect?"

Satisfied that he had clarity of the events so far he continued to read and added more events to the chicken-scratched timeline.

Abequea, the Indian woman who came to them with permission from her father, knew of a tribe who could shape shift just the same as the children. Packing up their belongings they traveled far looking for the shape shifting tribe. After two years of searching, they found the shape-shifters camp.

Facing slaughter, they had to prove what they said
was true about their children, so they waited until
night. After the children changed in front of the
chief and elders, they became accepted, welcomed
into the camp. After a while they learned the origin
of the werewolves, the *Blood Tasters* and a prophecy
as old as time itself that's intended to become fulfilled. It was just a matter of when.

The woman describes the origin of werewolves
to be similar to the blood ritual of *Blood Tasters*.
However, using the blood of wolves, mixed with
mortal blood and the blood of the guardian angels
of heaven. When the angels were battling against
the demons on earth, the angel's would call forth
men, women and even children to aid their fight.
They would become disguised as mortals, but
change into physically powerful, remarkably large,
beastly figures with abilities beyond mortal comprehension. These werewolves, with the elders of the
shape-shifting tribe, could change willingly using
the angelic symbol etched onto their body and the
will they had to do so.

The symbol would become etched onto them
as small as an unnoticeable birthmark and located
on the back of their neck inside their hairline. As a
precaution, they wanted the symbol hidden from
the evil *ground* spirit. If a tribe member died, they
would cut out the small patch and eat it. They believed that setting the body on fire, with the etching
still in place, would put the symbol directly in the
hands of Lucifer even faster. However, the elders are
the last and once they die the symbol will die with
the last consumption.

The prophecy describe of a time when a were-wolf will become filled with a *Hybrid*, a mixture of demon, angelic and wolf blood, born from natural creation. The *Hybrid* will aid the highest ranking guardian angel in the approaching battles and the final war of Heaven and Hell; the Apocalypse. Signs of a red moon will show in dreams or visions to those who are acute to notice them. Another sign will be the werewolf kind will expand greatly in a short amount of time, to ensure the safety of this child when it's born. The mother of the child will have a harder time transforming with her clan and therefore an easy target to spot. *Blood Tasters*, who are harsh, heavenly creatures, will notice the signs and find the woman who carries the *Hybrid*, taking her to a safe haven away from society.

With the final paraphrased words he scribbled down on the piece of paper. Gabrio flipped the last page on the book and in bold, beautiful handwriting, read the solitary word, 'Alexandria' and with that the book ended as well as his timeline. "Fuck, that's it?" He exclaimed as he sat back and calculated all the information he had acquired. After a few long moments, he finally understood what the dreams were about and who the mystery woman was. Alexandria. Her spirit was in his house to help him. He read the intertwining ties of how it all began, but it doesn't say how it will end or what it might deal with finding Esmeralda. However, he would go to Marrok and find out the other pieces of this story. That was the next connection. It had to be.

16

WHEN THE NEW ORDER KNOCKS

Esmeralda was sitting in a large high back hair ^(chair) with her legs tucked under her as she nibbled the pad of her calloused thumb. She stared into the roaring fire in the massive stone hearth while she recounted the slow moving days in her head. With each mental notch she marked her expectation for her release didn't falter. She waited, hoping for an opportunity to escape with the pleasuring fantasy of tearing out Conloach's entrails. After he told her of her pregnancy, her long lost brother and her relation to the infamous Laycerath, she'd moved from the dismal holding place. Then, she was transferred in a grand room of sage green and ivory design on the third floor of the castle were she remained under lock and key.

When first seeing the room, she noticed the radiant shine of the dark oak furniture, smelled the lemon cleaner and knew the room had become recently prepared for her long stay. There were even clothes in her size already laid out for her on the bed. She remembered looking at the closest later that night and saw the many styles of clothing in growing size. Esmeralda had not a doubt those were maternity clothes and probably chosen my Conlaoch himself. During the day, guards would stand outside her door, but come night they were gone. However, since Conlaoch knew she could just rip the door from the wall or bust out the windows to escape, he placed barrier runes on the doors and windows every night. Esmeralda tried escaping her first night by using her brutal force, but every time she would touch the wooden door she would instantly lose her memory. For an hour or so, she would reside in a foggy trance until the enchantment wore off her.

The luxurious room was her daily prison. Under different circumstances she would've gushed over such details and admire every inch of the room. She would've relaxed on the velvet to the touch, backless sofa while reading the workings of Shakespeare, Edger Allen Poe or the other various classic authors that filled the bookshelves. However, given the circumstance, she loathed having her freedom ripped from her and trapped in a seemingly ever closing room. The day after Conlaoch had her chained and drank her blood; he treated her with respect after finding out who she was. At least, a higher respect for whom she's carrying. She didn't know exactly which. Nevertheless, despite his overprotective attitude he still made outright advances. Her condition didn't stop him from looking at her like he wanted to take her. As always, his thick charm and nonchalant demeanor were obvious as he made passing comments consisting of telling her, even though she was carrying another man's kid he would be happy calling him stepson.

She remembered shooting him a look to kill and rightly told him to go have repeated relations with himself. He would walk away laughing. She felt so vulnerable and she missed her husband. She would wake up at night and swear she could hear his voice. She wanted to tell him that they had a baby. Finally, they had conceived. She didn't know exactly how far along she was, but she knew she was always ravenous. Now, she understood the night they attacked the bear, why she was so savagely famished for it.

Esmeralda longed to change. If she could only change into a werewolf she could escape from here and go home. She hadn't been able to change into her werewolf form since Conlaoch made her do so with his painful bite. She remembered other female werewolves being able to change while they carried. Why was she any different from the others? Esmeralda snapped out of her train of thought while ceasing biting her thumb. She looked to the window and saw it was dark. She looked at the elaborate clock that sat on the wooden mantel of the fireplace. *Eight o'clock. I'm sure Conlaoch's going be knocking any moment now to escort me to the dining hall.* Esmeralda thought, using her mind as a stable companion when she was alone, which was more often than not.

After a few soundless moments she heard forthcoming footsteps walk down the long corridor and cease at her closed door. The humming sound of the rune stopped, signifying the accursed enchantment had become removed from the door. Expectantly, the door swung open and Conlaoch stood in the threshold, leaning against the door frame with his right hand relaxed and tucked into his pocket. He looked indifferent, but on the inside, he was busy with observation and strategic thought. Esmeralda quickly looked him over, noticing he wore a black button up shirt with black casual dress pants. He rolled up his sleeves, revealing his tattooed forearms and the top two buttons on his shirt remained undone, revealing a silver cross necklace on top of his smooth chest. Esmeralda jaded by his melodramatic entrance looked away from him.

"Well, my lovely prisoner since you're finished looking over my body, are you ready for our dinner for two tonight?" He said smoothly and with a smirk on his face.

Esmeralda more than used to his crudeness, rose from the chair and wordlessly walked passed him and continued a brisk pace in front of his slow casual walk. She could hear him laughing behind her back. She must have looked ridiculous rigidly walking in front of him, but she didn't care. Esmeralda turned the corner, jogging down the swirling staircase. Watching her footing until she reached the bottom, she quickly looked up and ran into Conlaoch's broad chest."Damn it, Conlaoch! I hate it when you do that." She scolded him.

He smiled at her as he moved out of her way, extending his arm as if to guide her toward the dining hall. "Then you shouldn't bite the hand that feeds you. Yet, I do love your rebelliousness and the way your taught little ass looks in those darling jeans." He leaned his head to the side in admiration as he smacked her bottom. Slyly, he moved to the end of the elongated set table, before she turned around to strike him.

Esmeralda gritted her teeth and balled her hands hard enough to have her fingernails leave half-moon imprints on her soft palm. She pulled out her seat and plopped into it, as she locked eyes with the sneaky man at the opposite end of her.

Conlaoch spoke to her in a voice of teasing concern. "Why the sour disposition my Esmeralda or do you prefer the nickname you're husband gave you, Essie. Yes, that's it. Why the sour face, my Essie?"

Esmeralda crossed her arms as she bit her inner cheek to hold her words and ever increasing anger. She quickly tasted her blood and she wanted to regurgitate, but she held the feeling down until it passed. Nevertheless, the discomfort didn't remain unnoticed as she thought. Conlaoch looked at her, shaking his head as he clicked his tongue. He turned his attention to the glass of white wine that filled the clear goblet. He picked up the fragile item by the stem and took a gulp before he spoke to her. "I see your growing child has already entered that stage of maturation since you're already feeling the effects of it lingering within you. It's natural, of course, as well as you know. With that said, I'm glad I had the cook take fish and other upsetting items off the menu. In case you *accidentally* decide to empty your stomach all over the fine dinnerware and mahogany table." He said the last sentence in snide disgust to fluster her more.

She knew Conlaoch wanted to get a rise out of her and it worked. Esmeralda couldn't take it any longer and her nerves were buckling rather quickly since she has been there for several weeks and had no clear idea why she's held captive. "Why do you treat me like you do? I did nothing to you. You're the one that took me, remember? You took me from my home, my family, my husband and to bring me... where? I don't even know where the hell I am. All I want to do is go home. Then, you, you fucking bastard, always making sexual remarks toward me and what I'm supposed to do? Just take it, just fucking take it!" With that last outburst, she grabbed a silver two prong fork from the table and whipped it at him, aiming for his face.

Smoothly, without dropping a sip from his glass, he moved his head to the side as the fork missed aim and stuck into the wood of his chair releasing a thronging sound in his ear. He set the wine glass onto the table, reached behind him and pulled her makeshift weapon from his chair. Then he put his hands on top of the table, staring her down in eerie silence. It was as if someone put a drop of swirling black dye into a glass of crystal blue water. Esmeralda noticed the swirling black conquer the white-blue of his almond eyes. His pure black tribal tattoos turned the color his eyes once were.

In a flash he was already next to her, grabbing her hair to pull her up from her seat. He kicked her chair away from them, until the force made it fall to the floor. He forced her to bend over the table as he bent on top of her, pressing himself against her upright bottom to hold her still. His face rested against hers as he pressed her face onto the cold hard table top. He hissed at her through his teeth."The reason you're here, Essie, is so I can protect you! I don't think you understand how important your role is now. How dire would it become for you if you were in the wrong fucking hands of those who want to kill you and your baby? Those who you think you can trust, even love, could have hidden motives if they knew it were you. They would love to have the control over you and your child's powerful position."

Esmeralda growled through her gritted teeth. "You want to kill me, you even said so yourself!"

Conlaoch snarled at her as he shook her a bit, pressing her harder into the table. "You stupid woman, it's not just about you! It's about whom you carry. You will birth the magical weapon that allows the salvation of civilization to happen. The world once became destroyed by water. Now, it boils beyond the crust of the Earth. The fire awaits and it's getting hotter! The prophecy speaks of the apocalypse and how your son will help create order between the realms. He is part of the security the Father and the Son equip themselves with. However, the other members, including myself, know that we can prevent the end from happening by finding the creations *HE* needs destroyed for us to continue. It's not the mortals *HE* wants to punish, it's those that suffered their punishment long enough and are now spreading evil across the land! There are truer sins that still walk the earth and with each wave of destruction God's trying to destroy them. Two elemental waves are left, which mean's there are two people left. However, we don't know what, who they are or have become. We believe your son will lure them from hiding. Until then, it's my obligation to protect you until your son's born and your fate determined by us." He said through clenched teeth.

Their intense moment became interrupted by a man loudly clearing his throat. They both looked in the direction of the noise and noticed Samuel, the butler, standing in the middle of the threshold of the connecting kitchen doors. Next to Samuel were two servants holding large trays of various steaming meals. Esmeralda quickly saw that all three were horribly uncomfortable for intruding into their intimate quarrel. Conlaoch calmly rose off Esmeralda's bent body and wordlessly walked back to his seat with a look of smug across his features.

While the servants looked everywhere, but at them, Samuel focused his vision and followed Conlaoch with his eyes and noticed his tattoos were fading once again to the pitch-black ink. Then he snapped his eyes to Esmeralda, who was finally free to stand and did so abruptly. Her right cheek, which he pressed into the table, was pure red as if she put on too much blush.

Samuel, a kind portly man, signaled to the servants to set the platters of food across the table. Then, he fetched Esmeralda's knocked over chair and brought it back to her, rightly putting it in its place. Despite his polite gesture, he avoided eye contact with her, but hadn't become imposed to speak pleasantly to her. "Here you go, Miss. Now, you can sit and comfortably enjoy your meal. There's much to choose. I made sure each satisfying item became thoroughly digestible for your growing condition."

Esmeralda bitterly spoke. "I don't think I'm going to be doing anything with comfort for a while, Samuel. Especially with him around." She nodded toward Conlaoch.

In reply Conlaoch raised his wine glass and drowned his gullet with the sweet liquid and refilled it again.

Samuel was wise enough to keep his mouth shut and cast his dark brown eyes downward. He could already feel sweat beads from his thinning hair slid down his neck. He knew what his master was and understood he could kill him in a split second. So, he did what any wise man would do. Nothing. After the servants finished issuing the plates, Samuel quickly scooted the women away from the table and back through the kitchen doors. Commanded to return after she and Master Conlaoch, left the table, which became the nightly routine since her arrival.

He noticed, Esmeralda watched them leave, like he did. Only when Samuel locked the doors is when Conlaoch decided to speak to Esmeralda again. Loading his plate with dark meat from the already sliced turkey, he spoke to her in his usual manner. "First, I don't appreciate you trying to impale me with a fork. It's disrespectful. Second, Samuel with the other servants work for me. They won't help you escape from here. So, throw that thought far from your mind."

Having guessed her train of thought correctly, she glared at him and thought, *I fucking hate you.* Outwardly, she interjected smartly to his reply. "I don't care what you appreciate or find disrespectful. I'm only reacting to my barbaric treatment from you thus far." She could feel herself swell with tears and anger. "All I care about is going home to my husband, when I can see him again to tell him of our son and when am I going to get the hell out of here. " Anger began to outgrow her tears as she focused her point. "Cause when I do Conlaoch, when I do, I'm going to find a way to kill you. Only if Gabrio doesn't do it first when he finds me here with you."

Conlaoch took another sip of his wine as he chewed while he ignored her idle threats. "Second, we've been having silent, on your end, dinners for the past several weeks. So tonight, I think we're actually bonding more so than the first night you awoke." His tone suddenly switched. "Also, if you don't start eating to feed your babe right this moment I will shovel food down your slender throat and not tell you anything you want to fucking know. Got it, Essie?" He said both mockingly and threatening.

Esmeralda was too upset to eat, but she was starving at the same time. He made her become livid with the way he acted and how domineering he could become. However, she had no choice, but to comply. She felt her immortal strengths weaken every day. Now, he was stronger than her and he could force her to do his bidding, but she would still fight like hell and not make it any easier for him. Yet, she took the easy way for this round and scooped whatever food was in reach, onto her plate.

Conlaoch held a small smile as he watched her fill her dish with various sides of vegetables and meat. "That's a good girl. Now, you already know why you're here, chosen and so on. Only ask me what you want to know and nothing that you already do know. I hate repeating myself."

Esmeralda became shocked, after so many weeks he was finally going to comply with her and answer her questions. She didn't hesitate. "Where am I?"

Conlaoch had been just as quick to respond. "You're at Raven's Eye castle in the emerald green land of Scotland. Restored to it's natural, historical beauty, this castle was once the home of your mortal, great, great, great, grandmother, Alexandria before she fled to America carrying Laycerath's bastard, werewolf children. I thought buying the place would somehow be useful in the end. I was right."

Esmeralda quickly looked around and asked him another. "How do you know that this belonged to Alexandria?"

He raised his eyebrow at her. "You know this, Esmeralda. I drank your blood remember, but I'll humor you. Despite, your blood being absolutely scalding when I drank it, I gained a whirl-wind of several thousand different strands of lives. I could see every single one of their life changing actions, their thoughts, basically their entire existence. That's how I know who you are and where you come from. However, it would be unfair to not mention that her name had a scandalous attachment to this castle when her husband, Frances died on the same night she ran away. Folklore and superstitions are hard to kill around these parts."

Esmeralda pitched him another question, satisfied by his seemingly truthful answer. "When can I see my husband again? Does he know that I'm here?"

He swallowed another bite and sighed. "No, he doesn't know you're here and I'm not sure if you'll ever see him again after this."

His answer disturbed Esmeralda. Startling her, her stomach dropped as alarm rose her defenses and masked her voice at a higher harsher pitch."I won't see...? Yes, I will. I'm going to go home. You can't keep me here forever, Conlaoch."

Conlaoch shook his head. "It's just not up to me, Esmeralda. It's up to the order members, who are already on their way. Demon blood in a werewolf is rare. It's only in your bloodline. The prophecy doesn't mention what happens to the mother after the child's born. After you give birth and see your son, your demonic blood could turn you into a vile creature. It may cause you to take your own child's life. If you show any signs of turning throughout this pregnancy, we'll have to contain you until the baby's grown enough, take him from your womb and then you'll become eradicated."

Esmeralda's heart shattered in her chest as she thought of her husband. All these years they wanted children of their own. They planned, waited and nothing. Now, they'll have a son and she couldn't be there for him. Couldn't be there with Gabrio during all the milestones. For the first time in a long time, she started to weep. Her body slumped forward as she put her head in her hands. Tears leaked down her cheeks and into the slits her fingers created. Fear and loss struck her hard.

Conlaoch became uncomfortable at the crushing disposition of the whimpering spitfire. He didn't know if he should comfort her or if she would even accept his comfort. He did what he knew how by altering her emotions. He released a calm energy to fall over her. The invisible wave took effect immediately as her whimpering became silent and a deep sigh released; puffing out her cheeks. Esmeralda looked at him with weepy eyes and saw he stared at her, concentrating.

She instantly knew what he did for her and it took her by surprise. She wanted to hate him for tricking her senses, but she was thankful for it. "Thank you, Conlaoch." Esmeralda said humbly.

Conlaoch gave her a curt nod. "Women crying are a bitch to deal with when you're not used to them, but don't think I can't tell the difference, wolf. When or if the time comes, I'll not hesitate to kill you. I don't have much room for compassion, so don't even think about taking advantage of it. Do you hear?" He saw Esmeralda nod her head as she used the sleeve of her long black sweater to wipe her tears away. Her nod was answer enough to suffice, Conlaoch. "Good. Now do you have any more questions for me?" He spoke sternly to her.

Esmeralda nodded as she sniffled and cleared her throat before she spoke. Through shaky voice, he composed herself and asked another question. "What about Laycerath? Did your people even come close to killing him, given if he can even die?"

Conlaoch's eyes glared into tiny slits as he looked to the past. "He can become killed by one of our blessed blades. The blessed blades are made of the same swords the arch angels use during their battles. They're durable, completely unbreakable and they immediately kill. Once we came close to catching that fucking creature, but someone got in the way. The other members and I found him in Spain with an older woman. She alerted him of our presence and we began chasing him, but we were taken by surprise when the old woman was a sabotaging witch. She cast a quick spell to open the ground beneath him, sending him to the depths of hell. He became untouchable then. If he's here again because the prophecy, we won't be able to detect him until he reaches full strength. He's blended with the mortals and others when he's weak. Until then, we wait for him and we will kill him."

Esmeralda felt a bit safe at his certainty, but she knew not to put her all her hope into one solution. She was a silently skeptic for a second and then asked him another question. "What of this supposed brother of mine? You've seen him. Doesn't he have the blood of Laycerath too? What if one day he finds my son and tries to kill him."

Conlaoch finished the last portion of his meal and swallowed. He looked at her plate and seen only a few measly portions were eaten. "I'll only answer if you continue to eat and finish your plate while I speak to you."

Esmeralda quickly obeyed by grabbing her spoon and shoveled a blob of hot, buttered mashed potatoes into her mouth. She swallowed hard, making a gulping noise to prove to him it was gone. She even opened her mouth, sticking her tongue out to let him see nothing lingered behind.

Conlaoch smirked at her childish action and answered her

questions as he promised. "Your demon blood comes from your mother. Your brother is your father's bastard son from a brief affair before he met your mother. The night before the moon first called to him, your brother experienced an accident of sorts and his mortal mother died. He became prevented from initiating his first transformation. As well as you know, the very first one is the most important one, since it determines the cycle of the blood. The power the moon instills, couldn't find or accept him. This makes him a carrier of the werewolf blood, but not one himself. Not yet, at least. He lost a great portion of memory and time. Once in a while, he'll experience subtle changes within the passing moons. His truest nature is longing to break free from him. It has been a few years since he's stopped aging. However, I see he will gain his from changing out of pure will, just like your father."

She almost choked on the clump of food that she swallowed. She took a long drink of her white wine, clearing her throat to speak in a tone of disbelief. "My father? My father changes with the moon, just like my mother and me. How can he change willingly? That's not even possible. Is it?" Suddenly, a distant memory broke through and repeated the words she heard weeks ages ago. *Turn the father's sun.*" Esmeralda worked the words through and quickly it clicked. *Turn the father's son.* With her last strand of questions and revelation of fitting the pieces together. "Oh, my God."

Samuel stepped through the threshold of the dining hall, interrupting their productive conversation. "I'm sorry Sir, to interrupt, but I thought it important to let you know the rest of the other members have arrived and are approaching the front door. Should I let them knock or greet them with the door open?

Conlaoch looked at Esmeralda and with another sip of wine, he answered. "Let them knock first and then show them to their rooms. Give us some time to finish our food and let poor Esmeralda recover from her shock."

"Very good, Sir." Samuel said before he briskly walked away.

Esmeralda flicked her glassy stare at Conlaoch. She watched him for a few moments as she processed what he said to her and what it meant. "They're here, now. The others. When will I know of my fate?"

After the words were said, three loud knocks rang throughout the dinning hall, echoing through the castle. Conlaoch shrugged as he cut his meat and forked a large piece into his mouth. "Soon, Essie. Soon."

17

THE REVEALING

In the dark of the night, Gabrio walked the unusually lifeless streets of downtown Cadillac and realized he was the only soul around. The town was an eerie quiet, except for the sound of electricity humming life into the street lights and the occasional passing automobile. He snickered as he thought the surroundings could read his mind and knew the plan he conjured up after reading the old journal. All was silent, still and waiting for the result of his plan. Gabrio knew it needed to happen to find Esmeralda. He believed his prayer became answered by finding the old journal. Then, the dramatic flair of the apparition forced him to read the journal to become lead to the person who wore the ring. Everything anyone does a has a ripple effect, now the ripples waved toward Marrok. Gabrio shook his head on how complicated it became, but he knew everything had to connect somewhere and he was going to solve the riddle to find his wife.

As he walked past the darkened windows of a closed restaurant, the yellowish glow of the streetlights illuminated Gabrio's reflection in a large window. Catching a startling glimpse of his haggard and baneful appearance, he noticed his hand gripped around the collar of his coat to keep it close around his neck, keeping the biting November wind from him. The scruff on his square jaw matched the unkempt wildness of his rakish hair. Then, the stagnant look in his eyes, all made him look the part of an ominous man who hid a dark brutal secret. Gabrio scuffed and walked away. He was that man who held secrets, but he knew it was secrets that couldn't remain contained any longer. With that thought, Gabrio pushed his hand into the deep pocket of his coat. Clutching the leathery diary and the crisp folded paper that held the information of his findings, he headed to his destination.

He walked through the parking lot of Marrok's apartment complex and under the entryway. Gabrio scanned the last names of the tenants until he found Marrok's name and pushed in the button sounding a raspy buzz. After a few moments there was a short buzz, allowing Gabrio entry into the building. Gabrio ran up the three flights of stairs to become greeted by Marrok, who peered at him from over the railing on the top floor.

"Gabe, is that you?" Surprise and concern filled his voice as he met Gabrio at the top of the steps. "Oh my God, are you okay? It's almost two in the morning? What are... Holy shit, man, you look like hell." Marrok said.

Gabrio heard Marrok's greeting fade to worried concern. However, he walked passed him and through the open doorway into his apartment. Marrok quickly followed him and closed the door. As soon as the door shut, Gabrio spoke. "Marrok, there isn't much time to speak. There is something happening and I know you're the key. The key to help me."

Marrok became startled by the distressed plea of his friend. "Gabrio, what the hell?"

Gabrio sharply cut him off. "Don't ask me any questions, right now. I just need you to listen, keep an open mind, Marrok. That's important. I just need you to listen and keep an open mind to the impossible, because I'm desperate and I know you can lead me to my wife." Emotion swelled in his voice.

He shook his head as he looked over Gabrio. Marrok increasingly became overwhelmed by the almost hostile urgency from him. "Lead you to your wife... Esmeralda? Is she missing? Marrok asked incredulously.

Gabrio went silent and gave Marrok a haunting look and nodded his head.

Marrok eye's widened. "Since when? Have you gone to the department? Is that why you haven't been at work?"

Gabrio continued, only providing the information he could. "She's been gone for weeks. A month. I've tried my fucking best to find a starting place as to how I can find her, but that motherfucker didn't leave a clue behind for me to..."

"Someone has taken her? You know that for a fact and you haven't gone to the department?" Marrok exclaimed.

Gabrio ignored his questions as he became even more agitated. He roughly ran his hand through his hair as he ripped the diary from his pocket. He strutted to the black pub table in the small dining room and slammed the book down on the tabletop. Gabrio yelled sternly and passionately. He needed to get Marrok to stop talking, before it was too late and time ran out. He didn't know how much longer he could hold on before he lost it, in more than one way. "No, no, more questions. I don't have time for this. Listen, Marrok, this book contains information that led me here tonight. Call it fate, destiny or divine intervention, but there's a reason we became friends. Something *we* never do with your kind. I know in my soul it's the same reason my missing wife felt a connection to you when you met her at our home."

Marrok could see Gabrio was on the edge and emotionally, maybe mentally unstable as well. It was a side of Gabrio he's never seen and he didn't know how extreme the dangerous combination could turn out. Marrok, rubbed his face as he calmly walked passed Gabrio. He pulled out a kitchen chair opposite of where Gabrio stood and placed himself in it. Marrok wanted to put distance between them, just in case if the already intense situation turned into something worse and he could defend himself in time. Also, he needed to know all that Gabrio knew to assess the situation and determine his next move. In a sedated voice Marrok replied. "Okay, Gabrio. You have my attention. I'm listening."

Gabrio sighed in nervous relief and relaxed a little as he too pulled out a chair and sat atop the sleek, black stool. He reached into his pocket to grab the folded pieces of paper that held his notes. Gabrio could see the uncertainty in Marrok's eyes.

Marrok tensed as Gabrio's hand disappeared into his deep coat pocket. *If he has a gun, I'll have no choice, but do what's necessary.* He thought as he coiled ready to dodge whatever weapon Gabrio might pull on him.

Gabrio raised his free hand as if to give a signal that his next movement didn't mean to inflict harm. He then quickly ripped out the papers from his pocket and instantly seen Marrok release the depleted breath he was subconsciously holding in. Gabrio began to explain, getting right to the point. "Recently, I came into possession of this diary. In this book describes a ring. A pure silver snarling wolf's head. The eyes of the wolf are blood red rubies. I saw you wear this exact ring the last time we saw each other. I was going to comment about it that night, but Esmeralda spoke up first. I need to know how you came to own the ring."

Marrok became confused why Gabrio would go through all this trouble to ask him about his ring, which he religiously wore. Even now, as they spoke the ring rested on his chest, attached to a chain around his neck. There's been multiple times Gabrio could have asked about it. With nothing to hide, he answered truthfully. "My mother. I got the ring from my mother when she passed. She willed it to me, but she was going to give it to me the night she died. I wear it every day in memory of her. I don't understand. What does the ring have to do with finding Esmeralda?"

Gabrio again ignored his questions. "Did your mother ever tell you how she got the ring?"

Marrok quickly realized the asking and answering questions were a one-sided deal within this conversation. Marrok recollected the answer immediately. "My mother wore the ring on a chain every day. I was always curious about it and I remember one day, when I was a young kid, we were working with the horses and I asked about it. She told me a man she once knew gave it to her as a gift because he was leaving and she was sad that he was going away. She told me it was a token or some shit like that, to help her remember their friendship and the time they spent together. Then I remember she said something on the lines of the ring not being the only thing he left behind to help her remember him. I thought it strange, but I didn't push her for another answer when I saw tears in her eyes."

"Did she ever tell you the man's name? Think hard, Marrok. I need to know. I'm trying to piece it together." Gabrio implored.

Marrok placed his head into his hands, rubbing his face, trying to ward the exhaustion he felt creep into his heavy eyelids. "She never told me outright, but I heard her talking about him to my grandparents when they would mention he should know about me. If I remember correctly, it was like... Ryan? Roy? Fuck, for all I know he could be named Joe!"

Gabrio felt his questions and Marrok's frustrated answers were making things clearer. He helped Marrok along by saying a name of his own. "Raul?"

Marrok looked stunned as clarity struck. "Raul. My God, that was the name. Raul." He took a pause as he understood where the conversation was heading. Sternly, he asked Gabrio again, "What's that fucking man have to do with *you* being here tonight? Are you trying to scare me? Someone put you up to this. It was Eric, wasn't it. Fucking bastard!"

Gabrio couldn't believe it. Bewildered by the revelation that Raul, Esmeralda's father, was the one who gave Marrok's mother the ring. It's the only way it made sense. Gabrio decided to come forward and tell him everything he knew and show him *all* the evidence to proof what he said was true. He shook his head before he spoke."Marrok, this is the part where you need to keep an open mind."

Marrok silently nodded his reply as his heart began to race at the uncertainty that Gabrio made him feel.

Gabrio nodded his head toward the weathered, brown book that lay between them on the table. "That book once belonged to Alexandria O'Mara. She's the first woman in my wife's family to come to America. When she fled from her husband because she was carrying another man's child, twins to be exact. She took several items as she was leaving. Among those items, Marrok, was a ring. A ring her mother gave her on her wedding day, which described to be in exact detail like the one you wear. The same on your mother wore as she died.."

Marrok leaned back in his chair, skeptical of what Gabrio said. He chuckled. "Come on, Gabrio. You want me to believe that my family's related to your wife by an old ring?"

"It's not a common ring Marrok and I don't think that your family's related to my wife, just you. I know you are, Marrok. I can feel it to the very core of me. That man, Raul, is the name of my father-in-law. Esmeralda's father and your father as well." Gabrio raised his voice to make his conviction heard as Marrok shook his head in denial.

Marrok jumped from his seat, wanting to become removed from the uncomfortable conversation and began pacing the floor. "No, no, no. I just can't, I won't believe this. You're saying that your wife is my sister, and I'm supposed to know where the fuck she is because I'm theoretically related to her because of damn ring. Do you know how fucking crazy that sounds?" He said, outraged by Gabrio's insensitivity and the cruel joke he played.

"It's going to get crazier." He said through clenched teeth. Gabrio could feel his skin tighten and tear little by little over his body. He didn't need to at the clock to know he couldn't avoid it any longer. The *calling* has been alluring him for a while and denying it would make it worse. In a strained hoarse voice Gabrio intruded. "I told you to keep your mind open for the impossible, because I've just gotten started."

Marrok looked at Gabrio as he rose from the kitchen table, walking into the living room and stood before the large window. "What are you doing?" He firmly asked as he watched Gabrio carefully.

Gabrio pulled the blinds, revealing the view of the parking lot he walked through earlier and the moon that rested high in the starless sky. "Nothing in my world is impossible. You might not know who you are, but I do. She led me to you. She made me read the book and told me to come here. Well, I found you, Marrok. I need you to believe all that has been said. When you told me and my wife of the story of how your mother died, I knew there was more to that story. Please tell me the rest of it, but quickly." Gabrio spoke cryptically.

Marrok became hostile. "I'm not telling you shit. You come into my house...!"

Gabrio raised his voice even louder, but his voice was deeper, darker. "You tell me now, so help me God. Before I break...!"

Marrok didn't want Gabrio to finish his sentence for fear of what he threatened to do in his seemingly psychotic state and hurriedly rushed the occurrences of what had happened that night. "Okay, fine! On my tenth birthday, my mother was taking me out in the middle of the night to look at the moon. She said it was my birthday present. That and the ring I wear now. I didn't understand, but she was adamant. I became afraid and she was trying to comfort me from my fear of the dark. The horse became spooked and bucked us off his back. I hit my head on a rock and my mother broke her neck. I was in a coma for weeks. They said I had a horrible sickness and that my body was fighting with something, but they couldn't understand why I didn't wake right away. Eventually, I did and here I am. There, are you happy now. I told you the entire fucking story."

Gabrio smiled inwardly. "Your mother was trying to have you look at the moon, because it would've comforted you, but the accident prevented you from becoming who you really are. Preventing you from becoming more than just human. She knew, you would become this."

Marrok stood there watching Gabrio looking at him as if he's gone insane. He took a few brisk steps forward as Gabrio looked at the moon and the ground shifted, preventing Marrok from reaching Gabrio. He quickly watched his friend hunch over, grabbing his head. Then snap upward, arms outstretched as a beam of moonlight shot like lightning through the window. It struck Gabrio causing an implosion of shattering glass and wood.

Marrok turned his body to block against the scattering slivers of glass as he staggered his balance. He looked back at Gabrio, whom stood paralyzed, unharmed by the shards of glass and the white-hot light. He watched in horror as Gabrio's whole body expand in size. His clothes and skin ripped in long blood soaked streaks across his rippling back, exposing what looked like to be dark fur. Gabrio fell to the floor, clenching his teeth from the pain of his knees buckling backward as his arms and fingers became mangled and wayward. He rose to all fours, resting on the balls of his feet and his knuckles, finishing his transformation into a Beast Blood. Gabrio rose from the ground as a pitch-black silhouette in the shadowed apartment. He blocked the light of the moon and the town disallowing letting any light into the room. The top of his head was brushing the ceiling. He turned around in his monstrous form, making the room and everything within in appear miniature. Gabrio's eyes became illuminated spheres from the swinging pendulum light that hung above the kitchen table. Also, Gabrio focused his glowing eyes onto Marrok's shocked features.

He stood still, unwavering to let Marrok process all that he had witnessed and to not alarm him furthermore than he already was. For a few slow ticking moments, man and beast stood face-to-face.

Both unmoving and waiting for the other to make a sudden choice in the bizarre twist in events. Marrok swallowed hard, trying to moisten his throat that his fear made it bone-dry. Gabrio could hear Marrok's heart pound hard against his breast in the rhythm of his own and once again, he inwardly smiled.

Marrok tried to wrap his head around what just happened and began to search for reality within the insanity he felt. After what seemed an eternity Marrok swallowed again, pushing a hard lump down his scratchy esophagus. "S...so this is what you are? What you believe me to be one too because of my mother's ring?"

Gabrio nodded his reply.

"Jesus. I don't... I can't even comprehend how this is possible. Can you speak to me? Can you understand me?" Marrok exclaimed as he paced the floor, cautious of the glass to prevent his stomping bare feet to become pierced by the ridged particles.

Gabrio still stood in the shadows watching his friend become overwhelmed with the insight of the world he should've been a part of all along.

Marrok stopped and looked at Gabrio and repeated his earlier question. "Can you speak to me or do I have to be like you? You know a werewolf. That's what you are right, a werewolf? Marrok sighed and whispered aloud. "I must be fucking crazy. This isn't happening. I'm having a breakdown or a dream. Even a fucking prank, makes more sense. It's not like you see me sprouting fangs, claws in the middle of the..." Marrok paused in the middle of his sentence as he looked wide eyed at Gabrio.

Gabrio saw a connection link in his friend's disbelieving expression. *He now understands this is real. His life can now begin.*

Marrok explained his pause in an eerie, calm whisper. "I thought. No, I convinced myself I was still dreaming, you know, because it just wasn't real. It couldn't of been real. A few nights ago I awoke from a startling dream about my mother's and grandparents' deaths. I was so damn angry in my dream, when I woke up I noticed my hands, my fingernails..." Marrok mimicked his actions as he relieved his memory, flipping his hands over as if it was really happening. "Were receding from claws back into fingernails." He looked at Gabrio. The features across his face were that of a confused man, but then something swiftly changed within him. His teeth gritted together, creating a pulsing tick in his jaw. Marrok fully accepted the unfeasible now that he believed Gabrio's words to be true. Raul might be his father and Esmeralda, his sister. Then, in truth, he must have been stuck in a limbo of becoming like Gabrio because of the accident. "You didn't go to the department, because you don't think an ordinary person took Esmeralda?" Marrok asked in a sigh.

Gabrio shook his head.

"It wasn't another werewolf, was it?" Marrok asked.

Gabrio shook his head again.

Marrok looked at Gabrio's unwavering eyes and impulsively decided he needed to meet the man that Gabrio claimed to be his father. He wanted that proof to be sure of everything. Earlier today he was just a man, but now he knows something more sinister lingers in his blood. However, now the question was after all of this, does he want to be an ordinary man or become like the beast that stood in the middle of his apartment. *Would they kill me if I didn't become like them? How could I go back to work, look at people without thinking they're hiding a monster under their skin. Life will never be normal for me ever again.* Marrok knew he needed to make a choice, but it wasn't going to be now. "Gabrio, I need you to take me to the man you think is my father. I need to meet Raul, tonight."

Gabrio agreed with a hard nod.

Marrok scurried to the front door, grabbing his keys, coat and shoes. He hurriedly began dressing to leave. He looked around the apartment to make sure he wasn't forgetting anything. Then he spotted the diary and pieces of paper that still sat atop of the table. Marrok stomped to grab the items as he shoved them into his coat pocket as he looked at Gabrio and spoke with finality. "We might need them for proof, more for me and for Raul."

Gabrio snorted as he thought, *Raul is going to need the proof to prevent him from killing the both of us.*

Marrok pulled open the door, letting light from the hallway into his apartment. Marrok looked back at Gabrio. His mouth dropped open as he finally saw the detail of the ferocious, massively large creature Gabrio became. He was a creature that radiated destruction and death. Marrok felt a shot of fear enter his heart, but quickly gathered himself from his gaping. He looked down at the floor and spoke. "Meet me downstairs, Gabrio and lead the way. I'm sure you can make yourself known to me without making yourself known to others."

Gabrio nodded again and Marrok shut the door behind him while shutting out the light. *It worked. He's going to help me find my wife.* Gabrio thought as he turned around and jumped out the busted windows.

Gabrio stood hidden in the shadows of the back roads as he led Marrok to his father-in-law's home. Following close behind Marrok tried keeping the shining the headlights on Gabrio. Even though Marrok pushed the gas pedal until the truck reached its full speed, Gabrio still had to strain his pace. Continuously, Gabrio needed to remain seen and heard for Marrok. In record time they were on the outskirts of Mesick Township. Gabrio led Marrok down a remote dirt road and onto a long hidden driveway. Gabrio howled at their arrival as he ran ahead and jumped in front of the slowing vehicle.

Marrok saw Gabrio was at a dead stop, standing in front of the truck and quickly he slammed on his breaks. Marrok's body lunged forward at the sudden stop of momentum, raising his body a few inches off his seat and plopping back into it. He saw Gabrio's beastly figure standing in the headlights, once again, unmoving, except for the deep, rapid breaths, he exhaled into the air as they swirled from his scowling snout. Marrok turned the truck off, leaving the comfort of his truck to enter the unknown surroundings that were both dark and foreboding. He took a deep, shaky breath to try calming the mixture of adrenaline and nerves. He jumped out of the truck, shut the door and walked to Gabrio who waited for him. "What now? Do we go inside or wait for them to come out." Marrok asked unsure of what to expect.

Gabrio shook his head and released an echoing ear piercing howl.

Marrok cringed as it rang through the silence of the night and through his eardrums as well. They both stood waiting, listening. After a few passing seconds Gabrio's ears perked up as quickly as the motion light of the shed flicked on. Two large shadows stood emerged from the dark cover of the wood line and into the light from the shed. Marrok knew the standstill figures were werewolves, but he too stood his ground and straightened his spine. He deserved answers and possibly together they could find Esmeralda, if he chose to be a part of it all. He remained undecided. He felt insane trying to understand everything. It felt unreal, but it was real. It was happening to him.

Suddenly the two beings bolted from under the light and charged at Marrok. Gabrio grabbed Marrok by his coat and pulled him behind his physically powerful stance as he growled and snapped at them. He quickly executed his high position."Family aside, you will halt your movements, commanded by your elder!" Gabrio spoke to them.

Raul and Isabel halted immediately against their will and coward as they snapped and snarled, licking their teeth, in noticeable defiance at what Gabrio forced them do. Raul growled harshly. "Family? How dare you speak of family to us when you bring a mortal here to my home? Are you out of your fucking mind? You don't remember the great genocide of our kind, but I do. I was there as a soldier within the clans. I trained with your father and George and saw your mother. Swollen belly, with you inside. This is how it started, by the betrayal of Leonardo! Fires set in our homes, in the middle of the night, killing our kin, as we battled possessed mortals. Your mother and father! You betray them, Gabrio, by revealing us to one of them."

Isabel growled as her hairs rose along her spine watching the mortal and Gabrio carefully.

Gabrio powerfully spoke. "The both of you will calm down and you'll listen to what I have to say."

"I'll not listen to a fucking word you have to say until you remove your pet or I will do it for you." Raul didn't give Gabrio a chance to choose as he lunged at Marrok.

Marrok took several steps back as he witnessed the quarrel between the creatures. Gabrio bared his teeth as he evaded Raul's advance. He grabbed Raul by the back of the neck and threw him, causing him to slide across the grass. Isabel roared in distress as she remained torn between the safety of her mate and her son-in-law. Releasing a roaring cry, Isabel ran toward Marrok, hoping to rip out the mortal's throat. Gabrio saw her fly behind him in the corner of his eye. He hurriedly turned around, grabbed her by the back of the neck and threw her. She landed near Raul. Isabel rolled as she skidded across the grass. Digging her claws into the grass, she flipped herself upright and began to charge again.

Unaltered, Raul used the force of Gabrio's strength to twist his body and land on his feet; running back will full force, his claws ready to tear into Gabrio's black pelt.

He saw they weren't going to stop, but he knew if Raul did first Isabel would follow. Ready to fight further if they had it in them, but not wanting to fight the people he came to love and respect, especially for Esmeralda's sake, Gabrio yelled. "He's your son, Raul! He carries the ring you gave his mortal mother when you parted!"

Raul stopped in his tracks, incredulous of what he just heard. "What did you just say?"

Gabrio was thankful that made him stop. Now he knew they would listen to what he had to say. "He's your son. He wears the ring you gave his mother, Raul. You know it's not an ordinary ring. I know it's detail well. Made of pure silver with blood red rubies on a snarling wolf's head. He wears it and its not fucking coincidence why your daughter, my wife, felt a connection to him, when I invited him over to my house. This is the beginning of it all to finding my wife, your daughter!" Raul didn't say a word and Gabrio took that opportunity to speak further. "Listen to his heart. It sounded mortal until he's around us. Then, its beat is like ours. It's faster, harder and stronger than any mortals. He's one of us, but he's caught in a dividing line. That's why I'm here with him tonight. He wanted to me to take him here so he could be sure himself." Gabrio finished speaking and Raul was still oddly silent.

His features were fierce in skepticism, but on the inside, he remained floored. He's never told a single soul about Sophia. She was special to him. He was close to loving her, but she would never fit into his world because it wasn't the love their kind shared. It was too flimsy. It would've been easy to turn her. All he had to do was open a vein and make her drink, but she was a mortal with a family. It wasn't like George and Sheryl where Sheryl's family, unfortunately passed of sickness. Also, they actually fell in love with each other. Sophia was so naïve, wholesome and trusting. His felt his soul would've become damned if he took her and made her into what he was, especially since he knew she wasn't his life mate. He felt bad for leaving her that day, watching her baby blue eyes glisten with tears and confusion. He gave her a ring. A ring that changed his life forever, but now it's apparent that he left something else behind as well. Raul walked calmly to Gabrio and stood in front of him and gave him a curt nod. Gabrio nodded back as he moved out of the way to give access to Marrok. He saw the man was trying his best to remain fearless when the werewolf of soft brown fur, approached him and stared at him with glowing green eyes.

Isabel couldn't take it any longer and broke her silence. "Is it true, Raul? Did you have a son with a mortal woman?"

Raul assessed the blonde, well built man, whom he towered over. The man, despite the fear Raul could feel coming off him, never backed down. His features were so similar to him and Sophia. A perfect blend of each of them. Raul sighed and left him; turning around to answer his wife."It looks like I did, but I didn't know until tonight."

He could tell the answer shook Isabel to the core and became speechless. Raul then looked to Gabrio and spoke with authority. "I'm going to speak to my son."

Gabrio nodded his head. "It'll have to wait until morning, he can't understand...."

Raul briskly nodded and spoke callously. "No! Tonight! I speak with my son tonight! Especially, if Esmeralda felt a connection to him in her mortal form, maybe he can lead us to her!"

Gabrio wanted to argue with Raul, but he didn't have it in him to say anymore. Everyone's emotions and tensions have been already high and easily riled. "Go ahead."

Raul looked at the moon. It was the first time in over a hundred years that he had willingly changed back into his mortal casing, but tonight would break the streak. He stared at the moon as its silver gazed dared him to say the solitary word, which would allow him to talk to his son. Raul goaded as he thought the word in a language unknown to most. *Retrorol.* As soon as the word was thought, Raul became surrounded by a perfect circle of engulfing hot flames.

Gabrio lunged toward Raul, trying to save him from the flames. Isabel howled a blood chilling sound. Marrok was closer to Raul and rushed to the pillar of fire. As soon as he became close enough, the flames changed into a blue-white haze and released a windy blast of blinding white light, creating a force of its own. Marrok propelled backward, landing near his truck with the wind knocked out of him. Gabrio and Isabel shielded their eyes from the light.

After a few moments the white light dimmed and faded into the night and all was calm again. Gabrio, Isabel and Marrok stared at the wall of thick swirling smoke hoping their eyes didn't deceive them from the supernatural sight they witnessed.

In the dissipating smoke, Raul stood as a perfect specimen of a mortal man, unharmed and naked, in a charred circle of grass. Gabrio and Isabel were in awe. The man they knew survived fire, the one weapon that has killed their kind since the dawn of time and had willingly transformed back, without the light of day.

18

THE DYING REWARD

R aul knew the ability he had gained was one that all the werewolves would covet if they knew he possessed it. He would've
given the ability to Esmeralda and Isabel a long time ago, but he
swore secrecy never to reveal it to anyone until the right time came.
He made a promise and now here he was changed into a man to
talk to the son he never knew he had. Raul squared his shoulders
as he walked naked into his home without a single word said to the
others that stared at his naked back. He could feel their eyes and
knew Gabrio and Isabel would be crazed to know how he learned
to change and never die of the fire. He would have to tell them now,
but first he needed to get dressed and talk to Marrok.

A few moments later he emerged from the house, fully dressed in
a T-shirt and jeans and stood on the front porch. He didn't need to say
a word because all three surrounded the bottom steps of the porch,
ready for him to speak. So he did. "That was something, wasn't it." He
chuckled, trying to ease some comfort into this situation, but it didn't
work. He straightened his spine at their silence. "It's not yet morning.
Gabrio and Isabel, you two will stay out here. I know my wife still
needs to hunt and she's famished, Gabrio you will go with her."

Gabrio and Isabel began to show signs of protest, but he hindered them immediately and became commanding. "No! I'm going to take my son inside and we are going to talk. I want to speak to my son, alone." He then eased his voice as he spoke to his wife, his southern drawl becoming husky and warm. "Isabel, my love, please eat something. Essie wouldn't want you to wither yourself away and I can no longer see you pick at the scraps. You enjoy the hunt tonight and Gabrio will protect you. I trust him. I'll tell you everything in the morning, just give me this now."

Isabel's eyes softened, she gave him a light nod and looked at Gabrio, whom was looking between Raul and Marrok. Isabel fell to all fours, shook her simmering dark amber fur and trotted into the wood line.

Raul spoke to Gabrio. "It's okay. We'll find her and I won't hurt my own. So, go protect my wife as I greet my son. I have a feeling by morning we'll have a starting point to finding my daughter, your wife." He smiled.

Gabrio needed some hope and reassurance to feel some measure of sanity. All along he has been living with the pressuring guilt of being unable to protect her, but he would make it better. Together they'll find his wife and she'll return home. Gabrio dropped to all fours and ran in the direction Isabel did and met her at the edge of the wood line. Together they disappeared into the cloak of the forest.

Raul looked at Marrok a bit nervously and wondered if he should have waited until morning, but then he threw the thought aside. He had a grown son and was meeting him for the first time, of course he was going to be nervous. Waiting would only waste more time. Raul became uncertain how to speak to Marrok, but he cleared his throat to get his attention. Marrok looked at him. He addressed him as he would a friend. "Would you like to come inside, possibly have a drink or two. I think we both need and deserve it." Raul lightly chortled.

Marrok was irresolute. He didn't know how to take the man that claimed to be his father. Raul looked to be around the same age as him. Maybe a few years older. Despite his reservations he gave him a small smile. A drink would make sense, despite it being early morning and sounded good. "I think whiskey neat sounds like a damn good drink for the nerves."

Raul smiled back at him, while he moved aside to let Marrok up the steps and into the house. "That's the preferred kind for me."

In sequence, they entered the cozy, spacious living room of the brick house. Marrok lead the way, but once inside, he hesitated, unsure of how far he should enter the home. Raul saw the hindering movements of his son and knew the situation was just as awkward for him. He tried to make him feel relaxed and at ease as much as possible. "There's a coat stand next to you. Make yourself comfortable while I get the drinks."

After those brief words Raul hurried into the kitchen to pour the desired whiskey from his collection of crystal decanters. He was thankful that they always kept the wet bar well stocked. Raul, in his fast pace motion of preparing the items, took a large swig from the largest decanter out of the group. He wiped his mouth, poured the drinks to the rim, plugged it with the stopper and headed into the living room where Marrok awaited his return. Raul noticed he still wore his coat as he handed him his drink. He took another large swig out of the matching glassware, leaving the glass half empty.

Marrok was just as greedy with the whiskey. Once the glass was in his hands, he gulped the amber liquid despite the warm burn of the whiskey sliding down his throat. Once done Marrok pressed his lips together as he looked at the empty glass, wishing he had a bottle instead.

Impressed that Marrok didn't even flinch while consuming the potent substance, Raul blurted out without thinking. "Damn, son, you weren't kidding when you said you needed that drink." Raul lightheartedly exclaimed.

Marrok heard him use the word *son* and wondered if he did that out of habit because his obvious southern roots or if he was calling him *son* because that's who he apparently was. He didn't know which, but he decided not to dwell too much about it. He wasn't a sulky teenager for God sakes. "Yeah, I knew at some point tonight, it was going to come into play. A case would be good for something like this."

Raul nodded. Then the silence and tension began to grow. However, he caught it in time before it drew on too long. He quickly finished his drink, placed the empty glass on the oak coffee table in front of him and decided to deal with what they both had in mind. "Well, it's about time to talk about, everything. Starting with the obvious, your mother and I."

"I don't think that's the most obvious point here." Marrok said sarcastically as leaned his elbows on his knees as he rubbed his face with his hands and clasped them together in front of him. The whiskey was already kicking in as he could feel himself becoming more relaxed, which was a good because it meant he could be a bit more forthright. "I just want you to know that my mother was a proud woman who raised me on her own as best as she could. I was never without and I had a pretty normal childhood, despite my lack of a fatherly influence. I was damn lucky to have my grandfather be both people to me and my grandmother become a mother figure when mine passed. So, I don't want anything from you. I'm not scarred emotionally or mentally because you weren't there. Everything would've happened just the same, I'm sure. So, I don't want you to feel guilty because it's obvious she didn't let you know about me. Given what you are, what I might be, I have a feeling you would've been around, a lot."

Raul became shocked to learn that Sophia had passed. If she were still alive, as he thought her to be all of these years, she would only be in her early forties. "I'm sorry for such a sad loss, Marrok. I didn't know Sophia passed. She was an angel, that I had to leave. May I ask how she died?"

Marrok seemed like he was telling this particular story many times lately. It wasn't a memory he liked to relive, but he told him the story anyway. However, he gave Raul the short version. "My mother edged me out of bed in the middle of the night to take me horseback riding. She told me to look at the moon. Something spooked the horse, we fell off. She broke her neck and died. It was quick. She didn't feel pain. I bumped my head, which caused me to go in a month long coma. Gabrio believes the time I wasn't conscious, prevented me from being like the rest of you."

Raul shook his head. He didn't know how to respond to the information of the trauma his boy went through. *If only I was there.* Raul thought before he spoke aloud. "As you well know, she was a beautiful woman and so damn sweet. She was very dear to my heart. That was the very reason I couldn't turn her. I didn't truly love her. I know that sounds horrible, but love is different with our kind. When we find our life mate, it is a bond unbreakable by even death. Your mother wasn't my life mate and I couldn't change your mother if I didn't love her. It wouldn't be fair to her or her family. With that, I thought it best that I left. I didn't want her to believe the longer I stayed around, the more likely something more could come of it. I broke it off. It hurt me to do so, but it was honorable. I gave her the ring to remember me by. It was one of the most prized items I've ever had. Then, I told her if she ever thought of me to look at the moon and I'll always be there with her. I have to believe that night when she took you outside, she was about to tell you about who I was. There wasn't a way in hell she knew about me being what I am."

Marrok silently nodded at the explanation as he worked the connections through his mind. "I guess that makes sense." He replied in a monotone voice.

Raul thoughts switched as his mind took him to the single shred of evidence left that meant the man in front of him was his and Sophia's son. He couldn't help to be dubious, but the details of their affair remained their only secrete between them. This made him believe in the possibility of Marrok being his son factual, but there was one final method of proof. "So, you wear the ring I gave your mother. Do you have it on you right now?

Marrok nodded his head as he grabbed the thin chain around his neck and unhooked it from its hiding place. He lifted the heavy silver from under his T-shirt and handed in to Raul.

Raul did all he could not to snatch the item out of his hands. He looked over the ring as he turned it over, holding it lightly in his fingertips. He spoke bewilderingly. "My God, it looks just the same as the day I got it and the day I gave it away." He looked to Marrok and smiled. Warmth flooded his eyes, making them sparkle like jade jewels behind black, thick, fanned eyelashes. He starred at Marrok as emotion swelled, clogging his throat. "My Son. You're truly my son, there's no doubt in that. How in the hell did Gabrio find you? What are the odds of this happening and you are my son?" Raul asked Marrok.

Marrok became touched by the genuine questions of his father. He still couldn't believe it as the word flowed through his mind. *Father.* Past emotions of feeling alone, began to rise and fade as quickly as they came. It was an odd sensation of feeling complete and incomplete at the same time. Realizing he had a father and a family again, he found the point of closure. Emotions he hadn't felt in a long time began to overwhelm him. He felt them rise to the surface, turning his face red and causing his eyes to water. He cleared his throat and held it in. He refused to cry.

Raul startled Marrok from his thoughts. "I'm trying to put it altogether, still. How did Gabrio know how to find you? I mean, how did he know about you being my son? I never told anyone about Sophia and about this ring. God, this ring, I thought I would never see it again."

"I know Gabrio from work. He approached me one day after work and I was new, so I figured he was being nice letting me tag with him as he went and got a drink after work. We got talking, mostly about sports and we established a friendship. That was about eight years ago. As to how Gabrio linked us, he said he found it in a diary. Some relation to your family named Alice. No, sorry. It was Alexandria O'Mara. Apparently, she had that ring first. Here, I have the diary right here in my coat pocket." Marrok dug it from his coat and handed it to Raul.

Raul's eyes became widened. "Alexandria O'Mara's. You have her diary here. That's incredible. He spoke of her, but I didn't know who she was. This is all surreal." Raul took a calculating pause. Then he breathlessly whispered aloud. "Oh my God, the prophecy. All this time he was telling the truth about it all."

Marrok tried to understand the riddled exclaims. However, he couldn't figure out what Raul was talking about, but patiently waited for him to explain himself.

Raul rubbed the leather bound book as he looked at his son. He released a deep sigh as ages of dormant memory flashed fresh through his mind. "During the Civil War, I was an officer in the union army. In rank, I was a Lieutenant Colonial. Born and raised as a well-bred lad, I spent most of my days in the fine state of Louisiana. However, I didn't always believe in their ways. Especially when it came to other races and people. The things most of the plantation owners did to their slaves." He shook his head. "It's fucked up beyond comprehension. I won't go into detail about it, but when word broke about the declaring of war from Washington, everything changed.

Immediately, there was division in every household and in every state, especially in the South. Every single family experienced a drastic loss. Fights broke out between brothers, sons and fathers. Mothers, sisters, wives and children cried and begged for their loved ones to come home alive. That's when the Half-Born creatures ran rampant with chaos. Yet, the our kind remained together and strong. Some of us didn't care because it wasn't our fight. Yet, the ones that did care, most of them fought in the union Army. Those of us knew our gift with everlasting life on earth and thought we would use a small portion of our lives to fight for a good cause. When we first signed up and began preparing for the battles to come; we were together. Over time we became separated by one battle or another. The fires took many of our kind for that cause and I was thankful to still have my life.

Then one day, stationed in Iowa, I received orders from Lieutenant General Harvey Lukewater to help prepare and lead a small group of soldiers in Virginia. I had orders to pick my best men and sneak into an enemy camp that had been spotted trying to cross into Kentucky. We needed to wipe them out, which is strange because our kind can't kill innocent mortals. However, all is fair in love and war." He commented darkly and continued. "Proceeding with my duty, I selected my best men to take with me. I left the rest of the men in command of another Lieutenant Colonial named Samuel R. Robinson.

When we arrived at my given coordinates, we didn't expect to find what we did. As we moved through the middle of the night on foot, which thankfully that night there was a new moon and I didn't have to transform, we silently walked into their camp expecting a fight. We had our guns loaded, weapons sharpened and prayers already said as we charged into the silent camp. However, we quickly found out that all the confederate men already slaughtered. There were splatters of crimson staining the area. Their tents soaked with blood as if someone threw buckets of blood all over. When we gathered in the center, all thirty men of that small camp had become strategically placed around their smoldering fire pit in a circle. It was morbid that someone placed them that way and it was disturbing to see. Most of my men became a spooked by the sight and I ordered a search around the area. As we scanned the deep forest, I tripped over what I thought was a stump. However, come to find I stumbled on a wounded Indian.

Later, I learned his name was Anuk-Nusaye, which translated

similar to, *the last warrior.* He rushed to cover himself with moss
and earth to blend into the environment when he heard us coming.
When I was standing in his reach, he jumped out of the ground trying to attack me with a hatchet. However, before he did anything,
he stopped and grabbed at his stomach as if in pain. Then, I saw
fresh blood cascading from a small round wound at the bottom of
his stomach and knew instantly he became shot during his attack.
I remember his blood covered face stare at me as his eyes rolled to
whites and he passed out from lack of blood. Despite him attacking
me and having no clue who he was, I picked him up and carried
him back. I couldn't leave him there. There were too many unanswered questions as to why he attacked that particular camp and
if there were any survivors. So, that night, despite the men's objec-
tions, we took him to our camp. I commanded the men to prepare
another cot for him in my tent to keep a better eye on him and so
he could be at my disposal. At the time, I didn't know if I would
have to kill him or befriend him.

I got the medic to remove the bullet that embedded into his hip
bone and patch him up. He lost most of his blood, but he was thriving still. I looked over the seven-foot man, whose feet hung over the
edge of the small cot. The medic patched him up, cleaned his body
and chattered away as he went about his job. However, I didn't hear
a thing. I noticed a small tattoo behind Anuk's ear. It was a strange
little marking, but after that I didn't think too much about it.

At night I always took the patrol while the men slept. I could
transform without them ever knowing and become human before
they awoke. Well, the following night, after capturing Anuk, it was
time to transform again. Even though I could hear my men from
any range of distance and be in the camp quicker than the first
spark of light, I remained close. It didn't look like the man wasn't
going to wake up anytime soon. Yet, I didn't trust him at all and
I knew something was off, but I still had to patrol the area. So,
later than night, I transformed, hunted and scanned my route. I

remember the wildlife was unusually active, then after a few moments they went deathly still and silent. A tale-tell sign the world around us gives when you're not alone and you think you are. My hairs began to stand along my spine. I became ready for anything out of the ordinary and braced myself.

As I stood waiting in the pitch-black forest in Virginia, I suddenly became attacked. It felt like a fucking wrecking ball hit me and I didn't even see it coming. It side swiped me and the force of its impact launched me several feet. I hit the ground, but in my rage I savagely held my own. I heard him run past me and I caught a glimpse of his scent and I knew it was the Indian. I chased him down and tackled him. He got the best of me a few times, but ultimately I had him pinned ready to sink my teeth into his throat. He started laughing. The fucker started to laugh and honestly, it startled the hell out of me. It caught me off guard. He pushed me off him as he lifted himself from the ground, out from under me and leaned against a trunk of a tree, still chuckling. The conversation that followed I remember as if it had happened no more than two minutes ago. He told me in surprisingly perfect English. "I never would've thought you were a shape shifter, Lieutenant White-man. Yet, you here you are."

I eyed him as I thought. *How does he know which Union solider I am or if I'm not a rebel or even a native?*

Then he answered me immediately as if it were in the flow of natural conversation. He replied. "It's by your eyes, Lieutenant White-man. It's the same with all the children of the moon. Everything changes, but the eyes. The eyes are windows into the soul and the soul never truly changes. You should know this by now or else you're a newly made shape shifter and not born of the blood of the beast."

Stunned, but not rendered speechless. I needed to know more craving to understand what he was, who he was. I looked at the man and seen the spark of insanity residing in the depth of his black eyes as he unshakably gazed at me. His black hair waved in the slight breeze over his face as he smiled, revealing yellowed, rotting teeth. The man was truly insane and it made me think of the safety of my men right away. I spoke to him again through thought. "I take it you know who I am because you are a 'Beast Blood' as well. If this is the case, how are you not in your true forum and most important are my men still alive?"

He laughed again answering the second part of my inquiry. "Shape shifting White man, your heart is too big to swallow. Humans are useless. They're born to be our toys, our playthings.."

I didn't care for what he was saying so I cut him off to the quick, forgetting he didn't answer my first question. "My men had wives, children and families! They were innocent men not deserving..."

Anuk laughed once more and spoke. "Don't become so enraged, White man. I didn't touch your crew. They are alive, well and sleeping soundly, except one. As I left, he lain awake pleasuring himself with one of the camp following prostitutes. I'm sure you've smelled the infection those women carry, that's why you haven't mated with them, Lieutenant White man. They're stench isn't on you."

I remember cringing at Anuk's last remark. They were a reeking stench that followed his marching men. Despite their advances and knowing I couldn't obtain their sicknesses, I never went near them. The smell of their sickly bodies was horrific. However, I was glad my men were still alive and not torn to pieces, lined together in some gruesome display by the man who sat in front of me. Then I asked him about the dead men and why did he attack their camp. His eyes took a new light a sickening mixture of pleasure and anger. I could hear him grind his teeth together. Then he spoke in an eerie sinister calm and it's the most haunting thing I've ever heard in all my years. He said to me, "I'm Anuk-Nusaye. My father named me well since I am the last warrior of my people. The rebel men came in the middle of the night to slaughter my kin and I couldn't do nothing. I arrived too late. Their cries were clear even when I was nowhere near them. The sounds of their deaths rang in my head. I heard their despair all at once and felt the life fade from their bodies. I even knew when their souls left. They echoed for me in the mountains where I hunted and I ran to them as fast as I could, but I was too late.

Those mortal men killed my wife Rosie, whom taught me how to speak your language. She was my life mate and a werewolf. She didn't know about the symbol, but I convinced myself she wasn't the carrier of the *Hybrid*. When I came home I was going to entrust her with the emblem when I came back from my hunt. It was she whom I found first, chard in our home. I picked her up from the ground, crying, holding her in my arms. I didn't have to go far until I found my son and daughter dead, lying on the ground. My little girl's beautiful blonde hair that glistened like my wife's in the sun was dirty, dim and pulled from her scalp. Her body was bare from her clothes becoming torn from her undeveloped body. Her throat still bled. Her legs, still spread from them rapping her. The smell of fresh come and urine on her body made me vomit. I could smell their sex. All of them took their turn. My wife, my daughter and my son, are dead. I used to lie awake and listen to their growing fast hearts. They didn't even experience the sickness yet and were still too mortal to defend themselves. I found them lying on the ground and I changed back to my human form, held their bodies close in my arms for what seemed like hours and held a burial ritual in my custom. Then I searched for the men who took them from me."

Raul noticed Marrok's expression turn into one of sadness and scuffed in understanding his son's emotion. "I know. I felt the same way when he told me. I remained silent. Only listening to what he had to say. Finally, I understood his insane mannerisms and the brutality in the deaths of the rebels. However, he was just getting started and what came next changed my life forever.

I remember Anuk speaking again. He told me,"I see it in your eyes. Don't judge me, Lieutenant White-man. Do you know how hard it is burying your entire world, setting it aflame and knowing you'll never able to join them right away? They took my world away from me, so I did what I had to. I did what was fair. They were possessed and my vengeance was bitter sweet. It was later that evening when I hunted them down by their scent. I found and slaughtered them in my human form. I wanted them to know who I was and once the first few died they understood. Still in human form, I ate their hearts, their stomachs, sliced their faces and throats with my knife. I let their bodies lie in rotting ribbons. They killed my wife and children and they were never going to see their own, ever again. During my brutal slaughter, I became wounded by a bullet and my blood was pouring out. Yet, my skin was already mending around the metal. However, I quickly buried myself to camouflage within the woods when I heard you and your men approaching after I killed the last man. I was going to wait until you passed to get up and finish them even more so, but when I was watching you, you smelled the air. You were tracking my scent and no mortal could do that and be successful. You knew what you were doing. When you looked down at me is when I jumped up pretending to attack you. I punctured a twig deep where the bullet hole was to make myself bleed again and fiend to faint from the pain."

His story was sad, but riddled with occurrences that I didn't understand. I remember asking him why he would pretend to do such a thing and he told me because he needed another werewolf to do what he had in mind, because another werewolf would understand. If I did what he wanted he would reward me with the two most valuable possessions he had. It's funny how both are now priceless in the end." Raul paused only slightly and Marrok leaned in closer waiting for what was going to happen next in the incredible story he told. Raul didn't recess for long and continued, which Marrok was thankful for.

"Anuk took the ring out of his pocket and sure enough, it's the same one I hold in my hands at this very moment." Raul looked down at the ring in remembrance. "He told me the ring was his wife's, who received it from her mother when she died. I don't remember why I asked, but I wanted to know the name of Rosie's mother and he said, Alexandria O'Mara. Then, I remember he took out the scalping knife he hid in a small flap in a hidden pocket in his pants. The curved knife appeared newly sharpened, but no longer than an index finger. He lifted his long hair, pulling it away from the left side of his face as he took the knife to place it against behind his ear, pressing it to his scalp. With pressure and the flick of his wrist, he peeled a small portion of his scalp and cut the last thread of skin from his head. He began profusely bleeding down his neck and onto his chest. He then held out the piece of bloody flesh to me as he dropped the knife onto the ground. I held out my hand and he placed the flesh into my palm. Once I looked at the flesh I noticed it was the strange tattoo I noticed earlier. He proceeded to tell me the tattoo was a symbol. A talisman sent from the guardians of the Creator, which allowed those with the blood of the beast to become stronger. It protects them from fire, allowing them to change willingly and other abilities occur over time. He told me his tribe was the holder of the angelic symbol and it was their duty to give it to those who became worthy of it."

Marrok finally spoke, his voice a little hoarse. "So this is how you could change back to talk to me tonight and that's why you didn't burn in the flames."

Raul nodded. "Yes."

"What considered you worthy to have the symbol? Why did they keep it hidden? Did he tell you that?" Marrok asked.

Raul nodded again. "After giving me the symbol he told me of the prophecy, which detailed how it began by creating two species. *Beast Bloods* and *Blood Tasters*. Each became created by the Creator, aiding the angels against Lucifer when he fell from grace. It occurred when God questioned him about how he used Adam and Eve to bring sin into the world he created, then the battles begun. However, they didn't expect the werewolves to have a weakness to fire and change only by the moon. Knowing how to change the defect, an angel searched and choose a remote tribe, Anuk's tribe. They're the keepers of the angelic symbol and they choose to give it to whoever they find worthy. They kept the symbol to themselves passing it along the way. Then when the time came they sought for the release of death, their bodies would become set on fire with the symbol plucked from their bodies. Yet, having the symbol wasn't enough, there's a trick to use the symbol. There's a word, one word used to activate it and to reverse it. It's different for all guardians. They took every precaution to make sure Lucifer and his demon werewolf wouldn't get it. They were afraid of the repercussions if it became obtained by the evil they feared. See, the prophecy foretold a werewolf of demon blood would give birth to a mixed born. The power of the Hybrid would have powers and strengths that needed to become respected and feared. The demon werewolf would be the very opposite of the Hybrid and death, destruction with chaos would reign."

Marrok rubbed his face as he looked out the window and saw the traces of sunlight burst through the sky. Dropping his hands to clasp in front of him, he questions Raul. "So what did Anuk want you to do for him to give you the ring, the symbol and all the knowledge of his people?"

Raul answered grimly. "He wanted me to reunite him with his family."

Marrok's surprised overcame him in an obvious flash. "He wanted you to kill him? Did you do it?"

Raul slowly nodded and subconsciously rubbed his neck where the symbol became tattooed on him long ago. "Anuk was right. Only another werewolf would understand. If Isabel and Esmeralda were both gone, what purpose would there be for me any longer. I gave him what he craved most, his family."

Marrok nodded as he pieced the puzzle together. "So, the demon werewolf is a woman?" He asked.

Raul shrugged. "I thought that for a very long time, but I wasn't sure. Anuk told me there were signs to watch for, the increase of newly transforming werewolves and the blood moon. Also, he said that once the signs were occurring the *Blood Tasters* would find the carrier of the hybrid and secure..."

Raul suddenly paused, his mouth dropping open in his sudden realization.

Marrok became startled at the unexpected reaction. "What's wrong?" Raul was silent as Marrok searched his face, waiting for him to reply. After a few seconds of his obvious shock Marrok yelled his name. "Raul, what is it? What are you thinking?" Marrok asked deeply concerned.

Raul looked at Marrok. "It's Esmeralda. She's the carrier of the *Hybrid*. That's the only explanation. That night she suddenly disappeared, she became secured by a *Blood Taster*. She's a demon? Isabel's ancestor, Alexandria." Suddenly, he looked at Marrok. His piercing eyes, once a warm green, became cold as he lunged out of the chair grabbing Marrok's shoulders. Violently, he began shaking them as he pinned him against the couch yelling at him."I have to change you now. Let me change you. Gabrio told me she felt a connection to you in her mortal form. He told me. Did you feel it too? Can you connect with her? Marrok, can you? Do you know where she is? Tell me, I need to know!"

Suddenly, Gabrio and Isabel busted through the front door, human looking and dressing the part, as they were witnessing what looked like Raul choking his son."What the fuck is going on in here?" Gabrio yelled as he ran to pull Raul off Marrok. He set Raul in the chair he was sitting in before he lunged out of it. Gabrio looked to Raul, but he was silent, spacing out on nothing in particular. Then he looked at Marrok. "What the fuck happened to him? Why was he choking you?"

Marrok situated his coat and snarled in anger. "He knows who took Esmeralda."

Isabel stepped forward with hope leaping into her voice as she rushed to her husband. "He does? Who is it Raul?"

Raul shook his head. "It's not as simple as that. A *Blood Taster* has her, because she has demon blood in her and she carried the awaited child. She carries the *Hybrid*. She's a demon, because of your blood Isabel and because of your father's blood and his father's blood."

She became confused. "What are you talking about? You're not making any sense."

Gabrio interjected. "Yes, he is. He's making perfect sense." Gabrio couldn't believe he didn't piece it together sooner. He felt like the world sat heavier on his shoulders. His poor wife was pregnant and being held captive because they were the prophecy; they were living it. That's why they had premonitions in their dreams of the signs. Everything was finally clear and the plan was simple. A creeping thought clouded his mind. *Just like your father.* He shook his head. Now, the only obstacle he could see was Marrok not being able to transform to find her. They shared a different bond, unconnected and connected at the same time. A power was there, he just needed to get Marrok to change and unleash the beast that was clawing beneath the surface. Gabrio looked to Marrok and in a dead calm of conclusiveness he spoke. "Today you become one of us. Together we'll find my wife. Like it or not, you're part of this now. If you don't comply willingly I will cut open my vein and make you drink until you transform. Do you understand me?"

Marrok bore into Gabrio's hard eyes. "I have no choice, but to join you." He knew there would be no going back after what he'd encountered and the knowledge he had gained. Just like Eve when she bit the forbidden fruit, she became forever tainted with sin in her blood. However, he had the blood of a werewolf. Furthermore, he knew deep in his heart he felt a connection with Esmeralda that night, but until now he had denied it.

19

THE LAST CONSUMPTION

Laycerath stood behind swaying shrubbery as he spied on the woman he followed home from the bar the night before. A blinding wall of green, cloaked him well from becoming seen, as the morning sun poured through the leaves, illuminating them, making his cover more effective. He made a cozy spot for himself in the greenery of her backyard. Bored and growing impatient, his mind flashed to the events that had him standing, stalking, waiting for her to give him a sign of her awakening. He remembered how he noticed the woman right away as she foolishly fluttered around the bar, trying to snag a younger man. She would scan for her prey from the bar as she sat seductively on her backless chair, letting the smoke pour from her moistened lips. Then she would move to make herself known to them. When finally having one in her grasp, a few whispers of sweet nothings lingered between them and she took the young fool in the alley. He remembered the barkeep yelling the woman's name a few times throughout the night, telling her to remember their last conversation and to behave herself, giving the impression she was a wild regular.

He liked the wild woman's name. Jasmine. It fit her and

contradicted her because there was nothing delicate about the woman. He could see the color of sin hover around her. She would become a succubus if she continued her ways and entered hell. He was going to make sure she did. She would be a wonderful addition to his personal collection. The older barmaid that served him his drinks had noticed how he looked at her and felt she had to warn him about her, but if she only knew the half of it. Nevertheless, the older woman had a loose mouth and she was more than willing to tell him anything he wanted to know about the woman he watched. Everything, except where she lived. So, he dismissed her with a dark look. Finding out she was a married woman of ill repute, made him inwardly beam in dark pleasure. She was predictable as well. He didn't need to hear it to know it was so. The woman was transparent, she flaunted herself freely and didn't care. The barmaid told him Jasmine would go to that bar regularly, every time her husband was away at work, which was often and for long amounts of time.

She was perfect for what he had in mind, so he watched her. For the rest of the night he moved when she moved, but he kept his distance, like two magnets repelling each other. He wanted to study her and he did. He watched her from the darkest corner of the bar as she danced to the horrible music the bar played, drinking more liquor, more ale and saw her flaunt herself in front of a dark-haired man. When he saw her leave with the man, he moved from his seat and went outside. He watched from the shadows as she became pinned against the brick wall, her legs wrapped around the young buck's waist. He loved the way she fucked. It has been a long while since he felt the wet tightness of a woman. He grew eager to have her as he watched her. She bit her bottom lip in pleasure as she leaned her head against the brick wall. Her hot breath swirled within the while her lips parted and her pulse quickened. He needed her, wanted her for his own.

After they both found their release, he slipped her down the wall onto her feet. Jasmine kissed him lightly, then walked away, leaving the man to pull up his pants as he watched her walk away, stumbling to her car. When she drove off, he followed her with ease. He was mere inches from her as he saw her disheveled appearance walk awkwardly in her house. He looked through the windows, watching her undress for bed as she walked up the stairs and without more to do, she finally passed out.

Now, it was morning and he waited for the perfect opportunity to introduce himself. Such an introduction would've been easy the night before, but he wanted the hunt to continue. All the others died quickly, but this one was special. She would make him complete, which was why he starved himself for the last several days. He wanted to enjoy every ounce of her in every possible way he could. He watched the curtains flutter in the upstairs window of her home as he heard her walking around her room. In her skimpy nightgown, she pulled the curtains open to let in the morning. He smiled, as he obsessed about his plan. It was thrilling to watch their movements, their false sense of security behind shambles of crumbling walls. She saw that morning had come and a smile lightly touched her lipstick smeared lips. Jasmine raised her arms above her head as she yawned and stretched. Laycerath saw her nipples harden over the pleasure her body felt as she stretched her muscles.

His erection pressed up against the confining material of the black jeans he wore. *Calm yourself, not yet. Wait for the opportunity to arrive.* Laycerath thought as he eased his excitement and saw her leave the window. After a few moments of silence he heard a shrill ringing sound, then it stopped and Jasmine's husky voice sounded as she began talking to someone he couldn't hear.

"Hey, Tammy. No, you didn't wake me. I've been up for a couple of moments. What's up? I would love to go, but remember the hot neighbor next door? So what if he does. I don't care about his wife or my stupid husband...Tammy, he's gone on his business trips nailing his secretary. So, I get mine. I don't want to talk about this anymore. Because it's stupid to talk about! Whatever. Anyways, I

can't go today because Gabrio set me up with this irrigation company who could fix my plumbing. No, it wasn't a ploy. My walls
were really leaking water and I wanted to see if Gabrio could fix it.
Then maybe I could get him to stop thinking about the little bitch
he married. Yeah, I'm still hopeful. Very funny, Tammy. I'm not a
delusional nymphomaniac. Anyway, the woman plumber, he called
for me could only fix them temporarily because of how old they
were. Now, I have to stay here and wait for someone else to come
over. Then, they need to do something to them and all that bullshit.
No. I don't know who's going to show up. You don't have to come
over. I'm sure I'll be okay. God, you worry too much..."

Laycerath smiled, no longer paying attention to what he could
overhear. Finding his opportunity to introduce himself to the licen-
tious redhead, he realized he had to act quickly. He swirled the little
bit information he heard to make sure she believed who he said he
was. He made his way to the front door, trying to remain unseen.

Meanwhile

After her phone call with her longtime friend, Jasmine decided she
would jump in the shower to wash away the night from her body.
The hot water soothed her aching limbs. The water cleared her mind
and let her thoughts slide over last night's events. She thought of the
young man who loved her for twenty minutes or so against the bar's
brick wall. She couldn't remember his name and it didn't matter to
her. He was disposable and there were always other younger men to
enjoy. All were vibrant, stupid and easy to manipulate. They didn't
want anything serious and she didn't want anything from them, but
what they had in their pants. She already had money, a husband for
God-knows-what and she never wanted to deal with bratty kids. So,
as long as the young men remained stiff and they knew what to do
with their shaft, she was happy. On that last thought of her coming
against the nameless man's hard erection, she turned the water off

and lightly stepped out of the shower onto to marbled floor. Jasmine was finishing towel drying her hair in her downstairs bathroom when she heard loud knocking on the front door. Without delay, she wrapped herself in a long plush green towel, walked down the hallway and looked through the peephole. She almost purred when she saw the strong physique and the handsome face of the man that stood outside her door. Jasmine gasped and tenderly spoke aloud. "Look at you."

After already spending some time in front of the mirror, she knew how she looked and knew how to work with the clichéd towel act. She struck a pose to make a rounded hip and bent a showing slender leg through the slit of the towel. Once she felt she was ready, she slowly swung the door open to showcase herself to him. In a soft sultry voice she greeted him simply. "Hello."

Laycerath looked over her and it took all it could to contain himself. It's true, he's lain with more beautiful and younger women, but right now he saw how succulent her body appeared fresh from her bathing. A lot has changed from the world he once knew, but many things remained the same. The silky warmth of a woman's ivory skin when they soaked themselves in scalding water, was one of them. Knowing how tender her skin was, she looked mouth watering. He kept his poise as he heard her pulse quicken, saw how she pushed her chest outward while she stole glimpses to parts of his body. Underneath his cool demeanor, he was wild with desire as she boldly undressed him with her eyes. He knew she liked what she saw, but it didn't matter if she liked it or not. Either way he was going to consume her body. Laycerath smiled his most luring smile and lied through his teeth. "Hello, Mrs. Jasmine..." He paused, panicked she might not let him in. "I'm sorry they didn't tell me your last name."

Jasmine gawked at him, then quickly cut him off. "Oh, yes, yes. Please don't be formal with me. You can call me Jasmine. I know why you're here. It's for the leaking pipes in the wall upstairs.

Right?" She lightly touched her shoulder as she pointed behind her to reference toward the problem. "The woman named Rachel, said you would be here today."

Laycerath knew her last comment held a double meaning. Little did she know, he didn't plan to be proper and he knew she didn't plan holding onto any shred of scruples either. He kept his smile as he stepped into her home, but once the door shut behind him he became a predator. He kept close behind her, almost stepping on her heels. He was careful as she led him down the hallway and up the stairs.

"What's your name? I didn't catch it." Jasmine asked as he started up the trail of steps.

"Laycerath." He replied as he concentrated on her voluptuous curves swaying underneath the green towel.

"Your wife must love having a handyman around the house. Mine is for shit and can't do nothing, except grow balder and fatter." She said.

He knew she was reaching for information about him to see if he would be interested in her or not. His reply made it easier for the both of them to advance closer to the bedroom. "I don't have a wife because I've never wanted to marry. Life shouldn't become restricted by unrealistic boundaries people put on themselves. "I fuck when I want, where I want." He replied, knowing it would flame the lust she felt boiling in her loins. He knew her kind during his former life. He once had their bodies and saw their souls burning in the swirling pit of hell with him. They were easy to manipulate if you knew their trigger points. Sex happened to be hers, which worked to his advantage.

Jasmine stopped in the middle of the staircase, twisting around to see his face, but noticed how close he towered over her. She looked over his rough features and felt herself become moisten, ready for him. She could see it plainly, he wanted her, but there was something darker hiding in his reddish brown eyes. She almost wanted to run at the sudden burst of evil she felt from Laycerath. For a sliver of a second she wished she would've invited Tammy to sit with her, but the feeling quickly faded. Jasmine mentally shrugged. *He's young, sexy as hell and you want him. He wants you. Get it and get him out.* Despite her slight sense of feeling uneasy Jasmine smiled wickedly at him. She palmed his jaw and stroked the smooth skin on his face with her long fingers. She dropped her hand back to her side, turned around and lured him upstairs. In her mind, he was no longer there for the sole purpose of what brought him there.

Laycerath knew where she was taking him. He saw it in her mind's eye, but even if he couldn't see it, she was a predictable creature. She was taking him to her bedroom. Her frilly bedroom with cream painted walls and rose patterned bedding. However, created an illusion for them of a place in which they both fit in. Once Jasmine opened the white door to the master bedroom, Jasmine walked into a darken room. She looked around. It was no longer her room. Everything was different. Jasmine thought she was losing her mind. She blinked a few times to rid her vision of the sight that beheld her. She didn't understand and turned to Laycerath, who was already closing the door.

Jasmine became nervously confused. "This isn't my room. I don't understand."

Laycerath stepped toward her as he kissed her. He pressed his lips hard against hers as his hands gripped around her bare shoulders. Their lips parted and he spoke quickly, harshly to her. "This isn't your room, anymore. Today, this is our room." Laycerath whispered as he turned her around to kiss the back of her neck and shoulders.

Jasmine looked around the room. It was hard to miss the room smelled a strong mixture of burning incenses and candle smoke. She saw their blue smoke lazily rolled through the air creating, an aura of dreamlike temptation. The lighting was sparse, creating a dim candlelight glow throughout the room and seen that only the grand wrought iron chandelier, which hung in the center of the ceiling, lit the entire room. After her eyes adjusted even more clearly to the dim setting, she couldn't help but stare in shock as she took in more of the surroundings. She observed the expanded room and seen its walls were a soft black like a raven's wing. She noticed the stark white floor to ceiling blacked-out windows placed strategically parallel across from each other and donned in blood red silk curtains. *The windows must be open.* She thought, for all the red silk curtains puffed out as the bottoms of the cloths licked the air in a rhythmic pattern. Then she noticed the king-sized ebony bed that seemed so far from them.

Laycerath watched Jasmine in extreme intensity. In a firm, but smooth voice, his words coaxed her as his breath was hot on the nape of her neck. "I can hear your pulse racing and I can smell the thrill of your arousal already. By that alone, I assume you're ready for me."

Feeling mixed emotions for this man she met only a few moments ago, she experienced a turmoil to listen to her earlier instincts. She wanted to flee far from this dangerous man and then she wanted to become lured by the sweet challenge he offered. She spoke breathlessly to him. "Who are you? What are you doing to me?" She said becoming enchanted and lost in the illusion he created for them.

He smirked. "I am giving you what you want. What I want. I watched you last night, Jasmine. I saw how you suckled, danced, fucked and came. You are meant for me. There is no escape from this fantasy of ours. See, my Jasmine. We're cut from the same cloth. We both consume, can't get enough and so we demand more. Demand until we get what we want. As more me, I always get what I want and right now I want your heart. I will have your heart. Say it Jasmine. Say you'll give your heart to me."

Jasmine was mindless as the intoxicating smells, sounds and feelings he created sent her into a trance. She became lost with him without a care in the world. She only cared for the hungering release gripping tight in her chest and loins. She needed release. She wanted him hard and deep within her. Her nipples hardened under his almost painful pinching fingers. Jasmine heard him again, edging her to give her heart to him. She could feel his searching hand, slip under the folds of the towel, brush against her stomach and she gasped in pleasure as he grabbed her womanhood, shoving two large fingers inside her. Laycerath slowly began to tease her while he rubbed the nub that made her womanhood even slicker for his entry. "I give you my heart." She mewled, melting into his arms and welcoming hand.

Laycerath smiled, revealing his pointed teeth. The color of his eyes faded back to blood red. "There's a good girl. Now, whom I am doesn't matter. Does it?"

"No." She whispered.

"No." He sneered in pleasure. She became clay within his grasp. In a quick movement he stripped the towel from Jasmine as he turned her around grabbing her by the waist. He kissed her hard on her soft mouth. She succumbed to his assault and kissed him back with matching passion. Laycerath kissed her hard as he unbuckled his jeans and released his erection. Like a moth to a flame, Jasmine's hand wrapped around his throbbing member and began to move her hand up and down his silky shaft. Laycerath groaned. "Now, take me in your mouth, Jasmine."

Jasmine smiled and complied. Naked and on her knees, she took him into her warm mouth, swirled her experienced tongue around him and pressed him deeper into her throat in a rhythm all its own. She could feel Laycerath slowly thrust, back and forth in her mouth as he tugged on her bunching wet hair that he held tightly in his hands.

"Enough." Laycerath growled as he could feel himself getting ready to come in her slick mouth. He wanted to take her in a different way. She needed to be in place for what else he had in mind. He quickly lifted Jasmine to her feet, sweeping her off them. Interlocked he guided her toward the bed and lay on top of her. Without her noticing he reached for the straps that hid underneath the mattress. He lifted his lips from hers to see that he secured her hands above her head.

Dazed, she looked at him and noticed he was spreading her arms wide and taking each wrist to bind them to the opposite bedpost on each side of the headboard. Jasmine smiled at him as a thrill shot through her body to her loins. Laycerath knew he was now in complete control. She writhed under him after he tied the last strap and leaned back down to suck on her neck and bit her earlobe, flicking it with his tongue. She released a throaty moan in reply. He looked at her revealing heaving breasts. Laycerath trailed his hand from her neck, between her breasts and down her stomach; resting his searching hand on the mound between her legs. She was hairless and smooth. Something he's never encountered before, but his surprise didn't last long as the thrill of his plan falling into place fed his excitement. *Killing two birds.* He smugly thought. Laycerath hurriedly pulled his own clothing off as he leaned over her, their naked bodies pressed against each other. His chest brushed against her sensitive nipples as he took her hard, lifting her hips to enter her to the fullest. She gasped at the sudden, fulfilling intrusion of his hard flesh. Greedily, he slid in and out of her, over and over. Laycerath was careful to not have her come too soon. He was giving her enough and taking it away. During his repetitive torturing, she begged him for release. Laycerath spoke through clenched teeth between each brutal thrust. "What do you want, Jasmine? Tell me what you want."

Jasmine screamed at him. "You, I want you. Now, Laycerath!"

Laycerath didn't let her finish her sentence as he forcibly kissed her, biting her lower lip causing it to bleed. He suckled on her wound and loved the way her blood tasted; even though it was a bit polluted. "Come for me, Jasmine. Now!" He commanded her through his haggard breath.

She did as he demanded. Jasmine heard her own scream of intense pleasure as their enthusiastic thrusts sent her into a swirling spiral of sexual release. Laycerath pushed himself deeper into her while finding his own satisfying release. Spilling his seed deep into her, he groaned in agonizing pleasure. Fulfilling his sexual appetite, he collapsed atop of her, resting his head on her expanding chest. Laycerath could hear her heart and the shallow breaths she took. He peeked through his cloaking hair to look up at her. He saw she was still under his enchantment. He lightly placed his head back onto her chest as he withdrew his hand from her tangled hair to draw lazy circles over her heart. "You promised your heart to me, Jasmine." Laycerath stated.

Jasmine was in a haze as the room swirled around her. She felt drunk or on a stronger narcotic of some kind. She lolled her head to the side, lightly nodded, trying to speak, but it only came out as a subtle noise. "Mm-hmm."

Laycerath smirked as he lifted himself to lean over her, pressing his nose into her hair, still drawing lazy circles with his index finger. "I've enjoyed you well, my little slut. You're the best whore, I've had in over two hundred years. What I love about this arrangement Jasmine is once I kill you, your soul will join in my realm. Then, I get to enjoy you so much more. Jasmine, it'll be perfect, us surrounded by the hot flames, me, doing whatever I want to you for eternity. I could cut you." Laycerath's nails began to elongate and curl into a thick claw, from his hand, which still moved in the circulating trail he created. Then suddenly he pierced her skin with the sharp blade, cutting into the circle that he traced.

Jasmine wanted to scream at him and push him off her. She wanted to arch her back from the horrific pain she felt in her bleeding chest, but she realized couldn't move. She remained stuck in her own mind, hearing her own cries. It was like she was already dead at how unvoiced and motionless, she was, but he kept the paralyzing effect on her. The only visible life that came from her was the tears that streamed down the side of her face, staining the satin pillows in the accursed hell he created for them.

Gaining a different pleasure from what he did to her, Laycerath continued."I could rip your heart out." He snarled.

God, please. Please don't. Jasmine whimpered her plea within her head, with no use of being heard.

After cutting the crimson circle into her chest, Laycerath took his hand and dug into her chest, feeling her beating heart pounding against his fingertips. He licked his lips in expectation while he gnashed his teeth together. He wrapped his hand around the pulsing muscle and quickly pulled it out. With one last scream that echoed in her dying body, Jasmine was dead. Laycerath grinned as he rose above her lifeless body with her heart in his cupping hands. Blood ran down his arms as it dripped crimson droplets from his fingers onto Jasmine's flat stomach. His red eyes marveled at the pleasure of the small muscle that he held in front of his face. He sniffed in the intoxicating scent of the bloody organ. Savoring the moment and his prize, he licked the organ, gaining a tongue full of blood and swallowed. Crazed with the taste, he brought the organ to his lips as he consumed.

Finally, the last consumption was complete. The illusion became shattered as the sunlight flooded the room. The black walls faded to a creamy white, the blood red curtains were gone and reappeared were the white curtains. The room was back to normal, except for the naked blood stained woman, lying in the middle of disheveled sheets. Laycerath looked at Jasmine as her lifeless eyes stared back at him. He leaned down to give her a brief kiss on the lips and left the bed. Gathering his clothes he left the room, trotted down the steps and into the bathroom. After cleaning himself of Jasmine's blood and dressing, he left her house by slipping out the back door and running into the woods. *Tonight with the rise of the moon, my powers will become fully restored. Then we search for the carrier.*

20

THE BLOOD MOON TURNS

Marrok looked around the table as he observed the members of his newly found family. They all sat in a solicitous silence eating their late lunches and shoveling food into their mouths, except Isabel. She hardly ate anything since her last hunt, but she was still quiet like the rest. No one spoke to one another since early that morning when Gabrio stated aloud that he was going to turn him into a fully functioning member of the clan. He had reservations becoming a werewolf, but the mental arguments he created became outweighed when logic reasoned through them. He snorted at the thought of the word logic. Yesterday, nothing was logical about what had transpired today. However, today it prevailed. There was nothing else to stop him accepting his newly issued fate. He sighed and quickly rubbed his face, a twitch he developed when he was most stressed. Exhausted from the sleepless night and equally hindered nap; he needed more sleep. Raul and Isabel were kind enough to let him stay in one of the guest bedrooms. Gabrio took the other spare room, but he startled the household several times. He woke them up to the sound of him yelling Esmeralda's name while in deep, agitated slumber. Nonetheless, sleep didn't do any of them help to ease their troubled thoughts as everyone was still on edge at the uncertainty of what was to come. Fear was evident on the face's Marrok searched. Even he could feel it's creeping negativity crawl along his spine. Despite this, he was remaining strong with the others.

Raul finished his plate first and rose from the table to take the dish to the sink. He lightly placed the dish in the bottom of the tub and turned around to look back at the people who starred at him. He broke the tense silence. "Men, after you're finished eating. I'll grab my chisel and give you the symbol. Luckily, I have a photographic memory regarding the etching and can go by memory."

Isabel tossed a piece of broccoli around her plate as she lightly shook her head of long brown hair. "I don't want the symbol. I carry the blood of the demon werewolf and I just don't know if I can trust myself enough to have such a power." She swallowed a hard lump in her throat. "Especially if I ever need to be destroyed." Isabel dropped the fork on her plate as she choked out the last words. She tried pushing back the feeling to shed forthcoming tears, but it was useless.

Raul rushed to his wife as he consoled her. He wrapped her in his arms holding her tight. She hurriedly buried her head against his flat stomach sobbing into the folds of his gray shirt. "Hush now. Don't cry, Bell. Please don't cry. You have a blessed heart, a pure heart. The heart controls the blood, remember that. That won't ever change. I won't let it change." Raul whispered to his wife as he knelt beside her, never breaking their embrace.

Gabrio's lips pressed hard together as he folded his arms. He hated seeing how the turmoil edged deeper in his family. Thriving on the rooted anger within him made him all the more determined. "Let's do it. He noticed Raul looked at him waiting for his agreement. Gabrio nodded his head in reply. "I'm more than ready."

However, Marrok was still unresponsive. He wasn't too thrilled about having a chisel repeatedly tapped into the back of his head.

"Do you mean like a chisel, chisel? Like the tools they used to use to give tattoos?" Marrok asked balking.

Gabrio chuckled. His face becoming more relaxed instead of harsh looking as he found humor in what Marrok said. "Come now. Don't be a baby. A little pain from a medieval tool hasn't killed anyone, recently. Plus, the pain from a chisel won't compare with the pain of your first transformation. We're made for pain. You can take it."

Raul shook his head, speaking to Gabrio first. "The symbol won't allow you to feel pain when you transform once you have it on you."

Gabrio's eyes widened. "Holy hell! What a relief that'll be. After a hundred years of screaming in the middle of the night from the snapping of bones and tendons, we'll no longer deal with the agony." He paused. "Also, it works to our benefit when we search for Esmeralda. We'll have a new advantage of stealth. They wouldn't even hear us transforming. However, they might see us, unless we're hidden well."

Raul nodded at Gabrio's reply."But that's just it. With the symbol you can remain a werewolf for as long as you want, you just have to want to change when the day breaks." Then, he spoke to Marrok. "As for the chisel, it's clean. Old, but clean. It's made from the melted bullets of my gun. It was the only choice to do when you're in the middle of the woods. Wood was too porous. It soaked up the ink and blood. It was shitty. The one I have now had only been used just that once when Anuk gave me the symbol. Moreover, the symbol has to remain a secret. I wouldn't trust the random person at a local tattoo parlor. Who knows what they truly could be or if anyone should somehow know about the symbol try to track it down. I'm sure we're not the only ones looking for Esmeralda or this symbol. Anuk's tribe slaved to keep it unknown. For a longtime I was the last one with it, until now. Now, I've agreed to pass it to the two of you."

Marrok knew Raul made a good point and was about to say so, but Gabrio spoke before he could say anything. "I don't care if we do it with a razor blade and a broken ink pen. I'm up for it. I just want to find my wife and bring her home where she belongs after I wring the fucker's neck for taking her from me."

Raul nodded. Then he looked around the room and saw everyone was agreed to the plan, even Marrok. Raul looked into his son's startling blue eyes, Sophia's eyes, and could see Marrok's heart made him a genuine fighter for the greater good. Raul beamed at the uncommon trait his son possessed, but then in the same moment he felt just as guilty because he didn't see such a heart grow. Raul pushed aside his self-pity and dealt with the current problem they faced. After making sure Isabel was fine enough for him to leave her side, he raised himself from the ground and gave her a brief kiss on her cheek. "I'll be back. I'm going to grab the supplies." He firmly stated.

Meanwhile

Sheryl snapped her head as astonishment adorned her elegant aged beauty. Her ice blue eyes sparkled, smiling as she ran to her stepson and kissed him on his bloodstained cheek. Her long, bony hands framed his face as she radiated pure pleasure at the news he announced to her. She was still incredulous. She whispered loud enough for Laycerath to hear what she said as she paced the room. "Is what you say true? It is true. I taste the little whore on your flesh. The last heart - you're complete now. Well, you will be with tonight's moon. Finally, with your completion your powers will be supreme. The humans will panic, the *Beast Bloods* will gather and the *Blood Tasters* will protect the little bitch, but it'll be perfect. All these years of waiting it can finally happen because of us. It's all falling into place and no one knows the wiser. Esmeralda carries your blood Laycerath, your sweet, delicious blood and you'll know where she is. You can find her once you've transformed. Then I will complete the transfer using the symbols of the sisters once we have her in our hands."

Laycerath snarled arrogantly. "Why bother with those trinkets? We can overtake her."

Sheryl stopped muttering and looked at him realizing she never told him part two of the act. "After you die, the seals will be needed."

"You will not rid of me so easily, bitch!" Laycerath intruded as he jumped to his conclusion, ready to attack her.

Despite the candidly rude outburst, Sheryl didn't let it bother her as she lightly stated the rest of her plan. "As an energy source to transfer your soul into the newborn. The first heartbeat is life, but the first breath taken when the soul enters the body. You will already be there lingering inside before the child will draw breath. The child will grow quickly, thus you will grow quickly acquiring the powers of the Hybrid and the ones you'll gain tonight. Then you'll rule the heavens, hell and the world between. Then, I'll be at your side, seeing the long waited destruction of the world God created and we will start new. I survived the flood, but no one will survive what will come." She said darkly as she looked out the window watching the night blacken out the sun.

Laycerath wasn't sure if he could trust her, but her plan puts him in ultimate power. How could he deny the opportunity? He'd only have to relive death. He's felt the cool grip of it before, seen its blackened face. It was easy to die especially when an empty vessel waited nearby. "What do we do about the child's mother?" Laycerath asked.

She looked at him and snorted at his question. She replied. "That's easy. We keep her until she births the child and I raise you just as I have before. It'll be a fresh start for us both. However, I'll let you do what you want with her when we first obtain her from wherever she's at. Then, later on you'll have new playthings, a whole universe of playthings. Now, night is coming and we should gather what we'll need."

Laycerath watched Sheryl walk away as she hummed a tune. He looked outside as the wind began to flick the limbs of the trees. He could feel the air shifting already. The night was going to bring a storm and out of the rage a beast will rise with the power of the precious moon running through his veins.

Later

After several more pulsing stabs of the fine point chisel entering the soft flesh at the nape of Marrok's neck the symbol became finished. Raul dabbed away the small droplets of blood with a damp cotton wad and relaxed his hand in his lap, admiring the work he accomplished. "The deed's done. It's mighty fine job done, if I do say so myself." Raul gloated.

Marrok was grateful that Raul finished with the tattoo. "Finally, I can get up from this damn chair. I thought you were never going to end with that damn torture."

Raul shrugged. "It's a small symbol, but it's well detailed. Every swirl, every line and every circle have to align perfectly or else, well, you know." He mumbled, casting his eyes downward.

Gabrio raised an eyebrow as he lightly rubbed his tattoo on the back of his neck. "No, I don't know. What do you mean?" He asked unsure of the dire result was.

Raul slightly winced as he replied. "It can act as a self-destruct trigger if it's not properly done. It was another precaution taken by the angel and Anuk's elders." Instantaneously, he saw Isabel's mouth dropped. Marrok stopped in mid-movement as he was grabbing a bottle of water from the fridge. Gabrio dropped his arm to his side. Raul looked at everyone's stunned visage and quickly saw Isabel's expression first twist in response. "Are you serious and so you wait until now to tell them?" She exclaimed as everyone began fidgeting again.

Quietly, Marrok closed the fridge door and grab a large glass instead as he made is way to the cabinet stocked with whiskey filled decanters.

"I needed full concentration, a clear head to do it right and I got it. Overall, would knowing beforehand make a difference to what has to be done? This is our only hope of finding her and bringing her home to us." Raul defended.

Marrok chuckled while he poured the glass to the rim. "No, there wouldn't be any difference. It was needed. Either way we're going to go up in flames or out with a bang. However, a warning of what to expect would've have been fucking considerate." He downed the glass of the whiskey without a flinch. He began to pour another, but only to give the overflowing glass to Gabrio, which he unreservedly accepted.

Gabrio knock backed the whiskey with as much vigor as Marrok, but coughed at the harsh rush of burning liquid that slithered down his gullet. After he caught his breath, he spoke, rising to stand. "I'm as ready as I'll ever be and frankly the sooner the better since we no longer have to wait. Tonight we are finally in control." Gabrio walked from the room to head outside under the thickening pall of the night, leading everyone to follow him.

As they walked outside, the elements billowed around them. The wind stirred, bringing in a cold chill with the icy rain. Thunder rumbled above them as cracks of lighting whipped across the black sky. Gabrio, Marrok and Raul stood facing each other in the soggy farmland that expanded behind the house. To become heard, Raul yelled above the thundering noise. "To transform into and back into your forms, you need a certain word. A sole word from the language of the angels. I can't give you the word to use. They have to give it to you as a rite of ratification."

"They?" Gabrio questioned.

Raul nodded and pointed to the sky. "They."

Marrok looked up and saw the rain fall from the black sky. He searched the black void as a sudden clarity came over him. "I think

I understand what I have to do." He spoke while blinking the accumulating raindrops from his eyes. Standing silent while staring into the cloudy void, Raul and Gabrio watched him as the rain began to fall in slow motion around them. The symbol began to glow, slowly burning into the back of Marrok's neck. He cringed at the scorching pain that increased with the light of the gleaming emblem. His ears began to ring a high-pitched sound as if a loud explosion made him temporarily deaf. He looked at Gabrio and Raul. He saw their mouths moving, but couldn't hear them speaking to him. Then, he cast his sights toward the sky once again. Even the roar of the thunder after the strikes of lightning were lost to him and only the high-pitched ring remained. He grabbed his ears as the noise began to lower and become clear. The pitch took shape into an unknown voice, whispering to him. Marrok's eyes widened as he looked at Raul. He dropped his hands from his ears and licked his lips as he prepared himself. In his head, he repeated the word. *"Dhashay."*

In a flash Marrok's eyes glowed brightly as if the light of the moon were inside him. Then in a bursting explosion his body became surrounded by the same white-blue flames that engulfed Raul. Gaining the knowledge of how their breed came to be and their purpose. He quickly realized the symbol acted like the Calling and the word was the moon. Together they honed the power of both creating an ultimate force from within. As the color of the dancing flames changed to its primal color, his skin began to peel from his limbs revealing glimmering fur of gold. His joints cracked, but he felt no pain. He could feel the new strength of this power throughout his bones.

When he finished transforming, the flames became smothered and he knew he became marked by God. He had become a guardian, a protector of his kingdom and of those who proved worthy of his grace. His blue eyes had flecks of gold that shimmered in the dark of the night. He looked around him, seeing the world with even more meticulous than before.

Raul looked over Marrok. "You've done it. You heard the voice and completed the rite. Now you're marked to be a guardian, just like me and just like Gabrio. You're a *Beast Blood*, my son." He spoke proudly standing in his wolf form.

Marrok looked over at Gabrio and saw he had transformed as well. He tried to speak by using his mouth, but it only came out as a low grumble. Raul and Gabrio both shook their heads as their amusement became evident in their eyes.

"It's just like thinking. Direct your thoughts outward." Gabrio assisted.

Marrok looked at Gabrio and nodded to let him know he heard and understood what he meant. He tried to speak again and did so successfully, but in moderation. "I feel stronger. Everything's clear. I can hear everything, see everything. Smell everything, all at once. It's overwhelming." Marrok sparingly said.

"You'll become used to that in time, but control it. Learn to break everything up, narrow it down and put it altogether. Once you do it enough, you'll become used to it since you have all of eternity to practice." Raul advised.

"Can you find her? Can you sense her enough to find her?" Gabrio asked not wasting time.

Marrok looked at Gabrio and remembered the connection he first felt between him and Esmeralda. Once again the feeling was low just as it was when she first touched his hand. Marrok was about to shake his head. Then, with the flash of lightning the intensity of the connection escalated. Marrok grabbed his head, his claws digging into his scalp as a pulse of energy escaped his body pushing outward. Marrok was in the whirlwind of the farsightedness as the pulsing wave took him throughout the land, across the Atlantic sea in a gust. It was as if his soul left his body and he searched for her himself.

All the same time, he felt like he pushed toward her as a force repelled him from her. Cities and towns rushed passed him as the feeling became stronger the closer he was to her. Night became day as the scenery changed from the land to rest on a massive castle. He could feel himself circle the establishment. He felt her soul was there behind the walls. He could hear her heart and the almost soundless murmur of her child's heart underlying the strong current of hers. He found her by a window. She was looking out the window. He saw her ivory face in the stained glass. He screamed her name and she heard him. Esmeralda looked and seen him. She began to pound on the window screaming. Raven Eye, he heard her say. Marrok called out her name as he ran to her. Suddenly, a wolf with red eyes filled his vision. Startling him, the connection was broken and sent him back into his body. Gabrio and Raul surrounded him as they watched him intensely, waiting for him to speak.

Marrok felt mentally drained as he spoke. "I found her. She was screaming through the window. She's at Raven Eye. Then, another wolf with red eyes… I'm feeling so drained."

Gabrio looked at Raul. *"Raven eye. She's where it all began. She's in Scotland."* He spoke unambiguously.

The clouds began to break and a light of red cast over the land. The world around them looked bathed in blood. All looked toward the sky and saw a blood moon hung over them, low and foreboding.

Meanwhile

Laycerath looked at Sheryl as he snarled in his deep, unearthly voice. "Someone else had already found her. It's not just anyone either, It's a guardian."

Sheryl looked at the silhouette of the beast Laycerath had become with the blood moon. He was a magnificent sight to behold. She shook the remainder of her skin from her fur. "Don't tell me you're shaking in your fur. Your complete now and a guardian will be no match for you. Kill them and take their damn symbol. I'm glad we have an opposing team again. It makes things more interesting. So, what's a little more struggle in the race we're about to have? You know where she is, so let's go get her."

21

THE ORDER IS IN SESSION.

"Dream a dream for me tonight. Lay your head down on the pillow and dream a dream for me tonight. May you dream of flowers, may you dream of the skies so blue. You will soar through the clouds as you dream a dream for me tonight...." As Esmeralda rested on the velvet couch that sat in the middle of her room, she rubbed her expanded belly over the blanket she wrapped herself in, singing to the child that lay within. She warmed herself in the sun surrounding by the scattering colors from the stain glass window. She looked through its cascading colors as the morning sun began to rise into full bloom.

"I love it when you sing that song. You always have had an angelic voice, my Essie."

Esmeralda snapped her head as she looked toward the door and saw Gabrio entering through it. She became ecstatic as he slowly walked to her. The tears that she held back for so long flowed down her cheeks unrelentingly. She tried to rise from the seat, but couldn't manage to move quickly from the weight of her condition. "Gabrio! You found me, no us. You found us. Gabrio, there is so much I need to tell you. I thought I would never see you again. Come to me please. I need to hold you." She sobbed.

"You're pregnant?" Gabrio stopped walking to her and stood in shock when he saw her plumping stomach.

"I am. We're pregnant. Finally, we'll have a family all of our own. We did it my love, we did it. It'll be a son, you know, and he's special in more ways than you can believe."She replied.

Gabrio was silent as he stared at her in growing horror. Esmeralda became confused at his silence.

"What? What is it, Gabrio?" She asked.

"What did you do, Esmeralda? What did you do with our son? You murdered him. Our son is dead by your blood! " Gabrio yelled at her.

Esmeralda began to sob harder through her cries. "No, I didn't! I wouldn't harm my own son. I wouldn't." She cast her eyes from her husband, looked down at her expanded belly that hid under the white blanket and lightly touched her hand to the mound that protruded from her small body. "Gabrio, he's fine." She tried to reassure him, let alone herself as she unveiled her hand. Fear stuck in her throat as she caught sight of the piercing color of slick blood warm on her fingers. Esmeralda whipped the blanket from her body.

Her mind began to scatter as she seen blood covered her half naked body and her stomach was flat. "My baby, our son. Where is he?" She stammered as she cranked her head to look back at Gabrio, but he was no longer there. She tried to get up, but she became restricted by an unseen force. Her body was a motionless lump, except for her head. Confusion raided her senses while she looked around the room to the best of her capabilities and seen nothing was out of the ordinary.

On returning her view back toward the doorway Esmeralda quickly noticed an older woman wearing a black cloak standing in Gabrio's place coddling something close to her bosom. Esmeralda became startled as she looked closer and seen the woman was holding a baby, whispering words of motherly affections to the child. Instantly, Esmeralda knew the infant was her son in a stranger's caress and rage overwhelmed her. "Who are you? What are you doing holding my son? Give me my son before I fucking kill you." Struggling to rise from her invisible constraints she screamed at the mysterious woman, whose face remained hidden behind her long white hair. Esmeralda waited for a reply of any sort, but remained snubbed. The woman continued to coo at her son. She yelled again."Did you hear me? I said give me my baby! He's mine, not yours!"Esmeralda roared even louder at her.

A sarcastic laugh sounded loudly from the older woman as she flicked her long hair back revealing her face. Astonishment and relief flowed through Esmeralda when she recognized the woman who held her son."Sheryl. Oh, thank God. It's you. You have him, he's safe. Give me my son. I didn't get a chance to hold him." She softly pleaded. Sheryl flaunted an unsettling smile as she shook her head, speaking coldly. "He's no longer your son. He's mine now. My son. I'm going to raise him as my own, while you die, turning to ash. Freshly born with an old soul. His name is Laycerath, you know. He's your kin reborn, reincarnated. Isn't he beautiful with your husband's hair, your eyes and such an old soul? He'll be a great ruler of the new world."

"What are you talking about? Give me back my son. You can't have him. Give him back to me, now! Sheryl!" Esmeralda screamed loudly.

"Be quiet, Esmeralda. The baby is sleeping." Sheryl smugly said.

Esmeralda screamed again as Sheryl turned her back to her as her frantic petitions remained ignored. She headed out the wooden door, leaving with her child in her arms. Esmeralda saw the morning sun that shined its warm glow through the stain glass window began to turn dark as it shined a crimson glow throughout the room. Esmeralda remained paralyzed to her seat, still struggling to escape as she saw blood cascade down the patterned wallpaper. She looked above her, out the glass dome of her ceiling and seen meteors aflame, fall from the sky, leaving swirling trails of clouds and smoke. The earth was in sudden chaos. Esmeralda could feel the rumble of the ground shaking around her. She heard the trumpets of an army approach and the cries of thousands of people dying as the clash of swords rang just outside her walls. She snapped her head to the side to see out the stain glass window, but it crumbled down; allowing her to see the apocalyptic pandemonium beneath her.

Beast Bloods and Blood Tasters fought the demons of hell, protecting the angel's that flew high and fast above them. The angel's wings, large and shielding, protected them from the spears and arrows that flew through the air at them by the twisted souls that Lucifer cast on the earth.

The angel's swords of fire splattered flames across the land, waving fire toward the demons. Werewolves devoured the retreating creatures of hell, while the Blood Tasters cast their powers against the horde that ran toward them. It was a burst of light, earth, fire and wind in a raging battle. Esmeralda felt her heart was about to burst as she seen the beast rise from the fire and rubble. Fear overtook her and made her tremble as a distant memory tied within this reality. It was a werewolf, but it was like no other. The creature was as black as ash, with eyes red as blood and he noticed her. Esmeralda couldn't scream as fear choked her throat, the creature walked through the fire and the turmoil to get to her as blood dripped from his snout and claws. Fur rose on the creatures back into razor sharp points, as he snarled and snapped toward her. Through her fear the relation of the familiarity became known as she remembered the tapestry in the dungeon.

The creature, which was fighting God's arch guardian, Michael, stood there. She knew he was the same werewolf in the tapestry. However, he was no longer a weaved image. He was real and so close she could smell death on his breath. Esmeralda quickly found her voice as she screamed an ear piercing, ring when the demon werewolf raised his mangled hand to slice her throat. It came down in a swoop and Esmeralda heard her gurgling cry. Then all went white.

Esmeralda woke up in a panic, rolling over the side of the bed and began dry heaving. Eventually bile rose into her throat as she emptied her stomach into the large decorative vase next to her bed. Once she realized nothing else remained, she hunched into a small ball in the middle of the bed. Crying and holding her small expanded stomach; she began praying for her child's safety. She knew she had to go to Conlaoch right away and tell him what she had witnessed. She just didn't understand why Sheryl would betray her, even if it were to come true or just remain a dream, she needed answers and she knew where to find them.

Meanwhile

"Your blood has rushed to your dick too many times, disabling your brain, Conlaoch. She has to die after the child's born, if not sooner. When the child is strong enough to survive without the comfort of her, we take him out and raise him, protect him as we're meant to do. The child grows quickly. If we stall any longer and her demon side is stronger, she'll kill it while it lies in her womb, digging it out! She must remain contained, chained even, until the proper moment. You've stuck her in a gilded cage." Ja'Har yelled his deep, booming voice at Conlaoch.

Conlaoch glared into the lime green eyes of the tanned skin, white haired man that sat a few seats down from him at the rounded stone table. His hatred for Ja'Har began to grow stronger with the man's demanding arrogance and his thirst for blood lust. "I'm not going to kill an innocent just for the hell of it. She shows no signs as of yet of her demon side being stronger. True, it is there, but what if she's stronger, better than the blood that flows through her veins." He said just as sternly.

"What on earth makes you think she won't turn, if not now, but later when the child is a growing boy? You know you can't guarantee when the child's born, she won't eventually kill her own son. We can't rely on your word alone. We need to see her." Sabri, a slender woman of long silky red hair and large violet eyes, smoothly stated.

Conlaoch looked at all twelve members and saw their beautiful, hard faces filled with mixed emotion, except for Ja'Har, whom always acted impulsively instead of his brains. "I can't guarantee it. I only saw the child's purpose. I couldn't see anything else other than who she was and who she carried. The future was uncertain." He replied a bit downheartedly.

"See, the fool rants about what he thinks to be true with no proof of what is to come! All of you would bend over and fuck yourselves to side with this man." Ja'Har smugly stated.

"Will you shut your shit hole of a mouth, Ja'Har? What do you gain when or if she dies or lives? Why so eager to kill this woman when she did nothing to you?" Theon chimed, after remaining silent for so long. His ebony eyes glistened in the candlelight that illuminated the great room as he stared daggers at the boisterous man he addressed.

Ja'Har quieted as he looked around and seen that everyone had the collective thought resting on the tips of their tongues. Setting his gaze on Conlaoch's tight smirk and dancing crystal blue eyes, he became enraged even more so. "She poses as a threat. That's why she should die. If Conlaoch has a soft heart about it, send her to me. I'll take care of *It* and the woman." He yelled.

Quickly becoming annoyed of the bickering, Irion slammed his large hands on the table demanding to settle what he deemed to be a cock measuring contest between Ja'Har and everyone else. "You stupid man, the threat is already here and it doesn't lie with just her! We know this and that's why we're here tonight. That's why we've been here for the past five fucking days. Now, yesterday the blood moon hung high over America. My people tell me they're calling it the end of times, a freak of nature, but we know it was Lucifer's Hellhound completing his transformation. It's begun. His powers have revived and if he isn't already, he's going to try to find the *Hybrid*. We know he wouldn't be the only one trying to find the mother and child. We would all be fools to think so. There are *Truer Sins* that still linger the earth. The newborn will have a power between the realms. It gives an opportunity for those *Sins* to come forth. We need to be on guard, not just for the demon werewolf, but for anyone that's lurking in the woods surrounding us. Soon, the *Beast Bloods* will be here to protect her and last time I knew the guardians of the symbol have long since died out. Nevertheless, we have to remain united and by doing so the rest of us need to see the woman for our own individual evaluation. Conlaoch, will you please send for her now!"

Conlaoch looked at Irion and nodded at him. He held honor and respect for the diplomatic man. Immediately, he complied and waved his hand toward a nearby servant to go fetch Esmeralda. Given the order, one of Esmeralda's chamber guards burst through the closed iron doors with her in tow behind him.

The guard spoke suddenly and fiercely as he contained Esmeralda. "I'm sorry to interrupt your meeting, but she was frantic. She insisted she come and see you. She claims to have news and would not stop pounding the door. When I refused, she told me she was going to hang herself. Fearful, I opened the door and the little brute ran out from underneath me, running to find you and now here we are."

Conlaoch became confused. Overall amused by her tactic, but he dared not show it in the presence of the others. In a sobering voice he spoke. "Her strategy worked in our favor this time as we were about to send word to her. Yet, if she were to do it again, take her by the neck and put her back. Else she stays in my room and she wouldn't want that. Would you, Esmeralda?" He said hauntingly with a stern face.

Esmeralda looked at the group of people around the stone table. She saw their exotic faces starring between Conlaoch and her. They silently waited for her reply. She quickly noticed they all were warriors, baring similar tattoos on their showing skin like Conlaoch had on his arms and neck. She didn't cower from their watchful eyes. She squared her shoulders and stepped forward and boldly stated. "I'm sorry for my antics as you would call them, but I needed to come here and tell you..."

"What for?" Ja'Har snarled at her, revealing his fangs.

Esmeralda hadn't cowered by his intimidating snarl. She snapped her head in his direction and glared her fiery eyes at him. Immediately, she evaluated and hated him. She could tell he was an arrogant man who believed he was entitled to everything and anything he wanted. Tired of the villainous treatment when she was a victim of circumstance, she didn't hold back her thoughts of the man. "To tell him of my premonition, before you so rudely opened your fucking mouth. I've been in the room for less than five minutes and based on how everyone is looking at you, you're on their last nerve. Now, you're getting on mine. Get your cock out of your ass and stop being fucking rude. I'm not done speaking."

Irion laughed outright as the others tried to hide their smiles, except Conlaoch who smiled widely. Ja'Har became stunned at her outspoken vigor and readied to about to rant about it. Immediately, he lost his ability to talk and move. Phloxous, a beautiful woman with overflowing brown hair and turquoise eyes, cast her abilities over him enabling him to only listen.

"Thank you, Phloxous." Irion stated to the woman with laughter still in his voice and turned his attention back to Esmeralda. Irion leaned forward, looking her over. "Speak quickly about your premonition. You won't become further interrupted by any of us. Unless, he figures a way to release himself from her."

Esmeralda looked at the man who addressed her. She looked over his olive toned, weathered face. Despite his bright golden hair, his powdered blue eyes showed wisdom and understanding behind them, indicating he's a bit older than the rest or endured more. Feeling comfortable again enough to speak freely, she did so. "I had a vision of the world in chaos brought by the betrayal of a close family friend and a companion elder. In this vision she took my son and feigned it was her own. She kept calling him Laycerath and that he had an old soul. Then, I saw the world in flames and the battle that will become held over the extent of the land. I needed to know Conlaoch, did you see this when you bit me? You knew of my brother, my father, my son. I want my son to remain protected even if I have to die for this to happen. My son needs to be safe from all those who wish harm on him. Even if that means me."

Irion and Conlaoch made eye contact. They looked among the others for their reactions. They wanted to believe what she claimed, but they were skeptical because they knew evil beings would say anything; tell anybody what they wanted to hear to accomplish their own agenda. Ja'Har even remained still, calculating if what the woman said was either a lie or the truth.

Conlaoch replied. "No, Esmeralda. I could only see your child's purpose and who you were. I couldn't tell either of your fates. That's one reason why they are all here." Conlaoch directed his hand to the twelve beings that sat around the table. "They're here for the child's protection and to enable a constant safety as you so much desire, even if it means you die."

Esmeralda slumped in confusion when she saw most of the other members nod their heads in unison with the occasional mutter of their agreement escaping their lips. Yet, a man stood from the table. She watched him eagerly with the others.

Ya'Ru, a man with three scars running across the front of his bearded face, narrowed his gray eyes on the petite woman and addressed her as his glib tone broke through the quiet murmurs. "You're not afraid of death? You're so young not to fear death. You've lived for such a short life for your kind. What of your husband? Those years trying to have children, a family. You still desire your home, your husband's embrace and to live in a harmony that's denied you since fate called you here today. You crave life, but you are willing to die for your child because you still can't trust yourself. You're afraid your husband won't ever know what has become of you, know of his son and if your friend will betray you. Betray you for a reason you wouldn't even know why, until it was too late. A war is waging within you. Your demon blood is fighting with your angelic blood. It's a fight even our kind doesn't battle. However, I see that your heart is pure, but your soul isn't untouchable. However, that's why your chosen in your bloodline to have the Hybrid."

Esmeralda's guard became shattered at the words the man said aloud shook her to her very core. Everyone remained silent as they listened to the insight of Ya'Ru. Each one knew soul reading was one of the many abilities he possessed. He would read the deepest recesses of the subconscious of any mind, he chose, leading to the traits of their soul, which proved to be an undeniably accurate evaluation. He switched his erudite words and vision from Esmeralda. He readied his replies to for everyone in the room.

Conlaoch cleared his throat and spoke in a hollow voice. "What does this mean for her fate?"

Ya'Ru looked to Conlaoch, then to the others. "My people, I've seen this Beast Blood's soul. I decree before you on my life, my honor, she won't turn into what we fear she'll become. Not now, not ever. Since the day she was conceived, her cells and blood battled against the other. As she took her first breath, it allowed a strong soul to enter and it smothered the demonic side, unlike the rest. This made her pure enough to become chosen to carry the Hybrid. Yet, the blood will remain bitter on our tongues. It's proven in her words she spoke before us. Her life for the child's. There will be no need for her death. However, she will have to remained watched. She won't turn against her son on her own, but if a force were to try to inflict its own designs on her the consequences might be what we fear.

Esmeralda wanted to faint at the relief of knowing she didn't have to die. For so long she felt as if she was awaiting trial and she knew if the *Blood Tasters* decided she had to die, death was surely coming for her. However, if need be she was still willing to throw herself into its clutches for her unborn child's life and safety.

"What of the premonition? Is what she said true?" Sabri asked.

It was Jauni who answered. "I've read her mind. What she says is the truth. Her vision is still clear in her head and not altered by the brain."

Esmeralda looked from the ash-blonde, black-eyed man and back to Conlaoch as he started to speak to her. "Then it's decided. Esmeralda, Elder of Clan Santos, is not a threat to us, to her own kind and most importantly to her child. However, regarding your friend, Sheryl, the one that you've dreamed about this evening. What do you know about her and about her past?"

Esmeralda shook her head. "The information I know about her is what I have heard from her husband and mine. As well as the experiences I've had with her. She never talked about her past. Once, I directly inquired and she told me her past was too horrible for her to remember. So, it was to remain there. So, I didn't pry after that. We only went forward."

Irion gave a curt nod. "It was a sign for a reason. Being the mother of the Hybrid, you never take your dreams, visions and so forth for granted." Irion began taking command, addressing to everyone their strategic placement of his plan. "It's evident that we'll guard the castle as if it were the old ways of the world. The past is finally clashing with the present with this prophecy. What we do today will affect the future. We will use the unmarked vampire guards, Conlaoch created for this castle and set men at every post. They will kill any threat that tries to pass through. Pholxous, Ja'Har and Sabri you have the words to turn invisible. You will guard the castle from above and remain unnoticeable to those that think Raven Eye is ungaurded. Conlaoch, Theon, Ya'Ru and I will protect the center of the castle. Those who can shape shift, blend in the elements outside, be our eyes in the woods and watch for the other *Beast Bloods* and our threats. You'll know when you see the demon wolf because he'll look like no other. The rest of you will guard the various and vast dungeons and tunnels, inside and out. Never leave the posts you're assigned. Protect them well. Use every word and symbol of power *they* gave you to protect the castle from siege, but most of all to protect the woman and protect the Hybrid. Esmeralda is to remain in her room or with one of us, always. If we need to leave, she can't leave the castle unless they're at least ten of us to surround her. Is everyone in agreement to this plan?"

In unison everyone, except Ja'Har nodded, and spoke their agreement to the plan with a hardy enthusiasm. Esmeralda nodded as well, understanding the plan. She quickly prayed that nothing unholy would come for her and the plan wouldn't falter. She knew it was time to prepare for both the expected and for the worse to come. She could shake the sickening feeling that something worse was surely coming.

22

RUSH

Gabrio, Marrok and Raul stood on the jagged shoreline of Nova Scotia. The salt air droplets of the great Atlantic blew coldly through their muddied, bloodied fur as each stirring wave crashed against the rocks. The waves were choppy, rising higher with each peeking clash. They could feel the storm, they outran finally catching up behind them. Together they looked over the cloudy blue ocean that lay between them and their destination with a fierce determination.

"We are quicker, stronger than any ship or plane." Marrok propounded through the noise of the sloshing waves.

"That's true. Taking one or the other would only slow us down. We can do it. We're indestructible and nothing stands in our way. Why should this stretch of water?" Gabrio replied agreeing with Marrok's thought.

Raul remained silent as he calculated the mileage between the gap of where they stood and their destination. He pondered, knowing if they were fast enough, they could endure the increasingly large waves that rolled into the other without becoming overtaken. Nodding his head, he spoke. "We've already ran over eighteen hundred miles overnight and most of the morning. It's almost thirty-five hundred miles to Raven Eye Castle. It'll take us, at most, two days. Two days of running and that's with complications. I've never ran across the water. I never had to until now, but we are fast enough to not fall through. I've gone longer without hunting and so have you Gabrio, but Marrok." He looked at his son. "Your new hunger will make your frenzied enough to kill the first thing you see once you've hit land. Do you think you can make it?" Concern tinged his voice as he asked his son.

Marrok looked at Raul and Gabrio and gave a brief nod. "I can and will control it. I'll save it for anything that stands in our way and devour them."

"That's all I need to hear. Let's go." Gabrio growled. Pushing as hard as he could, starting a run at full speed into the water, he moved across the water as if it were solid land and Raul was close behind him.

Marrok watched Gabrio and Raul run across the choppy water. Quickly they were becoming faint moving objects the further they went. Lightning struck above him. He quickly looked to the jagged streak cracked above him. Despite the growing distance, Gabrio was still the easiest to spot as the blackness of his fur stood out among the grim dimness of the overcast afternoon. He noticed their forceful speed allowed them to slice through the waves that crashed into them without any hindrance. He readied himself, rushing to catch up with them, but stopped suddenly when he saw four blotches of black enter his peripheral vision, skimming across the water.

Snapping his head to his left to get a better look at the rapid specks, he narrowed his eyes and followed their direction. Stepping into the cold water to get a little closer, he saw they weren't running, but flying low across the sea. The razor tips of their thin, expanded wings skidded across the sea as they darted faster angling toward Gabrio and Raul.

"Oh, my God!" Marrok howled. Without a second thought he began to shoot across the water, running at full momentum and howling over the sound of the waves hoping to warn them before it was too late.

Gabrio turned to look when he heard the distressed howls of Marrok behind him. Immediately the sky became blackened from his view as he saw a distorted winged creature with large black eyes and pointed teeth, attack him from above. Sinking his claws into his back and biting into his neck, the creature lifted Gabrio from the water, rising them in the air. "We're under attack!" Gabrio snarled as he struggled to become released from the creature's gripping snare.

Raul saw Gabrio in the clutches of one of the flying creatures, hovering high above the water as another of the scaled, half human creatures released its curved talons from their sheaths. They readied to dig into his own back and Raul ran harder. However, the demon kept up with him.

Marrok heard the sickly pale creatures release their high-pitched screeches as they surrounded Raul. He scanned the water and couldn't see Gabrio. Fear struck him harder at the knowledge Gabrio could be dead and now his father was under the remaining creatures' advances. Their large black wings fanned above Raul as their long pointed tails flicked behind them, each tail taking a turn at trying to pierce the moving werewolf. Frantic, when he saw the largest of the three diving to kill his father, Marrok lunged toward the creature. He grabbed it by the wing with his snapping teeth. He pulled the demon into the water as the paper-thin wing ripped under his teeth. He heard the creature's ungodly scream piercing through his head like daggers. The creature tried to claw him, missing his throat, but Marrok flipped the creature making its human-like face gurgle underwater, choking on the cold liquid. He kept moving fast, until his paws touched the shore. Angrily, he took the creature from his mouth and smashed it against the rocks with a brute force until its blood, a black sludge, poured from its limp body.

Raul stopped, turned and lunged in the air, grabbing the long serpent tail of one of the swirling creatures that hovered above him. He hurriedly pulled the creature down until he had it by the neck, its scaly spikes piercing through his hands. Raul gritted his teeth as he felt the pain, digging his own claws into the throat of the creature. Without prevention the creature tried wrapping its wings around him to hold him close to tear out his throat, but Raul was swift. Holding a tight firm onto the neck of the demon, he ripped both wings from the demon's writhing body. The creature snapped its long barbed teeth trying to inflict injury, but before the demon could, Raul wrapped a large hand around the demon's head, snapping its neck. As the creature fell, it became engulfed by the navy water. Raul quickly realized he did not sink with the creature. He could feel the symbol under his fur burn as if it fine point tip of the chisel, from so long ago, was entering his neck again. He looked at Marrok and saw he finished killing another vile creature.

"Three." Marrok counted. He looked around to find Gabrio, but he was nowhere. He looked into the gray sky and seen Gabrio fighting the largest of the creatures above him as they were falling back to the water.

Gabrio burst through the dark clouds while lightning whipped in threads around them. He clutched the wings of the demon, holding back the razor blade points from entering his neck while he dodged the corpulent jagged tail from stabbing through his body. The creature screeched into his face, becoming angrier that he fought with just as much strength and prolonged the struggle. The creature released shards of spikes from his body. Gabrio roared as the barbs pierced into his body and in a fluid motion, he directed the razor points that brushed against his neck into the creatures large black eyes. The demon screamed as a tar-like liquid poured from its eye sockets. Gabrio took his large clawed hand and sliced the creature's throat. The creature's scream died in its throat as its massive flaccid body hit the water, creating an explosion of water around them. Gabrio hit the surface of the water as if he hit the rocky shore, knocking the wind out of him. The creature underneath him sizzled in the salty water, disintegrating into a mound of black foam, which faded away with the moving waves.

"Gabrio!" Raul yelled as he and Marrok ran toward where he lay lifeless. Marrok nudged him, hoping to get a response from his brother-in-law.

After a few long seconds Gabrio sucked in air to catch his breath. He rolled onto his back and looked up at the moving gray clouds as his body strangely swayed with the waves, but he remained in place. Suddenly Marrok and Raul were in his view as he looked to his side and seen the concern in their eyes. Inwardly, Gabrio smirked. "Such concern. Don't worry about me, I got that fucker." He smugly stated.

Raul snorted as he extended a hand to lift Gabrio upright. "You're lucky. For a moment there I thought it would've had you."

"What the fuck were those things? Did you hear their screams? It was nails on a chalkboard." Marrok spoke as he looked around them in case there were more they missed.

"If I were to guess, I'd say they're demons sent to kill us from whoever wanted us dead, which could be from the devil himself given the situation." Gabrio sarcastically said.

"I have to say you're right. If it wasn't the devil himself, it was a close second - the demon werewolf. Once complete, it'll rule the armies of hell." Raul replied.

"Well, they're gone now, but I wouldn't put it pass the bastard to send more of those foul creatures or others like them to try to kill us, preventing us from getting to Raven Eye." Marrok stated.

Gabrio rolled his shoulders. He could feel the few injuries he received from the impact of the fall already begin mending. "He's after my son and my wife. We have to move, now."

Raul and Marrok nodded in unison, but it was Marrok who spoke. "Especially since it's in the middle of the day and three werewolves are standing on the ocean only a short thirty miles from the coastline."

"Sounds like a bad joke, instead of the truth." Gabrio replied.

Raul snorted again. "It's a new power gained. It's already marked in our symbols. I felt it earlier during the attack."

"I did as well." Marrok said.

"So, did I, but I didn't hear anything from 'Them'. I think they mark us to endure the battles." Gabrio declared.

Raul shook his head. "It seems like that, but I don't know. However, we should go now and not waste anymore time here. I would hate for more of the demons to fly their ugly faces through here and try to stall us further."

"Agreed." Gabrio stated before he began to run, leading them forward.

Later

Several hours later Laycerath and Sheryl looked over the dark Atlantic Ocean and saw the slick black blood of the demons he summoned on the rocks of the shoreline, dripping into the sea. The large spinning beam of the lighthouse illuminated the body of the dead demon, which its body was already half disintegrated into the rising sea. Laycerath kicked the remains into the ocean as a receding wave took it with the current.

"The guardian was here." Laycerath stated as his red eyes glowed within the foggy darkness.

Sheryl looked over the ocean and seen the moon's wavy reflection in the water. "It doesn't mean he didn't die. The others could've taken his body into the sea and strangled him underwater, killing their own selves in the process." She reasoned.

He nodded. "Maybe. Or there's more of them and I only picked up on the one. Then together they evaded their attack and crossed the ocean."

Taken back for the briefest of moments, Sheryl's shocked faded as nonchalance replaced her surprise. "They can do that? No matter, we'll get Esmeralda before they do. We know the one thing that no one knows about the castle, even the fucking *Blood Tasters*."

Laycerath briskly took a few steps forward and slammed his foot onto the ground, as he moved his arms upward as if to raise something that wasn't there.

"What are you doing?" Sheryl asked, surprise forthcoming again, but this time it was noticeable.

Laycerath said nothing as he looked at the water and waited. The water began to gurgle. Sheryl watched the bubbling water and a body rose to the top, then another and another, until there was a singular line of piled bodies across the water as long as the eye can see. Sheryl looked to Laycerath and his red eyes bore into her crystal blue ones, fire and ice lingered together in the stillness of the night."Do you know how many men, woman and children have faced death by the sea? Wars, exploration, trade. The sea's filled with the bodies of those that remain lost to it. Tonight we are using their bodies to cross the ocean. Our night is their day. We'll remain in our wolf forms if we time it right." Laycerath proclaimed.

Sheryl shivered at the burst of power that rose within her. "Then we should make use of their poor decomposing bodies or else they died in vain." She brushed passed Laycerath and took the first step on the waterlogged body of a woman, covered in seaweed.

23

TUNNELING

Stepping off the reeking body of another bobbing waterlogged man who faced a watery grave so long ago, Sheryl finally reached the shores of Scotland. She felt Laycerath race passed her as they entered the western beach of the Isle of Mull. Both stepping onto the abandoned white, sandy beach still sheathed in their werewolf forms, they immediately began to prowl the land looking for signs of the guardian.

Sheryl breathed in the cool air, searching for a scent, but could only smell the freshly poured rain and the wildlife that surrounded her. "Can you find anything?" She asked.

Laycerath delayed his reply as he looked over the land as he strategically tried to place the guardian's whereabouts. "The land is vast. He could've come in this damn island from anywhere. If he rounded the coastline near Edinburgh, it would give us more time to get the woman and get out, without the guardian being nearby. We need to stay remote even more so since the mortals have overpopulated themselves across these once forsaken lands." He firmly stated.

Sheryl followed Laycerath as they crept further onto the land, keeping a watchful eye of their surroundings. "It doesn't matter if the guardian is already there or not. We need the woman for the child."

He looked at her as rage seethed within him. He dealt with her mindless tactic long enough."You're a stupid bitch. Now, I can see why ignorance was your downfall. The guardians have the ability to call the angels down from their posts. They'll take one look at us, know who we are and kill us both to protect the realms. If we die by their swords, their dogs and their blood sucking, ticks, then what can we do? Die, rot and burn? We can't do much when we're decaying in the seventh circle of hell." Laycerath snarled.

Sheryl became defensive. "You said you saw her in the room with the stain glass window. There's only one room, beside the chapel, with the stained windows and that's Alexandria's room. We go to Esmeralda and take her from the room using the same tunnel that you used to produce the bitch's kin. That's our advantage to her. We will remain unseen, unheard underground and between the walls. They won't ever know, until it's too late. She'll already be under lock and key while your soul rested in her belly, waiting to become reborn. Are you such a coward?" She conferred.

Laycerath sneered as they trudged through the darkness of the night. He hated the fact he needed her with him to get the woman and to use the forbidden spell. Witches and demons have remained linked since the dawn of time, but his step-mother was more than a mere witch. They've always needed each other. Although he often wished he could send Sheryl to an earlier judgment, he knew it wouldn't be long when the time came when he was in a position to rule the new world. Then he could send her to a tortured fate of his choosing. "I'm no coward, slut. Nor am I a dim-witted fool to run into a trap and risk my neck to end in an eternal torture at Lucifer's fucking leisure. Your neck, I don't care too much for and you can do whatever you like. If the tunnel is even still there, you will not linger when you reach the other side. You'll drag the carrier out of her bed, push her through the fucking tunnel and bring her to me. Do I make myself clear?"

Sheryl replied sulking. "Crystal."

He nodded. "Good."

Sheryl knew not to cross him since he attacked her and George saw the marks on her neck. She remembered that day well since it was the same day she ripped out George's throat. She didn't want to kill her husband, but how could she explain the scratches on her neck to him. She did what was best for her success. Before he could heal, she set him on fire with a simple spell, killing him as the flames licked his skin and torched the entire house. She slowly walked outside and watched the house burn around his charred corpse. After a few moments, he was gone. Sheryl did come to love the man in a way, but he was only another pawn used to cover her true identity. Her heart always remained with a man she betrayed so long ago.

"Is my castle in the highlands still standing or did it face ruin?" Laycerath asked Sheryl startling her out of her thoughts.

"No, it is in ruin. No mortal wanted a home in which all the servants and guests died in a mysterious brutal way, especially in a remote part of Scotland. Every owner that had it since you left only lived there for short amounts of time. They claimed the grounds were haunted by the your countless victims. The name the locals gave it is Black Water Castle. They say the blood was so thick of your killings the water turned permanently black." Sheryl replied.

Laycerath beamed in his pride. After all this time he remained infamous throughout history for his viscous slaughters and they locals still feared him. When he first became the demon beast his appetite for flesh wasn't controllable. Many were victims of his blood-lust and his hunger. Thousands died within those walls and became hindered from ever leaving. "That works to our advantage. I don't want to take her to the neighboring land of Raven Eye Castle. That'll be too obvious and the first place they'll look when they see she is gone. We'll take the carrier to the ruins of my ancestral home in the highlands and you can perform the spell. I see the seals are firmly in place around your neck."

Sheryl could feel the cold, thick silver medallion bouncing against her chest as she walked. It was her idea when they merged they created one piece. This secured the safety of each seal. She snorted knowing the decaying sisters didn't need them anymore. It took her years to find each sister with the correct seal and a few minutes to kill them all. They were still rotting in pieces in the middle of the woods. "They're secure." I still feel the weight of them around my neck." Sheryl stated.

"Good." Laycerath said as he began to sprint and then fully run through the damp grass.

Sheryl became pulled by the invisible current of his leading run as she followed suit, matching his speed and vigor. That was the last of the words said between them as they silently headed to the entry point of the tunnel in Raven Eye Castle's surrounding forest.

Meanwhile

Engulfed in the steaming water of her bath, Esmeralda submerged herself under, holding her breath as she closed her eyes, trying to release her thoughts from the constraints of her over analytical mind. However, no matter how hard she tried her thoughts always took her back to her dream. The look on Gabrio's face was pure horror at the sight of her being with child. The blood of the birth and Sheryl holding the sleeping child. The demon werewolf slicing her throat. All of it replayed in a loop in her mind. She tried to let it go.

Laying flat on her back underwater, Esmeralda's hair waved around her in flowing strands from the rising water level and a loose strand tickled across her nose. Impulsively, she wanted to inhale at the sensation. Coming up from the water, she deeply inhaled the warm air and rubbed her face to take away the itch. She opened her eyes and noticed Conloach's hard features and white, blue eyes staring at her from the side of the copper claw tub. Esmeralda screamed at the surprise of his intrusion, making Conlaoch release a spout of laughter. "God Almighty, Conlaoch! You scared the shit out of me! What are you doing in here?" Esmeralda exclaimed as she pulled herself in a modest fashion from his prying eyes seeing her any more than he already had.

Conlaoch chuckled at her modesty. It wasn't a trait he remained unaccustomed to seeing in a woman in this day in age when women in his experience became flustered if you didn't openly gawk at them. Then again, he dealt with mortal women, not women who grew within a different set of standards in society that will be no more. "I wanted to check on you. After dinner you seemed grim. Even after you're told you weren't going to die, at least, not by our hands. So, I figured it's the dream, that's still bothering you." He stated.

Esmeralda looked up at him looking back into his seeking eyes and seen he couldn't contain their stare as he flicked them to her exposed, plumping cleavage. She released a sound of disgust. "Ugh! Will you please turn around or something? Why didn't you send Sabri or any other women in your clan to make sure I was okay? It didn't have to be you." She scoffed, folding her body tighter against her raised legs.

Conlaoch laughed at her scorn as he turned around and leaned his back against the tub and looked everywhere around the spacious bathroom. "I couldn't send one of them and allow them to leave their place of duty. They're keeping a constant look out for anything amiss. So, it was just my luck that I'm assigned to stay in this section of the castle, which allows me to come in here and check on you. It's a constant requirement. Then for me it was a happy accident that you happen to remain soaked in hot, steamy water, naked with your perky, rosy nip..."

In a flash Esmeralda extended her arm and with her wet hand

smacked Conlaoch center in the forehead with her open palm. His head impelled backward, smacking the copper tub with a small thumping sound. For the briefest of moments the room was silent. Esmeralda couldn't help release a small chuckle that soon turned to blunt laughter.

Conlaoch became stunned at the rapid, wet hand smacking him in the head. It was an unexpected assault at which he wanted to become outraged over. If it was anyone else he would've raged about it. However, since it was the woman he came to admire and he heard the contagious laughter of that very same woman; he couldn't help himself by laughing with her. He noticed it was an endearing sound and realized it was the first time he ever heard her laugh.

He felt the water droplets from his forehead fall over his smiling cheeks as he touched the wet spot on his face. "You have fast reflexes, little wolf. I was not expecting becoming attacked by you so swift, nor the laughter that followed. You have a wonderful laugh, Esmeralda. Your husband is a very lucky man." Conlaoch told her softly with a touch of envy sneaking into his voice. He didn't mean to add that last comment, but it was too late. It's not that he loved her, but he came to love her in his own way. He protected her for all this time, dined with her, watch her sleep fitfully through the night and call for her husband. He knew she longed for her husband, would love her husband with a set faithfulness for all of her life. She still believed Gabrio would come for her, rescue her from her captor. However, in Conlaoch's mind, she was his and once he claimed what was his, he was like a selfish lonely child with a new toy. He kept it close for no one else to have.

Esmeralda's laughter diminished as the aura of the room changed into an awkward and increasingly uncomfortable silence, at least to her anyway. It was the first kind sentence he said to her since her internment at Raven Eye Castle, but she didn't know if it was genuine. It came out of the blue. She shifted in the hot water, lightly sloshing the bubbly liquid over the edge of the tub as she searched for something to say. She said the first reply that came to thought in a small, shy voice. "Thank you, Conlaoch." Esmeralda looked at the back of his head and saw him nod silently.

"So, what has your racing mind in a worried fit now that your neck has remained safely on your body?" Conlaoch asked a little too quickly wanting to change the conversation and think of something else less compassionate.

"How long will I have to stay here under your clan's protection?" Esmeralda spoke bluntly.

Conlaoch sighed, knowing she wanted to break free from her constraints, to leave the castle, to leave him and go back to her husband. Despite his feelings, he was an honest man and told her the truth. "You can't go home anytime soon. Here is the safest place for you and the child."

"Eli." Esmeralda interrupted Conlaoch softly.

Conlaoch turned his head to better understand what she said. "What did you say?"

Esmeralda cleared her voice and repeated. "Eli. That's the name of my son, the *Hybrid* as everyone is so fond of calling him. Eli is his name."

Conlaoch smiled. The name seemed fitting for the child, but he had a feeling it wasn't right. He kept his mouth shut and looked down at his hands in his lap. "You and Eli will remain protected here for now, with us. Majority of the your kind will come when your son begins entering his childhood, furthering the protection until he comes into a commanding age where he'll rule over them. They'll be his army to fight Lucifer's army and his demon Beast Blood. It's said that Michael will come for him when God plans to strike his wrath against mankind. In hopes to wipe out the truer sin and their corruption. There'll be a battle between heaven and hell over the world. Given our circumstance of never dying and the ideal fact of the light always conquers the dark, we should be okay." Conlaoch added lightheartedly, trying to turn the grim conversation less severe.

Esmeralda became flustered that she would remain held there for years to come without her husband, her family ever knowing what became of her. "I know all this, but what I don't know is the *truer sin*? What is this Truer Sin you're talking vaguely about. Who is it? Why can't you find them now just by biting their fucking neck?" Esmeralda harshly questioned.

Conlaoch lightly reasoned "Esmeralda it doesn't..."

Without warning, Irion's massive body burst through the threshold of the open bathroom door interrupting Conlaoch in mid sentence. "Conlaoch! Beings spotted and approaching the castle in haste!" Irion yelled his echoing voice into the large bathroom.

Surprise filled Esmeralda's shout. "What the hell is wrong with you vampires bursting into rooms with no regard for privacy?" She exclaimed at the sudden entry of the blonde haired giant man. She noticed his shoulders alone expanded the wide doorway, before she twisted her body to shield herself from his eyes as well.

Irion blushed almost scarlet as he noticed her scantly covered body, apart from her long hair plastering against her ivory skin in a wanton fashion. He hurriedly looked away at nothing in particular as he cast his eyes away from her. "I'm sorry Carrier, I did not know you were bathing, but it's of urgent news. Three beings approach fast, captured by our own! They were found in the woods by the shape shifters in flight. They put up a hell of a fight they said, but they brought them here. Now, they're on their knees and surrounded in front of the castle. Ya'Ru's heading there to get a read on them." Irion said.

Conlaoch lifted himself from the floor. "Is one the demon?

Irion shook his head. "No, their eyes remain normal, but they are of her kind. I'll leave you to bite them since you did so with her already, you can trace the blood."

Esmeralda perked up. "My kind? Three of my kind are here?" She stated, but remained ignored by both men.

Conlaoch relief became apparent. He was glad it wasn't the

demon werewolf. Yet, the threat is still lingering with those three werewolves alone. No one outside their circle's trusted. Especially, if the demon started to make replicas of himself using humans. "I'm going now, Irion. Head down and ensure the security of their capture as well. I'll be there right behind you to join you." He commanded with finality.

"Good." Irion replied. Turning around, he headed back through the door, leaving the both of them alone in the tense silence.

Conlaoch stared straight at the space Irion recently occupied and left. His face was grim, ready for a fight as he spoke, but he didn't look at her since he was respecting her insistent wish of modesty. He could feel the symbols on his body being to switch their colors. His tattoos began to glow as his eyes faded to blackness. "Please dress and be quick about it. Your doors and windows will remain enchanted once I leave. They will protect you from anyone breaking in here. However, if anyone does get through defend yourself the best that you can. Break anything to create a weapon. As a last form of defense use the angelic dagger under your bed.

"There has been a dagger there to whole time!" Esmeralda exclaimed in surprise.

He ignored her again and continued talking."Be careful with it! You have demonic blood and you're a werewolf- dying by this blade will- Oh fuck it! Just be fucking careful with it! I don't have time to explain why! Once I head down and find out the situation, I'll send Sabri and Phloxous to your room to sit with you and to protect you." He said sternly as the threat of Esmeralda and Eli's safety became finally challenged.

With his last word spoken, he swiftly left her to her deal with her racing thoughts. Esmeralda heard his pounding, echoing footsteps cross the floor of her room, followed by the squeak of the heavy wooden door to her room open-and-shut tightly. When Esmeralda knew she was alone, she quickly dashed from the bathtub. Her wet feet slapped against the wooden floor as she rushed to her closest to dress. A mixture of fear and hope rushed into her heart knowing a couple her kind where outside the stone walls of the castle. As she put on a loose shirt with slightly tight jeans, she deeply felt one of the detained beings had to be Gabrio. He was coming for her and their son. Then a stronger feeling came over her. She instantly recognized the feeling was the strange connection she once felt with Marrok. However, the feeling radiated through her and as quickly as it came it left.

It's my nerves. She thought, trying to calm herself. She moved from the open wardrobe to sit on the edge of the velvet, backless couch in front of it. Nervously biting the pad of her thumb, she became startled by the noise of a large thump. She cranked her head to look around the room and saw nothing was out of place. Her fear began to grow. The noise sounded again, but it was even louder, but followed by the noise of splintering wood.

Esmeralda jumped from her seat as she located the noise coming from the open wardrobe. Looking closely, she saw her clothes sway and slowly part. Out of the darkness was the face of a werewolf with crystal blue eyes. Esmeralda's stomach dropped as her face became ashen and her body became overwhelmed. Her fear paralyzed her from moving and making a sound. She looked from the familiar werewolf to her bed, devising a plan to protect herself from Sheryl's prowl.

24

THE TRUER SIN

Conlaoch stomped off the last step of the winding staircase into the great hall. His eyes were black as a stormy night sky as his symbols smoldered even brighter showing their continuous pattern through his clothes. He felt his muscles coil tighter as he began preparing for the worst. He knew Esmeralda and Eli were safe, so he pushed them from his mind. Marching toward the elaborate large iron doors, he clapped his hands together, moved them apart fiercely slamming the doors open before he reached them. Walking through the threshold of the castle entry into the lighted courtyard, his eyes quickly adjusted to the night. He looked over the scenery and saw a huddled group of his people surrounding the detained werewolves in a tight circle. He moved swiftly in his approach to see the werewolves writhing violently from the struggling hold of Phloxous and Sabri.

He noticed their thin, powerful bodies trembling. Their large black eyes narrowed as their teeth gritted in concentration. Together they pushed their powers harder to keep the werewolves from rising to their feet, but it was of no use. The incarcerated werewolves kept breaking through the invisible constraints, taking a few steps forward and falling back on their hands and knees. The routine was redundant. "What's going on? Why isn't anyone helping them?" Conlaoch demanded as he stood unnoticed in the small circle of people who kept their hard, black eyes on the massive, howling creatures.

Reison raised his head from the brawl to see Conlaoch ready for battle. "Good, you're here. I don't know how much longer the women will hold up. These beasts are strong. Once they get them down, the werewolves break the hold and get back up. I've never seen anything break through the holds before. It was a bitch just bringing them here." Reison exclaimed.

"I see that. Did you or the other shape shifters find anymore with them?" Conlaoch asked, looking briefly at the dark haired, golden eyed man.

"No." Reison replied firmly.

Conlaoch nodded as he answered. "You did well, Reison. Take the others, go back into the woods and keep your eyes peeled. It wouldn't surprise me if more are on their way." He didn't wait for a confirming reply from Reison when he pushed through the thinning barrier. Conlaoch saw Ya'Ru standing before the werewolves, apart from the circle, with a look of confusion on his face. He was about to ask what was wrong, but he became interrupted by his friend speaking first.

"I don't know if they're friend or foe. I can't get a read on them. There is a strong barrier over their minds. I've tried and tried, but there is always a high-pitched ringing in my ears and after a few moments it hurts like hell if I try pushing harder past it. It's like daggers in the ears."

"You can't read any of them?" Conlaoch asked as a mixture of astonishment and confusion coursed through his calculating strategy.

"Not one. They say there's a first for everything, but damn." Ya'Ru replied sullenly.

"Were their senses taken from them?" Conlaoch asked briskly.

Ya'Ru nodded. "Their eyes turn white and then quickly fade back to normal, which makes me believe the same happens when we take their hearing. Every symbol we have, we used on them. The only one that has been working decently has been the paralyzing effect, but they're pushing it off them. I don't get it. I've never seen this done before. I suggest you bite them soon before we have a massive fight on our hands and we'll have to set them on fire before knowing who they are. They seem almost indestructible."

Conlaoch scoffed. "They're strong. I'll give you that, but they're not indestructible. Everything has a weakness. What makes these prisoners any different?"

Irion walked next to Ya'Ru. Overhearing the conversation, he answered Conlaoch's question. "Bite them to find out what makes them different."

"Take the middle one first, Conlaoch. He has the most will within him." Phloxous yelled through her gritted teeth.

"He's the one breaking through the most often." Sabri snarled as she remained focused.

Conlaoch centered his attention onto the middle creature that gave them the most trouble. He noticed the pitch-black fur of the beast made the creature almost invisible even in the well lit court-yard. However, he quickly noticed when the light caught the creature's shifting golden-brown eyes it made him easier for the beast to become noticed, like now. Conlaoch couldn't help, but to feel smug as he thought, *See, there's a weakness already.*

Grateful the beast he focused his attention on breaking free, Conlaoch began to approach him. Immediately, the massive were-wolf took advantage of his closing proximity and lunged at him. His large clawed paw swiped the air, aiming for his chest, but Conlaoch stepped aside causing the creature to miss his aim. Falling back to the ground from the crushing weight of Sabri's and Phloxous powers, the creature snapped and licked his teeth as his hinged wrath fumed within him. Conlaoch growled low, his coiled muscles finally sprung to life from his withheld rage breaking free. In a flash Conlaoch was behind the massive, kneeling werewolf, when he revealed his long dagger like fangs. Conlaoch stabbed his fangs into the beast's neck, striking a warm vein.

Gabrio howled loudly from the gashing pain he felt. He could feel the black-eyed man's teeth slide into the firm, tensed muscles of his neck. His blood poured like wine into the man's waiting, suckling lips. A light breeze passed through the courtyard and Esmeralda's scent surrounded him. She's here. He knew she was in the accursed castle and the black-eyed demons were keeping them from rescuing her. Gabrio saw tunnel vision and sunk his teeth into the man's shoulder and seen a whirlwind of visions of his wife becoming captured and the duration of her time at Raven Eye Castle. He began to rise once more, but fell back to the ground.

Gabrio yelled to Raul and Marrok as he held firm into Conlaoch's shoulder. "I saw her! She's here in the castle, placed by this fucker drinking my blood."

"He dies first." Raul replied as he clawed the ground trying to lift himself from his knees.

"He'll die by my hands." Gabrio retorted.

"We'll have your back when you choose the moment to kill him." Marrok said as he was pushed back to the ground.

Conlaoch felt the pain sharp in his shoulder sharpen as the creature's stronghold became fierce, making him release a yell of distress into the Beast Blood's fur. His face cringed as he fought the pain. However, he didn't break his suckling hold from the creature, even when he felt him trying to rise again. Despite the creature's blood being clean of any demonic influence, Conlaoch still held him down with all of his might. He needed to know who the man hidden under the fur was. Conlaoch saw bursts of colors flood his mind's eye. The beast's identity was coming forth through. Conlaoch's eyes widened when it was clear to him, who they were.

He released his hold from the creature and saw the symbol for himself, glowing beneath the fur. He stepped away from the three beings and shock overcame him as he wiped his hand over his face to clean himself of the werewolf's blood. "Release them now." Conlaoch yelled at Sabri and Phloxous.

The women looked at each other and did as he asked them to do. Their hands fell to their sides and the auras of their powers were gone from the beasts they wrestled to keep down.

Gabrio, Marrok and Raul sprung to their feet from the ground in an instant. Their height and lean girth surpassed the black eyed demons. They towered over them. All thirteen members looked at the three Beast Blood's, ready to fight on command, except Ja'Har who looked more afraid at seeing the startling sight of the vicious creatures and had thoughts of running from them more than fighting against them. Gabrio turned around as he released a loud thundering roar when he knew Conlaoch stood behind him away from his kind. Immediately, Marrok and Raul guarded his back as the Blood Taster's began to step forward in their attack.

Before Conlaoch could react Gabrio had him by the throat. Forcibly, he pushed him against the stone courtyard wall with a heavy thud causing the some stones to fall through the other side. Conlaoch's' feet dangled several feet from the ground as Gabrio dragged his body up the wall and they looked at each other at eye level. Conlaoch could feel his windpipe becoming restricted from air as he felt Gabrio squeeze his neck slowly. In fluid movement, he hurriedly punched Gabrio in the face as he lifted his legs, pressing his back harder into the stone wall forcefully kicking him away. Gabrio propelled backward several feet back from Conlaoch's forceful attack, which allowed a long enough moment for him to fall to the ground on his feet. He saw Gabrio run at in a blur toward him, but he didn't back down. "I know who you are Guardian. You're marked with the angelic symbol, just as we all are." Conlaoch yelled at him while he peeled his shirt from his body to reveal the different swirling patterns over his muscled body.

Gabrio stopped a mere inch from Conlaoch. His snarling face fell into a dismal severity as he saw how the symbols swirled and blazed over his skin. Gabrio knew he was a Blood Taster, made of angelic, mortal and demon blood. However, what the man did to his wife- captured her, chained her naked for three days in her own filth as he lusted after her body- was reason enough for him to greet death. Gabrio craved to see the man's body bleeding out on the very ground they stood on, but he remained marked by the symbols. He knew Conlaoch was a guardian as well as Marrok and Raul.

Conlaoch could hear the subtle whispers among the Order about there being a remaining Guardian werewolf in their presence. Little did they know, thus far there were three Beast Blood guardians and all were in the courtyard with them. He kept his eyes locked onto Gabrio and took advantage of Gabrio's hesitancy as a sign to talk further. "Change in your human skin. You will not become harmed here. Not by us, at least." Conlaoch stated truthfully.

Gabrio was unsure of what do to as he looked at Marrok and Raul, whom stared blankly back at him. Not a word came through. He looked back at the black-eyed, dark haired man and seen his pulse was steady as his eyes. They held the truth, but he still wasn't willing to risk it when he was so close to getting his wife back. Gabrio growled at Conlaoch as a fair warning of what was to come.

"Esmeralda, Carrier of the Hybrid, your wife. She is safe as well as the Hybrid. Your son is safe. They're both safe inside and under the Order of Draco. The three of you, change into your human skins and I'll take you to see Esmeralda. We'll discuss what is to happen after that." Conlaoch stated, hoping they would lower their defenses.

"I don't think they're going to fight us Gabrio. I think that one next to you is their leader and they respect him enough to not try anything hasty." Marrok reasoned.

"We are just as strong in our human skin and indestructible as if we remained in our wolf forms. We're unsure if we should change back, but I need to see my daughter to know if she's okay. I know you need to see her too. More than any of us and I get that. With that said, we came to rescue her and now we're here. So, let's go get her." Raul appealed.

Gabrio's reply was hoarse as he looked at the cobblestone ground. "I'm nothing without her and if she's not there I just don't know what I'll do."

"We smell her on the air. These people have been around Esmeralda. They all smell of her. It's mild, but noticeable. She's here, Gabrio. If they moved her on our arrival I'll be sure to seek her out. However, we have to put our trust into their hands or else we'll be here all night wondering if we should or shouldn't." Raul rationalized to his son-in-law.

"If anything goes awry, we can always fight them." Marrok commented.

Gabrio knew he was right and gave a small, wordless nod.

I'll change first, Gabrio. I have nothing to lose if they were to try anything." Marrok dutifully said.

As instant as thought, Marrok became surrounded by the changing flame, before Gabrio or Raul could talk him out of it. When Marrok emerged from the swirling smoke, he did so naked. He flexed his muscles as he straightened his spine, appearing vulnerable and foreboding at the same time. He looked at the varying beautiful faces of the Blood Tasters giving them all a challenging look. Not one person moved from their unyielding stance. They looked at him with emotionless expressions. Raul quickly changed next, joining Marrok to stand before them while leaving Gabrio as the reluctant remainder. Gabrio gave a hard look at Conlaoch and sighed. He knew he had no other choice if he wanted to see his wife. He said the word that would change him back into a man and stood next to his kin. Together they stood naked before the group of Blood Tasters.

After a few moments Gabrio spoke. "We've changed, Blood

Taster. Now, take us to my wife." He ordered as he watched Conlaoch circle to stand direct in front of them.

Conlaoch nodded, turned around and commanded his people. "All know, these three beings are now under this roof as one of us. They are the Guardians of the Beast Blood symbol, the last of their kind. Not only are they Guardians, but they happen to be the Carrier's kin. They are our allies, not our enemy. They demand the highest treatment with respect and honor. Now, all of you get back to your posts in case any more visitors decide to crawl through the woods and try to breech our walls. We now have more men to protect Esmeralda- the Carrier." Conlaoch remained silent as he seen his people give him looks and nods of their understanding. Conlaoch began walking forward toward the castle, through the crowd of people. He spoke gruffly to the three Beast Bloods that walked swiftly next to him. "I'll have Samuel fetch clothes for the three of you to wear."

"Why did you take her from me- her family, Conlaoch?" Gabrio growled.

Conlaoch didn't want to discuss the reasons right at the very moment. He never thought he was ever going to face Esmeralda's husband. Let alone her father and brother to explain his actions. However, he felt what he did remained justified and spoke equally frank. "I saw the signs. Do you think the Beast Blood's increased only in the states? How many are there now? Two-three hundred? In Scotland there were about a hundred and fifty werewolves. Now, there is nearly three hundred here. Call it divine intervention, but I was lead to your clan. Then, they directed to your small town in Michigan. There, I found your wife. She didn't change right away and that led me to believe she was the carrier of the hybrid. Come to find out I was right."

Together the men stepped into the great hall and Conlaoch saw his faithful servant Samuel waiting for him. He ran an agitated hand through his hair as he approached the balding, smiling man.

"Samuel. Good you're already here. Find these men some clothes, they are..."

Samuel interrupted. "Our guests, but they're much more than that. I already know. I heard your voice carry from the courtyard into the kitchen. The hallways do echo very loudly. So, once I heard your commands, I decided to meet you here to find out what you needed from me to assist them."

Conlaoch smiled warmly at his servant and was never more grateful for his service than at that very moment. "Thank you, Samuel. All I require is that you find these men some clothes."

Samuel gave a curt nod as he slightly bowed. "Sir, I believe they're close to your size. No, they're a bit stockier in the chest and arms. I'm sure we'll have some items for them in the servants quarters. I'll be back quickly." Then he left them in haste.

Waiting for Samuel to become removed from their view, Gabrio resumed his questioning. "That still doesn't answer my question. Why did you take her?"

Conlaoch turned around to face Gabrio and the other two men. "You're not a foolish man. You can read people, just like I can and you know why I took her from the Ancient Ritual that night."

Raul spoke up, nearly yelling. "I'm her father. I don't know why you took her from us! For days on end, we worried about her. Not understanding why or how she could suddenly disappear while chasing our own. She grew up in our state. She knew those woods since a little girl and yet, nothing. We found nothing of her or of her captor! Now, we have. So, answer the fucking question!"

Conlaoch released a deep audible sigh. "I had to allure her to keep her safe and it was the smartest choice to make. By Gabrio's thoughts, all of you had no clue what was happening and why until a few days ago. For the past several weeks I've kept her and her child safe from those that wish to seek harm on them both. There are some that would love the power he will have.

Shocked, Gabrio looked at Conlaoch. "He. A boy. I'm having a son."

Conlaoch ignored him as he continued to speak. "Esmeralda would've died with your him in her belly and you wouldn't even know why or who did it! At least here, she remained safe from the very persons that would've left your wife's baby-less, corpse at your door."

Gabrio became angry again and yelled. "Kept her safe? For three days you had her chained naked as if she was your plaything! You admired her body and lusted after her. You treated her as if she was a prisoner. Brought to this fucking gaudy place for your sexual pleasure when you found it fit. It's true you didn't touch her, but you didn't think I was going to show up. You thought I was weak, would leave my wife behind and I would simply just move on, while you tried to fuck her. I should just rip your fucking throat out." Gabrio snarled as he dived at Conlaoch. Grabbing him by the throat, he began punching Conlaoch over and over in his face.

Marrok was about to join in the fight, but Raul held him back, shaking his head."No! It's a fight between them!" Raul explained and he and Marrok watched both men, fight with increasing vigor.

Sounds of fleshy pops, grunts and groans echoed loudly as both men threw their solid punches, making their desired contact every time one threw a hit. Conlaoch saw another fist was heading toward his face as he hurriedly grabbed the meaty, balled hand before it hit its mark again. He held firm onto Gabrio's tight fist as he took another punch at Gabrio's stomach, causing him to bend to the side. Gabrio threw an uppercut punch under Conlaoch's chin, throwing his head back.

Ya'Ru heard the noises of the brawl from outside the castle doors and ran inside. Immediately, he observed the fight between Esmeralda's husband and Conlaoch, as the other two watched in smug satisfaction. It was an equal match between them, each throwing and receiving their fair share of the quarrel. However, he knew their small army didn't need any division within the barracks. Especially when there were worse beings that could be coming for them, which they would have to deal with collectively. He didn't care how it started, but Ya'Ru planned on finishing it. He ran up to Gabrio, who was ready to throw another landing blow to Conloach's ribs, and turned him around to land his own heavy fist into the werewolf's face. The loud popping sound was the last one heard as it ended the fight immediately.

Conlaoch saw what his friend did to Gabrio and shook his head as he fought to find his breath. "Ya'Ru! That is not necessary! He was fighting for his wife and her honor. I would do the same in his situation." Conlaoch replied diplomatically as he wiped traces of his blood from his lip, catching his breath in deep inhales.

Ya'Ru didn't understand as he looked between the werewolves and Conlaoch. He saw Gabrio panting heavily as well, glaring at Conlaoch with the thick trails of glistening blood under his nose. He watched him use the back of his hand to wipe the blood away. Ya' Ru shook his head and replied just as so. "I don't understand this, but what I do understand is that we are not to become divided. Whatever the reason, we are not to become divided. We know why we're here. Now, all of you get your shit together before God himself decides to wipe all of us off the face of the blasted earth. We have a demon werewolf to watch out for and we have to remain prepared to destroy whatever comes in our path to make sure Esmeralda and the child's safe."

Silence filled the air as they looked at one another. Neither Conlaoch nor Gabrio felt shame for their fighting, but they knew Ya'Ru made a great point. They both gave each other a curt nod as if to call it a truce for now. Ya'Ru was about to speak again, but the silence became interrupted by the thumping waves of Samuel's heavy footsteps, followed by his voice.

"Here you are, gentlemen." Samuel walked closer to the group of men and seen Conlaoch's and Gabrio's bloody face and knuckles. Samuel began clicking his tongue as he shook his head. "I see there has been some disrespect of the guests and of the host. Not a matter now, I guess, since I see Ya'Ru's in here looking like he took the role of a scolding parent over a group of bickering children. Like I said, Sirs, here are your clothes. They should fit you well. I hope you find them to your comfort." Samuel observed and stated all in one flush breath as he handed the naked men their items of clothing.

"Thank you for your services, Samuel you may leave to prepare a meal for these men, as well as our own men and women. I'm sure everyone would enjoy a little more to eat and drink on an eventful night such as this one." Conlaoch kindly ordered.

"Very well, I'll go now." Samuel bowed and left the room once more.

Conlaoch turned to view the three Beast Bloods were finishing getting dressed in the well fitting clothes Samuel picked out for them. He spoke plainly to them. "Good. Now, that you're dressed, I'll take you to Esmeralda's room."

"Is she even in there?" Gabrio snarled as he followed Conlaoch up the wide steps and down the long corridor.

Conlaoch grimaced. "I'm many roles, Gabrio, but I'm not a liar. She's in there. I was checking on her when I became alerted of your arrival. Since, I found out who she was and who she carried, I took her from the dungeon and put her in Alexandria's old room. It's the most luxurious room in the castle. I thought she would have more comfort in there than any other room. It also had a connecting bathroom, which aloud her privacy given her condition. However, she was never to leave without someone with her. So, since her duration here, I've always put a symbol on the windows and doors to keep her in and everyone else out. I'm the only one that can release the symbol, once I've activated it."

Conlaoch's explanation helped ease their minds, but until Esmeralda was standing before them, they would remain on edge. Slowing their walk to stand in front of a lavish wooden door, that sounded a small pulsing hum, Conlaoch announced their arrival. He waved his hand over the door as he said a word and the symbol faded from the face of the door as well did the noise. Conlaoch turned the decorative, gilded doorknob and pushed the wooden door inward. As the door swung open, it revealed a ram-sacked room with scattered clothes, broken furniture and the strong familiar scent of Esmeralda. They scattered throughout the room, searching for her.

"Esmeralda!" Gabrio yelled as he finished searching the connecting parlor and bathroom. He caught a metallic, iron smell and knew it was her blood. Fear pumped his heart as he sniffed the air.

"She's not here." Raul bellowed.

"I smell her blood. Why would she be bleeding Conlaoch?" Did you leave her wounded?" Gabrio asked angrily, frantically looking around the room for her.

"Don't be a fucking idiot, Gabrio. Now that it's agreed by the Order she wasn't a threat to Eli, I wouldn't dare harm her, nor would any of my people!"

"Who's Eli?" Marrok asked raising a golden eyebrow as he lifted himself from looking under the large bed.

"Your nephew, she named him Eli. She was sick of people referring to her son as a nameless thing. So she named him Eli."

Touched, Esmeralda would honor his father, he commented."She named my son after my father. My selfless Essie, thinking of something as simple as a name when she's trapped here." His eyes furrowed as his heart pounded with fear. "Did any of you find anything?" Gabrio snarled as he swelled with panic.

Raul answered in short sentences as he concentrated. "I smell someone else. Someone else was in this room with her. I smell their scent on the air, it's fresh. I know that scent. I've smelled it before, but I can't place it."

He continued to sniff the air as it led him to the wardrobe. The scent of Esmeralda and the stranger became stronger. He saw the busted back paneling, a deep dark tunnel with a bloody hand prints surrounding the opening. He was sure it was Esmeralda's hand print, sliding from the smooth wood to the rocky foundation. He stuck his head inside the tunnel and seen it was endless. "There's a tunnel. Esmeralda's went through this tunnel." Raul yelled, his voice echoing through the dark tube.

"Like hell there is a fucking tunnel!" Conlaoch shouted as anger began to rise once more into his body. He pushed Raul out of the way to see for himself and his eyes didn't fail him.

"Are you trying to say that you didn't know about the secret tunnel behind the fucking wardrobe?" Gabrio hollered loudly.

Conlaoch became rigid as he began to scurry his mind to remember, but panic and fear scattered his brain. "No! I didn't know about the fucking tunnel or else I would've put her in another room. I've lived in this castle for hundreds of years and not once did I know about this." Conlaoch yelled.

"Who else would've known about this tunnel, then?" Gabrio interrogated.

Raul took one last deep breath inside the tunnel and the stranger's scent clicked with him. "Sheryl! That's who took her through this tunnel! That's her scent that's lingering around."

"Sheryl? What the fuck is she doing here and why would she take Esmeralda?" Gabrio asked Raul as he looked at Conlaoch's shocked features.

Gabrio's face furrowed as he began to snarl. "What's wrong with you Conlaoch?"

"Esmeralda's dream of Sheryl taking your son. Then the world was in chaos." Conlaoch mumbled as he pieced the shattered clues together. They began to take shape. Then suddenly he yelled, startling all of them. "Sheryl's the truer sin! She's going to hurt them both! We need to find your wife now before it's too late! Dawn is here and that's our advantage."

Meanwhile

Slowly coming to consciousness, Esmeralda could hear the small stirrings of snapping sounds and could feel the tiniest of sensations flooding her shaken nerves. She could smell the earth around her signifying she didn't imagine becoming carried from a hole in the ground to end in the middle of the woods. She was out of the castle. She felt as if she was swinging, but soon realized she was moving. She could feel the cradling embrace of someone carrying her. They were warm, too warm. Then the sensation became overwhelmingly hot as if she was roasting in the desert sun. Cringing against the burning heat she felt against her skin, Esmeralda fully awakened. Her vision began to fade into a clarifying focus as she wildly blinked her eyes lids. Everything was upside down. She could see the streaks of vibrant color of golden yellow cast through the sky as the morning began to creep over the entire land.

Esmeralda lifted her head and seen she was still moving through the forest. Still feeling uncomfortable and practically on fire, she struggled to free herself from the gripping hold of the werewolf's arms. Then she remembered seeing Sheryl's crystal blue eyes peeping at her from the wardrobe. Esmeralda struggled harder, remembering her dream; she wanted to be far from the person she knew wanted to harm her. "Sheryl! Put me down now!" Esmeralda demanded as she looked up and saw the blood red eyes of the werewolf from her nightmares, looking down at her. He was the one who carried her through the forest, not Sheryl. She grasped and released an ear-shattering scream through the forest, causing birds to leave the trees in a fluttering cloud.

"Let her scream all she wants Laycerath. We're already at Black Water. Once we change in our human forms. I'm going to perform the spell." Sheryl coldly stated, uncaring about Esmeralda's sudden fear.

Laycerath didn't reply only stared straight ahead at their destination. Walking through the ruins, which the wildlife and the creatures overran, they moved under the curtains of moss, various growing vines and roots. Once they entered the heart of the ruin, Laycerath dropped Esmeralda on the ground. She landed with a hard thud on the stone floor as tears fell silently down her cheeks.

"Strap her to the stone alter so she doesn't decide to run when we change." Sheryl demanded Laycerath.

Crying even harder, her heart wrenching sobs became lost on deaf ears as Laycerath dragged her through the dirt by the roots of her hair to the stone altar. Esmeralda screamed at the pain, burning in her skull from him pulling and pulled his hand down to her mouth to clamp hard onto his palm, taking a chunk of flesh from his hand.

He growled a yell from the pain she caused him. "You fucking bitch!"

Still holding on tightly to her hair, he took his free hand and slapped her hard across her face, releasing another scream from her. Then he lifted her from the ground, tossing her body onto the stone alter like she was a rag doll. Holding her down, he began to pull her arm above her head, to tie them to the stone posts that came from the corners of the altar.

Once she was secure Laycerath nodded his head at Sheryl and together they left the ruins to head into the sunlight. Esmeralda looked around and seen the damp, crumbling foundation of once a grand castle. She tried busting through the old leather straps and strong roots. Together, they were firm and unyielding around her wrists.

Sheryl's voice echoed through the ruins as if she was an unseen ghost. "Trying to break free, Esmeralda?"

Through deep sobs Esmeralda spoke to Sheryl, but she couldn't see her. "Why? Why are you doing this to me, you fucking cunt! I've trusted you." She sobbed.

Out of the darkness, Sheryl and Laycerath appeared. Their eyes illuminated from the darkness. Both remained naked, their long hair flowed around them in long waves as if they were wild savages ready to sacrifice their meal to the pagan gods. She caught sight of the glittering medallion hanging low upon Sheryl's chest. The salt from her running tears, stung the open bleeding gouges, Sheryl cut into her cheek from when she took her from her room. Sheryl's eyes were wild and her teeth bared as her lips curled over them. Esmeralda could plainly see that she had snapped.

Sheryl yelled increasingly. "Why? Because I fucking can, that's why! I have lived too long waiting for this moment to get my fucking revenge on it all! You're just a mere pawn in this fucked up plan called 'life'. Everyone makes choices, right or wrong and you're still fucking screwed in the end.

Cast out of grace, forgotten by the almighty creator. To watch your family, your husband and children die as well as their children and their children's, children. I remained behind to become continuously punished. All because of my lack of fucking knowledge, but it wasn't my fault. I was blind. Created by lack of sight about the world. I have been a pawn just like you!" She gave Esmeralda a cold stare.

Esmeralda became lost within her riddling rant. She didn't understand Sheryl's need to kill her for her unborn child. "Why my son? Why not have one of your fucking own?"

Sheryl looked incredulously at her as her eyes rapidly blinked as if she suddenly developed a nervous twitch. "Please tell me you're really not that fucking stupid. Here I gave you more credit than that. Let me explain it to you, slowly, so you can understand, why." Sheryl began to walk around the pale stone alter, lightly pressing the tip of the shinny, silver dagger into her fingertips, rocking the item in a back and forth motion. "Once upon a time the universe was dark and God said, "Let there be light" and light replaced the darkness. After that he created the night, the sea the air, land, water, creatures and then man. He saw that all were good. He named the man Adam."

Esmeralda saw Sheryl's eyes glass over as if she was remembering a memory and watching the replay in her mind's eye.

"Adam was a beautiful man with golden blonde hair and eyes greener than the green of leaves. He was a fine man and with a pure heart." Sheryl's expression turned even darker. "But, God saw the man was lonely. He created a woman for the man, using a rib from Adam and along came Eve. Together they thrived in the paradise God created for them. Eden. All three beings were happy and loved one another dearly. God would talk to them, teach them, but he still kept them ignorant like an overprotective parent. He forbade them to eat from the Tree of Knowledge. The Tree of Good and Evil.

Adam and Eve would walk by that accursed tree everyday and we were loyal. Always loyal to that one rule. Until one day, Eve wanted to surprise Adam and woke up before him to do so. She ran through the paradise to hurry before he awoke. Eve ran passed the forbidden tree and became stopped by a serpent hanging from its branch. The serpent was black and abnormally large. It hung in front of me and swayed back and forth in a hypnotic fashion, like a swinging pendulum in a clock."

Esmeralda caught on as Sheryl began describing herself. Then Esmeralda's understanding was a revelation of clarity. "Oh my God, you're Eve. You're the creator of the original sin. You're the Truer Sin that everyone's been talking about."

The rambling woman didn't hear Esmeralda and continued talking. "The snake began to talk to me, seducing me with its words and his sway and before I knew it, I bit the bitter fruit. The juice from the fruit was as red as blood, poured from my mouth in a crimson gush. I tried spitting it out, but it was too late. I knew shame, I knew violence and I knew hate. Sex, greed and even death. I knew everything and a doubted everything. However, my mind was not my own not just yet. The snake seduced me even further. Take the fruit to Adam; that's what the snake wanted me to do. I became forced to use his trust against him and he too bit the fruit."

Sheryl's past emotions and expressions had shown clear on her face now as she relived it. "After God found out what we've done, he sent his precious Michael with the sword of fire to cast us out of Eden. We became cast out of Eden without another word from

God. Without another word from that fucking serpent. All because of myself becoming created to be so damn naïve, I didn't know the repercussions. I knew nothing. Yet, we became punished! Day after day, I spoke to the Heavens to forgive us. I pleaded. Begged, but he closed us off forever. We still loved God even when we scrapped for food, savagely killing any of the animals we saw, that we once cared for, drinking fresh water only when it rained. The land was barren. It was a hell of its own, but we survived. Then we created our own world!" She turned back to reality as she spoke to Esmeralda. "It wasn't until my sons Caine and Abel, went into the field. Then, Caine was the only one to return. This is when my hatred for the Devil and the Creator began to grow. Yet, what made it bloom is when Adam died and what made it flourish is when God never took me. After all these years, God never took me. I remained a pawn and it cost me everything. So, I turned my back on both of them and I found my own power within witchcraft, the blood of the werewolves and other sources. Now with the birth of your son and how he's the prophesied one, it offers the chance to gain ultimate power over the sick tug-of-war of God verses the Devil."

Esmeralda was about to speak, but the woman looked at her and scolded. No, no, Esmeralda, wait your turn, I'm still talking. She watched Laycerath place a large, pressing hand over Esmeralda's mouth to quiet her further. Satisfied, she continued. "See, Esmeralda, a war is coming in the future and as well as you know your son will be on the right hand side of God. He will be Michael's guard dog, always close to his side. However, if we placed another creature in your son's place." Sheryl flicked her eyes over Laycerath to Esmeralda's slightly expanded belly. "If we transferred another werewolf's soul in place of your son's wholesome one, the new big, bad wolf can destroy it all, starting with Michael."

Esmeralda snarled at the woman. "You have another thing coming if you think that God won't protect me or at least, my child, from your fucked up revenge."

Eve walked over to Esmeralda and pressed her forehead against hers. Esmeralda tried to shy away, but Sheryl pressed the knife into her throat to keep her head in place. She gave her a smug look. "We will see where your faith gets you Essie, because so far it's taken you here."

Eve moved from Esmeralda and walked toward Laycerath. "What do you say, stepson? Do you think it's time for her final ritual or did you want to play with her first? Use her tight little body for your pleasures. I'll leave to let you do so."

Laycerath's deep voice boomed throughout the ruins. "No. I don't want to linger anymore than you already have, explaining your life's story. I'm as ready as I'll ever be."

Sheryl smiled. "Let's proceed."

25

THE SWORD OF FLAMES.

Eve's long white hair flowed behind her as she strutted to the end of the stone alter Esmeralda laid on. Her cold, twinkling eyes matched her tight smirk as she lifted her hands to remove the ancient looking medallion from her long neck. She stared at Esmeralda's whimpering silhouette in satisfaction as she twisted the seven seals from their melding hold and placed them in careful order on the stone platform. She noticed Esmeralda watched her as well with a quivering hateful predatory gaze. She scoffed and openly mocked her. "Essie, please don't hate me for doing this. It's not like I enjoy doing this to you. Well, maybe a little, but you can't blame me for that. This has been a long time of waiting. I was just like everyone else, waiting to see who it was going to be, when everything was going to line just right. Then when the signs came I looked even harder, but come to find out it was you, all along. You were right under my nose. Imagine my excitement." Her thoughts changed course as she scowled in her past frustration. "If that fucking Blood Taster didn't take you that night I was going to. Not that very night, of course, but I was going to take my time and use you when the moment was right. However, it all worked out for us. Now, you're here. Once everything is complete, we'll lose ourselves within this world. No one will track you for very long without having a constant chase."

Eve stopped her action of laying down the medallions for a brief moment once she circled the square platform near Esmeralda's head. She leaned over Esmeralda to stare into her blood streaked face and puffy red eyes that glistened with endless tears. She huffed at her again, resuming her task, placing a silver disk on the stone table, near the top of Esmeralda's head. Her slick tone of voice turned harsh. "Blood, tears and fear, you're so weak right now, Essie. It's not like you'll die today. You'll live, until Laycerath's reborn. Then, I'll make your death quick. It's the least I can do for you when you're going to give me the greatest creation since God sent his only son to the undeserving, withering fools of mankind. He could forgive those fucking idiots, but not me. He left me here to wallow in this shit-hole of a world, but you should be happy to be part of the new world. A better world."

"What makes you think I won't take my life as well as his fucked up existence? I'll just end it all for you." Esmeralda screamed.

"You won't. You might have the blood of a demon, but your heart is pure and once he's born, I'll feed him your fucking golden heart." Eve shouted at her. Then she slowly whispered in Esmeralda's ear. "So, you better become used to whom we really are Esmeralda. Because for the next, oh, I'm going to say about five months, it's only going to the three of us." She stood upright and completed laying down the last silvered disk and smiled widely as the large disks began to glow around Esmeralda's spread body. "Laycerath, come here. The disks are in place and now all we need is you." She said in a light, contented tone.

Laycerath walked from the shadows. His long black hair glistened in the streams of light that poured through the crumbling stone ceiling. Even when the light hit his skin, he seemed always to be in constant shadow. Esmeralda saw he was just as evil in his human skin as he was in his werewolf form. She saw his naked body had scars crossing in large puffed streaks across his chest, back, stomach and one circling his thick neck. He stared down at her with a fierceness of pure evil as he stood next to Eve, then he smiled revealing his pointed teeth. Laycerath leaned down over Esmeralda smelling her cascading hair, releasing a sound of pleasure. She thrashed her head to the side, but he grabbed her beautiful face back into his view. His gaze lingered over her features for a brief moment. Suddenly he thrust his tongue on her skin as he licked the side of her cheek, leaving a wet streak of rancid saliva. Esmeralda's fear clogged her throat as she unwillingly lingered her gaze on him. She felt Sheryl tugging on her shirt to show her expanding belly. Laycerath moved his hands from the side of her face and allowed her to see what Eve was doing next.

Eve marveled at the revealed skin and rubbed a bony cold hand over the showing mound. The tiny infant began to stir underneath, pushing against the skin from inside the womb. She looked at the moving child in a daze. Her voice was wispy as she spoke into herself. "Look how beautiful life is. Someone so tiny will grow into someone so powerful. He'll be mine." As soon as the words became uttered from her mouth, the well placed medallions around Esmeralda began to glow brighter. They sparked and turned into columns of flames, creating a cage of inferno around her. Esmeralda looked around her as she stared in horror. She could feel the hot flames around the edge of her body, singeing her skin when the flames swayed too close. Quickly she snapped her head to the side and saw Eve grab the silver dagger she had once placed to her throat. She began to circle the stone platform headed toward Laycerath with the dagger tightly placed in her hand.

The blaze of the fire illuminated the large shaded ruins. The red glow of the fiery beams filled the room, making darkest of shadows appear deeper. The flames danced in Eve's wide eyes as he slowly walked closer to Laycerath."This dagger will kill you. Your blood's needed next. It'll pour on her stomach from your throat, over the unborn. Your blood will soak deep into her skin as if it craved it. Your death will be swift, releasing your soul. You won't see, you won't hear, but you'll feel the flames that surround her. Then you'll be drawn to your blood and her blood mixing. Your soul will enter the womb Then, all will become completed. Are you ready?" Sheryl asked.

Laycerath looked into Eve's eyes as he curtly nodded signifying that he was ready to face death. Pleased with his answer, she lovingly touched his cheek and spoke tenderly. "It'll be all ours. My greatest revenge and your ultimate power. Nothing will stop us. I'll make sure of that. See you soon, my son. I love you."

Eve quickly raised and pressed the angelic dagger to cut the thick, roping scar around Laycerath's throat. Laycerath saw a quick darting shadow run behind his stepmother and merge within the darkness. He narrowed his eyes as he searched the darkness. Seeing nothing at first, he waited and became greeted by fiery golden, brown eyes staring at him. Laycerath's face twisted as he shouted in a deep booming voice, pushing the moved the dagger from his already pricked neck. "They're here, behind you."

Eve twisted her naked body to look behind her and saw Gabrio's massive body lunging at her in the form of a Beast Blood. Fear crossed over her as she saw the sheer intent of her death within his familiar eyes. "Gabrio. No, he can't be the guardian." Eve whispered in horror. Reacting quickly to his advance, Eve turned her body and in fluid movement, she sliced deeply into Gabrio's chest.

Within his pain, Gabrio loudly roared as he took his large paw and smacked Eve across the face. Sheryl's head cracked against the stone alter as she fell to the floor. The dagger fell from her hands and skidded across the ground with a metallic clanking, landing near Laycerath's bare feet.

Laycerath looked at Eve's naked body lying unmoving and quickly saw the small puddle of deep red blood creating a morbid halo around her head. He glared at Gabrio becoming enraged he roared loudly. The ground began to shake violently while the walls crumbled down around them, revealing the sunlit field. The earth cracked loudly. The stone floor shattered like glass in a large circle around Eve, Laycerath and the fiery stone table. Esmeralda screamed loudly as she struggled to break free. The floor disintegrated creating a black immense sinkhole around them and the small surrounding army of Beast Bloods and Blood Tasters.

Gabrio jumped backward, bumping into Marrok and Raul preventing from becoming swallowed by the sinking ground. "Move! The demon werewolf is sinking the ground around them!" Gabrio yelled.

"Where is she? Is she okay?" Raul bellowed as he saw the increasing mass of the widening abyss.

"They have her strapped to the stone altar. She's struggling to break free." Marrok loudly replied through the increasing noise.

A dark, unearthly groan came from the large, surrounding depths and the morning sky, once fully bloomed with the sun, began to darken. A black orb, larger than the sun moved across its lustrous light creating an eclipse. All was under darkness.

"Anuk fu' resio!" Laycerath's snarled in a deep, demonic voice as he raised his clawing hands above his head.

Suddenly the depths of the hollow circle exploded with a burst of fiery light. A black oozing sludge snuffed the blinding light and began to boil, arising out of the sinkhole. It overflowed, spreading across the ground. The sludge began to bubble upward as distorted figures formed within the sludge, creating mangled and twisted bodies slicked in glistening black.

Irion narrowed his eyes through the dark. "Are those what I think they are?" He asked incredulous.

"The demon werewolf is with the Truer Sin. He's raising the others Destroy them! Kill them all!" Conlaoch yelled his order as he ran toward the speeding horde.

Leading the others to do the same he used a battling word triggering his angelic symbols. His symbols became streaks of light as he whizzed like a bullet through the field. He watched the creatures of hell, coming closer, overlapping one another in a disturbing wave of high pitched cries and twisted bodies. They clawed their way through, eager to kill those before them. Quickly coming up with an impromptu plan and with his blessed blade in hand he suddenly stopped before the demonic crowd. As if he was giving a halting stance he outstretched his arm with his hand splayed before him and screamed. "*Frieno.*"

In his heightened sense of awareness, Conlaoch saw everything as if it was in slow motion. Several feet lay between him and the ocean of demons. He could see their muscled arms, overly large clawed hands reaching out and his glowing reflection in their black soulless eyes when a blinding burst of light projected from his hand and onto them.

Movement became normal again as he watched the demons burst and burn into charred corpses as they fell to the ground. The heat from the inferno made the beading sweat, turn into streaking droplets on Conlaoch's skin. The smoke billowed, the smell from their bodies made his eyes sting as he held firm. He saw the other demons remained diligent in their attack as they crawled over the scalding corpses.

Beast Bloods and Blood Tasters released their battle cries as corrupted creatures of hell burst forth through the thick, sludge releasing their high-pitched squeals in unison. Thousands of demons slithered, crawled, scurried and flew through the darkness in an overwhelming horde toward the opposing few. In a thudding clash the battle had begun. "There's millions of them still rising!" Conlaoch snarled through gritted teeth warning the others as he defended himself from the demons' rapid attacks.

"Then we kill every one of the bastards!" Sabri replied with a fierceness in her voice as she darted through the ash and fire while taking her angelic swords from the sheaths on her back. Her agile body jumped into the air and landed with a killing blow through a demon's skull. She swung her weapons in finesse as she used a battling word to paralyze them for a split second and run her blade across their necks. Having a moment to look around her, she noticed Marrok became overwhelmed by them. He flailed while becoming unbalanced as he reach behind him to pull them off him, but once one was gone several more would take its place. She saw the creatures were biting into his body and draining him like leeches. Sabri hurriedly sliced through a demon's neck and boldly ran through the battle to aid him before the bleeding creature fell to the ground. She meshed her blades together to create a larger sword, raised the blade over her head. In one clean sweep the demon's that clawed into Marrok's back became sliced in half.

Marrok heared the puncturing sound of the sword going through the demonic creatures. He felt their grip loosen and the weight of them fall off his back. Standing upright, he noticed Sabri, splattered with demon blood, standing beside him fighting the others that came at them. He noticed Raul and Phloxous fought side by side. Their opponents fell with slices on their chests, throats, often times with severed limbs pooling blood at their feet. Looking to Gabrio he saw a demon slithering on its belly, flicking it's dagger like tail behind it heading for Gabrio as he battled it's brethren. Marrok didn't have time to get to him as another mass of demons surrounded him and Sabri. He let out a warning howl to him, but the sound was lost through the demons higher cries.

Already healed from Sheryl's stabbing dagger, Gabrio ripped and sliced through the attacking mass with a violent strength of mind to get to Esmeralda. Covered in his blood and demon blood Gabrio finished killing another winged demon when felt a sharpening pain in his leg. He growled at the disturbance as he saw the slithering creature sinking its rows of pointed teeth deep into the back of his thick, furred leg. Raising it's tail in a swinging force to strike through his torso. Gabrio saw the attack just in time and prevented the attack by grabbing its tail before it could puncture his stomach. Through gritted teeth, he plucked the suckling creature from the ground and from his leg. The demon thrashed wildly in his gripping hands, screeching loudly in its mindless rage as Gabrio's blood poured from the demon's mouth onto the ground. Quickly he sunk his teeth into the demon's body. Feeling his teeth pop through the thin, pale skin he clamped his jaws tightly together and pulled his head back from the demon's chest. He left a gaping gouge in the creature's chest, exposing the chest cavity. Black dregs of sludge poured from the hole and he threw the limp corpse from him as he saw more running from the sinkhole to him.

As if motion began to slow down, he looked through the opaque darkness to see everyone paired together in the midst of battling the vicious creatures that came in unstoppable waves toward them. Chaos reigned as blood and the lifeless bodies of the demons littered the ground into increasing puddles.

They're easy to kill, but they're never going to stop. Gabrio thought as he looked back at the stable center of the collapsed ring of fire. Flicking his eyes the stable ground in the middle of the sinkhole, he saw Laycerath lifting Sheryl onto her feet. She clutched to him, steadying herself and once she could stand Laycerath smacked the handle of the silver dagger in her hand and readied the dagger near his throat. Gabrio saw Laycerath nod his head and knew instantly the demon werewolf was going to try to finish the ritual. "No!" Gabrio screamed when he saw the knife glide across Laycerath's throat. Another around of demons attacked him, preventing him from stopping Laycerath's death. Simultaneously, as the demons tore into his skin, he felt a strange pressure squeezing his head. He felt as if his skull was about to crush under the weight. His ears began to ring and sound became lost to him. Gabrio fell to the ground, kneeling atop of rotting demons. Gabrio shook his head, trying to rid of the numbing sensation and of the writhing creatures attached to his body. The ringing began to increase in volume as the pressure continued, creating an unbearable pain. He couldn't take it anymore. Gabrio arched his back as he released a howl that echoed vociferously through the deafening noise of the battle.

The sky began to rumble in reply as a stark beam of white light broke through the black orb that covered the sun and fell over the raging combat like a focused spotlight. Spontaneously, the demons' skin started to smolder under the intensity of the sun's light, eventually catching fire. Their shrill wails of tormenting pain gurgled through their blood filled throats as their bodies melted in their inferno, killing them.

Eve looked over the falling demons and saw her defenses were failing. Her eyes fell upon Laycerath's lifeless body and noticed his soulless eyes looking at her. His head rested awkwardly on the ground and blood gushed from his throat. Quickly casting a look at the blinding light, she winced against the pain it caused her. She covered her face from the light with her clumping, blood soaked hair as she dropped to the ground to scoop the crimson liquid into her hands. Holding back tears, she trembled in anticipation as she felt the warm blood of her stepson seep into the hairline cracks on her cupped hands. She looked at Esmeralda, who was still roped and surrounded by the columns of flames. Eve rose to stand, wobbling until she found her footing. She knew there was no going back now. She had to finish what she started and do it quickly.

Having the last of the demons fall to the ground, Conlaoch hollered their victory. He rightly joined his people, who cheered with him. Conlaoch looked around him and saw everyone, covered in dirt and blood, cheering loudly. Everyone, but Gabrio's voice wasn't heard. Panic struck him as he scanned the horizon to find Gabrio running to the edge of the sinkhole and jump the abyss that separated him from his wife. "Gabrio, don't jump!" Conlaoch yelled and everyone looked to witness the same sight. Gabrio jumped as he became engulfed in the changing white-blue flames.

"He's turning himself back. He's not going to make it." Sabri screamed as she watched with uncertainty.

Everyone was on edge as they watched Gabrio soar over the gaping trench as a werewolf, aiming to land on the solid ground on the other side in his human form. He became lost within the cloud of settling dirt as his fur and the eerie darkness camouflaged him from their sights.

"I don't see him anymore. The fucking dust is too thick. Did he make it?" Marrok asked Raul with worrying concern.

"I'm not sure. I can't see him either." Raul replied while he prayed for his daughters and son-in-law's safety.

In the corner of her gaze, Phloxous caught sight of several darting figures coming through the streaming beam of light. She raised her hand over her eyes to block the radiating luminosity from impairing her vision and focused. From the great distance she saw the figures were wispy silhouettes of light, taking shape in a human form. Watching the hovering creatures in front of the eclipsed sun, she noticed they're built like well-trained men of battle. Strong, warrior like and they didn't move until the last figure of light revealed itself from the beam. Their transparent glow began to solidify into a tangible mass as they darted down to earth. On recognizing the most noticeable part of the beings Phloxous couldn't help, but to smile widely.

Holding on tightly to the rigid edge of the ground, Gabrio gritted his teeth as he pulled his dangling body over the edge. The sharp rocks cut into his naked body as he dragged himself upward. He barely had made it as he jumped the trench as a werewolf to land on the other side in his human skin. He knew there was a slim chance of his survival, but it was a risk he had to take. Lifting his dusty body off the ground, he took several steps forward. He saw Sheryl standing next to the flaming stone altar. Esmeralda thrashed and screamed as she tried to plead for her child's life. Sheryl remained lost in a trance as her cold eyes held the flame, her naked body covered with blood and dirt. She looked the image of a satanic witch. She held her hands, full of Laycerath's blood over Esmeralda's stomach and spoke in a soft tongue, what he figured was a spell. "You get away from her." Gabrio growled as he took cautious steps toward the stone altar.

Esmeralda stopped moving when she heard her husband's voice. An odd mixture of hope and fear radiated throughout her body. She lifted her head as he tried to see where he was, but couldn't get a good view. She could only see the flames and Sheryl. She leaned her head back and tried chewing through the straps, but they wouldn't break. Wrestling her constraints she yelled. "Gabrio, kill her. She's Eve, the mother of sin! Please, stop her now. She's going to kill our son if you don't. Please, Gabrio."

Eve looked down at Esmeralda and flicked her gaze to Gabrio and continued harshly whispering her spell, her mouth moving unnaturally quickly. Her cold stare never left him, but she ignored him like an insubordinate child. The few seconds they watched each other, felt like an eternity. Gabrio could feel the sliver of his remaining sanity grow hot and explode from his lungs. "Leave her be." Gabrio roared at Eve as he charged at her.

Before Eve could get away Gabrio had bitten her in the collarbone to drop her hands, but he stuck paralyzing a nerve. He heard her scream as her muscles tighten as she cringed against the attack. Her blood coated his mouth as he could taste the strange mixture while her ancient existence revealed all who she was and pretended to be since the beginning of time. He ripped himself from her skin and he stumbled back, incredulous of what he witnessed. The remaining blood held visions of the beginning of time, Adam, God, the garden of Eden and time moved forward. He saw flashes of his parents, an unknown man with twisted features and lastly, it flashed to George's death. Her hands held the flame. His eyes returned to see the present and landed on Eve, which tried resuming the spell. "You are Eve!" He said wide-eyed. Then his features quickly changed. "And a murderous bitch!" He snarled leaping to attack her again.

In an instant a blast of light and earth exploded behind Eve, causing them to lose their balance as the fierce impact of the demolishing force violently shook the ground. Eve's hands fell to her side as she tried protecting herself from falling and seen Laycerath's blood drop to the ground. She screamed with dismay and began scanning the ground looking for his puddle of blood. She saw the dark black puddle on the ground. In a scurried frenzy she scooped more into her hand, but had noticed the blood on the ground was already gone, mixed into the earth. The clumpy fell poured from her hands as she looked for Laycerath's body. Gabrio read her thoughts through her expression and rushed to Laycerath's dead body. Just before she could reach Laycerath, Gabrio kicked the man's lifeless body over the ledge into the endless sinkhole.

Eve released another tortured scream as she saw her beloved stepson's body fall and become lost in the darkness of the abyss. Her years of planning destroyed. She killed Laycerath with the angelic blade and could never bring him back. He was gone forever. Her plan had backfired and she was once again left in her own bitterness. Rage overwhelmed her as she looked at Gabrio's figure heading toward her. Ready to attack, she charged toward Gabrio, but became stopped in mid step. Quickly she whisked around by a gripping hand.

She became confronted by a glowing profile of a massively large man with golden-brown hair and eyes of the purest blue. His expression was one of grim sadness. His jaw set in his determination. She couldn't believe what she saw. She noticed the man wore glittering black armor, which stood out against his contrasting enormous dusty gray wings. They fanned behind him proudly. She knew the man right away and looked for his signature weapon. Fear overcame her as she noticed a sword of flames remained held tight within his hands. She looked up at him as she swallowed hard past the lump in her throat. She began weeping. "Michael, let me explain."

Michael wanted to speak and warped time to stop. It was only him and her midst an ending battle. He looked around at the darkness and destruction she caused. Fire spread across the land, lightning struck the ground around them, the sinkholes that surrounded them, the littering bodies of demons and the stench of bloodshed. It was chaos. He looked back at Eve and seen the fear in her eyes and he knew she saw he had a duty to uphold. Finally, he spoke clear and simple. "Ask and you shall receive, Eve. Forgiveness has been always yours, but you couldn't forgive yourself. Bitterness and hate clouded your heart. It ruled your soul and you couldn't accept anything else. You broke the ties, not Him. Now, it's time."

Eve's eyes widened from his revelation. Time resumed. In a flash Michael, whipped the sword of flames through the air, making contact with her frail neck. In a clean sweep he had decapitated her. Eve's stiff body fell to the ground in flames as her head rolled into the dark abyss.

Gabrio heard a short, echoing cry escape Eve's throat as her body became a pillar of flame and then ash. He quickly saw a man with large beautiful wings, sheathing his sword of flames at his hip. He stood over Eve's burning body, staring at the charring corpse expressionless. Gabrio knew who the man was, what he was. He stared at him for several moments incredulous at the vision that was real. Gabrio found his voice and in a low, whisper he said the man's name aloud.

Michael heard the subtle whisper of his name and looked at Gabrio. Their eyes connected and Gabrio fell to his knees as emotion overcame him. Michael wordlessly crouched to the floor and flatly laid his hand on the ground. He looked up at the beaming light and in a swift motion, he flicked his wings, causing a warm brushing wind over the ground. A moment later, the earth groaned as it shifted, moving closer as the land began to mend, causing the large sinkhole to disappear as if it was never there. The rotting piles of demon bodies turned to ash and blew across the land with the warm breeze from Michael's wings. The eclipsed sun broke through in shooting rays, revealing it's healing light across the land. When the dust settled, the world around them was as it should be.

Michael rose to his feet and saw the small gathering of the chosen people running toward them. Beast Bloods and Blood Tasters, bloodied from battle, but remaining the strong, forceful creatures they became to be. Knowing he completed God's plan of action, Michael spread his wings and propelled upward into a shooting ray of light. He joined the others that hovered high above them. Not lingering for a moment more they became lost in the day's light. Everyone stood in awe at the majestic sight. However, Gabrio ran quickly toward Esmeralda as he knocked the medallions from their posts, briefly scalding his hands in the process.

"Gabrio! Oh God, Gabrio." Esmeralda exclaimed as tears of joy streamed heavily down her dirtied, bloodied face as she watched him eagerly use his teeth to free her from her biting constraints. He made quick work of the task.

"There." Gabrio yelled as he pulled the remaining straps from her wrists and questioned her. "Are you hurt? I saw your blood! Where are you bleeding from?"

Once free, Esmeralda sprung herself from the table and met Gabrio's embracing arms. They clutched to each other tightly, both afraid to let go. "No. I'm not hurt. She gouged my face, attacking me before I grabbed anything to defend myself with. She grabbed the blade from under my bed. I'm fine, the baby's fine. Oh, God Gabe. I'm just so glad you're here with me. I thought I was never going to see you again. Now, you're here. You're finally here." Esmeralda choked on her sobs as she cried into Gabrio's neck.

Gabrio held her tightly. "God, Essie, the world doesn't spin without you. Nothing will keep you away from me again! I'll make damn sure of that. I've missed you so much Esmeralda. I love you so much." Gabrio looked down at her, nuzzling her face with his as he left trails of kisses. Unsatisfied, Esmeralda greedily grabbed his head, closed her eyes tightly and pressed her lips to his in a feverish need, putting all her unyielding love for her husband in the reuniting kiss. With equal passion and longing Gabrio kissed her back.

After several moments their lips reluctantly parted. Smiling warmly at each other, they pressed their foreheads together, lingering in the content bliss they felt. They no longer had to become denied of each other. Hearing the soft footsteps, Gabrio twisted his head to see Marrok and Raul leading the group of Blood Tasters as they jaunted toward them. He smiled. "Look behind you Esmeralda." He said lovingly, swallowing a growing lump in his throat.

Esmeralda turned around and instantly spotted her father in his Beast Blood form and in the middle of the day. A squeal of excitement broke from her lips as she moved from the hated stone altar. More forthcoming tears stung her eyes and fell down her cheeks. Running to her father, she swiped the salty water from her face. Raul greeted her as if she was a little girl once again. He crouched to the ground and met her in a long awaited embrace as she dived into his arms. "Dad!" She softly cried into his fur.

Raul coddled her tightly as he began thanking God she was safe and still here with them. He must have been holding her too tightly as he could feel her writhing away from him. Once he let her go, Esmeralda took a deep breath, hugged him again and spoke in a trembling voice. "You're a werewolf, in the middle of the day! I can't believe that. I can't believe you're here with Gabrio. How? How did you guys find me? Sheryl... Eve, she took me from the castle, from my room. She brought me here to preform this fucking spell on me and eventually take my son when the time came. She revealed it all to me. Her entire plan. The entire time she was the Eve. The Truer Sin. And Laycerath, he was the demon werewolf." She broke her embrace from her father and looked up at him, wiping her eyes, then looking at the crowd of people around her. "What about George? Did he know? We have to tell him when we get home about what happened." She stated.

Gabrio didn't want to tell her until they went back home, but now was as good as any. "No, Essie. He didn't know. There will be no telling him when we go home." He answered vaguely.

"Why not? We have to tell him. They were..." She ranted as Gabrio interrupted her abruptly.

"Because he's gone. He died by fire and Eve was the one to set it aflame. She killed him while he was the house to cover her tracks about Laycerath and who she was." Gabrio spoke calmly as he quivered his jaw, causing his cheeks to pulsate.

Esmeralda felt sadness and dread fall on her once more. She rushed to him and hugged him tightly. "I'm so sorry, honey. I know he was like a father to you."

"The only one I truly knew." Distraught with emotion from George dying by the woman that raised him and then having his wife back alive and in his arms. Gabrio couldn't say anymore, except hug her and nod.

"How did find me? Know where to go?" Esmeralda's shock and racing mind poured the questions in rapid-fire, hardly allowing herself to catch a breath between the sentences.

Conlaoch stepped forward from the crowd. Esmeralda gazed her puffy eyes at him and raised an arched eyebrow. "You, Conlaoch? You brought them here to me? You were here so fast there wouldn't have been enough time to find them, then me?" Esmeralda asked confused, yet grateful.

Conlaoch shook his head. "Your husband, father and brother are Guardians. They are keepers of the talisman such as we are, but for their kind. Marrok can trace you. He can find your essence, no matter where you go in the world. He can do that with anyone he chooses as long as he reads a strong enough connection to them. He's the one that found you with us."

Esmeralda looked to the golden werewolf and walked toward him. Her expression was blank as she searched his eyes. Then she released a stark, beautiful smile. "My brother- the whole time, you were my brother. I felt a connection to you the first night we met, you know. It was so weird to me. The signs were there, weren't they? A werewolf in disguise. Now, it looks like you can become trusted." She smiled as she gave him a lingering hug.

Marrok nodded as he stared down at his sister, with a growing compassion for the woman. There was no denying it now. He knew became fully accepted into the family. He couldn't be happier at who and what they were.

Gabrio stood next to his wife, held her tightly and snorted his reply. "More signs than you'll know; from the book, to the ring, to the ghost in our house..."

"Ghost? What ghost?" Esmeralda interrupted and exclaimed in disbelief.

Gabrio nodded his head. "Swear to God, a ghost. I don't know who she was, but she helped me find you." He paused for a moment. "Now, that I think about it, she looked very familiar. Do you think it was Alexandria, getting her revenge?" He asked knowingly.

Esmeralda arched her eyebrow again as she looked at him with mixed emotions of pure joy and disbelief. "There's many details to this story that I don't know yet, isn't there?"

"I'll fill you in later, when I get you home. To our home in Michigan!" Gabrio challenged Conlaoch with a defying stare.

Conlaoch smirked as he nodded his head. "You called on the angels, made the demon werewolf take his own life and the Truer Sin became decapitated by the leader of the archangels. Importantly, Esmeralda and the baby are both safe and very much untainted, for now." He was purposely vague knowing the future held more in store.

"Thank you for protecting me and Eli. Even though you were difficult to be around most of the time, but I'm going home. I don't have to stay here any longer, Conlaoch." Esmeralda stated firmly, but was still uncertain what might come next.

Conlaoch laughed heartily. "Don't be so heartbroken she-wolf. You knew what we had between us. Nothing serious would've ever come out of it. I protected you, your child and now you're in more than capable hands, but we'll always be around, closely watching you and your family." He acted nonchalant while in reality he felt empty knowing she would be gone with the excitement. "However, if you ever become bored of your husband sooner, I'm always at Raven Eye. We'll make use of those chains once again, but in a more *pleasurable* manner." Conlaoch said irreverently to Esmeralda's for Gabrio's reaction.

"Battle's over now. We don't need to remain united anymore and I can freely find a way to kill you." Gabrio growled and he began to move forward, but Esmeralda held him back.

Conlaoch began laughing at the expected reaction he coveted from the Beast Blood's demeanor. "You could try Gabrio, but I rather not fight a naked man. You might enjoy it too much."

Esmeralda rolled her eyes as she looked at Gabrio, moving him a few feet away from Conlaoch. "Don't pay any mind to him. Please take me home, Gabe, I'm ready. I'm so ready to go home and experience life in our normal way."

Gabrio smiled at his wife. "I'm ready too."

"No, seriously right now. I'm ready to leave right now. I've been here for way too long and we only have about five months to prepare for our son. He's very important, so I'm told." Esmeralda said with laughter glittering in her eyes.

Gabrio softly chuckled. "That's right, Eli, our son, whom you named after my father."

Esmeralda nodded. "Eli Santos-Mackley. It seemed fitting to honor him through our firstborn son."

He gave her another kiss and smiled warmly at her

thoughtfulness. "Thank you, but our son will be his own man. He'll grow into his name, not be burdened with the tortured memory of my father."

Esmeralda lowered her eyes just as quickly as she flicked them up again. "I understand. Different man, different fate." Then, she outburst suddenly another name. "Thaddeus. I like that name."

He laughed. "I like that name too." Gabrio's smile bloomed as he saw how the sunlight played with her hair and across her skin. He loved the twinkling blue in her lively eyes and the succulent pout in her lips. He loved her with all of his heart, she is his life mate, his Beast Blood and there she stood in front of him when he once doubted he ever would. In a flash he picked her up, hugging her tight and releasing a shriek of surprise from her. "Be careful, Gabrio. Remember, I'm pregnant." She chuckled, marveled at hearing the words pour from her mouth.

Gabrio shook his head as he lowered her down his body and gave her a long hard kiss. "No, my wife, we're pregnant. We're a growing family. I'm going to take you, the both of you home. Where we belong. It'll be a different beginning for us all. You, me and our son, the Hybrid."

EPILOGUE

Cairo, Egypt

He puffed on his cigarette as he watched the sunset fall below the horizon. Soon the darkness would spread over Egypt and he would become plagued by sleep, then enchanted by the dreams of *her*. He loved *her*. The dreams had started over twenty years ago and every night she offered him hope and destiny. A cool breeze swirled inside his small apartment, rustling papers and the cheap teal curtains that hung from the silver rod over the window. He took once last drag and let the smoke slowly pour from his nostrils. Finished, he put out the remaining cigarette on the back of his hand. He let it linger as he welcomed the burning pain. He was happy could feel pain again. A sensation he hadn't been able to experience since the death of Christ, which meant Eve had finally died. *So, she was finally taken.* He thought, wanting to laugh aloud. He thought he was loosing his mind when he could taste the food he consumed was full of flavor and the wine he drank was sweet. He could smell again, feel again, taste again. He was restored of full life since her curse became lifted from his body. Then made him remember, he could die. After all this time he could finally die. Yet, he no longer desired death's release. It didn't matter if he did desire it, since only those with a soul could die and gave his away a very long time ago to a demon and a small, sickly boy, whose own desire was greater than suspected.

He closed his eyes, leaned his head back on the chair and took a deep breath. Air filled his lungs and he took pleasure in it. Life surrounded him and he marveled in it. He could hear the people upstairs, fucking to the sounds of some porn as the man across the hall laughed at what his wife had said. He could even hear the woman crying in the apartment beneath him. Life was good and it was going to get better when he found *her*. The woman of his dreams. At first he doubted them, thinking at first they were his subconscious telling him he was lonely and in need of a woman's comfort. Yet, every night the dreams became more detailed, more elaborate, until they had pointed him to where she was. Then, last night he was able to find her name within the dream. He loved it. Loved the sound of it as he repeated it aloud to himself for most of the day. He became overwhelmed with excitement at the memory of her name. He opened his eyes and looked down at the passport that sat on his lap. He smiled as he spoke aloud. "Soon, Miss Jezebel. Very soon our dreams will be our reality."

CPSIA information can be obtained at www.ICGtesting.com
Printed in the USA
LVOW11s1410061115

461417LV00001B/19/P

9 781480